"Is that your handkerchief, then, also?" Drayton asked casually. "I think I accidentally dislodged it while I was loosening your bodice."

She blushed, remembering. "Yes, it is. Thank you for returning it."

Drayton reached out and unfolded the handkerchief. There in the corner were three initials: a small R, a large M, and a small R, picked out in the lace trim edging the cambric. "I had always thought," he said, "that the large initial, the one in the center, was the family name."

She had thought herself clever, choosing a name so close to her own. Rachel improvised again. "The handkerchief was made in Spain, Captain Drayton. There it is customary to use the mother's name as the family name for an unmarried daughter."

This was true, as Drayton knew. But he also knew more than Rachel guessed about handkerchiefs. "Try another, my girl," he said grimly. "I didn't spend three years squiring Cyprians around London without learning my linens. That's Brussels lace."

He reached out and seized her shoulders in an iron grip. The hasty club she had made came undone; her hair spilled out and curled down over his fingers. She made no movement, only looked at him with an odd mixture of pleading and defiance. For a moment they stood like that, their gazes locked.

Then, without thought, without volition, he bent his head and kissed her.

A QUESTION OF HONOR

Nita Abrams

ZEBRA BOOKS
KENSINGTON PUBLISHING CORP.
http://www.kensingtonbooks.com

ZEBRA BOOKS are published by

Kensington Publishing Corp.
850 Third Avenue
New York, NY 10022

First Printing: March 2002
10 9 8 7 6 5 4 3 2 1

Printed in the United States of America

For the real Rachel

Chapter One

Spain, March 1813

"Captain's in trouble again," observed a stout dragoon, standing in the doorway of the barn and peering out into the mist. It was a raw, windy morning, and intermittent bursts of rain scudded across the wet stones, obscuring the uniformed figure on horseback and the servant who stood arguing with him in front of the farmhouse. "That's Lodge, from the general's staff." His companions, crowded behind him and watching the scene in the yard, did not disagree. A messenger who arrived before sunrise demanding that their captain post up to headquarters immediately was unlikely to be a harbinger of good news.

"Did something happen last night, then?" asked the smallest trooper, trying to see over the shoulders of his larger comrades. "I heard the Fifty-second invited our officers into the village for a celebration after the French pulled back."

"They did," affirmed a corporal, his eyes intent on the two figures in the farmyard. "Robson was there waiting on table, though, and apparently it was all quite civilized. Stewed rabbit, half-dozen bottles of port, cigars, a few local *señoritas*—the usual sort of thing."

"It won't be so civilized when someone wakes Drayton at this hour of the morning and tells him he has to ride four leagues in the rain," muttered the stout man. "Especially if he had his share of that port." There was a moment's silence.

"Robson wouldn't make one of us wake him, would he?" one of the new recruits asked nervously. As if he had heard them from across the yard, the small serving man turned and looked straight at the group huddled in the doorway. An instant later the watchers had vanished back to their pallets on the other side of the horse stalls. Drayton's patrol might be curious about what the messenger was saying to Robson, but no one was going to venture out of the warm barn into the drizzle to find out. Especially if it meant they might be sent into the house to face the caustic tongue of their captain.

Not surprisingly, Robson had come to the same conclusion as the troopers, and was unsuccessfully trying to persuade the messenger to dismount and give Drayton his orders personally.

"No, no, I think I should be on my way," said Lodge politely, concealing a smile. Robson's arguments about regulations did not fool him for a moment. "I'm rather pressed for time at the moment." A sniff greeted this remark, and he added defensively, "I've three more packets to deliver. And he won't thank me for dripping horse-flavored water all over him. You're his batman, Robson. *You* wake him."

Robson jutted out his chin and glared at the muddy rider. "What if he doesn't believe me?"

"Give him the letter," was the curt reply.

"But this damned letter makes no sense whatsoever!" shouted the bald little manservant in frustration. He was trying to protect it from the damp, but now he took it out from under his jacket and waved it at the messenger. It was unsealed, and written in the practiced script of an army bureaucrat:

Captain the Honourable Richard C. Drayton, 14th Light Dragoons

Sir, this to advise you that notice of your injury has been forwarded to Colonel Sawyer and Colonel the Earl of Bridgwater as of the 3rd instant, with approval for medical leave, as per the endorsement of Surgeon Major Hopp.

I have the honour to be, etc.,

E. G. LeSueur
Secretary to the Adjutant-General

"This is dated tomorrow, the captain is not injured, he has requested no medical leave, and I've never heard of this man LeSueur!"

The messenger gathered up the reins of his horse. "I wouldn't pay much attention to what the letter actually *says,*" he advised. "Not if it comes from Tredwell's office. Just pass on the orders: He's to report to Tredwell, up at headquarters, and you're to follow with his gear and go to the field hospital. Best roust him at once, Robson; the road is a bog. He'll need to leave soon to be there by eight."

"Wait, Lodge; wait, man," appealed Robson anxiously, putting his hand on the bridle. "For pity's sake, just tell me, What is it? Some sort of disciplinary hearing?"

The messenger softened. Robson, he knew, had been with Drayton's family for years. "Well, for what it's worth," said Lodge, "in my experience, reprimands come from the regimental command, not headquarters. And when Tredwell is involved, you're more likely to be getting into new trouble than hearing about old trouble, if you take my meaning."

"I don't take your meaning at all," said Robson, scowling. "Who is this Colonel Tredwell?"

"Ho!" Lodge grinned smugly, glad to air his superior knowledge. "Haven't run into Tredwell yet, eh? His title is Deputy Adjutant-General, and officially he manages requisitions. But in fact, he supervises military intelligence for the whole Peninsula. Reports directly to Wellington." And twitching the bridle away from the dumbfounded Robson, he nudged his tired mount gently in the ribs and trotted out of the yard.

Robson stood frozen for a minute or so, watching the horse disappear into the gray half-light. Then he came back to himself. Lodge was right; he should wake the captain straightaway. He headed for the farmhouse and gave a disgusted snort as he opened the door. The stove had gone out, as usual. That meant no hot water. Lucky thing he would need to stay behind and pack. Drayton was not going to be good company on the long ride up to headquarters.

"Captain Drayton, sir," announced a shy subaltern as he opened the door of a side parlor in the stucco-walled tavern. The tap room they had come through was dim, cold, and empty, but a litter of maps and dispatch cases on the tables suggested that the house was not currently open for regular business even at more civilized hours. Drayton saw with relief that there was a fire in the parlor; he could feel the heat from the doorway. Two hours of slogging through the rain had chilled him to the bone.

"Morning, Captain," said a small man of forty standing next to a makeshift desk opposite the door. "Gentlemen, Captain Drayton, of the Fourteenth. Drayton, my assistants LeSueur and Houghton; this is Colonel White, from London, and his liaison officer, Captain Southey." Drayton nodded to two blond young aristocrats who stood on Tredwell's left, gave a respectful greeting to the colonel, a tall man sporting enormous salt-and-pepper mustaches and a savage scowl, and then grinned at the redheaded young man nearest the door.

"Hullo, South," he said. "Didn't know you had signed on." Southey, an old friend, grinned back.

"Can't all be getting named in the dispatches every two weeks," he said. "Break the poor riders' arms carrying the cases were they that heavy."

Drayton flushed. He had been conspicuous in the dispatches in more ways than one. At Salamanca, he had been cited for bravery after his futile attempt to save Harry when his brother's line collapsed. And he had been part of a group which had done an extraordinary job sapping the fortress wall at Burgos while under enemy fire. But he had also been reprimanded twice for dueling, and had come perilously close to a demotion the second time.

Tredwell looked down at a document he was holding and carefully folded and unfolded the pages several times while frowning slightly. Southey coughed and lowered his eyes, and Drayton turned back towards the colonel. He was feeling rather conspicuously unshaven and disheveled. His boots and breeches were filthy, his hair was damp and windblown, and he suspected that his hasty attempts to smooth it had smeared mud on his cheek. "My apologies for my appearance, sir," he stammered, "but my man told me it was urgent."

"Yes, yes, that is right," muttered Tredwell, still looking over the papers. Drayton caught several glimpses of his own name. "Quite the fire-eater, I see. Not exactly what we want, but we have no time to be choosy." Finally he raised pale blue eyes to Drayton. "Captain Drayton, I have asked your commanding officer to place you on medical leave. Your batman will take your things to the field hospital at the convent in San Luis, two miles from here." He turned to LeSueur. "Was there a skirmish yesterday in Drayton's area?"

"Yes, sir, just before the second French division pulled out."

"Very well, Drayton has been wounded in that skirmish. Advise the senior medical officer immediately. And put his regular horse somewhere inconspicuous."

"Yes, sir," said LeSueur and swung out the door.

"And find Rodrigo and get him over here!"

LeSueur put his head back into the room. "He's on his way, sir. He's a bit in shock, still."

Waving his hand vaguely, Tredwell gestured for Drayton and the junior officers to be seated. White had already taken a chair next to Tredwell at the tiny desk, where his long legs bulged out beside the spindly boards supporting the desktop. As he sank down next to Southey, Drayton murmured, "Any hints for an old schoolmate? Am I supposed to know why I am here, or rather, in the hospital with a nonexistent wound?"

Southey looked at him apologetically. "I'm afraid I suggested you," he whispered.

"I waited for Captain Drayton to arrive," said Tredwell with sudden energy, "but we won't wait for Rodrigo. LeSueur and Southey already know our bad news: Rover is dead. He was killed during a pursuit near Jarandilla two days ago." White gave a startled exclamation; Houghton's eyes widened in dismay and he muttered something that sounded to Drayton like a stifled curse.

"Rover was our most reliable and experienced reconnaissance engineer," said Tredwell, turning to Drayton.

"He was more than that, by God, Tredwell!" said White, quite shaken. "He was the heart of our courier service! The general told me once he was worth an entire brigade! A brave man, a very brave man. And irreplaceable."

"Well, White, I pray your fourth statement is wrong, although I must agree with the first three," said Tredwell wearily. He sighed and rubbed his forehead with one hand. "Drayton, we hoped you could help us finish collecting the information Rover was after before he died," he continued after a moment. "It involves a series of small bridges in the hills southwest of Madrid. There are six of them, and we need all of them inspected to see what weight they can bear, in case we need to take gun carriages over them. Rover got to two, but one of those is too frail, and we must have at least three secure possibilities. We need someone with some knowledge of engineering, who speaks Spanish and has a good chance of passing undetected behind French lines."

He paused, looking at Drayton's thick, dark hair, the level brows and nearly black eyes in a slightly square, clean-lined face. He was tan from months on campaign. Perhaps a little on the tall side, but he would do, Tredwell decided.

"Little Rover, another one of our couriers, is on his way from England, but we cannot wait; if he is delayed he will not arrive in time. The general may decide to advance as soon as five weeks from now. Southey remembered that your mother's family was part Spanish, and your dossier says you did some engineering at Woolwich before you joined the Fourteenth. I see you were involved in that wall fiasco, in fact."

"Yes, sir," said Drayton numbly.

"Why did you leave Woolwich?"

"My father insisted that I withdraw, sir."

Tredwell grunted. He had heard rumors that Alcroft had quarreled bitterly with York, the commander-in-chief. Apparently they were true.

"Am I to infer that your father preferred your subsequent career among the peep-of-day boys in London?"

Drayton shifted uncomfortably in his chair. He was not proud of his wild years following his departure from the academy. "The peep-of-day boys, as you call them, sir, have no board of governors. My father was not, therefore, in a position to compel me to leave, as he did at Woolwich."

"But he eventually bought you your colors? Why did you not return to Woolwich?"

"My brother and I purchased our own commissions, sir, when we came into some money from our mother's side of the family. My father could not prevent it; we were both of age. And I did not return to Woolwich because I wished to be with my brother." He closed his eyes briefly. He had been with Harry. For two months. And then Harry had fallen at Salamanca.

"Everyone wants to be a glory boy on a horse," muttered the colonel. "What we need is more engineers. What about your languages? *Do* you speak Spanish?"

"Yes, sir, a bit. Harry and I—our nurse was Spanish, and I have been here nearly a year."

"Practicing in the village bedrooms?" snapped Tredwell, brandishing the papers angrily. "This is not a game, Captain Drayton. I accept your engineering credentials, which are at least in part verified by your competence with that blasted fortress wall. But I will have Rodrigo check your Spanish as soon as he arrives, and I will ask you to understand something: You are going behind enemy lines, out of uniform. You will not necessarily be considered a prisoner of war if you are captured. You are responsible for your own safety, for the accurate recording of the information we need, and for the safety of Rodrigo, who has volunteered—*volunteered*, I say, since he was Rover's family retainer and has no official connection to us—to return to the area as your guide. Arrogant, hotheaded behavior like these ridiculous duels over your local inamoratas will put you, and your guide, and our campaign, in danger."

"Tredwell," interrupted White sharply before Drayton could reply, "have you perhaps forgotten that you have no right to command any subordinate to undertake missions not in uniform? You seem to take his consent for granted. We do ourselves no favors when we bully young officers into accepting assignments they cannot handle."

The smaller man looked up, startled, and then suddenly his face relaxed; he laughed and regarded Drayton in almost a friendly manner. "You are correct, White; I assume too much. But"—with a challenging glance at White—"I would stake my entire salary that the young devil with this dossier would no more deny such a request than you would cut off your mustaches."

Drayton gritted his teeth. He was finding Tredwell's offhand comments more embarrassing than the formal reprimand he had received three months earlier. "Yes, sir," he muttered.

"Yes, what?" White leaned forward. "You're certain you are willing to undertake this sort of thing, Captain?"

Drayton lifted his head and smiled suddenly. "I'm afraid surveying sounds almost appealing compared to organizing patrols and posting vedettes, sir."

Tredwell considered the unshaven cheeks, the eyelids red-rimmed from wine and cigars and lack of sleep, the mud streaked lightly on one side of the square jaw. But the dark eyes met his firmly, and Tredwell felt a stab of something like remorse. Of all the unpleasant aspects of his job, sending amateurs behind enemy lines was the worst. Tredwell was perfectly sure that Drayton had not the least idea of what reconnaissance work was about.

There was a light knock at the door, and Houghton sprang up to admit a lanky, olive-skinned figure dressed in civilian riding clothes. "Ah, Rodrigo," said Tredwell. "Captain Drayton has arrived. Drayton, could you go on out into the taproom with Rodrigo and see how your Spanish sounds to him? You can spread the map out on one of the tables out there. Houghton, get them a lamp; it's another infernal gray day and even at the table by the window I'll wager they can't see properly."

Drayton stood, and the man called Rodrigo stepped back to let him pass through the door, then escorted Drayton politely to a table. Pulling out an oilskin map pouch, he addressed Drayton in the flawless Castilian of a Spanish grandee. How long had he been in Spain? Was it true that his grandmother had been from Valencia?

Drayton replied, at first haltingly, and then more rapidly, and to his surprise, Rodrigo suddenly began speaking in a coarse peasant argot, interspersing questions with insults and crude jests. Drayton had more difficulty following the questions now but was still able to respond to his interlocutor's satisfaction. There followed a few sentences in what Drayton recognized as Portuguese, but he could barely stammer a reply in that language. Rodrigo switched back to Castilian.

"Good, let us examine the maps while we continue to talk. Look"—he pointed with a thin finger—"we are here. The French line is currently here, five leagues beyond us; and the bridges are in these hills ten to twenty leagues farther on. Tredwell says he has found you a horse who can handle the hills and who will not look like an army mount. It is very rough country, and we must avoid both the French army and the Spanish partisans. Most of the latter are very good men, but a few are little better than bandits, and our horses will attract them. Also, the French suspect that we are interested in the bridges, although my master was able to mislead them about our actual route before he was killed." He paused for a moment, staring bleakly into the lamp. Drayton said nothing. His own wounds were too raw to allow him to offer meaningless condolences to a stranger.

After a minute, the Spaniard resumed. "You will have to inspect and sketch mostly at night, for this reason, and since it is nearing full moon it is best that we leave at once, to take advantage of it. I have drafting supplies and some small surveying instruments outside, ready to go, in my saddlebags, along with suitable clothing for you, but you should check to make sure I have not omitted anything necessary."

Drayton looked over the maps for a few moments. It was mountainous terrain, with few roads. The bridges would be of crucial importance. He began to make a list in his head of what he would need and shoved aside his chair. "Let me see what you have brought," he said to Rodrigo. The older man bowed slightly, and waved Drayton out to the front of the building. Drayton's gray gelding, Cloud, was gone. In his place was an ungainly roan with a scar on its neck and a tail which looked as though it had been hacked with a kitchen knife. Rodrigo was unbuckling the saddlebags of a stocky chestnut, but when he saw Drayton staring in dismay at the roan, a gleam of mischief came into his eyes.

"Do you not like your horse, Captain Drayton? His name is Relámpago, 'Lightning.' " Drayton gave a shout of laughter. "He is quite fast, *señor,* in spite of appearances."

"Oh no, you don't understand," said Drayton, still laughing. "I'm acquiring a complete set of weather horses, like one of those commemorative china services. My charger here is named Cloud, and I have a mare at home called Sleet."

"An unusual name for a horse," commented Rodrigo.

Drayton's expression was wistful. "I've had her since she was a filly. She's a gray with tiny silver streaks down her face and withers, like an ice storm. She was a gift from my brother."

Tredwell's shadow fell over Drayton's shoulder. "How is he?" he asked.

"As you suspected, sir," said Rodrigo in accentless English. "He must be my servant, since his Spanish pronunciation will not serve for more than minimal conversation. He follows well, though, even when I spoke in dialect. He has almost no Portuguese, but we will not need it."

Drayton had turned at Tredwell's approach. Tredwell looked at him soberly.

"Keep your head down, Drayton, and no heroic posturing. If you're to pass as the servant of a landless Spaniard, humility must be your watchword. Meet no man's eyes unless your pistol is trained on him."

"When should we be ready to leave, sir?" asked Drayton, hoping to be able to see Robson, perhaps shave, and pick up some of his spare clothing.

"Now," replied the colonel grimly. "Leave your uniform and gear with Houghton; that includes your weapons. Rodrigo will provide you with replacements which are not army issue. Take nothing which can identify you in any way."

Chapter Two

It took them most of the first day to get behind the French lines, because Rodrigo would gesture a halt every half mile and leave Drayton with the horses while he disappeared to reconnoiter on foot. Before they started out he taught Drayton how to lay his hand in a certain spot on the bridle of each horse. "It is not foolproof," he said, "but even in the presence of other horses we have trained them not to whinny if you hold them here. Usually, they remember." Human talk was discouraged as well; many attempts on Drayton's part to ask questions were cut off by Rodrigo with an imperative gesture for silence.

The silence continued on the second day, even though it no longer seemed required for safety. They saw almost no one, even from a distance, for the whole day, although Rodrigo went into a village to buy provisions late in the morning, leaving Drayton concealed. Drayton found it strangely restful to spend hour after hour riding through the spare hills hearing nothing but the soft fall of the horses' hooves and the occasional skitter of a small animal shooting off down a rocky slope. For months, he realized, he had rarely been in a quiet place for more than a moment, constantly surrounded by the coarse jokes of his men, the singing, the grumbling—all the noisy stratagems of soldiers in exile, desperate to ward off fear and boredom.

On the third day, they turned into much rougher country and had to dismount and walk the horses several times. Rodrigo was more talkative, and pointed out landmarks as they rode. Several times he impersonated a French officer and interrogated Drayton about his papers. Rodrigo's imitation of French soldiers speaking Spanish made Drayton laugh until he recalled that a Frenchman might equally well be able to hear his errors. After that, he paid more attention to Rodrigo's corrections of his pronunciation.

Towards evening, Rodrigo guided them to a tiny valley between two brown hills. It had rained in the morning, but now the afternoon sun had come out, and the clearing was lined with elongated shadows from the rocks overhead. Drayton's spirits lifted when he saw that Rodrigo was preparing to build a fire. They had been too close to the French troops to have a fire on the first two nights, and March was cold in the hills even during the day.

As the twilight settled in, he was chewing on a piece of dried sausage and looking at the fire when he heard Rodrigo say something.

"What's that?" he said.

"Excuse me, *señor,* but I need to see you walk," Rodrigo repeated. Puzzled, Drayton got to his feet. He was still not sure exactly what his relationship to Rodrigo might be. Certainly the man was nothing like Robson; if anyone was in charge of this expedition it was in fact, if not in name, the Spaniard. Rodrigo treated him with an odd mixture of deference and exasperation which Drayton found unnerving. But the man knew what he was about; they had seen not one French soldier during that tortuous first day, and Drayton felt fairly certain that there had been at least three patrols within a few miles of the pass they had taken through the hills beyond the British lines. So Drayton paced back and forth a few times in front of the fire, and then paused.

"As I thought," muttered Rodrigo angrily, and jumped to his feet. "Look," he commanded, "this is how you walk." He set off in front of Drayton with an exaggerated version of the haughty swagger typical of Wellington's cavalry. Drayton had to laugh.

"It is not a matter for amusement, *señor,*" said Rodrigo. "No one will believe you are my servant if you walk in this way. You must walk like this." Before Drayton's eyes he seemed to shrink; his shoulders hunched slightly, his head bent down, his stride shortened, and he added a slight shuffle. Drayton tried to imitate him, but Rodrigo frowned. Two more attempts were equally unsuccessful.

"Captain Drayton," said Rodrigo with great seriousness, "tomorrow we approach the first of the four bridges. To reach it, we must go through a town, right through the middle of it. There is no way around. We can camp on the other side and go back to the bridge from the uninhabited country after dark, but we cannot avoid the town itself, and when I passed through with . . . earlier—" He paused. "When I was there last, there were French troops quartered there. They may well examine our papers, and if we do not look like the people described in those papers, it will not be a good thing."

"I do not think I will ever be a success on the stage," said Drayton somberly.

"No, you were not made for this work," agreed Rodrigo, but without condemnation. "Somehow, however, I must teach you to walk properly before tomorrow."

"The poverty dance?" suggested Drayton with a twinkle in his eye. Rodrigo laughed.

"Perhaps that is not such a bad way to think of it," he said. "Let us try having you go step by step, as though you were learning a new kind of quadrille." He was as good as his word, fixing Drayton's arms and head for each movement of a set of six paces, and then forcing Drayton to repeat it some fifteen times before he was satisfied. At the end of an hour, Drayton's neck ached fiercely; the balls of his feet were sore, and he was dizzy from looking over his shoulder at Rodrigo.

"I need a brandy," he said through clenched teeth. Rodrigo laughed and went to the saddlebags.

"We have earned it," he said, bringing over the flask. They sat down by the dying fire, and Drayton stretched out his long legs with a sigh of relief.

"What was he like?" asked Drayton suddenly. "Rover, I mean."

"He was incredible," said Rodrigo simply. He stared into the fire and switched to Spanish. "He was the best courier I have ever seen. What I have just shown you—that was nothing to him. He could be a woman, an old man, a young man with a wound in a particular spot, a nobleman, a mountaindweller, anything. He could move in complete silence, even over gravel or leaves. He could finish an accurate sketch of a building in minutes.

"He escaped from enemy captors three times, although once his children helped him. *Ai!* I was not with him, that time. The younger child, our Little Rover, was then only twelve. They were tracking him with dogs, and the children drew them off until he could get clear. Another time he was held in a cell for a month and was sending and receiving information the whole time in his cell."

"Jove!" breathed Drayton, awed not only by the speech but by the face of the speaker.

"Why did you come back with me?" he asked after a moment. "Tredwell said you are not one of our men. Why didn't you take Rover's back pay and effects home to England, to his wife and children?"

"To finish what he started," said the other man slowly. "To have something to do while I waited to meet Little Rover. There is no back pay to go to the children in England, in any case. Your army did not pay him. In fact, I believe he recently loaned Wellington quite a bit of gold, to pay the Portuguese auxiliaries. And his wife is long dead, or you may be sure those children would not have been able to persuade the groom to take them into France to find their father. They are a wild pair."

Just before noon on the following day, they reached the hills above the town. Rodrigo nodded with satisfaction as he saw the streets crowded, and numerous parties of travelers moving in both directions on the main road they were about to join. There was safety in numbers. Even so, Drayton, practicing his shuffle as he led the horses, did not look up until they were a league beyond the river and had turned onto an unfrequented track. He was soaked with sweat, and his hands were shaking. They had not been stopped; but two other travelers ahead of them had been questioned as they were going by, and Drayton had been frantically rehearsing proper intonations in his head until it dawned on him that the town was behind him. Rodrigo was completely unruffled and whistled a little tune under his breath as he looked around for a watering place for the horses.

"How do you do that? How can you just walk along while the patrols look at you, as though you were strolling through your own garden?" Drayton gasped in Spanish. Rodrigo had set a new rule: no English except in camp at night. Rodrigo smiled.

"Practice," he said. "We must stop here now and rest. Tonight you can be an engineer for a while."

In comparison to the agonizing masquerades required whenever they were forced into contact with people, Drayton found his inspections easy. Rodrigo would stand guard, watching the tall, angular body swing with surprising agility under struts, sketching, balancing the dark lantern, and measuring. No matter how late it was when he finished, Drayton always transferred the plans and numbers to a tiny roll of onionskin that same night. Then he would burn the originals. Rover had simply inspected the bridges and made his own judgment about their capacity without recording anything on paper; Drayton, as a junior officer without full training in engineering, did not trust himself to do more than transmit information, and he was determined to make that information as precise as possible. Now it was Rodrigo's turn to be impressed.

"How can you write in such small letters?" he asked. "And make those very thin lines?"

Drayton grinned. "Practice." He rubbed his hands; it was very cold at night and he longed for the fingerless gloves he had used sometimes at Woolwich, copying diagrams in the unheated study hall.

"Why must it be done now? Would it not be easier in daylight?"

"Yes," said Drayton, "but if I had missed anything, or if the numbers did not tally properly, we would lose a full day waiting until nightfall to remeasure."

Rodrigo looked at him with respect. "You are no actor, *Señor* Captain," he said, "but you are more of a courier than I thought."

At the beginning of the third week, with all four bridges recorded and a mere five leagues to the no-man's land beyond the French lines, Drayton made a disastrous blunder. Ironically, the problem was not his Spanish but his French. They had come up a small side road to a lovely pass between two valleys and were resting near a farmhouse. A thin warmth came from the sun overhead, the first sunshine they had seen in several days. Both were off their guard, perhaps, feeling as though the worst was behind them. Rodrigo even sent Drayton to the farmhouse to negotiate food and drink.

"After all," he pointed out, "you are the servant. I would have to hide you if I went in, or it would look very odd, and there are not many places to hide up here." He was right; it was open, bare country, and they could see for miles down the shabby track to the lower hills where the shrubs and trees began again. Drayton had no trouble purchasing some cheese and a flagon of wine. The farmer's daughter, who brought out the wine, was a lively girl with a flounce to her walk. She was markedly underdressed for the cool spring weather, and Captain Drayton of the Fourteenth would have put his hand on her almost-bare shoulder when she handed him the flagon. The courier remembered to look at his boots.

Just as he had turned out of the farmyard, however, the two soldiers rode up. Without even looking at him, they tossed a coin onto the dirt and shouted in poor Spanish that he should hold their horses. Then they strode up to the house and, calling loudly for refreshment, duplicated Drayton's purchase, but with the addition of the pinches and caresses for the winebearer. And as they walked back towards the gate, glancing at Drayton, they began to speculate in French about him and the girl, whom they took to be his sister, and to make increasingly crude suggestions as they strolled over to reclaim their horses. Later, Drayton, apologizing frantically, told Rodrigo that of course they had no idea he could understand them. All he had to do was grin stupidly, hand them their horses, and watch them ride off. But at the time he realized nothing except that he had stopped breathing, the sky had turned black, and he was screaming insults in French at the top of his lungs while he knocked the first soldier down with a left to the temple.

The pain in his knuckles sobered him at once, and he looked over to Rodrigo in horror. The second soldier stood stupefied for a moment, gaping at him in rage and astonishment. Gathering his wits, Drayton vaulted onto one horse while still holding both sets of reins, and rode towards Rodrigo, hauling the second horse along, shouting in Spanish to take their own horses and follow. If there were no other soldiers on horseback nearby, they could easily reach the thickets below and disappear. The two Frenchmen would never catch them on foot. But he had forgotten they had pistols. Fifteen yards down the track, Drayton heard a series of sharp cracks, and something slammed into his left shoulder.

For a count of ten, perhaps more, he felt nothing. Suddenly, his arm was on fire. His back arched in pain. His entire left side seemed to collapse, and he dropped the reins. The second horse pulled away, and his own mount slowed to a walk and then halted. He was falling forward over the horse's neck. Then a familiar, ugly roan head appeared next to him. Rodrigo was cursing at him, dismounting from the chestnut, sliding him over the back of the roan, riding next to him and talking, shouting, telling him to stay on the horse; they were almost to the trees, don't slide, hold the neck with his right hand, it was just a flesh wound, here are the trees; just a few more minutes, pulling him off the horse and wadding up a neckcloth to make a bandage, forcing brandy down him, pushing him back on the horse, riding, riding, there is a gorge, we will look for a cave, I think there are caves in this area.

There was a cave. Drayton had been sitting in it for years, it seemed to him. His back was propped up against his saddle, with a wedge of cloth inserted to leave an empty space under his left shoulder. It was not a flesh wound. The ball was sitting inside him, burning the back of his ribs with waves of agony. Next to his right arm was a leather water bottle, filled with ice-cold water. More cold water dripped from the walls of the cave, but Drayton was hot. Periodically he dipped his fingers into the water and drew it across his face or dribbled it down his neck. He could not go to sleep, because in case he was found he had to be ready to grab the pistol, which lay by his right thigh.

Rodrigo had gone off on the chestnut, leading the roan. "There is no use leaving you a horse," he had said. "He will just add to the risk that you might be discovered. What we need is a wagon, and some help. If we are near Escalona, and I think we are, there is an inn where I have found help before." Drayton had tried to give him the little onionskin packet, but Rodrigo had refused.

"That is your responsibility," he said shortly, causing Drayton to apologize again, overwhelmed with remorse, until a fit of coughing silenced him.

"Stay awake," Rodrigo said gently. "Listen for a whistle"—he gave a peculiar two-note call—"so that you will not shoot me when I return." He had backed quietly out and down the hill to the horses. But Drayton had thought that the gun would not be aimed at the entrance of the cave if it went off. He had worried for a while about his notes. How could he protect them if the French found him? A grim solution had come to him, and after a painful struggle, using his left hand as little as possible, he had been satisfied that he had done the best he could. He had settled back to wait.

* * *

It had been just before sunset when Rodrigo left. The hours went by, and Drayton caught himself again and again sliding off into semiconsciousness. He tried to count to keep himself awake, first in Spanish, then in French, then in English, very softly. It was too monotonous. He did not dare sing, and in any case deep breaths were agony. He began to recite poetry under his breath, everything he could remember from school, from his nursery days, from recitals at grand salons in London.

"Adieu, adieu, my native shore fades o'er the water blue," he murmured and then gave a wheezing chuckle as he thought of the hot, crowded ballroom where he had heard Byron's lines three years earlier declaimed by an intense young debutante who had preferred mouthing poetry to dancing. Even that soft laugh brought agony to his back; he hissed and concentrated on holding his ribs motionless. No more poetry, he decided. Too painful. His thoughts drifted to Miranda Waite, the girl his sister thought he should marry. She laughed at poets like Byron and had once corrected the metrics of a swain unwise enough to recite his verses in her praise under her window. He had competition, certainly. Miranda had plenty of suitors. She was attractive, although not beautiful, lively, unspoiled, and very, very well dowered.

Did he regret not having married younger? Then he might have left children behind him for his father . . . although there was his nephew William, of course. What a mercy he was no longer in line for the title. Sara was right; he should settle down. Miranda would be a good mother; her younger siblings idolized her. It was always noisy and cheerful at the Waite house—not like this cave, where the only sound was the drip of water and the rasp of his own breathing.

Suddenly he heard a noise on the hill below the cave and grabbed the pistol, sending a sear of pain through his left arm. Then there was a whistle, the most wonderful two notes he had ever heard. Vague shapes shadowed the moonlight in the cave entrance, a tinderbox sparked a small lantern, and Rodrigo was bending over him.

"Thank God," he said weakly.

Someone else was with Rodrigo; he caught a glimpse of a young man with dark, curling hair, and a cultured British voice said quietly, "Easy, old chap, the relief forces are here now. How are you feeling?"

Drayton ignored this question and held out the pistol. "Unload it," he croaked. "Carefully."

The stranger emptied out the powder and started to tap the bullet down the barrel. Sitting in the barrel, in front of the bullet, twined in a tight spiral, was a tiny roll of onionskin. The newcomer whistled.

"Not so amateur after all!" he said. "We shall have to load you into a wagon. It's about half a mile away. Can you walk?"

"Probably not," said Drayton honestly.

"Well, Rodrigo and I have not changed for dinner yet," said the stranger with a friendly laugh. "You can bleed on us a bit. We'll unhitch the mule and bring him as close up to the cave as we can."

The wagon ride was very bad and very long, but Drayton was only conscious for part of it. The wagon had a false bottom, which meant that he had no space to move, and no way to protect his shoulder. Once it was safe, Rodrigo and the stranger took off the stifling panel covering him and settled him more comfortably, but when they finally lifted him out of the wagon, he was covered with blood that had leaked out through the bandages and had a raging fever. He heard Rodrigo's voice, but he didn't see him, or the other man, and then he was carried into a room with long tables, and figures began bustling about with basins.

"Surgery," he thought. "I made it to the hospital after all." Someone was cutting off the rest of his shirt and sponging the blood off his back. A familiar face appeared at the foot of the table: Southey.

"This is Drayton, of the Fourteenth, wounded in the skirmish two and a half weeks ago, surgeon," said Southey crisply. "He's had a relapse. Your idiot junior surgeons appear to have left the ball in his shoulder."

"Tell Tredwell to go to hell," growled a deep voice over his shoulder. "Prestwick, get me a bullet extractor and a set of small knives." Drayton braced himself—he had seen bullets removed before—and then remembered something important.

"South! Are you still here?"

"I'm here, Richard. What is it?" An anxious face loomed over him.

"Have the dispatches gone yet? With the casualties, I mean? With my name?"

"No, we . . . er, delayed reporting your injury until you—until now."

"Until you knew whether I was dead, wounded, or whole, you mean." Drayton managed a grin. Then his face grew serious again, and he said faintly, "Must it be a skirmish? The bullet went in from the back."

Their eyes met.

"My, how self-conscious you heroes can be," drawled Southey lightly. "Very well. I'll have LeSueur change it to a sniper."

Chapter Three

England, Late March

Sara sat in the parlor of her suite at Mivart's and wished for the fourth time that day that she had opened the London house. She had come up from Kent Monday afternoon, thinking that her business could be conducted Tuesday morning and at worst on into the afternoon; it was surely not worth it for the servants to bustle around readying rooms when she might be staying only one night. But now it was Friday morning and she was no closer to finding a new governess than she had been on Tuesday. The current candidate was seated opposite her in one of the hotel's ugly gold-and-white armchairs, looking very nervous. Sara glanced down at the card next to the coffee tray. "Rachel Maitland Ross," said the notes. "Italian, French, German, history, mathematics. Young. Experience? References?" This last word was underlined twice.

On her side of the table, Rachel was trying to keep her hands still in her lap. Her mouth was dry, and she felt a bit faint. This was the most absurd scheme; it would never work. She, too, had glanced at that note card. Even upside down she could read the last two items on the list, with their damning question marks. Her coffee sat untouched; she did not dare try to drink lest the trembling of her wrists give her away.

Not suffering from this handicap, Sara picked up her cup and mechanically took a sip as she studied Rachel carefully. Only twenty-four or so, she concluded, most likely too young to take charge of a hoyden like Caroline. And she did not look anything like a governess. More like a princess of some minor European royal house, traveling incognita. The dark hair was beautifully dressed. A green silk gown fell in soft folds around the chair like the draperies in an Italian painting. The trim on the shawl matched the dress perfectly, and delicate half-boots were visible beneath the skirts. Rachel's interviewer, who did not herself indulge in expensive clothing, was nevertheless knowledgeable enough to estimate that the shawl alone had probably cost as much as her own outfit in its entirety.

Sara set her cup down firmly in its saucer. "Let me explain my situation to you, Miss Ross. The governess is required for my eight-year-old niece Caroline. She and her younger brother William are the children of my late brother, but they have been residing for the most part with us at Leigh End. Their mother died when William was an infant, and my brother subsequently went out with Wellington, so even before his death they were used to make their home with us. Legally, they are now wards of their uncle Richard, but he is still on the Peninsula and has entrusted their care to me.

"Caroline was quite ill for a time after her mother died, and although she is perfectly well now she refuses to settle down to lessons. She has grown more and more impossible, especially since my own two boys went off to school last year." Sara sighed. "She is a master strategist, I am sorry to say. She took to her bed with the first governess, who left after two months of Caroline's convenient 'illnesses' during lesson times. The rest she has terrified with spiders, or snakes, or some other creatures—she adores animals—or she has spread rumors about them among the servants, or, in the last case, she woke the poor woman every night making horrid noises in the wall of her room."

She paused cautiously, awaiting the reaction of the potential victim, and saw a frown. Stiffly, she said, "Please do not feel that you need to stay for the rest of the interview, Miss Ross, if my niece's behavior would make the position unacceptable to you."

Rachel was still frowning to herself. "Does Caroline have a nurse?" she asked abruptly. She no longer looked so anxious.

Sara looked thoughtfully at the younger woman. "Indeed she does," she responded dryly, "and you are the first person with the wit to ask me that question. Caroline has her own nurse, because she was so ill when William was little that we hired a second woman to take care of him. Mrs. Mott is devoted to her, and Caroline exploits her shamelessly."

"I would guess that Mrs. Mott is not heartbroken when a governess leaves."

"Not at all," confirmed Sara. In spite of herself she was impressed. "Does this mean you might consider taking the position?" she asked hesitantly. "Could you tell me something about your training? Your previous pupils?"

"Yes, my training," stammered Rachel, fixing on the safer of the two topics. "I am afraid that I am not proficient in all of the subjects a governess usually teaches. I can instruct her in modern languages, of course. Also, I read Latin, and have done a bit of Greek and Hebrew. I was tutored with my brother for several years," she explained, seeing Sara's surprise. "Hence the mathematics, also. I am not at all artistic, however. My sketches have a distressing tendency to look like a draftsman's rendering of the scene, and you will have to have a separate music teacher, because my singing is dreadful and no pianoforte is safe in my hands.

"As for your second question, I must be honest with you, Lady Barrett. I have never been a governess. I have been much with children, though—I took charge of my brother when I was twelve and he was Caroline's age, and when my young cousins visit, I am always their guide and playmate, since they cannot see anything of London with nursemaids who speak no English." At this piece of information, Sara gave a slight start.

"In spite of my lack of experience, I am quite certain I could handle Caroline, could you but find an excuse to send Mrs. Mott away for the first ten days I am there. Has she a sister or an aged mother, or something of that sort? Perhaps they could be induced to request a visit?"

"She has an aunt," said Sara, thinking hard, "who is the widow of my brother's lodge keeper and might well agree to help us." She began to feel somewhat hopeful. This candidate was more promising than she had thought at first. Then she remembered something. "You mentioned in your letter that you only wished to take the position temporarily? How long did you have in mind? A year, perhaps?"

"Four months," admitted Rachel with some trepidation, gripping the fringe of her shawl tightly.

Sara stared at her in astonishment. "Four months?" she said weakly, picturing herself repeating the horrors of the past week in the heat of July in London. "Miss Ross, why on earth would you wish to take a position for only four months? I have never heard of such a thing!"

The fringe of the shawl was being twisted into a tortured spiral; Rachel forced herself to drop it. It uncurled over the top of her leg and lay there accusingly, crumpled and bent. "Lady Barrett, I find myself in a rather difficult situation." Her voice was strained, and she kept her gaze fixed on the battered fringe. "I was not educated to be a governess, nor will I pretend that financial embarrassment forces me to seek work. The truth is, my family is conspiring to send me abroad, and I have very pressing reasons to remain in England. Perhaps it was foolish, but I thought that a temporary post of this sort would allow me to remain here."

Without looking up she could sense the other woman's uneasiness. "Please do not imagine that I am an undutiful daughter, or that I am in disgrace," she said hastily. "It is quite the opposite, in fact. My father is out of the country at the moment and may be gone for some time. I promised him, before he left, that I would watch over my younger brother. He is just now of age, but rather wild, and my uncle, who has taken us into his household, does not get on with him at all." Here she gave an expressive grimace which was instantly familiar to Sara, whose hot-tempered sire had been quarreling with his younger son for as long as she could remember. "My father does not solicit such promises lightly. I know why he is concerned; my brother is a rebel who seems to take a perverse delight in being as reckless as possible. When he was serving on the Peninsula, he did not always listen to his colonel, any more than he listens to my uncle. And he takes offense very readily; my father and I are forever intervening to prevent duels."

"What was his regiment?" Sara asked, leaning forward, her uneasiness forgotten. This wild younger brother sounded just like Richard.

"The Ninety-fifth, the rifle corps. But he is now back in England, doing government work in London and Dover." She stopped there, not daring to say more. "I must also tell you that it has been understood for many years that I would marry one of my Italian cousins." A merry smile appeared suddenly. "One of the older ones, who has outgrown nursemaids, of course." She summoned up her courage and looked directly at Sara. "Please do not imagine, ma'am, that I am not sensible of my obligation to my family to make a proper match. But now my uncle, that is, the one who resides in London, tells me that my cousin will visit here this spring and that he expects me to return with this cousin to Italy as his bride. I cannot go abroad and leave my brother alone. And I cannot tell my uncle of my promise to my father; he and my brother would be furious. Besides, my uncle would not consider such a promise of any weight in comparison with the expedience of sending me to Italy under my cousin's protection."

She continued in a lower voice, "I have been trying to think of how to manage, and I hit upon the idea of taking a position as a governess for a few months, and telling my uncle that I was going to Germany to visit family there and would meet my cousin as he returned to Italy. In this way I thought that I could remain near my brother. I would have to bring our family groom with me to serve as a messenger, of course, as well as my maid. Could you perhaps use another groom temporarily? I would privately reimburse you for his wages, but I think that it is not customary for governesses to have their own grooms."

"No, indeed," said Sara, in a trance. "Nor even usually their own maids; we have been used to assign the governesses one of the upper maids part time."

"Once my father returns, I could sail to Italy and be married. I assume that as a governess I would not go into society much, and the children are probably left in Kent during the season . . . You do not host Lord Wellington or his senior officers in Kent, do you? They might recognize me, and they know my uncle well." She recollected herself and said despondently, "In any case, I see now that it will not serve. It was a ridiculous notion. I am sure you would not wish to hire someone for such a short time. Especially someone who has no experience and who cannot furnish any references. I had forgotten that even first-time governesses would be expected to provide testimonials."

Sara was astounded by the implications of this strange recital, but she said after a moment, "Yes, of course—letters from the vicar, or a great-aunt, or something of that sort. And it is quite unthinkable to hire a gently bred woman as a governess without the knowledge of her family. Were you underage, we could be charged with kidnapping if we housed you without their consent."

"I see that now," said Rachel quietly. She looked very discouraged. "I am five-and-twenty, as it happens, and my brother would know where I was. It seemed to answer so well; that was what prompted me to write to you when I saw the advertisement. Your estate is close to both London and the coast, and there were no older boys in the family. I had heard that younger governesses could not normally find places in households with marriageable sons." She spoke lightly, but blushed and lowered her eyes. "I must thank you for your time, Lady Barrett."

She rose politely. Sara rose also but neither moved towards the door. Rachel stood still, considering the pleasant, open face before her. There was a long silence. "Lady Barrett." She swallowed. "If I tell you my real name, will you consider assisting me, or at least making a trial? But I must have your word that you will tell no one my secret, not even your husband or brother, without my permission."

"Agreed," said Sara slowly. She thought to herself, I must be mad. Rachel tugged open her reticule and gently offered her a card.

"My uncle's card."

No wonder she never inquired about the wages, thought Sara, stunned. The name on the card was well known to her. He was one of the richest men in England—no, in all Europe; an intimate of Wellington, a man with the ear of princes and kings in six countries. Not a man to deceive lightly. She made a faint sound of protest and unconsciously moved back, away from the outstretched hand and the little square of pasteboard.

Rachel, watching her, turned perfectly white, and her eyes blazed. She cursed herself for a fool. What else had she expected?

"Pray excuse me," she said with an effort. "I apologize for my presumption. I am sure you quite see now why I have no letter from the vicar. You would be in dread every time I escorted Caroline to church that a bolt of lightning would strike, would you not?"

Sara's brain began to function again. She reached out and took the card. She read it twice. She looked at Rachel. "Your brother was truly in the Ninety-fifth? Was that not rather difficult for him?"

"Do you imply that he was not fit for it?" demanded Rachel, flaring up again.

"My dear," Sara said calmly, "if your brother is as hot-at-hand as you are, I am very sure your father is right to have someone looking after him."

Rachel's face slowly relaxed its guard. A rueful smile appeared. "You may find this difficult to believe, my lady, but I am the prudent one in my family."

"I had thought I could say the same of myself," muttered Sara. She frowned. "The servants will be the most difficult. You are most unlike any of the previous governesses, and they would not be fooled even if you bought an entirely new wardrobe. I think it will be best to claim you as a distant connection, perhaps the niece of a school friend. You are from a wealthy family; your parents are odd and do not approve of society . . . You are a bit of a bluestocking, with some theories about female education. It is fortunate that you have studied mathematics and Latin; that will give credence to the notion that you are willing to undertake Caroline's education as an experiment to confirm your theories. Your parents are abroad, and for our mutual convenience you have consented to act as governess temporarily, but as a guest rather than an employee. This will explain the presence of your own maid and groom, and will allow you to dine with the family."

Rachel was looking at her with delighted astonishment.

Sara was still thinking. "Aunt Estelle is so inquisitive," she murmured. "We had best make it someplace countrified . . . I have it! Shropshire!" She turned to Rachel. "Your father's family is originally from near Shrewsbury. But your eccentric parents have lived mostly abroad or in London. Will that do, do you think?"

"Lady Barrett," said Rachel with great earnestness, "I believe I will feel quite at home in your household. You remind me of my father. He concocts false identities faster than our cook makes pastries."

Sara was not quite sure whether this was a compliment or not.

Chapter Four

Ostlers were hitching up the new horses at Maidstone, and Rachel stretched briefly, feeling quite pleased with herself. Her farewells to her uncle and aunt had gone smoothly, and Maria and Samuels had behaved perfectly. She blessed Lady Barrett for proposing that she be more of a guest than a governess. Governesses, she supposed, did not ride in carriages. But she was not quite certain. And there were a host of other questions she need not answer now: When real governesses arrived at the house, which door did they use? Did they give vails to the servants? Could they go riding without the excuse of escorting their pupils?

Well, she could have her own horse and groom with her, and her own maid. She could go for rides, the wonderful long rides which were impossible in London. She could wear her own dresses and jewelry. She would have a guest room, and not a room near the nursery, where it might be more difficult to slip out at night to send Samuels with messages to James. Certainly she would still make some errors—after all, she was used to her odd life in London and was not familiar with the way of things on country estates. But Lady Barrett's story would provide an excuse for her lapses.

Maria was still asleep. "Confound the woman," thought Rachel, who had been hoping to review her script once more with her maid, "she has been sleeping for this age!" She leaned over and shook a round shoulder gently.

"Señorita?" mumbled the maid.

"Don't call me that!" said Rachel at once. "You are supposed to be Italian. Lady Barrett and I agreed that was far less suspicious."

"I am sorry, Miss Rachel," said Maria apologetically.

"Tell me my name," demanded Rachel.

"Miss Ross, Rachel Maitland Ross," answered Maria, pronouncing *Maitland* as a three-syllable word, "Mai-te-land."

"And my parents? Where are they?"

"Germany, se—Miss Rachel. With your brother."

"And my aunt? The acquaintance of Lady Barrett?"

"Miss Eugenia Ross, your father's sister. But you know, Miss Rachel, these are not the things I will be asked. The servants, they speak always about how the mistress behaves, and does she slap you if you tangle the comb in the hair, and is the brother one of those who pinches girls."

"And is he?" asked Rachel coolly.

"Miss *Rachel!"* said Maria, scandalized. But in a few minutes her head was nodding again and her plump arms sagged against the cushions. Rachel sighed and closed her own eyes.

Samuels's voice woke her. The carriage had pulled up for a moment; he was asking directions of two children playing by a gate. Then he turned off the main road. Mossy walls glistened in the early April sunshine, and gentle hills rolled off towards the south. It was very quiet and green, the gentle spring green as trees first begin to leaf again. There were no other vehicles on this smaller road. Suddenly Rachel was no longer so comfortable. What if her cousin Juliette did not post her letter back to her uncle from Germany? What if someone had seen Samuels leading her mare away from the livery stable? What if her uncle checked with the master of the ship—the ship she would not be boarding? What if someone visiting the Barretts recognized her? What if she could not manage Caroline? And beneath all these worries, the real fear: What if her father did not come back this time? And what if James got himself killed trying to help him?

"Stop it," she scolded herself. "They have always come back before. We have always managed somehow." But looking down, to blink away the tears in her eyes, she missed the turn onto the drive of Leigh End. She did not realize they were no longer on the road until a few minutes later, when the carriage drew to a halt.

Samuels handed her out of the carriage, and she stood looking with silent admiration at the house. The fashion now was for Italianate villas, but with the perversity of one who had visited Rome frequently, Rachel preferred crooked Tudor floors and plain, rectangular planes to the curves and columns of modern houses. This was her favorite kind of house: square-fronted, brick, mellow, and old, covered with ivy. English. The windows on the upper story had all been replaced, but at least two of the ground-floor rooms retained the mullioned windows like the ones in her father's study in the London house. He had refused to let her uncle put in sash windows. Rachel could see from the line of chimney tops that the house formed a *U*-shape facing back to the gardens.

One corner of the garden was visible, and a small human form was crouching down at the end of a path. Rachel narrowed her eyes. The shape appeared to be female, hatless, and under four feet tall. "Caroline, I'll wager," she thought. "Going in search of some dreadful insect to put in my bedchamber. Two can play at that game." She took a small hinged container out of her reticule.

Thus it was that when Lady Barrett, escorted by Minton, came down the steps to receive her, she found Rachel on her knees in the plantings by the front terrace carefully packing a small and very wriggly spider into a ring box.

"Oh, dear!" said Rachel, scrambling to her feet. "I had not realized that Samuels had knocked at the front door yet. I was just collecting a . . . er, a gift for Miss Caroline."

"So I see," said Sara, trying not to laugh. Minton maintained a majestic calm. "I hope your journey was not too tiring? I will show you to your room straightway; you will wish to refresh yourself before tea, will you not?"

Rachel looked down at her pelisse, which now had several clumps of dirt attached to the lower hem. "Thank you," she said gratefully. "Perhaps

Maria can help me make myself presentable again."

"Have no fear," said Sara in an undertone as Minton stalked pompously ahead of them into the front hall, "Minton is most discreet. He confides only in Mrs. Tibbet, the housekeeper. By the end of the servants' teatime, Mrs. Tibbet will make sure that everyone down to the gardener's boy knows that you are just as eccentric as I have painted you."

"I thought I would steal a march on Caroline," said Rachel, embarrassed. "I saw her in the garden, and it looked as though she was capturing some little crawling ally to launch her campaign to drive me off."

"Very likely," agreed Sara, smiling. Caroline had a surprise coming, she thought, and it was not confined to the ring box.

Tea was served in the small drawing room, which had French doors opening onto a terrace which ran the width of the back of the house. Rachel's confidence had been somewhat restored by a change of clothing and a hasty wash. Sara looked up from the tea tray and noted with approval Rachel's neat cambric gown and lace fichu.

"Aunt Estelle," she said, "may I present Miss Ross? Miss Ross, my husband's aunt, Miss Lutford." The other occupant of the room leaned forward and peered at Rachel. She was a tiny, restless woman with implausibly dark hair and a hawklike face.

"Ross," she muttered. "Ross. Any connection with Lavinia Ross? The one who married that Italian count? Or Edward Ross, that good-for-nothing?

He was one of my suitors. From Essex, both of 'em."

"No, ma'am," said Rachel, casting a beseeching glance at Sara. "I'm afraid my branch of the family is not well known." Rachel had seen this game played in London drawing rooms before but had never been a participant. She knew, however, that expert players—and Miss Lutford looked to be one—could trace the genealogies of dozens of county families out to the third cousins, and recall something scandalous about each twig on the family tree in the process.

"I told you, Aunt Estelle," said Sara calmly, "Miss Ross's people are originally from Shropshire. But Miss Ross has lived in London or on the Continent, for the most part. Would you care for some tea, Miss Ross? I have asked Betsy to bring Caroline in to join us."

"I infer," said Rachel with a smile, "that I might be well advised to fortify myself before she arrives?"

"Oh, no," said Sara. "Caroline always behaves perfectly when her great-aunt is present."

"Hmmmph," snorted Miss Lutford. But she looked gratified.

Rachel seated herself and accepted a cup of tea and a seed cake. Her enjoyment of these items was somewhat hindered by Miss Lutford's persistent questions about her family. Fortunately, her inquisitor was easily distracted by Rachel's descriptions of the various places she had lived with her parents, and in the midst of a discussion of the perils of Italian inns, a freckled maid opened the door and gently ushered in a young girl.

"Caroline!" said Sara. "Come and make your curtsy to Miss Ross. Miss Ross, this is my niece, Caroline."

The girl was small for her age, Rachel saw, and wiry. She had fine, curling fair hair and blue eyes which glared fiercely at Rachel for an instant before she came over and made an awkward bob. Rachel observed that the maid had not managed to get all the dirt out from under Caroline's fingernails.

"How do you do, Caroline?" she said. "I hope we may be friends." Instantly, she regretted the second phrase, which she herself had loathed hearing as a child. Caroline woodenly made a second dip towards the floor.

"Well, I hope you may teach that girl to make a proper curtsy!" snapped Miss Lutford. "Five governesses and not one could even manage that."

"You raise a complicated question, ma'am," said Rachel. "That is, what is a proper curtsy?" She was feeling reckless. Springing up from her chair and shaking out her skirts, she continued, "For example, in Germany it is most improper for unmarried young ladies to lower the shoulders when curtsying. It is considered immodest." Rachel sank gracefully to the floor, keeping her back and head completely upright. "In France, however, the head must always incline." She repeated the movement, this time bowing her head until it nearly touched her knees. "Those are full curtsies, of course, for court occasions. And then there is the question of handling different types of skirts. The placement of the hands is crucial."

Miss Lutford was staring at her in astonishment, and Caroline's eyes were like saucers. Rachel hastily regrouped.

"Caroline, I brought you a small gift," she said, turning to the girl. She fished the ring box out of her reticule. "I think you had best open it out on the terrace."

"Why?" said Caroline, accepting the box with a puzzled frown.

"Because Lady Barrett and Miss Lutford will not like it if you open it in here," replied Rachel enigmatically.

Intrigued, Caroline tugged open the door and went out onto the terrace. Rachel forced herself to stay seated and appear calm. She was expecting to hear a shriek but instead heard only a small scrambling sound, and then Caroline reappeared.

"It got away," she said, disappointed.

"Well, it was a very small one," said Rachel. "They are quite fast, and difficult to catch."

"Aren't you scared of spiders?"

"No."

"Snakes?"

"Some snakes. Anacondas, for example."

The two other women were sitting with their teacups suspended in midair.

"What is a Naconda?" asked Caroline.

"A snake found in the East Indies, yards and yards long. It hangs on trees, looking like a vine, until you walk underneath it."

"Ooooooh," breathed Caroline. Then she recalled her mission. "What else are you scared of?" she asked eagerly.

"Caroline," said Sara in forbidding tones.

Rachel looked at Caroline. "Everyone has things which frighten them," she said. "But usually we only tell our special friends what they are."

"Then," said Caroline in her most grown-up manner, "I also hope we may be friends."

* * *

Dinner was a quiet affair. Sir Charles had just returned from London, accompanied by a portly older man who looked vaguely familiar to Rachel. He was introduced to her as Mr. Castell, and since he did not appear to recognize her, she relaxed. Sir Charles himself looked a bit like his aunt: the same hawk face and piercing hazel eyes, the same slight build. He did not seem like a man who missed much, and Rachel wondered how long it would be before she would have to give Lady Barrett permission to tell him who she really was. But conversation at dinner took no dangerous turns, and since three of the party had been traveling, Rachel was able to return to her room fairly early. Maria was waiting for her.

"I found it, Miss Rachel," she said triumphantly. "In your washbasin, under the pitcher." She held out a cup, inverted over a saucer. Under the cup was a very small frog.

"Hmmmm," said Rachel. "I expected worse. Did you look all the way through the bedclothes?"

"I remade the entire bed, Miss Rachel. *And* took the bolsters out of their cases."

Rachel went over to the wardrobe and shook each garment vigorously. Nothing. She inspected her hairbrush and ruffled through the pile of chemises in her trunk. Two books on the nightstand were examined. She turned her nightcap inside out. At the last moment she thought to look inside both pairs of boots.

"Aha!" she said. A large chestnut-burr emerged from the toe of one riding boot.

"Now," said Rachel, "I think we can go to bed. Could you take the frog downstairs and put him outside, please, Maria? And wake me very early tomorrow morning."

"I want Mottsy!" wailed Caroline, gripping the coverlet as Betsy tried to remove it.

"Now, miss!" said poor Betsy, exasperated. "You know Mrs. Mott is gone to visit her sick old aunt. You're to have a lesson today with Miss Ross, and you should have been dressed this hour and more. Your porridge is gone all cold."

"I don't want any porridge," said Caroline sullenly. "I feel ill. I want my nurse. My stomach hurts."

"Good morning, Caroline," said a voice from the doorway. "Thank you for my frog, but I thought he might be too hot in my room, so I had Maria put him back outside." Rachel was in her riding habit. Caroline could not help it; she sat up and peered hopefully at the boots. Rachel fished the chestnut burr out of the pocket of her jacket and handed it over to Caroline. "Maria and I found it last night," she said dryly. "My toes are intact."

"Miss Ross," said Betsy apologetically, "I know I was supposed to help Miss Caroline dress and be ready for lessons, but she says she is feeling poorly."

"Yes, I heard," said Rachel, eyeing her charge. "Thank you, Betsy, that will be all. I am quite an experienced nurse, and I am sure I can tend Caroline this morning." Greatly relieved, Betsy fled.

"What seems to be the matter?" she asked Caroline, very solicitous.

"My stomach hurts," said Caroline warily. She had counted on dealing with Betsy, who knew that Mrs. Mott brought her candied ginger to suck on when she was ill and let her cut out paper dolls in bed.

"Mmmmmm," said Rachel thoughtfully. "Let's have a look at you." She peered into Caroline's eyes and felt her forehead. "No fever. Do your elbows hurt?"

"Oh, yes," said Caroline, falling neatly into the trap. "Most awfully."

"No lesson this morning, then," said Rachel crisply. She marched to the windows and ruthlessly closed the curtains. The lovely April morning disappeared from view. She rang the bell. "Lie down now, Caroline, and we'll have you feeling better in a few days. You must rest and not tire yourself. I will sit here where there is a little light and read to you. I bought a book just for you in London, about proper deportment for young ladies." Betsy reappeared.

"Betsy, could you ask Cook to make some thin gruel for Miss Caroline? And please send Maria in; she has my case with the tonics. I am sure Miss Caroline needs a dose of Dr. Darkhouse's elixir."

"I . . . I think I might be feeling a bit better now," said Caroline.

"Now, now, dear," said Rachel. "Don't try to be brave. I have nursed my little cousin frequently, you know, and she is getting on very well. She can walk with a cane now, and they thought she would be confined to an invalid chair forever."

"Oh," gasped Caroline.

Then Rachel repented; she did not want to terrify the child. "I am just teasing, Caroline," she said gently. "But you are not really ill, are you?"

"No," said Caroline in a small voice. Rachel motioned to Betsy, who discreetly withdrew. She would have a tale for Mrs. Tibbet, so she would!

"Ladies do not tell fibs," said Rachel sternly. Then, recollecting her own situation, she added, "Unless they need to do so to protect someone else."

There was a long silence.

"I am very sorry, Miss Ross," said Caroline reluctantly. She added quickly, "Are you going to punish me?"

"Do you know what we were going to do for our lesson?" asked Rachel.

"French?"

"No, go riding and then do some nature drawing. Samuels found some birds' nests in the lower wood."

"Oh, famous! Can we go? I have a new horse, a real horse; she is taller than me! Aunt Sara said you like to ride. I'll get dressed right now, I can dress myself. I'll be very, very good, I promise!"

"Caroline, do you think I should take you riding?" said Rachel, looking her in the eye.

The blue eyes fell. "No," she whispered.

"What do you think would be fair?" said Rachel. "You said you were ill to avoid your lessons."

"You could whip me," said Caroline hopefully. She had seen Sir Charles cane one of her cousins once. Whippings were over quickly, and Ned had told her that it only hurt a little. "Or . . ." She swallowed. "You could make me lie in bed all day." Her eyes filled with tears.

"All day is too long," said Rachel gently. She was smiling; the girl was a handful, but she liked her, at heart. "If you will lie still for an hour and then eat your breakfast, we can go riding after that. I promise you that an hour will seem very, very long in a dark room when you are thinking about riding your new horse."

"Will you stay with me?" whispered Caroline. "Or can Betsy come back?"

"I'll stay," said Rachel. "I brought a book." She held it up. It was not a book about proper deportment for young ladies. Caroline squinted at the letters on the binding.

"Oh! It's a novel! What if I had asked you to read to me about deportment?"

"I think I could have found something to tell you," said Rachel, her eyes twinkling. "I never finished my lecture about curtsies, you know. Now lie down, so that we can go riding before lunch."

Rachel was under no illusions: She had won the first battle, but the war was not over. After riding, in fact, she made a tactical error. She should have taken luncheon with Sir Charles and Lady Barrett, but instead chose to join Caroline and William in the nursery and have a tray sent up. Her fear of awkward questions from Sir Charles or Miss Lutford, she realized, had led her astray. Left on her own with William and his nurse, Caroline would probably have looked forward to rejoining Rachel for lessons after lunch. But now, having gulped her food in ten minutes, she was sitting on the floor next to Rachel cutting out paper dolls while Rachel ate her meal in a more civilized fashion. She had good adult company, she was fed, she was happily occupied—how was Rachel going to get her to do a lesson?

"Shall we go for a walk?" suggested Rachel tentatively once she had finished eating. "I have not yet seen the garden."

"Oh, yes, do let's," said Caroline, too promptly. Something was wrong. But what? Rachel looked around. William's nurse was cleaning off his tucker and getting ready to take him off for a nap. The nursery seemed friendly and clean; the toys were in their places. The door to the schoolroom was open, and Rachel could see nothing amiss in there either. Caroline's face was guileless. Rachel sighed and went to fetch her shawl. She would find out sooner or later what that little imp was plotting.

It was sooner, as it turned out. She had not even reached the bottom of the front staircase, where Caroline was waiting for her, when she heard a gasp of dismay from Lady Barrett, who was just below her in the hall.

"Miss Ross! Whatever has happened to your dress!"

Rachel looked down and at first saw nothing wrong. She twisted to the right, and then the left, peering over her shoulder. Then, to her horror, she realized that the entire left seam of her skirt had been nearly slit in two. Her petticoat was exposed all the way to her thigh, right through the banister of the staircase. And to complete her mortification, Sir Charles and Mr. Castell, who were preparing to ride out for the afternoon, had just emerged from the dining room and were looking straight at her.

"Oh, heavens!" she gasped. "How clumsy of me! Lady Barrett, pray excuse me!" She folded the seam over under her left hand with a convulsive twist. "I was cutting some cloth out for Caroline up in the nursery and I must have cut through two layers without realizing it." She did not look at Caroline, nor at the two men, who were more amused than shocked. With some attempt to preserve her dignity, she turned as calmly as she could and retreated with a stately tread to her room, clutching the ripped seam. Maria was there airing her bed, and she threw her hands in the air with a shriek when she saw the side of Rachel's skirt.

"*Señorita!* Miss Rachel, you went out with that terrible hole in your skirt! And I gave you your shawl myself and never have noticed!" She folded down onto her knees beside Rachel and inspected the damage. "It is right along the seam, Miss Rachel; it will be easy to mend. Did anyone see you?"

"Yes," said Rachel. "Everyone." She started to laugh. Caroline burst in.

"You didn't tell! You knew I did it! Why didn't you tell?" she demanded furiously.

"Caroline," said Rachel firmly, "ladies do not enter other people's rooms without knocking. Go out and try again." Caroline gave her a smoldering look but marched out, head high, closed the door, and knocked.

"Maria," said Rachel loudly, "please tell whoever is at the door that I am not dressed yet. I will be ready shortly."

"You should beat her," said Maria fiercely as she unbuttoned the cambric dress. "Look, there is a small rip in the petticoat, also."

"Never mind," said Rachel. "I don't want to put on a new petticoat. Just give me my blue walking dress and the other shawl." She dressed as slowly as possible and let Maria take a long time rearranging her hair. At last she nodded to Maria to open the door. A small figure sat forlornly on the floor outside.

"Maria," said Rachel, "ask Miss Caroline to come in." Caroline came in slowly. She was angry, and puzzled. Aunt Sara had said Miss Ross was odd, and she certainly was. Grown-up ladies were upset if even their ankles showed in front of gentlemen, and Caroline had made Miss Ross show her whole petticoat, and she had laughed! Caroline had heard her, through the bedroom door.

"Why didn't you tell my aunt and uncle it was me?" she asked again. "I did it when I was pretending to cut my paper dolls. You know I did. You told a fib."

Rachel sighed. "I did, yes. But remember I said ladies sometimes told fibs to protect other people. The rules for being a lady are not easy. For example, ladies do not carry tales. And that rule is more important than the rule about not telling fibs, especially if it is a very small fib."

Caroline nodded. "I know about that rule. Jamie and Ned told me. They said tattling is worse than almost anything. Boys who tattle at school get sent to Cob-tree."

"What?" said Rachel. "Oh! Coventry!"

Caroline hung her head. "Will you make me pick my own punishment again?"

"Do you want to do that?"

Caroline shook her head. "Yours are probably nicer than mine."

"Can you sew?"

Caroline made a face. "Yes."

Rachel glanced at Maria, who was looking horrified. "Not well enough to mend my dress properly, though. I shall ask Mrs. Tibbet to give us some linens which need mending, and you shall sew up the equivalent of twice the length of the seam you ripped."

"That will take hours," said Caroline mournfully.

"Yes, no French lesson this afternoon, what a shame," said Rachel casually. "And I had such a lovely plan. It will have to wait until tomorrow." Stealing a glance at Caroline's face, she concluded that she had made up at least some ground. She had best think of some clever plan for a French lesson before the morning.

Sara hurried up the stairs and down the back hall to the nursery. She had hoped to see Rachel at breakfast this morning and find out how she was getting on with Caroline. Yesterday's tale of Dr. Darkhouse's elixir had made the rounds of the entire household already. And Sara knew perfectly well who had cut Rachel's skirt.

They had had no chance to talk after dinner last night because Aunt Estelle had prosed on for an hour about the new vicar, who had already in less than a month managed to offend that rather conservative lady in ways too numerous to recount. Then Sara had received the letter at breakfast, and her need to find Rachel became even more urgent. Fortunately, Betsy had been able to tell her that Miss Ross and Miss Caroline had already returned from a ride and were up in the schoolroom. Sara paused outside the door. She could hear voices inside. They were speaking French.

"*Merci bien, mademoiselle,*" said Rachel's voice.

"*Je vous—je vous,*" stuttered Caroline. Sara heard a whispered prompt. "*Je vous en prie,*" said Caroline happily.

Sara heard a step beside her. It was Betsy. "Oh, my lady!" she whispered. "You should peek in. It's as good as a play, it is! Mrs. Tibbet gave Miss Ross all them old things from the trunks upstairs, from Sir Charles's grandmama, and Miss Caroline has been as careful as careful."

Opening the door slightly, Sara peered inside. Rachel saw her at once and nodded in a friendly way. Caroline had her back to the door, however. She was wearing a white ball gown which had been made for a very small lady, but it was still pinned up everywhere. She carried, as though it were made of eggshells, an ancient ivory fan. Her blond curls had been powdered and piled on her head. A mirror had been carried in from one of the dressing rooms, and Caroline was admiring herself. She looked so animated and happy that Sara almost withdrew without interrupting. But then Caroline caught sight of her aunt in the mirror.

"Oh, look! Look at me, Aunt Sara! I'm a French lady!"

"Tiens, petite," said Rachel, scolding. *"Pas en anglais, s'il te plaît."*

"Ah, oui," said Caroline carefully. *"J'ai . . . j'ai oublié.*

"Please excuse me," said Sara. "I came to see if you would like to come into Haythorn with me after lunch, Miss Ross." Rachel could see that she had something more to say. She stepped out into the hall and looked at Sara doubtfully.

"Is there something wrong, Lady Barrett?" she asked quietly.

"Yes—no—not really," was the disjointed reply. "I have had a letter from my brother. He has been wounded but is recovering well, and is on his way back to England. He will be here in a sennight or so." Misinterpreting Rachel's look of concern, she added, "I am sure he will be happy to have you continue working with Caroline, and will be eager to meet you."

"Oh, that is not at all what I was thinking," Rachel blurted out. "My own . . . I have known," she corrected instantly, "so many people who have friends and kinsmen fighting with Wellington. You must be very worried about your brother."

"I am," said Sara, feeling her throat go tight and tears start up behind her lowered eyelids. "But I am so happy that he is safe for the moment, at least, and that we will see him. Please don't tell Caroline; if he were to be delayed she would be so disappointed. We will let it be a surprise. I am going into Haythorn to order some of his favorite things from the grocer; he is always complaining about the food in Spain. And it is a beautiful village; I thought you might want to see it."

"That would be lovely," said Rachel sincerely.

"How are you faring with Caroline?" asked Sara, tearing her mind away from her concern about Richard with some difficulty.

Rachel softly opened the door to make sure that her charge was out of earshot. Caroline was at the other end of the nursery, practicing walking in a pair of ancient red-heeled pumps.

"Well," said Rachel with a smile, "I'm not routed yet. But she is a resourceful girl, your Caroline."

"Yes," said Sara. "She takes after my father. As does my brother. He has always landed on his feet so far. I am sure he will be well again very quickly."

"And then he will go back."

"Yes," said Sara heavily.

Rachel sighed. "He sounds just like *my* brother."

"Men!" said Sara. She felt better. Her inexplicable impulse to share her news with Rachel first had been right. She went back down the hall, humming lightly and plotting extravagant orders at the grocer's in Haythorn. She must remember to send down to Sussex for Richard's horse. With luck, Sleet would be here waiting when he arrived.

Chapter Five

White's was thin of company this evening, and when Drayton and Southey entered, they were surrounded immediately by young bucks hungry for news of the campaign and glad of fresh faces. "It's Drayton!" called out George Chapman as card players emerged from the side parlor. "Name your seconds, everyone!" Drayton flushed. Had he really such a name for being a hothead? But he soon forgot his momentary embarrassment as long-missed friends greeted him with unfeigned warmth and concern and deluged him with offers of drinks, dinners, horses at bargain prices, and introductions to the latest belles. Southey had at first stationed himself strategically to prevent newcomers from clapping Drayton on the shoulder, but when one of his acquaintances drew him aside, Drayton was left unprotected and winced visibly as a hand grasped him from behind.

"By Jupiter! It *is* you, Drayton," said a laughing

voice, which changed almost immediately to an embarrassed one. "I've hurt you! Didn't know you were wounded. I beg your pardon, old man!"

"Corey!" said Drayton eagerly, turning. Ferdinand Courthope, a shy young lieutenant with brown hair and light brown eyes stood smiling apologetically. He was wearing dress regimentals, as was Drayton.

"I came in on the other transport and spotted you at Portsmouth," said Courthope. "I was hoping we could travel together up to London, but you gave me the cut direct."

"Never!" protested Drayton. "I did not see you, you gudgeon. To tell the truth, I was not feeling quite the thing until a day or so ago. There wouldn't have been room in the post-chaise in any case; I shared it with Southey. Why on earth would I cut you? Haven't seen you in ages!"

"Well," said Courthope honestly, "the last time was when I was seconding Fielding, and he was an hour late."

"Oh, that!" said Drayton. "Anyone can get confused about which park has been agreed on by the seconds. I am staying with Fielding at his lodgings, in fact. I had forgot all about that silly duel."

"Speak not so loudly," advised Courthope sardonically. "At least five of your opponents in those 'silly duels' are within hearing distance."

"Hullo, Drayton," said a smiling dark-haired young man at that moment. He was wearing the uniform of a captain of rifles. "I believe I am one of the victims just mentioned. How are you?" And he clasped Drayton's hand with obvious pleasure.

"Victim?" said Drayton. "You winged me, as I recall. I only grazed your ribs. You don't appear to be in such good form at the moment, however," he added, frowning. The new arrival was leaning on a cane, and bandages were visible under the breeches above his right knee. "Evrett, you know Courthope?"

"Oh, yes, we've met," Courthope nodded. "Evrett has been a regular visitor at headquarters until recently. What happened?" he said, turning to Evrett.

"My horse was shot under me, and it rolled over my knee," said Evrett, making a face. "Curst nuisance; my lieutenant is an idiot and I've had to come home and hope my unit can still remember how to present arms by the time I get back. Are you going to the charity ball?" he added, looking at their elegant uniforms.

"No; I had thought of it," said Drayton, "but somehow I can't stomach the thought of a whole ballroom full of people jostling me. Are you?"

Evrett shook his head. "I'm safer than you," he said, laughing and brandishing his cane, "but not exactly in dancing form. I take it you're wounded?"

"Just a trifle," said Drayton cheerfully. "I took a ball in my left shoulder. Home on leave for a bit."

Evrett looked up to see an older man bearing down on him. "Ah," he said. "Winters wants his revenge for last night. I predict he will have my winnings and more." And he strolled off towards the card room.

The two friends stood for a moment in companionable silence.

"Are you going down to Sussex?" said Courthope abruptly, looking carefully at his schoolmate.

Drayton shook his head and answered curtly, "No."

So Alcroft and his son were still not on terms, thought Courthope.

"I'm paying a few calls here in town and looking in on my man of business, and then I'll go down to my sister's and see Harry's children. I am their guardian, you know."

Courthope looked at him with sympathy. "I heard about Harry. Very bad news. Splendid fellow."

Drayton mumbled an acknowledgment and, groping desperately for a change of subject asked, "And you? Going up to Lincolnshire?"

"I think not. No one there right now but the servants. My mother has gone to Bath with my grandmother. I suppose I'll have to trundle over eventually, but I despise the place, and my grandmother gives me the fidgets. She thinks m'father and I are both about to get killed over on the Peninsula every minute, even though we are both safe at headquarters doing nothing except writing memos." This last was said with some bitterness.

"Come down to Leigh End with me for a few days, then," said Drayton impulsively. "You can go on to Bath from there if you must. My sister would be delighted to see you, and you can protect me from Barrett's aunt." He groaned. "I think she can read my mind. She always knows every dreadful thing I have done while I have been away, but she won't rake me over the coals in front of a stranger. Southey is riding down with me most of the way; his place is quite near Leigh End. I owe you some hospitality for neglecting you at Portsmouth."

"A very kind invitation," said Courthope, meaning it, "but I think I should stay in town for a bit. I have woefully neglected my social duties, and my belated appearance in Bath will be more palatable if I have visited some relations and been introduced to a few more damsels. My mother is pushing hard for a marriage, although why she thinks anyone in the middle of a campaign against Bonaparte ought to get hitched is beyond me."

"That is precisely the point, you dolt," said Drayton harshly. "Our beloved parents have us neatly cornered no matter what we do. I am denounced because I did not marry and beget an heir before I tore off to join Wellington, and my brother was denounced for leaving his motherless children behind when *he* tore off to join Wellington. You are all your mother has, and she wants a grandchild before you get yourself killed. Otherwise she'll have to leave those lovely Funds to your pimply cousin."

Courthope said nothing.

"Sorry," said Drayton with a rueful grin. "I'm a bit touchy on this subject. I'll do you a favor with your mother: I'll take you with me tomorrow morning when I call on the Waites. Miss Waite has some cousins visiting, and one of them is said to be a real stunner. You know the Waites, do you not?"

"I know Frederick, of course," said Courthope, frowning. "He was at Cambridge with me. And I've seen his sister, but I don't think I've ever been introduced."

"What!" said Drayton lightly. "You haven't had a touch at the fair Miranda? And you named Ferdinand! I'll let you add yourself to the lists, my boy. Fielding told me last night she is not yet betrothed."

"I thought there was some understanding between you and Miss Waite," said Courthope bluntly.

Drayton shook his head. "I fancy my family would

not object, but she has never shown any partiality for me."

"Don't think I'm much competition, do you?" Courthope laughed. "Very well, I'll take you up on that offer, even if I must decline the invitation to Leigh End for the present."

Two very presentable young men were accordingly ushered into the Waites' parlor next morning at just past eleven. There were already several callers.

"Unfair!" cried Fielding cheerfully, who had risen to take his leave of Mrs. Waite and the three attractive girls she was guarding. "You military men steal all the ladies with your tales of derring-do."

"Well, but you have all those months while we are away on campaign to persuade them back to you," retorted Drayton, laughing. He presented Courthope to Mrs. Waite and Miranda, and both young men were introduced to Miranda's cousins, the Misses Cole, and to two older women, friends of Mrs. Waite.

Miss Cole was indeed a beauty, with fashionably dark hair and an ethereal air, and her younger sister showed promise as well. Both were far prettier, at least in the classic sense of that word, than Miranda, whose charm depended more on her sunny nature than on her undistinguished features and pleasant but not elegant figure. In addition, all three girls wore the pale muslins appropriate for young ladies, and Miranda's light brown hair and gray eyes did not look as well with pastels as the more dramatic coloring of her cousins. But Miranda clearly did not care a jot that she was sharing her sofa with two girls who outshone her, and Drayton admired her for it. He thought cynically that her enormous dowry would outweigh Miss Cole's beauty in the eyes of most suitors in any case, and then reproached himself. Miranda deserved better.

Visitors were continually leaving and arriving, and Drayton gave up on having a private word with her. He would probably see her at Leigh End, in any case. Mrs. Waite had told him quietly that his sister Sara had invited them, and he doubted that she would have mentioned it had she not intended to accept. Instead, he set himself to be agreeable. Since the ladies were as eager for news from the front as the men had been the previous evening, he and Courthope were hard put to leave in a timely manner. Fortunately, Southey came in at half past the hour, and with some banter about relief forces, Drayton and Courthope excused themselves.

They walked down towards St. James in silence at first, enjoying the sensation of being back in London, and each somewhat abstracted as a result of their call on the Waites. Drayton was thinking that while Miranda was no beauty, he far preferred her spirit and warmth to the fragile coldness of Miss Cole. And he was wondering about Miranda's greeting to Southey, which had clearly suggested that he was a frequent and welcome visitor. He grinned. Fielding would object even more to Southey's courtship, if that was what it was, since Southey was based largely in London, working for Colonel White. But Drayton was, in the main, preoccupied with some gossip he had heard.

"Do you know Southey well?" he asked Courthope suddenly.

Courthope started; he had been deep in thought.

"I suppose," he stammered. "He was ahead of me at Winchester; you both were. Most brilliant chap in the whole school. You know him better, of course. Why?"

Drayton frowned. "Doesn't seem like himself. His father died a year ago, you know, and Fielding tells me that while I've been in Spain he's been acting rather wild. Drinking, women, you know what I mean. Not his sort of thing at all. When I saw him last month in Spain he was fine, and he nursed me valiantly on the trip back, but at White's last night he was over the oar before half the evening was gone, and apparently that's not unusual now. I heard the old biddies muttering something at the Waites' to that effect."

"His father died in a hunting accident, did he not? I remember hearing about it."

"Yes, that's right, but I'm surprised he took it so hard. They didn't get on, and hardly saw each other. And this is more recent, just the last six months or so. Why would he suddenly miss a father he hated, six months after the man rode his horse into a ditch?" Drayton knew that that was one of the things that had forged such a bond between him and Southey at school. The difference was that his father despised him, whereas South had despised his father. A hard-drinking, lecherous old fool, South had called him, and Drayton could not dispute that assessment very far. Nigel Southey had treated his wife dreadfully, had gotten himself blackballed from every decent club in London, and had not been seen sober after six in the evening for as long as anyone could remember.

In Drayton's opinion, Southey had expended all his energy—and it was considerable—in making himself as unlike his father as possible. His father was slovenly; Southey was neat as a pin. His father had left school; Southey was the top student in his year every year. His father was a womanizing sot; Southey was notoriously modest with women and rarely took more than a glass or two of wine in an entire evening—at least until recently. His father loved guns, hunting, and fishing; Southey was an expert fencer but never hunted. Part of Drayton's surprise at seeing Southey in uniform was born from this knowledge; the one successful period of Nigel Southey's life had been his brief stint in the army, where he was promoted twice before selling out and marrying Southey's mother.

"Perhaps he's regretting not mending his fences with his father before he died," said Drayton slowly. "Or perhaps his mother is putting pressure on him to marry, and he's chafing. He certainly did not seem a reluctant visitor at the Waites'."

Courthope did not respond. Drayton glanced at him.

"Corey! You haven't been listening to a word I've said! What ails you, man? Must I fret myself over you as well?" Then, narrowing his eyes and recognizing the symptoms all too well, he groaned. He recalled Courthope's awkward shyness in the Waites' parlor, which he had wrongly attributed to youth and lack of social finesse.

"Don't tell me. The Cole chit. You're smitten."

"Miss Cole?" said Courthope hotly, coming to life. "I'm sure she is a pleasant enough girl, but surely you don't think she can hold a candle to Miss Waite?" He turned a radiant face to Drayton. "I can't imagine why I didn't realize it when I saw her a few times last year. She's a diamond of the first water. Absolutely the most beautiful girl I have ever seen."

"I see," said Drayton dryly. "At least I see now. I have apparently been blind for the last hour. Well, I am going to prove my friendship for you, Corey."

"What do you mean?" said Courthope, bewildered.

"I'm going to renew my invitation to Leigh End. You'll hear the news from someone else soon, in any case: My sister has invited Miss Waite and her mother down for a visit. I suspect Sara is plotting in my favor, but I can't leave you up here in London wandering around with that sick mooncalf expression on your face."

"I do not look like a sick mooncalf!" gasped Courthope, affronted.

Drayton grinned. "This wound has its advantages, you know," he commented. "No one can call me out. I can say all sorts of outrageous things. And you do look ill, old man. I think you had better take me up on my offer. If not for the sake of your health, then at least to give Southey some real competition. His estate is just the other side of the river, you know, and if Miss Waite comes down I rather fancy we may see a lot of him at Leigh End. It's not such a long ride from London, and he must have some leave coming after that trip to Spain."

"The whereabouts of Michael Southey are not my concern," said Courthope with an attempt at hauteur.

"Stuff!" said Drayton briskly. "But I should warn you: I'm safe enough as his rival, if he really does mean to have Merry Miranda. He can't ask me to pick up a pair of foils until I'm healed up. You, on the other hand, my dear boy, might consider brushing up on your fencing."

"Don't care for dueling," said Courthope soberly. "Never could understand your predilections in that line, Drayton. Lucky thing the French officers are not as besotted with such affairs as we are, or Boney could simply wait for us to slaughter each other on the field of honor."

Pacing along beside him, Drayton looked over at his friend and saw that he was looking unusually serious. Courthope had fought one duel, forced on him by a loud-mouthed bully hoping to make himself a reputation at the expense of an inexperienced country lad—or so he thought. The younger man had put a bullet in his opponent's wrist before he had even leveled his weapon. With a generally peaceable demeanor, and an understanding that his marksmanship was superior, Courthope had been able to avoid further encounters.

"Believe it or not, Corey," Drayton said slowly, "I find I am beginning to share your opinion."

Chapter Six

The house was in an uproar. Maids were scurrying everywhere with clean linens, two more girls had come in from the village and were driving Mrs. Tibbet to distraction with their slovenly ways, carts from the grocers were driving the wrong way round to the kitchens, and the gardener was complaining that there would be no flowers left in the garden if Miss Lutford did not stop cutting blooms for vases. Leigh End was preparing to house more guests than it had seen at one time in many years. Lady Barrett's brother was coming, and bringing a friend; Mrs. Waite and Miss Waite were arriving the following day, and two friends of Sir Charles were expected by the end of the week. Sara and Sir Charles did not count Rachel as a guest any longer, but Mrs. Tibbet did. Rightly so, since she was in one of the biggest guest rooms.

Rachel fled. She knew that her peaceful rides and quiet evenings were over now, and her carefully negotiated truce with Caroline, which was blossoming slowly into something more promising, might not survive the arrival of Caroline's guardian. It had barely survived the return of Mrs. Mott. Seizing the chance for one last lovely day—and it *was* a lovely day, mild and sunny and dry—she had sent Maria to the kitchen to beg for a picnic basket and had escaped with Caroline and the horses down to the river.

"I am a coward, Caroline," she confessed as they watched Samuels tether the horses a few yards downstream. "I did not even dare go to the kitchen myself. I sent Maria."

"Mrs. Tibbet was *swearing* this morning," said Caroline. "I heard her. She said 'blast.' " Both contemplated for a moment the awesome forces which must have been exerted to bring such a word to the normally genteel lips of Mrs. Tibbet.

Belatedly recollecting her duties, Rachel admonished Caroline, "Ladies do not say that word. Even when they are reporting the remarks of others."

Caroline sighed. "Ladies never do anything fun," she said. "I would rather be a gentleman."

"Gentlemen have lots of rules to follow, too, Caroline," said Rachel. "Most of the same rules that ladies do, and while it's true that they can swear and ride astride"—Caroline was fascinated by these two accomplishments—"they must be forever defending their honor, which means lots of fighting, and shooting, and getting hurt."

"They can take their shoes off and go in the water."

It was warm, one of the first warm days of the spring, and they were sitting by the bank at a particularly tempting spot. The river eddied in here to make a grassy beach, and next to the beach was a little inlet, shallow and reedy. Caroline was peering into the water there.

"Oh!" she breathed. "Tadpoles! Thousands of them!"

Rachel looked around. There was no one in sight except Samuels. Furtively, Rachel concealed the jug of lemonade she had just taken out of the basket. "Samuels!" she called up the bank. "Would you mind very much going back to the house and bringing the lemonade? It seems to have been left out of the basket, and I don't think Miss Caroline should drink the river water."

"Certainly not, miss!" said Samuels. "Will you be all right here without me?" He knew that it was not proper for Miss Rachel to ride unaccompanied in London. He knew that Miss Rachel did not always do what was proper, though, and in his view, her residence at Leigh End under an assumed name was so improper that it swamped lesser considerations.

"It is quite safe here, I am sure," said Rachel. "And it will not take you long."

"So you say," muttered Samuels. "Fat chance I have of getting into that kitchen, much less finding anyone to fetch me a jug of lemonade." But he swung back onto his horse and cantered back towards the house.

"You told another fib," said Caroline accusingly.

Rachel sighed. "I do seem to be telling rather a lot of them these days, now that I have met you," she acknowledged. "I'll make this one right, though." And she picked up the jug of lemonade and deliberately poured it out at the base of a bush.

"See? Now we have no lemonade, just as I told Samuels. And you can use this jug to collect tadpoles."

"But they're out in the middle of the stream," wailed Caroline. "There are only a few little tiny ones over here by the part where I can reach in."

"I know," said Rachel. "And ladies must not show their ankles where anyone can see them. But now Samuels has gone, and there is no one here to see. So take off your boots quickly and I will take off mine, and I will hold your hand so that you can step into the water and dip the jug into the soupiest piece of tadpole water." Caroline had her boots and stockings off in an instant. She held up the skirts of her habit and waded out into the inlet, tilting her thin little face up to the sun.

"It feels deleck-ible," she said, experimenting with a word she had overheard in the kitchen.

"Wait there," commanded Rachel, struggling with her boots. "I'll have to help you hold up your skirts while you dip the jug." It would be dreadful if Caroline got soaked just when all the guests were arriving, so she dared not let her try drawing up the water without supporting her. She pulled off her stockings and waded out next to Caroline, holding up her own skirts. Then she took her skirts and Caroline's in one hand and gave her other arm to the girl.

"Lean on me, and scoop from the bottom if you can," she said. Concentrating intently, Caroline swung the jug down into the reeds and pulled it back up. It was a large jug, and filled with water was very heavy. Caroline's wrist shook.

"Quick, take your skirts back," said Rachel. With her free hand she grabbed the jug. Caroline hopped ashore and Rachel handed it to her.

"It's just *full* of them!" said Caroline in delight. Rachel laughed and waded towards the bank. She was enjoying the feel of the cool water on her feet, and the tremulous brushes of the tadpoles against her ankles. With a pang of regret, she stepped onto the grass, holding her skirts high.

"Caroline!" said a man's voice from the top of the bank. "Whatever are you about, you wretched minx?" Rachel looked up in horror. A rather fierce-looking young man was sliding off his horse and striding down the hill. He had a full view of Rachel's bare feet, her ankles, and a good portion of her calves.

"Uncle Richard!" screamed Caroline. "Uncle Richard! No one would tell me who was coming! It was you! Oh, I am so glad!" And she set the jug down so hastily that a third of it slopped out and flew in her bare feet to hug him. Then she was tugging him down to meet Rachel, chattering breathlessly.

"Uncle Richard, this is Miss Ross, she is a friend of Aunt Sara's; no, wait, her aunt is a friend, and she is staying here and being a little bit like my governess, only much better. She is teaching me botany, and drawing, and Latin, and French, and deportment, and I have a piano teacher, because she is dreadful at music, and she is not afraid of spiders, and she has the most beautiful horse, almost as nice as Sleet. And I have my own horse now, a real horse, and we go riding every day, even when it rains. And Mrs. Mott says she is a coaching female, but I am doing all my lessons now and my favorite is French! And I always used to think French was horrid! And look at my tadpoles!"

Rachel's face was flaming.

"You must be Captain Drayton," she managed.

"Coaching female?" inquired the young man, raking her up and down with his stare.

"I take it Mrs. Mott called me an encroaching

female," muttered Rachel, clipping the words between her teeth. She was mortified. She was angry with herself for allowing this ridiculous situation to occur, but she was even more angry with this supercilious young man, who was taking every advantage of her predicament to humiliate her.

"How nice to meet you, Miss Ross," said Drayton, his voice icy. "I have been hearing so much about you from my sister. It is gratifying to think that Caroline is becoming a young lady. So kind of you to help us while your parents are abroad, is it not? And such an ambitious curriculum! Latin, do you say? I trust your knowledge of Latin is better than your knowledge of deportment?"

"Oh!" said Rachel, goaded beyond endurance. "You, sir, are the rudest man I have ever met! I may have been guilty of a lapse of judgment in allowing Caroline to collect her tadpoles, but I would never stand and stare at you in such a brazen fashion did I come upon you in such disarray! Is it too much to ask that you turn your back for a moment so that I can put my boots on? Or are you afraid that I will be teaching Caroline Latin curse words in sign language while you are not watching?"

Drayton made no move to turn his back. He raised one eyebrow.

"Are there Latin curse words?" he said with some interest.

"There most certainly are," Rachel informed him with some asperity. "And if you think I am going to retail them for your amusement, you may think again. Caroline has a prodigious memory for new words, and with my luck would repeat them to the vicar."

Drayton gave a shout of laughter. "Touché, Miss

Ross! I will retreat and allow you to restore your propriety. But I mean to speak to my sister about your visit here; I warn you fairly. Caroline is my ward, and her education is my responsibility." He was about to offer to wait and help them remount when Samuels returned, out of breath, bearing the lemonade. Drayton mounted—a bit awkwardly, since he was still favoring his left arm. Once up, however, he rode off gracefully, with a grave nod of his head to Rachel and a kiss of his hand to Caroline, leaving Samuels staring at Rachel with a disapproving frown. He did not fail to notice the jug and the tadpoles.

"Dished again, by gum!" he muttered to himself. "If she gets up to her tricks, she can be as bad as that James!" And shaking his head, he dutifully carried the jug of lemonade down the hill.

Caroline was tugging at Rachel's skirt. "You are cross," she said unhappily. "You didn't like him. And he is my favorite uncle, and my guardian."

"Let's have some lemonade," said Rachel. "You are right, Caroline, I am cross. Perhaps I am thirsty."

Sensing that Rachel was unhappy, Caroline cast about for something to make her feel better. Lemonade was a start, and she sipped it thoughtfully. Then she had an idea. "Miss Ross," she said tentatively, "do you think we are friends now?"

"Yes," said Rachel after a moment. "Yes, I think so. Why?"

"I'll tell you what I'm afraid of," said Caroline. "I'm afraid of the dark."

"So was I when I was little," said Rachel. "I think most children are, at some time. It will get better."

So Caroline remembered that conversation in the drawing room, she thought. And knowing what was expected, she did not tell a fib, for once.

"There is something I am afraid of, Caroline. You will think I am very silly."

"What is it?" said Caroline, her eyes wide.

"Dogs. Very un-English, is it not? I was chased by dogs once when I was younger, and now I am afraid of them, and they know it, and it makes me more afraid."

"Poor Miss Ross!" said Caroline, tears of sympathy in her eyes. "Dogs are wonderful! They are my favorite, next to horses. We have two big ones, out in the kennels, named Bertha and Belinda, and Belinda is going to have puppies."

She said with sudden confidence, "I will teach you how to talk to them and not to be afraid. When Belinda has her puppies you can play with them. No one is afraid of puppies. Then you can learn to like dogs again."

"Thank you, Caroline," said Rachel, squeezing her shoulder briefly. "That would be very nice."

Dinner was going to be an ordeal. Rachel arrayed herself for battle: her best silk dress, of an unusual deep brown which was very flattering, an amber pendant, and matching earrings. Maria fluttered about her. She recognized the look on Rachel's face and her heart sank.

"You look lovely, Miss Rachel. The amber is so beautiful with this silk. And your skin is so fine, what a pity you cannot wear the lower necklines; you have such lovely shoulders. Let me put a ribbon in your hair, though."

"No ribbons," said Rachel shortly. "And even if

I could wear low-cut necklines, décolletage is not appropriate for a governess, especially one whose credentials in the matter of deportment have been questioned by her employer.''

Maria held her peace. She knew fairly well what had happened this afternoon—Caroline was a prattle-box—but when the *señorita* was in this mood, it was best not to argue with her, and to try to distract her with other topics.

''Did Samuels have news of your brother, Miss Rachel?'' Samuels had ridden out very early that morning to meet with a messenger from James.

''Yes. He is well, and his man has set a regular time to meet with Samuels at the posting house in Charing.'' She bit her lip. ''Evidently James will be wanting some French money, Maria. You will need to go up to the attic and take some twenty-franc pieces out of the hidden compartment in my trunk.''

This was not a good distraction, thought Maria. She tried again. ''Have you met the other guest yet? Lieutenant Courthope? I saw him talking with Hickman and Samuels by the stables. He seemed the nice young man. Very shy.''

''I was introduced, yes,'' Rachel said. She hoped, in fact, that Courthope would be seated next to her at dinner, but she was the only female guest, and she had a sinking feeling that that privilege would be allotted to Captain Drayton. At least it was only for one night, she consoled herself. Tomorrow the Waites would arrive.

Her entrance into the drawing room happened, unfortunately, to coincide with a brief pause in the conversation, which allowed Miss Lutford's remark, meant only for Drayton, to be quite audible to Rachel. "Such want of conduct!" said the piercing voice. "Now the *Essex* Rosses—Edward Ross was one of my suitors, you know, Richard—the Essex Rosses, I say, have always been known for their odd starts. It would not surprise me to find that her family is originally from Essex." Drayton, looking toward the door over the head of the tiny form of Miss Lutford, saw Rachel halt in dismay and gave her a savage smile. Sir Charles immediately drew off Miss Lutford with a dexterity born of long practice, and Lady Sara steered Courthope over to Rachel, but she knew that it was only a temporary reprieve.

"Dinner is served, my lady," announced Minton, appearing like a magician at the inner doors leading into the dining room. Her heart sinking, Rachel saw Drayton making his way towards her to escort her to the table. Her arm felt like a block of wood as she laid it over his elbow and went through the folding doors. Drayton placed her carefully, like an exquisitely fragile piece of china, in the chair between his own and that of Sir Charles, and the servants began to carry in the soup.

When two people have, in the first minute of their acquaintance, accused each other of gross discourtesy, it is not to be expected that it will be easy for them to sit together for two hours at a formal dinner. Rachel responded mechanically to the civil conversation of Sir Charles, on her left, and waited for the first sally from the enemy on her right. It came during the second course, as Sir Charles turned to speak with Miss Lutford.

"I hear, Miss Ross," drawled Drayton, "that you brought a rather unusual gift to Miss Caroline when you arrived two weeks ago." Courthope, who did not know the story and was in any case a scrupulously polite young man, continued very properly to converse with Lady Sara. Miss Lutford, however, abandoned even the pretense of conversing with her nephew and perked up her ears.

"Every good guest," responded Rachel coolly, "endeavors to discover something of the interests of her hosts before she selects a gift."

"Indeed?" said Drayton. "But then, it is more usual to obtain the gift elsewhere, rather than plucking it from the host's shrubbery on the way in the front door."

"I see that you consider the gift to have been what was contained in my box," responded Rachel, beginning to enjoy herself. "But, from another point of view, since spiders are so common, the gift might be said to lie in the act of containing the spider. And I did provide the box."

Drayton tried another tack. "Yet I believe it was our jug that was used this afternoon? For the tadpoles? And Caroline did the containing herself."

Rachel gritted her teeth. If everyone in the household had not heard about her disgrace this afternoon already, they would be aware of it now.

"Ah, but Captain Drayton," she managed to reply, "that was not a gift. We were studying biology."

"Biology," murmured Drayton. "Yes, I believe I have seen some rather unusual specimens by the river. I have neglected this area of my education, clearly. I shall have to visit the spot more often."

"Indeed, sir, you are right," said Rachel with spirit. "I am quite sure that I myself saw a beast there this very afternoon." Her sense of humor got the better of her then, and she laughed. To her surprise, Drayton laughed as well.

"Truce!" he said. "I cry a truce, fair preceptress! I would not play Benedick to your Beatrice to the neglect of our fellow diners."

Rachel took the hint and turned back to Sir Charles, but when the ladies retired to leave the men to their port, she gave Sara a look of such distress that Sara quickly drew her away from Miss Lutford and said in a low voice, "My dear, pray do not refine too much on my brother's remarks about what happened at the river this afternoon. He is still ill from his wound, and worried about the children. I will speak with him tomorrow morning. I would not like to have you leave us just yet. Caroline is a different child now you are here, and I have come to enjoy having you here for my own sake as well."

Rachel was amazed and touched by this last remark and, much heartened, was able to converse cheerfully when the gentlemen joined them, instead of retiring early with a headache, as she had originally planned.

Drayton sought his sister out as soon as she had breakfasted the next morning. Rachel and Caroline were out riding, and Courthope not yet downstairs, but they went out on the terrace and walked into the garden in an unspoken alliance against the prying ears of Miss Lutford. Sara sat down on a bench and looked up at her brother. How tired and pale he looked, she thought. And he had not asked about their father. She sighed.

"Sara," said Drayton, "this arrangement with Miss Ross seems most improper to me. How much do you know of her? How can she be a guest and a governess at the same time? And no,"—he lifted his hand to stop her—"do not tell me again about her odd upbringing and her parents' trip abroad. If she is an unsuitable person to have charge of Caroline, and you wish to have her here as a guest, then let us engage a proper governess and have done with this farce."

"Richard, you have no idea what you are saying," said his sister, setting her chin. "Caroline drove away five governesses—*five,* Richard—in as many months. I spent half a week in London interviewing candidates and found no one. Miss Ross's interest in trying her educational theories on Caroline was providential." She reached up and laid her hand on her brother's arm. "Richard," she pleaded, "don't you trust me? If her theories had been useless, and if Caroline was being badly taught, I would interview fifty governesses, if I had to, to find someone suitable. But that is far from being the case. Do you remember what Caroline was like when you visited last, after Harry's death? Think, dearest! She was pale, and tired, and fretful." Like you, she added silently to herself. "She is so happy and healthy now! She rides every day, and draws, and behaves well in company. And she has learned more French in two weeks with Miss Ross than from all her other governesses combined. Miss Ross speaks it like a native, and has the most wonderful way of teaching her."

"As she teaches biology?" said Drayton, with an edge to his voice. "Sara, I wish Harry had not left the children under my guardianship. I am not fitted for it. But he did, and the less fit I feel myself, the more I sense an obligation to be sure that they are well cared for while I am out of the country. I do not want Caroline turned into a hoydenish bluestocking."

"And was Miss Ross a hoydenish bluestocking last night at dinner?" retorted Sara.

Drayton flushed. He remembered Rachel standing in the doorway, looking oddly vulnerable and lonely as Miss Lutford's disastrous remark greeted her.

"I apologize for last night. I was most uncivil, and she set me properly to rights. I have nothing against her personally, but I wish I knew more about her and her family."

"She is perfectly respectable," said Sara, lying. "Her parents are a bit eccentric, but there is nothing wrong with the Shropshire Rosses, and I have grown quite fond of her. She has elegance and address, and those are certainly not qualities I associate with bluestockings."

"Lady Barrett!" said a voice behind the bench. Southey swung around the hedge and bowed over her hand. "Miss Lutford sent me in search of you. I hope I do not intrude."

"Not at all; how lovely to see you!" said Sara, smiling. She had always liked Southey. He was dear to her because he had been such a good friend to Richard during his difficult school years, and more dear now because of his great care of his mother, who had become her neighbor and friend when she had married Sir Charles and taken up residence in Kent. She added, with a twinkle in her eye, "What a coincidence to find you here just when the Waites are coming for a visit!"

Southey laughed. So, thought Drayton, his pursuit of Miranda had become an established thing recently.

"Don't count on having her all to yourself," said Drayton with a lazy grin. "I expect to command some sympathy for my valorous wounds, and if she prefers someone healthy, I brought Courthope down here as well."

Southey snorted. "Courthope! The boy is so shy, I'll wager he can barely hold a conversation with his mother."

Sara laughed. "Don't preen yourselves in front of me," she said. "Save it for Miss Waite. Though if you strut like this in her presence she may well prefer Lieutenant Courthope to either of you, you conceited things!" She rose, and they strolled back to the house together. Sara left them at the terrace, hurrying off to the greenhouse to consult about fruit for dinner.

Southey turned to Drayton. "Care to see my new horse?" he asked. "She's in your stable right now, eating your hay. Might as well have a look, don't you think?" Drayton was puzzled. Southey had never been one to talk about horses; he left that to his father. He rode them, but he treated them as conveniences and ignored them whenever possible. Drayton could not even recall the name of any of South's horses, and they had known each other for fifteen years. He followed Southey obediently around to the stable and waited while the horse was led out by Hickman, the head groom. Hickman was grinning broadly.

"The devil!" said Drayton hotly. "What sort of a joke is this, South? That's Sleet! You think you and Hickman can put a new saddle—" he broke off. "It's not Sleet, is it?" he said slowly.

"No, it's a five-year-old from the same dam," said Southey. "Amazing resemblance, isn't it?" Drayton agreed. Now that he was looking more closely, he could see differences—a darker coat, fewer markings on the withers, higher stockings on the forefeet, a narrower mouth—but it was uncanny.

Sleet's coloring was so unusual; he had never seen another remotely like her. And now he was looking at her twin—her younger sister, at least.

"I sold all my father's hunters," said Southey, after a pause. His voice was strained. "And the man who bought the best one, the chestnut, had visited down here several times and had seen you on Sleet. And he told me this one was for sale. I couldn't resist."

Drayton stroked the mare's nose. "What's her name?" he asked.

Southey made a face. "Her previous owner was a nincompoop. But she's answered to the name for five years, so I'll have to leave it for the moment. It's Silver. You'd think someone with the wit to buy this horse would have more imagination, would you not?"

"Have you met Miss Ross yet?" asked Drayton. "My sister's rather odd guest, and Caroline's pseudo-governess?"

"Yes, just now," said Southey. "She and Caroline were just going in to change when I rode up."

"She has a beautiful mare; I saw it yesterday. And Caroline told me its name. Peekhole."

"The deuce it is!" said Southey, shocked.

Drayton grinned. "I think Miss Ross has not yet taught Caroline any Italian. I surmise that the horse's real name is Piccola." Southey burst out laughing. "Are you coming in? You are welcome to stay for lunch, you know."

But Southey was mounting up. "I simply rode over to pay my respects to your sister," he said. "Invite me again another time."

"You mean you rode over to find out when Miss Waite was arriving," said Drayton, chuckling.

"You're welcome anytime, South. She's expected this evening before dinner."

"See you at dinner, then," said Southey cheerfully, and rode off towards his own lands, muttering to himself once he was out of hearing, "Shropshire Rosses, eh? And not a bad-looking girl, at that."

Drayton went back into the stable. He almost felt the need to reassure himself that Sleet was really there, after seeing her near-double trotting out of the yard. He went over to her box and patted her as she nuzzled him affectionately. Piccola was in the next stall, looking jealous. Seeing the mare, it occurred to Drayton that Caroline and Miss Ross might be having a lesson up in the schoolroom. Perhaps he could look in on them. He trusted his sister, and yet something about that Ross woman made him uneasy. He went in the side door from the stableyard and went softly up the back stairs to the nursery door.

His hand on the latch, he paused, hearing voices inside. Caroline sounded tearful. "Why can't we have our French lesson, Miss Ross?" she asked. "Where is the hamper with all the nice dresses, and the little shoes?"

"Betsy took it back upstairs to the attic, Caroline. I am very sorry. I think your uncle does not approve of my style of giving lessons. He is quite cross with me because I let you wade in the river yesterday, and I am sure he would not like to come up and find us playacting in French in Grandmother Barrett's ballgowns."

"Couldn't we do it and not tell?"

"No, Caroline. Look what happened at the river yesterday."

"Could we ask him if I might have my French lessons the way you do them? He might say yes."

"Very well," he heard Rachel say. "Perhaps if you write him a letter in French. I will help you."

Well, thought Drayton, this might not be the best time to observe one of Caroline's lessons. He wondered suddenly what had been so dreadful about allowing Caroline to wade in the river for a moment to collect tadpoles. Was he turning into a prig? He turned quietly and went back down the stairs.

Chapter Seven

Rachel was dressing for dinner when there was a knock at the door. Maria opened it to admit Mrs. Mott and a very clean Caroline. The little girl was wearing a tatted shawl, presumably borrowed from the nurse, over her nightclothes.

"I asked Mrs. Mott if I could come and show you my note," Caroline said breathlessly, "because I couldn't read all the words. Betsy brought it up while I was having my bath. I had to have a bath because I spilled the treacle in the kitchen, and it went all over me."

"Beg pardon, Miss Ross," said Mrs. Mott stiffly, "but she was that set on it, and Betsy thought you was not gone downstairs yet."

"It is no trouble at all," said Rachel, happy to see her rival willing to share Caroline even for a moment. "But Caroline, you read so nicely. Who sent you a note? Is their writing hard to read?"

"It is from Uncle Richard, Miss Ross," said Caroline, her eyes glowing. "He sent an answer to my letter. And he wrote it out very clearly. But it's in French! And look what came with it!" Parting her cupped hands, she revealed a folded sheet of note-paper. Inside the folds were two rosebuds, a tiny yellow one and a larger red one. The note was very brief. It read:

Ma chère Caroline:
Ta tante me dit que tu aimes bien tes leçons maintenant. Je te donne ma permission de les continuer. Mes devoirs à Mlle. Ross.
Ton serviteur, R.D.

"I know 'Dear Caroline' and that I love my lessons, and 'permission.' What is the rest?"

" 'My dear Caroline,' " translated Rachel slowly. " 'Your aunt tells me that you like your lessons quite well now. I give you my permission to continue them. My greetings to Miss Ross.' "

"Which rosebud would you like?" asked Caroline shyly. "I think the yellow one is for me and the red one for you."

Rachel started to say that she thought they were both for Caroline, but she did not in fact think so, and ladies did not tell fibs.

"I expect you are right," she said. "Thank you, Mrs. Mott, for bringing Caroline down to show me the note. She has been very sad to think we might not be able to go on with our lessons."

Mrs. Mott did not reply to Rachel, but there was a slight thaw in her manner. "Come along now, Miss Caroline. If Lady Barrett sees you a-galloping around in your nightclothes at this time of an evening, it'll be as much as my place is worth."

"Good night, Miss Ross," said Caroline obediently, putting her face up to be kissed. "I'm glad we can have our lessons again. Perhaps we can invite Uncle Richard to come, since he speaks French. After I've learned more words."

"Good night, Caroline," said Rachel. She was relieved to hear that they could resume their French make-believe, which she enjoyed almost as much as Caroline. And she would somehow contrive infinite delays to the proposed invitation. Then she recollected the state of the household, and warned, "I'm not sure Betsy will be able to get the hamper back out from the attic for us in time for a lesson tomorrow morning, Caroline. The maids are very busy, and the guests' trunks have been piled up in front of the entrance to the storeroom where the hamper is kept."

"We can't have a French lesson tomorrow even if Betsy finds the hamper," said Caroline, after thinking a minute. "Aunt Sara told me I will only have morning lessons while all the guests are here. And tomorrow you must have your first session with the dogs. Belinda has to learn about you now, otherwise she won't let you touch her puppies after they are born."

"I see," said Rachel weakly.

The interruption had delayed Rachel's toilette, and she and Maria hurried to fasten up her gown and dress her hair. With the memory of last night's scene in the drawing room still vivid, Rachel did not want to be the last to arrive for dinner. She emerged from her bedchamber just in time to see the door opposite hers open. A young woman stepped out into the hall. She was slightly shorter than Rachel, and more rounded in figure, with an appealing energy in her movements. It could only be Miss Waite, thought Rachel. She had heard the Waites arrive, but it had been so close to dinner that they had gone straight up to their rooms to rest and change.

"How do you do?" said Rachel, advancing. "You must be Miss Waite."

"And you must be Miss Ross," said Miranda cordially. "My mother is already downstairs, I am sure. It will be nice to go down together; I am always the last, and Mama scolds me for my tardiness."

A shy smile accompanied these words, and Rachel felt a pleasant anticipation begin to take the place of her anxiety about the arrival of new guests. She had been prepared to like Miss Waite simply on the recommendation of Lady Barrett, whose opinions she respected greatly. In fact, even if Lady Barrett had not spoken of Miranda so warmly, Rachel was ready to welcome anyone who would distract the terrifying Captain Drayton. Surely he would not pay much attention to a guest who was half governess when the girl he might marry was here! Rachel looked at the sparkling gray eyes and began to consider liking Miss Waite for herself.

The light in the hall was dim, but Rachel thought she saw a rather strange expression replace the grave smile on Miranda's face. She was staring at Rachel's gown. Rachel's first thought was that Caroline had slashed another seam, but then she looked more closely at Miranda.

"Oh!" she gasped. "Your gown! From Miss Russell, I'll warrant! How awkward! I will go and change at once!"

"No, pray do not on my account," said Miranda at once. "I . . . I was just surprised for a moment.

Miss Russell does not usually make up such similar gowns for two different customers. That is why she charges so much, my mother says."

"Similar!" retorted Rachel. "If we were more of a height, we could exchange them and no one would notice the difference, save for the colors! And they are very distinctive," she added ruefully. "It's not as though we were wearing round gowns. I understand what has happened," she added after a moment. "Miss Russell knows that I do not go into society much, and when I saw this in La Belle Assemblée and asked to have it made up, she thought I would never appear in the same company as you." And, she added to herself, normally she would have been correct.

The gowns were silk, and deceptively simple. Two bands of flat trim crossed at the breast, forming an *x*-shape which defined the bodice, and continued around the back to form the border of a demi train. Rachel was right: They were the latest cut, and quite distinctive. Miranda's was rose, trimmed in lighter pink; Rachel's dark gold, trimmed in white. It was Rachel's favorite new gown; she could not wear most low necklines, but to anchor the crossed bands under the breast, two broad straps of ribbon came up to both shoulders, concealing her scar.

"We cannot change," said Miranda with decision. "We would be dreadfully late. Men never notice what women wear, in any case. Let us go downstairs together, and if anyone remarks upon it, we can say we planned to wear them together."

Another dramatic, embarrassing scene, thought Rachel miserably, hoping Lady Barrett would not be offended. She followed Miranda down the staircase and in a moment of bravado moved next to her so that they entered the drawing room side by side.

It was dramatic, but far from embarrassing. The two made a stunning picture, framed in the doorway: rose and gold, light hair and dark, gray eyes and brown. They were the last to arrive—dinner had in fact been put back a quarter of an hour—and the other members of the party were all assembled: Sir Charles and Lady Barrett, Drayton, Courthope, Southey, Miss Lutford, Mrs. Waite, and the vicar, who (to Miss Lutford's annoyance) had been invited to fill out the table.

"Jove!" said Southey, putting up his quizzing glass.

Courthope stood staring. Even Sir Charles was taken aback. Drayton was the first to recover. He strode gracefully over to Rachel and Miranda and made an elegant bow exactly midway between them.

"Mesdemoiselles," he said, "I have never before wished to be a twin, but I would gladly double myself at this moment."

"Oh, how pretty!" said Miranda, dimpling. "I vow Spain has improved you, Captain Drayton." Then, more seriously, "Save for your shoulder, of course." She peered up at him. "Are you quite well?"

"I am healing rapidly," said Drayton, "but claim the wounded soldier's guerdon of escorting you to dinner." He shot an apologetic glance at Rachel as he said this, and added, "I'm afraid I am not always the most congenial dinner companion, as Miss Ross could tell you."

Rachel was surprised at this new civility but replied promptly, "On the contrary, Captain Drayton, I take great pleasure in recollecting our conversation of yesterday evening."

"As well you might," said Drayton, laughing. "You won every round, I believe." He turned to Southey, who had come up behind him. "Be warned, South: Miss Ross is as fine a fencer with words as you are with swords. Cross her at your peril. I believe she is seated with you tonight."

"It will be my pleasure," said Southey. He was hoping to learn more about Miss Ross.

As Southey took her arm to move into the dining room, Rachel looked at the little court that had formed around them and murmured wickedly to Miranda, "I thought you said that men never notice what women wear."

Miranda did not answer. She was looking at Courthope. His eyes had not left her face from the time she had entered the room. Absently, Miranda laid her hand on Drayton's elbow. In another moment she had collected herself and was making some laughing reply to Rachel, and turning back to Drayton.

Well, said Drayton to himself as he sat down between Miranda and Mrs. Waite, perhaps there is something to being a mooncalf after all. Corey will need those fencing lessons quite soon, or I miss my guess.

For Sara, it had been a very long day. The Barretts had not entertained much at Leigh End since the children had been born, and she had forgotten how much work was involved in receiving guests and organizing a formal dinner, even for such a small group. She closed her eyes. Sedale had taken her hair down; it felt wonderful. When she wore it up it had to be anchored with so many pins that her scalp seemed covered with metal.

"Thank you, Sedale," she said to the dresser. "That will be all." She looked longingly at her bed, but Sir Charles had given her one of his looks when she served him his tea after dinner. That look meant *I need to speak with you in private.* So she crossed through her dressing room, which led into his, and emerged into the master bedroom.

"Oh, dear!" she said, looking at the corded valise by the door. "You are leaving again! Is Fidder going with you this time? I think Richard may still need him to get into his jackets properly, with his shoulder."

"I am only going for one night," said Sir Charles. "And I agree with you, so I told Fidder to stay here. It would be different if Robson had come home with Richard, but he did not."

"You've been going to London so often recently, love," said Sara sadly. "I can see it is tiring you, traveling back and forth like this. Perhaps we should open the house in Harland Place. Although then I will feel even worse about that enormous bill from Monsieur Mivart, for the five days I stayed in his stuffy hotel."

"Nonsense," said Sir Charles in a brisk tone. "I will stay at the club, as I always do, and get my business done far more quickly than if I had to deal with all those servants and that enormous house."

"Is that what you wanted to tell me?" asked Sara. "That you were leaving again?"

"That, in part," was the reply. "But I heard something in London on Monday which gave me pause. Sara, do you have something to tell me about Miss Ross?"

So, the moment she had been dreading had

arrived. She took a deep breath but did not reply. Sir Charles looked at her shrewdly and changed his question.

"My love, *can* you tell me anything about Miss Ross?"

She shook her head.

"Swore you to secrecy, I'll wager. Well, I cannot pretend I do not admire the girl. I collect she has done Caroline a world of good, and I can see that you enjoy her company as well. But . . ." He fell silent. He began pacing up and down in front of the linen chest at the foot of the bed.

"All these trips to London," he muttered. "You know I prefer to spend more time down here, especially at this time of year. And Ned and Jamie will be home for the half-holidays soon, so it is especially vexing to have this business come up now. But it cannot be helped. I may not tell you the details, my love, but I am advising the minister on some rather complicated financial matters, and there are several other men working with me. And one of them is a very influential gentleman whose niece is allegedly in Germany."

"Oh," said Sara. Somehow she was not surprised.

"He is a very astute man, my dear. But I believe he is not unhappy that Miss Ross, as we will call her, is staying with us. He asked after her, under the name Ross, most politely."

"You are not angry, Charles?" said Sara in a rush. "I hated to deceive you, but I thought you would soon discover the truth in any case, and it was very important to her that no one should know she was here."

"No, I am not angry," he said quietly, a smile in his eyes. "I hope that we trust each other enough to have secrets occasionally. If I may not tell you everything which I do in London, you need not tell me everything which you do here."

Sara blushed. "Did you see Lieutenant Courthope looking at Miss Waite?" she asked. It was not quite changing the subject, since Sir Charles's smile had somehow made her remember the incident before dinner. "He is far gone, poor boy."

"Miss Waite did not seem to mind his look," observed Sir Charles. "Do you? I know you had thought she and Richard might make a match of it."

"I am not sure now," said Sara slowly. "I had thought of the match, as you know. I have made no secret of it these two years. That is why I invited Miss Waite to visit. But Richard has never looked at her the way young Courthope does. And she has never looked at Richard the way she looked at young Courthope."

"Puppy love," growled her husband. "Miss Waite has been courted by fortune hunters for so long that she is dazzled by someone with the least spark of romantic feeling for her."

"Perhaps," said Sara. "But you looked at me in just that way, you know. You still do, sometimes. Right now, for instance."

There was a noise outside Rachel's door. Two people were arguing in low voices. Rachel got up and opened the curtains. It was misty outside, and there was dew on the lawn. The clock on the mantel said it was just before seven. She threw on her wrap and went to the door. Maria did not normally come and wake her until eight.

"Caroline Drayton!" said Rachel in a fierce whisper. "What are you about, coming down to the guest rooms at this hour?" She drew them into her chamber and closed the door.

"I told her it was not proper," said Betsy, looking very worried. "Mrs. Mott was helping Amy with William, he is that fussy this morning. And Miss Caroline told me that you had agreed to go out to the kennels with her, very early. So I dressed her and brought her down, but when I saw your door closed, I made sure she was hoaxing me and meant to serve you some trick."

"I'm not! I don't!" said Caroline, indignant. "I never play tricks on Miss Ross, not now, leastways. Tell her," she appealed to Rachel. "We're going to have a dog lesson, aren't we?"

"But Caroline," said Rachel, "why must it be now? I thought we could meet the dogs after we went riding."

"Don't you know anything about dogs?" said Caroline scornfully. "You have to come and feed them, of course. That is the way to make them like you the fastest. Some people won't let anyone else feed their dogs, just for that reason. But Jem lets me feed them all the time. They eat very early. So we have to hurry. They like to eat at the same time every morning. If Jem tries to wait for us, they'll howl and wake everybody."

At this threat, Rachel capitulated. She did not even ring for Maria, but had Betsy help her into her riding habit and boots. She and Caroline went quietly down the back stair and walked over to a small shed in back of the stable.

"This isn't a very big kennel," said Caroline, enjoying her chance to be the teacher. "The spaniels stay in the house, of course. And Uncle Charles doesn't keep a pack. So we just have Bertha and Belinda out here. You're not scared of the spaniels, are you?" she asked, worried. "If you are, Bertha and Belinda might be too big for you. We could go back into the kitchen and feed the spaniels."

Rachel would have loved to go back into the kitchen. But she forced herself to answer honestly. "No, I am not frightened of the spaniels. Only of big dogs. Like the ones who chased me."

Caroline was relieved. "I would have been surprised if you had been afraid of Tug and Lion," she said. "They are so old and silly, and all they do is sleep."

A gangly boy with white-blond hair came out of the stable and grinned at Caroline. "Morning, Miss Caroline. I didn't believe you, but here you be with Miss Ross, just like you promised." It was Jem, the stablehand who doubled as the kennelmaster at Leigh End. He was carrying two bowls of something which smelled like a mixture of meat and porridge. He lowered one bowl so that Caroline and Rachel could see inside.

" 'Tis a special mash for Belinda, now that she is so near her time, but we have to give it to Bertha, as well. She gets right jealous, else."

He opened the shed door and gave a low whistle. Two of the most enormous dogs Rachel had ever seen flung themselves out the door and barked joyously at Jem. They were so large that at first she could not tell which was about to whelp; the distended belly was dwarfed by the massive shoulders and neck. They were as tall as Caroline.

"Now," said Caroline, "we get to feed them, but they have to settle down first. Jem says it's bad for their digestion to eat right after they've been leaping about the way they do when he first calls them out. If they try to jump on you, you hit them on the nose, like this." She banged Bertha on her black nose with a smart slap as the bitch tried to lick her face. "Down, Bertha," she said sternly. Bertha sat.

Jem grinned. "Miss Caroline is a marvel with the dogs," he said to Rachel, as Caroline called the dogs to heel and walked them around the yard. "You watch her."

Rachel felt as though she were in a dream. The dogs were so gigantic, Caroline so tiny. They paced around the yard behind her like creatures in an ancient legend, enchanted by some magic spell. And she was bringing them back to Rachel. Rachel closed her eyes. She forced them open. This was her chance, her chance to stop shuddering every time she heard a deep bark or saw an unleashed canine form in the park. She took a deep breath. From a distance, she heard Caroline say, "Now you can take the bowls, Miss Ross, and put them down in front of you." They will come after me, she thought, and then shook herself. They were well-trained, hungry dogs. She put the bowls down and waited. Caroline had one hand on each collar.

At that moment, Drayton emerged from the kitchen clutching a slab of bread and butter and wearing his riding boots. He took in the scene and raised his eyebrows.

"More biology, Miss Ross?"

Rachel ground her teeth. Why on earth did that pestilential captain have to appear every time she did something the least bit outré?

Caroline turned to her uncle and stamped her foot. "Shush!" she said imperiously. "This isn't my lesson, it's for Miss Ross. She's afraid of dogs, and I'm teaching her not to be."

"Are you?" he said, looking at Rachel thoughtfully. "Afraid of dogs?"

She nodded. "Only of large ones," she said with an effort. "I was attacked once." Her face was very pale, Drayton noticed, but she was standing quite steadily.

"You are doing the right thing," he said seriously. "And Caroline is simply amazing with animals. You may trust anything she tells you. Barrett's farrier thinks she is a wonder child."

Rachel was stunned. He was not laughing at her. He was sympathetic. He did not think she was an idiot, standing here at this uncivilized hour, guarding two bowls of reeking dog food and waiting to be overwhelmed by those elephants masquerading as hounds.

"Are you going riding after you feed the dogs?" asked Drayton. "Might I join you?"

"Would you mind waiting until we have some breakfast?" said Rachel. She looked grimly at the bowls at her feet. "If, that is, I have any appetite left after this."

In the event, Rachel's elation and relief when the dog feeding had been successfully concluded left her quite hungry, and it was past eight when the riding expedition got underway. Sara, who had appeared just as they were finishing breakfast, had promised to join them, and they rode out towards the river at a slow pace. Drayton drew up under the lee of a hill a short way from the edge of Barrett's land and said to Caroline, "Let us see you ride, little imp. You seem to be getting on quite well for someone who was still on a pony last time I visited. But no adventures, mind. No gallops, no jumps."

Overjoyed to be the center of attention, Caroline

turned her stocky little mare and headed off along the side of the hill at a sedate trot. Then she cantered, moving easily with the horse. Rachel was impressed.

"She has a beautiful seat," she said. "I have always ridden right next to her, of course, and could not see this well."

"My sister is one of the finest riders in the county," said Drayton, still following Caroline with his eyes. "I am sure Caroline has been very well taught." Then he narrowed his eyes suddenly and let out a groan. "I might have known." He snorted. "The brat cannot behave for more than ten minutes at a time, can she?" Caroline had given in to temptation and spurred her mare to a gallop. She wheeled in a circle round the meadow under the hill, and returned triumphantly to her critics, pulling up in a show of stamping and snorting very alien to the natural preferences of her quiet bay. Sara chose that unfortunate moment to ride up on her own horse.

"Richard!" she exclaimed. "How could you let her go off like that! What if she had lost control of the horse? You were a quarter-mile away from her! Did you think yourself to be training her for your regiment?"

Rachel gave Caroline a speaking look. The round little chin quivered, but Caroline took a deep breath and said to her aunt, "Uncle Richard told me not to gallop, Aunt Sara. I—I forgot." Another stern look from Rachel. "I mean, I did not listen," said Caroline miserably. "Oh, Miss Ross, does this mean I cannot go riding tomorrow?" Tears trembled on the ends of her lashes. "I love riding with Uncle Richard, and he will not be here for very long."

Drayton was stunned. Caroline might still be willful and unpredictable, but was this the whining, spoiled child he had left last spring? Sara shot him a glance which said *I told you so.* Then she spoke hastily, before Rachel could pronounce what would have to be an irrevocable sentence.

"You may ride tomorrow, Caroline, since it is important for your uncle to spend time with you while he is here. But you must help Jem groom both your horse and Sleet when we return." This was no punishment in Caroline's eyes, and she bounced up and down in her saddle with joy.

"Have you taught her to gallop?" Drayton asked his sister. "She handled it beautifully."

"Yes," replied Sara with a mock glare at Caroline, "but she knows perfectly well she is only allowed to gallop with someone riding alongside her." Caroline hung her head.

"Well, take her out again, then," said Drayton cheerfully. "And Miss Ross and I will admire your handiwork."

Rachel sat absently patting her mare as she watched the two figures, tall and small, tearing off back towards the river.

"She was never in any great danger, you know," she said to Drayton. "I could have caught up with her easily, even riding sidesaddle, on Piccola."

"Am I to infer that you do not always ride sidesaddle?" said Drayton, looking at her quizzically.

Why can I not mind what I say? thought Rachel in exasperation. No point trying to conceal the truth, though. It would fit in with her eccentric character. "When I was younger, Captain Drayton, my family lived for a year in the hills of Spain. And I am embarrassed to confess that my brother and I often went off for the day with no one, or just a groom, and I would change into boy's clothing and switch the saddles as soon as we were out of sight of the house. It was very mountainous country, and I found the sidesaddle hard to manage."

"My grandmother is Spanish," commented Drayton. "Where in Spain were you?"

"North of Zaragoza," answered Rachel. They had started to trot after Caroline and Sara.

"Is your father an artist, then?" asked Drayton, frowning. He was trying to think what a rural English gentleman would be doing in northern Spain.

Rachel sighed. "My father never does anything for very long, nor stays in any one place for very long," she said. "But you could certainly call him an artist, at least at times."

Chapter Eight

The wisdom of Lady Barrett's decision to cancel afternoon lessons soon became apparent. Rachel was badly needed elsewhere. It was not to be expected that the younger guests would wish, as Mrs. Waite did, to sit and chat for hours with Lady Barrett, or go on genteel walks to the village. Every day Drayton or Southey would propose a long ride, or an expedition to Scotney Castle, or a visit to the old ferryhouse. A party of three young men and two young women was far more comfortable than three young men and one young woman, and did not require the same careful chaperonage.

"Thank goodness Miss Ross happened to be here, Mama!" said Miranda, one morning a few days after their arrival. "It would be dreadfully awkward were she not. Captain Southey joins us nearly every afternoon, and to have three gentlemen forever disputing over who should hand me into the chaise or fetch my reticule would drive me to distraction."

Mrs. Waite glanced fondly at her daughter, gratified by the modesty and good sense displayed by this remark. Miranda's fortune had attracted such a crowd of eager and persistent suitors that a girl of vainer temperament might well have come to think the attentions of three young men at once no less than her due. When Mrs. Waite had accepted Lady Barrett's invitation, however, she had not anticipated the presence of these other courtiers. Lady Barrett did not seem troubled by the unexpected additions to the party, but Mrs. Waite knew that both she herself and Drayton's sister had originally conceived of Miranda's visit in quite a different light.

Now she said slowly, "Miranda, are you disappointed that this visit is not the quiet family party we first planned? I had thought you were looking forward to renewing your acquaintance with Captain Drayton, and I expect that you have scarcely had two words alone with him since you arrived."

This was a very broad hint indeed, and Miranda did not pretend to be ignorant of the real question her mother was asking. "Captain Drayton has been a valued friend, Mama," she said quietly. "And I know that you and Lady Barrett hoped that he and I might discover, on this visit, whether he might become something more than a friend." Miranda already knew the answer to this question, had known it since the first evening. But she was enjoying Rachel's company, and Lady Barrett's easy manner, so welcome after the rigid protocols of the London Assemblies, and she did not yet dare to wonder whether a certain lieutenant would follow her should she cut her visit short and return to London. So she dissembled, "I think, Mama, that I have been enjoying the respite from town life so much that I have not wished, as of yet, to think of more serious matters."

The afternoon following Miranda's conversation with her mother saw Miranda, Rachel, and their three gallants riding out to look at a ruined church which had belonged to a small priory sacked by Cromwell's forces during the Civil War. It was a romantic spot. The remains of the church stood at the top of a gentle hill. Tendrils of ivy twined through the roofless arches and along the edges of the windows, which still retained, in a few places, remnants of what must have been beautiful stained-glass decoration. Miranda cried out in delight and took out her sketchbook.

"Do you not sketch, Miss Ross?" asked Southey, who was somewhat artistic himself, and thought the scene well worth recording.

"I do," acknowledged Rachel, "and I have been teaching Caroline to draw from nature, but I have learned not to draw buildings, or at least, not to show those drawings to anyone else."

"Why is that?" asked Drayton, with some amusement.

She laughed. "I'll demonstrate." Borrowing a leaf from Miranda's book and a stick of charcoal, she set the paper atop Miranda's watercolor box and proceeded to make a rapid outline of some dozen strokes. "Voilà. A perfect plan of the building, should you wish to attack it with a cannon. I have no romance in my drawing." The three men looked at her sketch, and then at the half-finished effort of Miranda, which even incomplete evoked perfectly the elegiac pleasure of the scene.

"A gentleman ought never to contradict a lady," observed Southey. "And yet it would be discourteous to agree with your self-condemnation, Miss Ross. I will therefore abstain from giving my opinion on the aesthetic merits of your sketch."

Courthope was not as polished as Southey. "By George," he said impulsively, "you might be an engineer, Miss Ross! That is very well done. Where did you learn the trick of it? Surely you were not at Woolwich with Drayton?"

"I was tutored with my brother for two years, Lieutenant, and drafting was one of his subjects. I found to my distress that once I had learned to sketch plans in this way, I could not unlearn it. I would prefer to be able to sketch what I see with my memory and my heart, not simply record on paper the dimensions of the nave."

"And what do you see with your memory and your heart, Miss Ross?" asked Miranda, who had stopped work on her own sketch.

Rachel's face closed. "I see," she said quietly, "people who were killed because they prayed to God with different words than the men who commanded the troops. And those troops, not content with taking their lives, smashed the stained glass, and the tombstones, and the decorations on the choir stall, and the tracery on the windows, in case anyone might later remember the people when they looked at the beautiful church they had built. Miss Waite's sketch honors those builders and their loss. Mine does not. It merely provides information for the next troop, so that they may destroy the church with the least expenditure of ammunition."

They were very quiet when she had finished

speaking. Drayton said at last slowly, "There is more than one way of drawing, Miss Ross. I think we will not forget the picture you showed us just now." And although, a few moments later, the rest of the party was laughing and chatting as they walked back down the hill to their horses, Drayton lingered behind. Scowling to himself, he walked over to the rock where Rachel had been sitting. Forgotten on the ground was the despised sketch. He picked it up and tucked it into his jacket.

The day had been fine when they set out for the church, but the skies were darkening when they rode back through Haythorn, and the wind was beginning to blow in chilly gusts. Southey had left the party early, since he was going up to London that evening, but he promised to call in a few days when he returned. The other four spurred their horses, hoping to reach Leigh End before the rain. Drayton and Rachel made a bit of a race of it, setting the two mares over a hedge and cutting across the south pasture. They arrived, breathless, at the head of the drive just as the first drops began to fall. There they were met by Samuels, very agitated and already mounted.

"Captain Drayton! Miss Rachel! It's Miss Caroline! Mrs. Mott has been looking for her this hour! She says one of the village boys told Miss Caroline a vixen was down in the ravine in the lower wood with cubs, and she is afraid Miss Caroline has gone down there without waiting for you and Captain Drayton to return. It is very steep down there, Miss Rachel, and a vixen with cubs can be dangerous, little though Miss Caroline might think so."

"Are you sure you have searched properly?" said

Rachel, shocked. "Perhaps she is in the garden. I cannot believe Caroline would go off like that, without leaving word or asking for someone to accompany her!"

"I can," said Drayton grimly. "Miss Ross, you have brought out the better side of Caroline's nature, but I have known her to do things very like this many times. We must get down to the ravine at once; it can fill with water in heavy rain." He turned his horse, and Rachel and Samuels followed, worried. By the time they reached the lip of the ravine it was raining hard, and it was difficult to see down into the tangle of growth.

"Caroline!" called Drayton. "Caroline!" They dismounted, and Samuels led the horses away from the edge and into the shelter of a large oak. Drayton and Rachel began to pick their way cautiously down the slope, peering into the hollow, calling Caroline's name. Suddenly Drayton heard a noise behind him, a choked cry. He turned and saw Samuels lying motionless by the horses. A masked, hooded figure with a cudgel stood over him, and two more hooded figures were running towards the ravine.

"Quick!" yelled Drayton to Rachel. "Back up to the path! We have no chance of escaping them on this hill!" He picked her up and slung her, none too gently, back over the lip, then leaped up after her. The two men were on them, brandishing thick clubs. Drayton tried to push Rachel behind him, but a burly fellow reached him first. All Drayton could think of to do was to swing out with his riding crop, which he was still clutching somehow. It landed feebly on the collar of the ruffian's coat, and he laughed. Infuriated, Drayton struck out and connected solidly with a paunchy stomach. The man made a belching sound and sank down.

Drayton turned to face his second attacker, in time to see Rachel block the cudgel aimed at his ribs with her left hand and then land a solid punch under the ear with her right. Her opponent coughed and staggered slightly but recovered quickly and knocked her roughly aside. Horrified, Drayton sprang to help her and left himself unguarded. A powerful blow landed, and with a cry of agony he sank to the ground, clutching his left shoulder.

"Oh!" cried Rachel, infuriated. "If only I had my pistol!"

Words of ill omen, because at that moment she saw the masked man, the one who had clubbed Samuels, standing quietly about ten feet away. In his hand was a large pistol, pointed at her. To her amazement and horror, he addressed his two comrades in Spanish.

"You fools! You were not supposed to hurt them! He has a wound in that shoulder! Tie them up, and not too roughly."

The first man, still kneeling on the ground and clutching his stomach, peered over at Drayton. "We won't need to tie him, *señor,* he is unconscious."

"Idiot! They will be in the cart for over an hour! What if he wakes? Tie him!"

Dazed and bruised, Rachel felt her hands pulled behind her back. A leather cord was laced around them. It was tight, but not painful. The man with the pistol was motioning for her to climb into a cart standing behind Samuels's prone form. She looked at the body in anguish. Was Samuels dead? Then she saw his chest rise and fall slightly. The pistol nudged her ribs. She climbed into the cart. The other two men were carrying Drayton over; they laid him down next to her.

"You know where to go?" said the man with the pistol sharply.

"Yes, *Señor* Commander."

"Good. I will see you after you have delivered them. Drag some bracken over the marks made by the cart wheels here in the mud. I do not want them found too quickly." He turned, checked Samuels briefly, made sure the horses were firmly tethered, and then strode away.

At first Drayton thought he was back in the cart in Spain. It all seemed the same: his shoulder hurt dreadfully; he could feel blood seeping onto his back; it was gray and wet and cold and he could hear two men talking in Spanish as they drove the cart. Every rut sent a wave of pain through his left arm. At least that damned panel was not pushing his shoulder down into the floor of the cart any longer. Then he caught sight of Rachel's face as she bent over him anxiously and he remembered where he was. There had been a fight, he had been attacked in Barrett's woods, Caroline was missing . . . Did these villains have her, as well? How could he be in Spain if he had been attacked at Leigh End? What was Miss Ross doing in Spain? It was all so confusing. He closed his eyes again.

His head began to clear, and he accepted the astounding truth: He had been kidnapped, in the middle of Kent, by Spanish-speaking bandits. He was in a cart with Miss Ross, being taken God knows where—perhaps to the coast, to be put on board ship. He gave a faint groan and opened his eyes.

At once he saw Rachel's face bending over him. Her lips formed one word: *sleep*. Just in time, he closed his eyes again.

"Is he awake?" asked a voice from the front of the cart. He felt a movement above him and held very still.

"No, still unconscious."

"Is everything there in the hut?"

"The commander said so; he saw to it himself." There was a coarse laugh. "I would not mind being forced to marry that one." He used a Spanish pronoun which referred to a female. "The commander will not let the others find them until tomorrow; they can have their honeymoon before the wedding, eh?"

"Quiet, you fool. He could wake at any moment." A flask was passed from one speaker to the other, and the cart bounced on in silence. It was full dark by now, and the man next to the driver cautiously lit a lantern. Drayton opened his eyes momentarily at the light, which gleamed on the iron rails of the backboard. The cart slowed, and then inched forward.

"Here it is. You can see the tracks from the commander's trip last night."

The cart turned clumsily and rumbled into a wooded copse. It drew up outside an ancient square tower, and the two men climbed out. The original doors to the tower were long gone, but there was now a tall iron grill across the arch, closed with a padlock. The driver unlocked it, and his companion turned to Rachel with a mocking grin. Making an elaborate bow, he assisted her from the cart, untied her hands, and escorted her through the gate. The interior of the tower had been gutted, forming a roofless courtyard. Against the rear wall of the tower was a small hut. After a moment, the two men reappeared, carrying Drayton, and disappeared into the hut. They emerged, bowed silently to Rachel once more, and went out through the gate, locking the grill behind them. Rachel heard their voices murmuring for a moment more, and then the creak of the axle as the cart rumbled into motion. She ran to the grill and shook it desperately, staring after the receding shape of the cart.

"Stop!" she screamed. "What do you want with us! He is hurt! You cannot leave us like this!" There was no reply. In a moment, the last flicker of the lantern disappeared into the woods and she was alone. For the first time since the attack at the ravine terror swept over her. Up until now she had been stunned, unable to comprehend what was happening, concerned for Samuels and Drayton. She had barely had the presence of mind in the cart to tell Drayton to lie still so that their captors would keep talking. But their remarks had only bewildered her further. Why had they been brought here? Where was Caroline? Who was the commander? Tears of anxiety and despair rose to her eyes. She shook the grill again, then kicked it. It was solid and rose high into the roof of the arched doorway. She would never be able to climb over it.

When she turned back to the hut she was surprised to see a faint light inside. The door was open. Drayton was on a plank bed against the far wall, watching her gravely as she entered from the courtyard. She saw that his hands had also been untied, and a small candle was burning on a rough chest next to the bed. There was wood in the fireplace, and a jug of water next to the candle. On a table by the door was a loaf of bread, a second jug, some crockery, and two lumps wrapped in napkins. Drayton saw her looking at the table.

"Our dinner, I believe," he said. His voice was weak but steady. "I had not planned on visiting another ruin so soon after this afternoon's expedition, but I gather that we will be picnicking here."

"And breakfasting, as well, belike," said Rachel bleakly. Her eyes met his. "Did you—did you hear what they said in the cart? They did not know I understood Spanish."

"I heard," said Drayton. In the candlelight he saw a fiery blush rise on Rachel's throat. "You are soaked," he said. "You should light the fire and take off your jacket and skirt." She stepped away from him with a shocked gasp. "Don't be so missish!" he said in a sharp tone. "I have already seen your petticoats at the river. There is a blanket here on the bed that you can wrap yourself with while your skirt dries."

Rachel peered behind him to try to find the blanket and then suddenly noticed his pallor. Belatedly she realized that he had not risen when she entered, nor offered to make up the fire. Without answering, she took the candle and held it up so that she could see the back of his jacket. A dark stain was spreading down underneath his left arm.

"I think we must tend to you first, Captain Drayton," she said. "You are even wetter than I am. And your wound has reopened."

"How perceptive of you," he drawled.

Rachel ignored him and set about her tasks. First she made up the fire. She was very thankful that it had already been laid, because the wood she had seen piled outside the hut was likely to be quite damp. Drayton was right; there was no point in being missish. As soon as the fire was going steadily, she took off her jacket and hung it precariously from a rough projection on the stone wall behind the fireplace. It began to steam gently. Then she turned back to the bed.

"Would you like to try to take off your coat?" she said. "Or should I cut it off?"

"If you help me, I think we can get it off," said Drayton. "It is ruined in any case, but there is only one blanket, and we might need it as a cover if the night grows cooler."

Rachel thought that it was already quite cool; she was shivering in her damp blouse. Gently, she tugged Drayton's right arm out of the coat and then pulled the coat around to the back and eased it off his left arm. It dripped as she carried it over to the fireplace and hung it next to her own.

"I must cut your shirt, sir," she said. She looked around for something to use.

"Try the table," said Drayton. "This appears to be a very well-equipped kidnapping." He was right; next to one of the napkins was a small knife. Rachel sliced expertly through the shirt and folded back the cloth square. A small trickle of dark blood was oozing from the depression left by the bullet. Worse, Rachel realized, the edges of the wound looked red and angry. Her attempts to clean the wound did not help.

"This has not healed properly," she said, frowning. "How long ago were you hit? Did they get the bullet out?"

"Yes," said Drayton, calculating frantically. "F-seven weeks ago."

Rachel raised her eyebrows but said nothing. She held the candle closer to his back. "You need a physician," she announced. "There must be a fragment of the ball, or a bone splinter, still in the wound."

"At the moment, Miss Ross, I fear that you are the only physician available."

"Well, I have tended bullet wounds before," she said to his surprise. "Please lie down on your stomach, sir. I will try to make a bandage from one of the napkins. Our own garments are far too wet and muddy." She crossed back to the table and inspected the napkins. One was wrapped around several slices of cold meat. But the other held two hunks of hard cheese, and the outside appeared dry and clean. She folded it into a pad and bound it into place with a strip from Drayton's shirt. Then she picked up the blanket and, ignoring Drayton's cry of protest, sliced it in two.

"Your half, Captain Drayton," she said with a curtsy, as she handed him one piece. Then she went over to the table, and returned with something in a small cup. "This is indeed a well-equipped kidnapping," she said wryly. "As your nurse, I must warn you that I will only allow you two small cups. But it appears to be what Sir Charles would call quite a decent claret."

It was very late by the time they had dried their outer clothing and boots. They had eaten wrapped in the blanket halves. Rachel had portioned out the food carefully, but neither felt very hungry. They were exhausted and apprehensive.

"Do you know where we are?" said Rachel at last.

"Yes. Bettham's Keep. It is very old; Norman, I believe. And quite isolated. Calling for help would be useless." He looked at her steadily. "There is no avoiding the issue, Miss Ross. Our hosts have the right of it. You will have to marry me."

"I most certainly will do no such thing! It is completely impossible!" blazed Rachel. Drayton felt a great mixture of relief and shame flood through him. His mistrust of Rachel had almost led him to suspect that she might have engineered the abduction herself, and he was for some reason absurdly pleased to have been wrong.

"Are you already wed?" he asked.

She shook her head.

"Betrothed?"

"There has been an understanding between myself and one of my cousins, but no marriage contract or announcement."

"Are your affections engaged, though?" He looked down at his bandage. "I fear your cousin will have to wait to call me out."

"He would not do so, sir. I have not seen my cousin for five years; he has not that sort of claim upon me."

"Then why the devil do you say it is impossible to marry me? I realize," he added sardonically, "that your notions of propriety are less gothic than my own, but surely even you must see that you will be completely ruined by this night's work unless we are wed?"

"It is not to be thought of," said Rachel obstinately. "Are you so poor-spirited, sir? Is it not obvious that—for some reason I cannot fathom—the villains who struck down Samuels and abducted us have exactly this outcome in mind? I would not so gratify them, even if I were otherwise minded to accept your very obliging offer."

"As I take it you are not?" he said, with some

hauteur. There was no polite reply to such a question, and Rachel compressed her lips in silence.

"If it is not to be thought of," said Drayton after a moment, "perhaps you have some scheme in mind to prevent it? You surely do not think that you can simply return to Leigh End and continue as you were, once it is known that we spent the night here?"

"We could try to keep it a secret," said Rachel hesitantly. She knew, as Drayton did not, that she could always make Miss Ross disappear. She could go on to Germany, and then to Italy, and probably no one would ever be the wiser. But then James would be left to his own wild devices, and she would be breaking her promise to her father. Rachel did not admit to herself that she had grown very fond of her life at Leigh End—of Caroline, of Lady Barrett, of the beautiful countryside and the joyous hours of riding.

Drayton's reply was two words: "Miss Lutford."

"But surely—even if it becomes known—your wound—you can barely stand!"

"I assure you, Miss Ross, that that will not serve as a defense." His eyes twinkled. "Come sit on the bed next to me and I will demonstrate why." He looked at her appreciatively. Her hair was still damp and curled around her face. Her blouse clung to her slender shoulders. She was very attractive, he thought, detached. Not his style, of course. But she and Miranda had made a very pretty picture the other evening.

A smart slap across the face interrupted his thoughts. "Maria is right!" said Rachel furiously. "You are a rake!"

"Now you are behaving like a well-brought-up young lady!" said Drayton, amused. "I am surprised you did not give me a right to the jaw, as you did to that oaf who attacked us."

"Oh," said Rachel in a small voice. "I had hoped you would not see that."

"Or hear you wish for your pistol? What other subjects did you study with your brother, Miss Ross, in addition to drafting?"

Rachel looked down, miserable. Why had she ever imagined she could carry off such an imposture? She was not good at masquerades, like her father and James. She was always stepping out of character and revealing herself. It was lucky she had not forgotten and spoken in Spanish to the kidnappers! She tried the truth, or some of the truth.

"My family is a bit odd, Captain Drayton. My father—my father and mother travel frequently, and have not always thought it right to take us with them. For quite a while, my brother and I have been in the charge of my uncle, who resides in London. He does not approve of my father's wanderings and hoped to make a scholar of my brother."

"It did not work?" queried Drayton.

"No. My brother was uncooperative, and because he has always been very close to me, my uncle offered to have me join the lessons. They were very good lessons," she added. "Our tutors were excellent. I enjoyed them very much. But my uncle would not at first hear of engaging instructors for boxing, or fencing. So my brother determined to teach himself, and he practiced on me, in the schoolroom. We had to swear Maria to secrecy; I had so many bruises!"

"You seem to have learned at least the rudiments," commented Drayton, recalling her block of the cudgel.

She shook her head. "I am out of practice. There is a place on the neck, below the ear—if you hit it just right, you can make your opponent swoon. I missed. My brother taught it to me. My uncle realized several years ago that my brother would never be a scholar and allowed him to hire proper instructors."

Drayton did not recall learning this particular trick in his own boxing lessons, but he let that pass. "I did not thank you, you know, for trying to defend me, at the ravine," he said abruptly. "Talk of swooning! Most young ladies would have fainted away at the first sight of those blackguards."

"As always, I behaved most improperly, did I not?" said Rachel with a laugh. Then she caught her breath. "Captain Drayton! I have an idea! Would you feel obliged to offer for me if it were known that you had been unconscious the whole time we were here?"

Drayton thought about this. "Probably not," he said slowly. "But it is not true, of course."

"I could say that you had been unconscious."

"When we are found—and I presume our captors will arrange that we are found—our rescuers will see very well that I am not unconscious."

"You could pretend."

"I am not an actor, as my friend Rodrigo has told me." Rachel gave a slight start at those words. "I cannot imagine myself trying to lie still while Hickman or Sir Charles hauls me out of this silly hut."

"Well, that was what made me think of the

scheme," said Rachel. "I rather suspected you would not wish to pretend. It would be better if you actually were unconscious when we were found. We must wait until we hear people coming, and then I will knock you out."

Chapter Nine

Sara hurried into Rachel's room, where Maria, her face grim, was standing over her mistress while she drank a steaming mug of broth. Rachel's hair had been brushed out and she was in a flannel nightdress, but she was not in bed. She was sitting in a low armchair, looking very anxious. The stained riding habit was in a heap on the floor.

"Oh, my dear!" said Sara, tears in her eyes. "We are so glad you are safe! What a dreadful thing!"

"Is Caroline all right?" said Rachel. She started to get up, but a ferocious glare from Maria sent her back to her armchair. "Sir Charles told me that they found her asleep in a pantry, but that she was very difficult to rouse. Is she ill? Does anyone know why we could not find her?"

"She is very poorly," said Sara, distressed. "Miss Ross, I cannot believe it, but I think she was *drugged!* She told me that she had some milk which tasted odd and then grew very sleepy, and she has been retching now for hours. I must go back to her, but I wanted to see you, just for a minute."

"I am fine, perfectly well," said Rachel, although she looked white and haggard. "I think it nonsensical to make me go to bed in the middle of the day. I ought to go and see Samuels, and make sure he is comfortable. And I could help nurse Captain Drayton. Is he awake yet?"

It had not been difficult for Rachel to pretend concern about Drayton. By the time their rescuers had appeared early the next morning, Drayton was feverish and weak. He had stayed unconscious for the whole trip home, and Rachel knew that she had not hit him very hard. Since the search party included not only Sir Charles and Courthope, but nearly every groom in the county, Rachel felt fairly certain that her reputation was safe. She was less certain about Drayton's health. They had rebandaged his wound while they waited for a wagon to be brought up, and Rachel saw that his whole shoulder had turned purple.

"Yes, he is awake now, and has asked after you. But he does not look well at all. The village doctor has been here, and he has managed to reduce the swelling somewhat, but he agrees with what you told Sir Charles at the keep: We must send for a good surgeon. Courthope has ridden in to Maidstone to find Mr. Harvey. Please do rest, Miss Ross. I will come back after Mr. Harvey has been here, and report to you. We will ask him to look also at Samuels, and make sure his arm was set properly. Hickman says he is lucky that his head is not broken, as well."

Rachel obediently got into bed, and allowed Maria to fuss over her with warming pans and plasters. But after Maria had withdrawn, pointedly closing the curtains and tiptoeing away, Rachel lay on the bolster with her eyes wide open, trying to make sense of what had happened. When she had first heard their attackers speak Spanish, she had been horrified, sure that somehow her identity—and her role as liaison with James—had been discovered. But it had rapidly become clear that the kidnappers had no idea who she was. They did not realize that she spoke Spanish, and they obviously believed that she moved in social circles that would require her marriage to Drayton after a night spent together without a chaperone.

On the other hand, they clearly knew quite a bit about Drayton. They knew he was wounded, and where; they knew he understood Spanish, which many of Wellington's officers did not. And he had mentioned Rodrigo. She frowned. It was a common name, of course. But—and this was most puzzling of all—the kidnappers were not Spanish. She had become certain of that after hearing them speak in the cart. They were French. If Drayton was connected with the Rodrigo she knew, she could easily understand why French agents would want him killed, or captured. But why on earth would they want him married to Rachel Ross of the Shropshire Rosses? Drayton's wound was another mystery. She was no expert, but she would have said that that wound could not have been more than a month old. She sighed. The village doctor was an idiot, according to Sir Charles. Drayton had best hope that Harvey, who was unlikely to be so ignorant, was at least discreet.

She lay in bed dutifully until teatime, when Miranda poked her head around the door very quietly. Rachel pushed off the coverlet, swung her feet out of bed, and stood.

"Miss Ross, please do not get up!" said Miranda, looking guilty.

"You are my excuse," said Rachel, crossing the room towards the bell rope. "And I need an ally, or Maria will push me back into bed."

"I saw Maria going out to the stable loft to check on Samuels," said Miranda. "She told me I might look in on you, but not to let you get up."

"Excellent!" said Rachel. "That means that Betsy will answer the bell. I am quite well rested, and if I do not get up and get out of this horrid nightrail I will begin to roast. I did not even want to bring this one, it is so heavy, but Maria is convinced that no one but my uncle has warming pans for their beds." She tugged on the bell.

At that very moment, Betsy appeared. "Please excuse me, Miss Ross," she stammered. "But Sir Charles asked me to see if you was awake, and well enough to come down to Captain Drayton's room. That Mr. Harvey is here."

In a few moments, Rachel and Miranda were following Betsy across the stairwell to the other wing of the house. A knot of uneasy people stood outside one of the bedroom doors: Fidder, Courthope, two footmen, and the vicar. Courthope's face brightened as he saw them approaching. He was still in riding clothes and was spattered with mud.

"Miss Ross! Happy to see you in better frame!" he said. He turned to Miranda. "I hope you and Lady Barrett did not fret when I was gone so long; it took me an age to find the fellow."

Sir Charles emerged from the sickroom, looking worried. He came straight over to Rachel. "A word with you, Miss Ross?" He drew her into a side room and closed the door. The room faced west; the sinking sun lit the wainscoting with gold highlights. Sir Charles, the light full in his face, looked at her levelly.

"Miss Ross, I do not want you to think Lady Barrett has broken her word to you."

Rachel's heart sank. So Mr. Castell—if that was his name—had recognized her after all. She was bitterly ashamed; she had come to like and respect Sir Charles. "Sir Charles," she began, "I most deeply regret—"

He cut her off. "I work with your uncle, and he knows you are here; that is of no concern at the moment. We can discuss it later if you wish. Your aunt is sister to the king's physician, is she not? I mentioned her to Harvey, and he tells me she is a notable nurse in her own right. I saw the pressure bandage you contrived for Drayton, and hoped that you might have a bit more skill than Mrs. Mott or Lady Barrett. Harvey thinks he has now cleaned the wound properly, but someone who knows what they are about must change the dressings every few hours for the first two days. He wishes to send for a nurse from Maidstone. I am reluctant to do so. The more I think about this business, the more I believe that the fewer tongues wagging the better."

"Do you also know who my father and brother are?" she said in a very faint voice. He nodded. "Then you will understand that I have had considerable experience nursing wounded men, in addition to what I have learned from my aunt."

"I rather suspected as much," said Sir Charles. He turned to hold open the door. "You may not believe this," he added gently, "but I would have been glad to invite you here under your own name."

* * *

Drayton was lying on his side, waiting for Rachel to come in with fresh bandages. She was very prompt; he could set his watch by her. He knew that Harvey was right, that his shoulder would never have healed properly if the bone splinter had stayed in the wound, but it was very hard to go back to being an invalid after he had thought himself almost recovered. In some ways it was worse than the first time, in fact, because Harvey's instructions for draining the wound as the dressings were changed did not make it a pleasant operation for the patient. He had not had such careful attention at the field hospital. A shadow fell over the bed, and he looked up, expecting Rachel. It was a spruce gentleman with graying dark hair, impeccably attired in sparkling white linen, broadcloth, and pantaloons. He regarded the patient with a frown.

Drayton's jaw dropped, and he pushed up onto his elbow. "Sir!"

"Don't get up," said his father. "I see you're a bit better than you were when Harvey was here day before yesterday. He said you were limp as a fish."

Drayton was struggling to sit up.

"Don't be a fool," said his father curtly. "I'm not staying long. I ran into Harvey in Brooks, and he told me you had been attacked. Did some of your London friends decide to pay you a visit and play pirate?"

Drayton did not answer.

"He also told me that he had to go digging in your wound from the Peninsula. It was a most interesting conversation we had, in fact. His impression seems to have been that the wound was a month-old pistol wound. And yet," said Alcroft, looking thoughtful, "I was almost certain that your sister had told me that you were wounded eight weeks ago. By a sniper. My curiosity was sufficiently aroused that I actually went down to Whitehall and looked at the dispatches. Is it not odd that although your unit did indeed engage the enemy in early March, the casualty report was not filed until the end of the month?"

Drayton looked at his father's fine-featured face. It was very cold.

"You know," said Alcroft, "in spite of your general's successes, I have found no reason to revise my opinion that our war office is grossly mismanaged. I have been trying to think how I could explain this discrepancy in your medical history, and the only thing that occurs to me is that you have been dueling. Again. Which is not a surprise, but to think"—and here his voice broke—"to think you took the damned ball in the *back!* And they covered for you! My God! Even with all the rest, I did not think you a coward."

His face white, Drayton stared at his father.

"As William's guardian," Alcroft said, after a pause, "it is not possible, in justice, to deny you access to the London house, or to Alcroft Hall. But I would appreciate it if you would confine any visits required by the exercise of your responsibilities to those times when I am not in residence."

There was a sound in the doorway. Rachel stood there, a basin in one hand and a roll of lint in the other. She looked horrified.

"Your servant, ma'am," said Alcroft. "Good day, Richard. I wish you a speedy recovery."

Mechanically, Rachel stepped aside, and Alcroft swept out. She put down the basin, and the lint, and closed the door. She stared at Drayton, her lips compressed in anger. He looked back at her calmly, his expression remote.

"How could you!" she said. "How could you let him believe that . . . that ridiculous nonsense!"

Drayton's eyes glittered. "How do you know it isn't true?"

Rachel had no evidence except her own conviction, but that did not dissuade her. She was in a high temper.

"Of course it isn't! You are torturing that poor old man, all because of your idiotic pride!"

"*My* pride! Poor old man! My good girl, are you mad? My father is so arrogant, the Duke of Clarence sometimes forgets and bows to *him!*"

"Well, then," said Rachel fiercely, "I know where you get it from. Turn back on your side please, sir." She began to peel off the bandages. She was not gentle, and Drayton flinched several times before she was through. But when she rose to leave, still clearly very angry, he stopped her.

"Thank you," he said quietly.

She looked at him suspiciously.

"For not believing it."

Rachel's eyes filled with tears, and she turned hastily away. She was very tired; it was not easy to be awakened every few hours, and she had not slept at all in the hut. "I don't know what to believe anymore," she said in a low voice. "Everything is a muddle."

His father was not Drayton's only visitor that day. Towards evening, he heard a light knock at the door, and Southey came in. He looked very agitated and came swiftly over to the bedside, peering anxiously at Drayton.

"For God's sake, South!" said Drayton irritably. "Don't you begin fussing at me as well. I've had Courthope, Miss Lutford and even Caroline in here mooning over me as though I were at death's door."

"I just got back from London and rode straight over. Dammit, Drayton, this is unbelievable! A mile from Barrett's pasture! In broad daylight!"

"I am finding it difficult to fathom who they were and what they wanted," said Drayton.

"Are you?" said Southey, looking at him keenly. "Barrett tells me your abductors spoke Spanish."

"Yes, Miss Ross heard them talking," said Drayton, remembering in time that he had been unconscious. "But I had thought my brother-in-law more discreet than to let that particular detail out."

"He is very discreet," said Southey dryly. "He is so discreet that he is actually permitted to be aware of my real appointment at Whitehall. I would be surprised if he had told anyone save myself about the nature of your abductors."

Southey began to pace back and forth. "Do you think this is connected to that business with Tredwell?" he said, concerned.

"That was my first thought, of course," said Drayton. "But they did not seem interested in questioning me, or even harming me. Southey, I will have to swear you to secrecy if I am going to tell you any more."

"You have my word," said Southey, "of course."

"South, the whole affair seems to have been a scheme to force me to marry Miss Ross—or her to marry me. We heard them talking in the cart. They did not know Miss Ross speaks Spanish, and I pretended to be unconscious."

"You pretended! Do you mean . . . you were in fact awake with Miss Ross in that hut?"

Drayton nodded. "I have your word, Michael? I have told no one else, not even Sir Charles. It is not so far from the truth—well, at least towards morning, when I think I was rather feverish. When we first arrived I was still fairly lucid. My extended sleep, if you would like to call it that, was Miss Ross's idea. She was very keen on frustrating the goals of our abductors."

"Was she?" muttered Southey. "It certainly worked. Even Barrett's Aunt Lutford assured me that no one thought Miss Ross at all compromised, under the circumstances."

"She is really a remarkable girl," said Drayton pensively. "Would you like to know how she made sure that I could play my part when the rescue party arrived? Take a look at that." He indicated a livid bruise below his left ear.

"By Jupiter!" said Southey. "She *hit* you? Hard enough to knock you out?"

"It took her two tries," admitted Drayton. "But, as she said, she was out of practice."

Miranda and Rachel had a difficult time keeping Drayton in bed for the prescribed week. Sara had given up in disgust. "He always could wind me around his little finger," she said candidly to Miranda. "You and Miss Ross may have more success in getting him to listen." When Rachel came into his room on the sixth day after the surgery, she found him looking so much better that she was not at all surprised to see him sitting on the edge of the bed, dressed. He had the grace to look guilty.

"I bribed Fidder," he said. "I couldn't bear to be in a nightshirt one more minute."

"Have no fear, Captain Drayton," she said, happy to see him so much stronger. "I will not make you undress again."

He slanted an oblique look at her. "I would not object if you did," he said provocatively. "Under certain circumstances."

Rachel chose to consider this evidence of returning health and merely laughed. He seemed much better . . . Perhaps now she might venture to probe a bit about the mention of Rodrigo. She was not good at indirection, she knew. Her father would have had the information he needed days ago. She had postponed pursuing it out of cowardice, but now her excuse—his frailty—was clearly gone. So she said lightly, "You said some very odd things while you were ill, you know." He had not in fact been truly delirious, but she was fairly certain he could not know that. "You kept talking about Rover, and Spain. Is he your dog? I did not know soldiers could keep pets while on campaign."

"They can," said Drayton shortly, struggling to turn back his cuff without moving his left arm. "And mistresses. And children. But no, I did not have a dog. Rover was a—a colleague, another soldier. I did not actually meet him," he added honestly. "I only heard about him."

Rachel had heard only one word. Her heart stopped beating. "Was?" she said.

"Yes, he was killed," said Drayton absently. "A great loss, I gather." Then he recollected that it was perhaps not politic to discuss intelligence couriers, even dead ones, and he changed the subject. "Miss Ross—" he began, looking up from his cuff.

But Rachel was sliding down the side of the bed and crumpling to the floor. She had fainted.

Frantically, Drayton staggered over and tugged at the bell. What were you supposed to do when females fainted? He had a vague memory that you loosened their stays, or threw water on them, or gave them smelling salts. He cast an anguished glance around. No water or smelling salts met his eye. Dropping stiffly down onto the floor beside Rachel, he propped up her head and pulled aside the top of her gown, ripping several guineas worth of braided floss in the process. She was wearing a gold chain and he tore at it, with some confused notion that it might be strangling her. On the end of the chain, to his surprise, was a small two-noted whistle, in solid gold. "Odd sort of locket," he muttered. Her handkerchief was tucked into her bodice, and he pulled it out, thinking to dab at her forehead, but then remembered that he needed water or cologne in which to dip the handkerchief. He set it aside. Finally he found some promising-looking laces. With a desperate yank he ripped at them one-handed; her bodice loosened, and he gave a sigh of relief. Then he caught sight of the inside of her right shoulder and froze.

There was a small scar there. He remembered now that she rarely wore anything low-cut. It was a round, dimpled scar, not unattractive, really. It was, unmistakably, a bullet wound.

Rachel gave a small cough, or groan, and opened her eyes. She saw Drayton's blurred face above her and realized she was lying on the floor.

"No!" she said, aghast. "Did I faint? I *never* faint!" Then she saw her dress, and the torn laces of her bodice, and cried out in dismay. She sat up and clutched her dress around her.

Drayton was staring at her, his eyes narrowed. "Miss Ross," he said, "I think you really will have to marry me this time."

"What? Why?" Rachel looked down at her dress in horror. "How long have I been unconscious? What have you been doing? Surely it is not improper for you to assist me if I swoon?"

"That is not what I mean," said Drayton. "I refer to your shoulder. We must be destined for each other. I see that we have matching scars."

Rachel's eyes flew to his face. He looked grim, and his jaw was set. "You saw it, then," she whispered.

"Yes. Would you care to explain, Miss Ross, how it is that you have a bullet hole in your right shoulder?"

"It was—an accident," she said desperately.

"You are not a good actor, Miss Ross."

"It *was* an accident," she said hotly. "It was when we were being chased by the dogs. My brother had a pistol, and when the dog caught me he tried to shoot it. But he was not a very good shot."

Now he will ask me why we were being chased by the dogs, she thought, and then what will I say? That it was really my father who was being chased by the dogs?

And then, with a gasp of anguish, she remembered why she had fainted; she heard again the dreadful words *he was killed.* Scrambling to her feet, she ran from the room without even looking at Drayton, sobbing in despair. When a breathless footman arrived, apologizing for the delay in answering the bell, he found Drayton sitting on his bed staring numbly at a tiny gold whistle and a lace-edged handkerchief.

Chapter Ten

The morning sun slanted in through the window in the back of the shed. Its beam was filled with whirling motes of sawdust, and if you tracked the golden band all the way to the floor, you could see what was stirring up the shavings: five wriggling puppies, struggling to clamber over each other to their mother. Belinda lay on her side, looking at the puppies with tolerant scorn. Caroline and Rachel were doing plenty of cooing and mothering in her place. They had stopped in for a visit on their way back from their morning ride.

"Aren't they the nicest things ever?" said Caroline dreamily, turning over the smallest pup and stroking its pale belly gently.

"They're marvelous," said Rachel, meaning it. In the past two days she had escaped down here many times when she could not hold back the tears. She realized suddenly with a sense of wonder that she was finding the presence of Belinda and Bertha comforting; that she had not hesitated to come to the kennel alone.

"May I come in?" said a voice from the door. It was Miranda, with the hood of her pelisse pushed back, holding her gloves in her hand.

"You'll get your pelisse and gown all over sawdust," said Caroline practically.

"I don't mind," said Miranda. She stooped over next to Belinda and was met by a friendly but unmistakable growl.

Rachel laughed. "Ah, sweet reward for my devotion to duty! All those early mornings stumbling down to offer these hulks their food have finally proved their worth. She does not growl at *me.*"

"You have certainly earned your reward," agreed Miranda. "It must be nice to have one patient who is grateful and obeys orders." The two exchanged wry smiles. Drayton's health had been improving rapidly, at the expense of his temper. He had insisted on going riding the previous afternoon, and had refused to take any mount except Sleet. When the skittish mare objected to carrying this odd, rigid person who only used one hand, Drayton had stubbornly prolonged the expedition far beyond his original intention and had been white and stiff-limbed for the rest of the day.

"The secret of my success with Belinda and Bertha," said Rachel in a confiding whisper, "is that I don't give them any orders." Then she noticed Miranda's dark-blue traveling dress under her pelisse. "Are you going off in the coach for the day?"

"Yes, but not for the day," said Miranda. "I stopped in to say good-bye."

"Good-bye! Whatever do you mean?" said Rachel, scrambling to her feet and shaking sawdust off her habit. "We will come out and say farewell properly, of course. I did not know you were leaving."

"Neither did I," said Miranda, "until last night. It was very sudden."

Last night, thought Rachel. What had happened last night? Lieutenant Courthope had gone back to London just before dinner . . . that had been rather odd as well, come to think of it. He had been so upset and embarrassed when he stammered his farewells that Rachel had wondered if he and Drayton had quarreled.

"It did not seem right to stay on in the home of one suitor's sister," said Miranda shyly, "when I had just given another suitor permission to seek out my father in London."

A more elegant version of the same scene was being enacted in Lady Barrett's private parlor. Mrs. Waite sat on the edge of a cream-colored divan and peered anxiously at her friend, waiting for her reaction to the announcement.

"It is wonderful news!" said Sara sincerely. "Truly, I am very happy for Miranda. I could see how they felt about each other from the first evening you were here. And how lovely for Miranda that he is so wealthy; she will never doubt his motives in offering for her."

"Do you think Richard is very much cast down?" asked Mrs. Waite, worried.

"Much as it hurts my pride to admit it, no, I do not," said Sara, with a whimsical smile. "I had thought that Miranda would be the very girl for him, could I but contrive to keep him in one spot for more than a few days so that they could become better acquainted. They seemed such good friends, and have known each other for so long. They are still good friends, but that is all. He is in a foul temper at the moment because he wants to be healing faster than he is, but his black mood has nothing to do with Miranda. I saw him when Courthope broke the news to him before he left yesterday evening, and I am sure his congratulations were completely honest; he has never been able to hide his feelings well."

"When I saw that Richard was not serious about Miranda," Sara continued, "I admit that I had some hopes that Miranda might look kindly on Captain Southey's suit. He is Richard's dearest friend, and I have known him since he was twelve. While his father was alive he did not come home very often, but in the last year he has been very attentive to his mother, who now relies on him completely. There is a younger sister, also, only a few years older than Caroline, and he is wondrously gentle with her. I was happy to think I would have Miranda so close to me, just a few miles away—it would be delightful to be neighbors again, although of course Miranda was very little when I left Sussex to be married. But now I have heard some worrisome rumors and think it is perhaps just as well that they did not suit. It would have been simply dreadful if Miranda had developed a *tendre* for him, only to have her father forbid the match."

"No," said Samuels. One arm was still in a sling, but he folded his arms anyway. "Your father would have my head, Miss Rachel. And Master James would slice up anything what was left after your father was done."

"You cannot ride to Charing! You cannot even ride around the stableyard! You have dizzy spells constantly!"

"I only had one today," said Samuels stubbornly. "It's not fitting, Miss Rachel, and you knows it. You're a grown lady now, not some harum-scarum schoolgirl. If Maria knew you had Master James's clothes in that saddlebag, she would burn 'em."

"If Maria knew," said Rachel coldly, "it would be because you broke your sworn word and told her. Someone has to take that French money over to Charing tonight, and you are not able to do it. It will take but two hours, and no one will trouble me if I wear James's clothes. I need only to know where the meeting place is in Charing, so that I can find Silvio." And, she added silently, when I find him, perhaps he will have more definite information about my father. She had not said a word to Maria or Samuels about Drayton's casual remark.

They were standing by Piccola's stall in the stable. Rachel was absently feeding her bits of apple from a small bucket. Usually she only fed her two or three, but she had become absorbed in the argument and Piccola was not about to demur. She swallowed her sixth apple chunk and nuzzled for more.

"No," said Samuels. "I won't tell it, and you're not going. If I can't ride tonight, Silvio will return on Wednesday, as we agreed. I should be able to ride by then."

"You think a broken arm and a cracked head will be mended five days hence?" asked Rachel scornfully. "Besides, we already missed the last meeting. If James does not get the money, he might do something desperate.''

''Such as riding out dressed in boy's clothes, as is most improper and dangerous?'' asked Samuels.

''No,'' snapped Rachel. ''Such as going over to France without it! And let us not forget what happened when my father tried that!'' They were both silent, remembering: The unpaid Frenchmen had kidnapped Rachel's father and held him to ransom. She glared at Samuels. ''If you do not tell me where I am to meet Silvio,'' she said, pronouncing every word distinctly, ''I will go to Charing and ride through the entire town, every inn, every barn, every public square, every smithy, until I find him. If it takes until daylight.''

Samuels capitulated. He always did, in the end.

Drayton was having trouble sleeping. And no wonder, he thought savagely. If a man was plumped onto couches all day and prevented from getting out in the good fresh air, and forced to lie down and have his wounds examined, which was all right when they were in real need of attention but was getting downright embarrassing now that he was nearly healed—well, insomnia was the natural result, surely, of such nonsense. He stamped into his dressing room and stamped back out. If Robson were here, he would be sleeping in the dressing room. He would at least be company, even if he were snoring while Drayton talked to him. But Drayton would not rouse a maid to wake Fidder in the middle of the night simply because he had the megrims.

And why, he said to himself, pulling on his dressing gown and slippers and taking a candle from the nightstand, why are you so blue-deviled? Are you jealous of Courthope? A fine friend you are! You don't care for Miranda in that particular way, so how can you begrudge Corey his happiness? He is a fine fellow; Miranda is glowing like a Christmas candle, and what is it to do with you? He stalked out the door and down the hall, muttering to himself. Everyone said he was healing well; he could feel himself that his shoulder had a fuller range of motion than it had before Harvey's surgery, although it was still very tender. But he was impatient; he had had enough of being an invalid. He wanted to be up and doing.

He had arrived at the end of the hall, where the east wing of the house formed the top right-hand end of the *U.* There was a large bay window at the end of the hall, looking out onto the terrace above the garden. And in the moonlight he could see that someone else was up and doing. It was a man, carrying something that looked like a cloak, walking round the edge of the house toward the side court which led to the stable. Walking very carefully and slowly. As though he did not want to be heard.

At once Drayton's melancholy dropped away. He dashed back to his room, sliding the last five yards on the polished boards of the hall like a schoolboy. Shedding the dressing gown and slippers, he threw on a shirt, not bothering to insert his left arm, and pulled on his breeches. Boots were still hopeless; he didn't even consider them. It was nearly May; he could go out unshod. Exhilarated, he sprinted down the stairs and through the silent kitchen out to the side yard. He could see a lantern flickering in the stable. He was too late, though. A dim shape was pushing open the stable door, leading out a saddled horse. The rider had some difficulty mounting, but Drayton knew he would be off before Drayton could cross the yard, so he remained concealed.

As soon as the rider was gone, Drayton slipped into the stable. The thief had gotten away, but with luck, he could come up with him, especially if he did not know he was pursued. Drayton had ridden barefoot before. He began the delicate task of inserting his left arm into the sleeve of his shirt as he walked down to Sleet's stall. Then he paused, stupefied. Sleet was gone. The thief had taken Sleet. And hanging neatly over the door of the loose box was a petticoat, a cambric dress, and a shawl. He recognized the shawl, at least. It belonged to Miss Ross.

Drayton was so bewildered that he let his back slide down the rough wall of the stable until he was sitting, knees under his chin, gazing across at Sleet's box with its improbable bunting of feminine garments. The dogs had not barked, he realized. Someone from the house, someone known to them, had come into the stable and taken his horse at one o'clock in the morning, and left these garments behind. Miss Ross seemed to be the likely culprit, so a bit of investigation was in order.

One: She had left her clothing. So, she was returning, and he had no need to follow her. He could wait here.

Two: She was not wearing her dress; therefore she had changed. Presumably into male attire, which was why he had thought the figure was that of a man.

Three: She had not taken her own mare. This was a puzzle. Impatient, he shook his head and left it.

Four: If it was Miss Ross, she would not be in

her room. He frowned. Which was her room? Did her maid sleep with her? He thought she had the front guest room, which did not have a maid's room attached.

He loped over to the house again and ran lightly up the back stairs. What a mercy Miranda and her mother were gone; he need not fear going into the wrong guest room. All were empty save for Miss Ross's. A nasty thought struck him: What if Miss Ross was, in fact, in her room? And awakened to find him there, checking her bed? He chuckled at the idea. It would certainly not be the first time he had crept into a guest room in the middle of the night, although it would be the first time he had not been invited by the occupant. He moved silently around to the front of the house. The door to the central guest room was ajar. Cautiously, he slipped in. A candle had been left burning by the bed. It was empty.

"Well, well, Miss Ross!" muttered Drayton. "I think you will have some difficulty explaining this as one of Caroline's lessons." Leaving the door exactly as he had found it, he withdrew. No one would go to this sort of trouble for a ten-minute moonlight ride. He had time to get dressed. He might even be able to get his boots on, if he was very patient. Then he dismissed that thought. Miss Ross would hardly be able to criticize him for wearing pumps in the stables if she was herself dressed in breeches.

A vague memory flickered at him as he rounded the corner of the hall and headed toward his own door. It nagged at him as he pulled on stockings and slipped his feet into the shoes. He slung a jacket over his shoulder and was about to leave the room when it solidified at last. Back into the dressing room he went. Opening up the old snuffbox on the top shelf of the armoire, he shook out a crumpled piece of fabric and a gold whistle. Then, stuffing them into his pockets, he strode out of the room. A minute later he was back. He grabbed the candle again, and a book. He might be there for hours.

It was just past three when Rachel rode back into the yard and slipped wearily off the back of the horse. She was tired and dispirited. Silvio had not had any news of her father, and she had not dared to tell him what Drayton had said. James was evidently involved in something even more dangerous than usual, because Silvio had been looking quite worried, and he did not worry easily. They needed more French money, Silvio had told her, and very soon. Before next week. Rachel was trying to remember exactly how much she had brought with her. She hoped it was enough; there was no hope of getting more from her strongbox in the London house without giving up her masquerade, which provided the only means of delivering the money. On top of everything else, she had discovered after Silvio had left that her money pouch had folded over on itself. There were still three gold pieces left, trapped in the bottom of the bag. But surely James would not miss three coins; he must have requested more than he actually needed to pay his people. She sighed. In fact, it would be very like James to request exactly what he needed to pay the boatmen and the informants. Boatman, forty francs; informants, three at five Napoleons each . . . seventeen Napoleons total. Forgetting that he might need to eat, or bribe someone, or hire a horse, or stay overnight at an inn.

She led Sleet into the stable and took off the saddle. It was heavy, and she staggered slightly under its weight, but she got it over to the bench without falling. She picked up a towel and began to rub Sleet down. She had almost forgotten that her clothes were over the door of the mare's box; when she opened it to lead her in she stared at them in surprise. She leaned against the horse for a moment, overcome with fatigue. Days and nights of nursing, combined with dog breakfasts, had taken a toll, and even now that Drayton had been on his own for a few days she had not quite recovered. Sleet let her lean.

Watching from the shadows, Drayton was boiling with anger. The sight of his horse, who was normally rather standoffish, accepting attentions from this usurper irritated him, but there was something else, something he could not explain, which made him feel almost as though he wanted to spring out and strangle the girl. He contemplated waiting to emerge until she had stripped off her boy's clothing. That would put her at a disadvantage. His innate civility intervened. She was at enough of a disadvantage already, and it was in theory possible that there was some reasonable explanation for her behavior. He tried to think of one and failed. She had started to reach down to pull off the shirt, so it was time to move. He stepped out into the lantern light and pointed the pistol straight at Rachel's chest.

"Good evening, Miss Ross. Or should I say, good morning?"

Rachel gave a stifled shriek and dropped the

pouch she had removed from her shirt. It fell on the floor with a betraying chink.

Drayton's eyebrows lifted. "Pick it up," he said curtly. In silence, Rachel obeyed. "Empty it into your hand, and hold your hand out where I can see it." Glittering in the faint light, the three French gold pieces lay on her palm. He noted with astonishment that her hand was not trembling. He looked at her face. It was expressionless. He had thought the bag might have valuables from the house in it—silver, or jewels. This was worse. He began to feel slightly sick.

"I am sure," he said, "that you have a reasonable explanation for all this. I would be delighted to hear it. At your convenience." The pistol was still pointed at her heart. "You can skip the costume change; we will take that as a given. Let us begin with destinations."

"I went to Charing," said Rachel quietly. Drayton thought for a minute, calculating. Forty minutes there, forty minutes back, some time to meet someone or deliver something.

"Fair enough. Why?"

"To deliver some money to a servant of my brother's." Her brother—he remembered now, her brother was abroad with her parents.

"I thought your brother was with your father and mother."

"No—he is estranged from them. He needed money, and I promised to send it to him. Samuels cannot ride, and I could not think of any other way to deliver the money."

"Charing by daylight is also a lovely town," he said conversationally.

Rachel was improvising desperately, trying to stay as close to the truth as possible. "My brother's servant is French. It is very dangerous for him to be seen here."

"And you did not trust my brother-in-law's grooms?"

"The servant would have fled if a stranger tried to approach him."

Drayton nodded. "Very well. Why did you take my horse?"

Rachel's face lost its impassive stillness for the first time. "I apologize for that, Captain Drayton. It was very wrong of me. You had told me that I should ride Sleet while you were ill, to give her some exercise, but I know perfectly well that you meant something quite different from this type of long ride. It is just that when I reached the stable I realized that I only had a sidesaddle ready for Piccola. Your saddle for Sleet was right there, and I was in a hurry."

Drayton blinked. Here she was, caught red-handed, dressed in male clothing, a thief or worse—probably much worse; he had little doubt about what the French coins portended—with a pistol trained on her, and she was apologizing politely for tiring his horse?

Fumbling awkwardly with his left hand, he reached into his jacket and fished out a small cloth bundle. "Take it," he said, gesturing with the pistol. "It's yours. You left it in my room the other day."

Rachel put the coins back in the pouch and set it down. As she reached over to take the crumpled roll of cloth, their hands touched briefly; startled, Drayton jerked away his arm, then swore under his breath as his shoulder flared in pain. Rachel's head was lowered; she had unwrapped the handkerchief and was staring at the whistle. With some annoyance, Drayton realized that she did not seem to be concerned about the pistol. Since he was getting tired of holding it, he released the trigger and tucked it into his breeches.

"Thank you," said Rachel, looking at him. Tears were standing in her eyes. "I looked everywhere for it; it was a gift from my father. I should have realized that I might have lost it when I fainted."

"Is that your handkerchief, then, also?" Drayton asked casually. "I think I accidentally dislodged it while I was loosening your bodice."

She blushed, remembering. "Yes, it is. Thank you for returning it. But it is a trifle compared to the whistle."

Drayton reached out and unfolded the handkerchief. There in the corner were three initials: a small *R*, a large *M*, and a small *R*, picked out in the lace trim edging the cambric. "I had always thought," he said, "that the large initial, the one in the center, was the family name."

So, the return of the whistle was a trap! She had thought herself clever, choosing a name so close to her own. Rachel improvised again. "The handkerchief was made in Spain, Captain Drayton. There it is customary to use the mother's name as the family name for an unmarried daughter."

This was true, as Drayton knew. But he also knew more than Rachel guessed about handkerchiefs. "Try another, my girl," he said grimly. "I didn't spend three years squiring Cyprians around London without learning my linens. That's Brussels lace."

He reached out and seized her shoulders in an iron grip. The hasty club she had made came undone; her hair spilled out and curled down over his fingers. He could feel her collarbones shifting under his hands, but she made no other movement, only looked at him with an odd mixture of pleading and defiance. For a moment they stood like that, their gazes locked.

Then, without thought, without volition, he bent his head and kissed her. Her lips were cool and soft and tasted of salt. She trembled lightly in his arms, but she did not jerk away or turn her face aside. Only gradually did the significance of the salt come to him; he pulled back and frowned down at her mouth. On the gleaming curve of her lower lip a drop of blood was welling up. So, underneath that forced calm she *was* afraid, so afraid that she had bitten through her lip. Mechanically, he reached up with one finger and gently blotted away the tiny red drop.

At that careful touch she seemed to awaken from some sort of trance; with a startled gasp she attempted to step back. But he gripped her harder, struggling to make sense of a bewildering jumble of anger and admiration which was flooding through him. Tears were sliding down her face, although she made no sound.

"Who are you?" he said at last. "Damn it, who *are* you?"

"My real name is Rachel Roth Meyer," she said, her voice very faint.

"Roth? As in Eli Roth?"

"He is my uncle."

"You are a Jewess," he whispered in disbelief.

She flinched at his tone but inclined her head in acknowledgment. "Sir Charles and Lady Barrett know my real name, Captain Drayton. Lady Barrett kindly offered me the opportunity to visit here and teach Caroline so that I could remain in contact with my brother. My father is away, and my brother has quarreled with my uncle. I apologize for having deceived you. I will leave first thing in the morning."

"It *is* first thing in the morning," he said savagely.

"Then I will go and begin packing my things now," she said.

Three hours later, all she had managed to do was to change back into her own clothing. She was sitting frozen in misery in the armchair next to the window when she heard the sound of wheels on the drive. In slow motion she rose and drew the curtains back. It was fully light now, and she could see a chaise disappearing towards the north end of the drive, out toward the village. She dragged herself back to the armchair and sat down again. Forty minutes later there was a timid knock at the door. A footman entered, hesitating, with a note. She managed to take it, and thank him, but sat with it still folded for a long time before she could look at it. It read:

Madam:

I must beg your forgiveness for my conduct earlier today. As Sir Charles and my sister are aware of your identity, my only proper concern is with my ward, and for her sake I beg you to consider remaining at Leigh End for the moment. Certain items of business call me to London, which may ease any awkwardness you might feel about continuing as her instructor.

Please accept the apologies of one who remains

Your devoted servant,

R. C. D.

Chapter Eleven

"What is he doing?" said the newcomer, pausing at the door and addressing Courthope. Drayton sat with a frown at the card table, a drink at his right hand and eight cards in his left. Three cards lay faceup on the table. The other players looked at him expectantly.

"You mean besides getting drunk?" said Courthope bitterly. "Playing whist."

"Whist? Drayton? Thought he said whist was for dowagers in their drawing rooms."

"Not at these stakes," said Courthope with an unhappy grimace. He was leaning against the door frame, watching the play and feeling more and more that Drayton had lied to him when he assured him he was delighted at Miranda's acceptance of his proposal.

"I take it an interruption would not come amiss?"

"Well, I would not take it amiss. He might. He's

ahead to the tune of several hundred pounds. Why?"

"Just came in, and there was someone at the door asking for him. Name of Robson."

Courthope turned in astonishment and looked out towards the front of the house, then strode over to the card table and addressed Drayton in an urgent whisper. Astonished, and clearly uneasy, Drayton excused himself to the rest of the foursome and strode out to the entryway as quickly as he could through the throng in the main room. A small, balding figure was arguing with a manservant in the front hall.

"Robson!" he said, perturbed. "What the devil are you doing here? You were supposed to stay in San Luis. I'll be going back in ten days or so. Is there something wrong? Your father ill again?"

His batman glared at him belligerently. "Master Richard, do you know what I've been through trying to find you since I landed in Southampton? First I stopped at Miss Sara's, thinking you might be there, and they told me you was come up to town. Then I go to Berkeley Square, and they haven't seen hide nor hair of you. So I go to Sussex, and they don't know anything, and finally I come back here and just start a-walking around to any place I can think of. And given your habits the last time you was residing in London, that is a lot of places, some of 'em mighty ugly."

This scolding, since it was customary, was ignored. "You didn't answer my question," Drayton pointed out.

"I am here," said Robson, with a quelling look, "be-cause Colonel Sawyer told me to come back to England. You've been reassigned to Colonel White. You should of got the orders three days ago."

They had probably been sent down to Leigh End, Drayton realized. And Whitehall didn't know how to track him as well as Robson did. Colonel White—surely there were not two of them? It must be Southey's colonel, the one he had met in Tredwell's office in the tavern outside of Frenada. His heart sank. Evidently his idiotic fistfight with the French soldiers had not been enough to discourage Tredwell; the man must be desperate.

"Let me just excuse myself to the table," he told Robson. "They'll be delighted to see me leave; the cards have run my way all night." Lucky at cards, unlucky in love, he thought as he made his way back into the side room. Courthope probably thinks I'm sulking about Miranda. His conscience pricked at him, half drunk and wretched though he might be, and he stopped on his way out to murmur some disjointed reassurance to Courthope.

"Sir, you don't need to leave on account of I finally came up with you," said Robson earnestly as Drayton rejoined him. "You ain't going to call on Colonel White at this hour."

"No," said Drayton, "but I'll need to start sobering up right now if I'm going to see him tomorrow morning. I've only met him once, but he didn't seem the type I would want to confront with the handicap of a pounding head."

In the event, it was not morning by the time Drayton was ushered into Colonel White's office. Robson had not been able to give him any information beyond the name, and no trace of the letter with his new orders could be found at his father's house in Berkeley Square, or at Fielding's, where he was staying. He went perforce to the porter's desk in the Horse Guards, where he was directed to a dusty set of rooms in a disused corridor on the third floor. There he sat for an hour waiting for someone—anyone—to appear, and when a subaltern finally arrived at half-past ten, he scrutinized Drayton carefully, asked him to wait, and then disappeared again before Drayton could tell him that he had already been doing plenty of waiting. After a quarter of an hour he reappeared, out of breath, and told Drayton that he was to go out to Greenwich.

"Greenwich?" said Drayton, thoroughly confused. "That's the navy."

"Yes, sir, but Colonel White has another office over there, in the observatory. I've checked, and you're to go across and ask at the Royal Naval College for Ensign Lawrence. He'll direct you to Colonel White's office."

Muttering to himself, Drayton made his way back out to the Mall and looked for a hackney. Naturally, there were none in sight. In the end, he walked down to the Tower pier and caught a boat.

Ensign Lawrence, a cheerful young man with a very round face, led him through what seemed like an endless maze of corridors in the instrument collection attached to the observatory and knocked at last on a door set into a corner of the hall at an odd angle. Drayton was immensely relieved to see a lieutenant open the door; at least he was back in the right branch of the services now. Over the lieutenant's shoulder he could see a peculiarly shaped room, with two square interior walls and then three angled ones, each with a window. One square wall was covered with maps; the second had a door leading into a small inner office.

A familiar tall, mustached figure emerged from

that room as he watched, carrying a portfolio so full of folders that Drayton was surprised it did not burst. The scowl was familiar as well. White caught sight of him and set the portfolio down with some difficulty on his desk, which was already covered with papers, stacked, in many cases, several inches high.

"Drayton!" he said without preamble. "Where the deuce have you been, sirrah? We've had messages sent to every blasted address we could think of."

"I beg your pardon, sir," said Drayton. "I left Kent in rather a hurry a few days ago and neglected to give my sister's butler my direction in London."

"Don't have to give your sister's butler anything, as far as I'm concerned," said the colonel testily. "But an officer on leave must report any change of address to Whitehall, or to the county garrison; you know that, Drayton. Well, never mind. Sit down." He pointed to a chair. It was covered with paper, which the lieutenant smoothly removed and placed on the floor nearby. Other piles of paper on the floor suggested that this was not an uncommon practice. "Where's Southey?" he said, turning to the lieutenant.

"I believe he is down at Hythe, sir," said the lieutenant.

"That's right, so he is. That will be all for the moment, lieutenant." The junior officer withdrew discreetly into the inner office and closed the door.

"Heard you were injured again," said White. "And a good thing, as it turns out, or you would have been on your way back to the Fourteenth by now, I suppose. Southey tells me you were attacked and then had to have surgery on your shoulder."

"Yes, sir, but it is healing well now," said Drayton.

"I had thought I would report in next week and let Whitehall know I was fit to ship out."

"We would prefer that you remain in England, for the present," said White. "Still on leave, in theory. How much do you know about our courier service?"

"Almost nothing," said Drayton frankly.

"You saw something of the type of work the reconnaissance officers do in Spain," said White. "Tredwell tells me that was a damned fine job you did with those bridges, by the way." Drayton was astounded to hear this, but the colonel swept on. "Needless to say, there is a lot more involved than the sort of thing you did. We have messengers, informants, and reconnaissance people in both Spain and France. And we have a group of couriers who check periodically at appointed meeting places near the coast, both here and in France, so that the French informants can send reports over here on a regular basis. Recently, there have been a number of disturbing incidents involving these couriers. Messages have been intercepted, and in one case, French soldiers raided a landing site in Brittany only hours after our informants had passed on their papers to our courier. Apparently information is being passed to the enemy via secret meetings at inns along the Dover road." At these words Drayton felt a cold hollow open in the pit of his stomach.

"Southey has been trying to look into it, but he is needed here in London. It occurred to me that you were most excellently placed to investigate without any suspicion falling on you. Southey may well be known to the French counterintelligence, but you have only the one mission under our aegis, and no one has questioned the story that you were invalided in early March."

"There you are wrong, sir," said Drayton, his mouth tightening at the memory. "My august parent took exception to the backdating of my medical leave and concluded not only that I had funked in the middle of a duel, but also that I had persuaded Colonel Sawyer to falsify the records to correspond with the last-known engagement of my unit."

"And you did not enlighten him," said the colonel, looking keenly at Drayton.

"I did not."

"Naturally," said the colonel dryly. "Your father, who is an acquaintance of mine, is a very intelligent man. I am not surprised he put two and two together. It is odd that he came up with five as the answer, but that is no matter. He is privy to much more information about your wound and your whereabouts than the French, who should have no reason to be interested in you."

Drayton wondered if he should tell White about the Spanish kidnappers but decided that Southey must have already done so. It was all pointless in any case; he had a very good idea of who was interfering with the couriers on the Kentish coast. Was it possible for him to refuse this assignment? No, he had to see it through. It would be ghastly for Sara, and Sir Charles. And he had heard that Roth, the uncle, was a close friend of Wellington, and had practically financed the Peninsular campaign out of his own pocket at first. What a stinking mess.

"Southey will work on the London end of the problem," said White. "Someone at Whitehall is obviously smuggling messages out of the city to a confederate who then passes them on to the French. If it is feasible we should like to know who the confederate is and how the information is conveyed to French contacts." A guest in my sister's house, thought Drayton drearily. Someplace in Charing. Oh, God. "Southey will fill you in on the incidents so far; he will be back in London tomorrow and will come down to Kent the following day. Can you return to your sister's house by then?"

"Yes, sir," said Drayton. "I have finished my business here in London." After all, his business in London had been to run away from what he had seen at Leigh End. And that was no longer possible.

There was to be a guest for dinner, Maria told Rachel, and since he was returning to London afterwards, dinner had been moved forward. It was time to change her gown, and leave off looking through picture books pretending she was finding scenes for Miss Caroline to copy. At least she was remembering to look at the book today, thought Maria. Yesterday she just stared out the window all afternoon.

"Do you know who it is?" said Rachel, reminding herself that Drayton would not be considered a guest, and would almost certainly not leave afterwards.

"A friend of Sir Charles, Miss Rachel, that is all that Minton told Mrs. Tibbet."

Rachel hoped that it was not the mysterious Mr. Castell. It would be awkward to pretend to be Miss Ross all evening in front of someone who had identified her to Sir Charles. She picked out a very quiet pale green gown and let Maria put up her hair in the Spanish style, with combs. Then she made her way downstairs and entered the drawing room. Lady Barrett and Miss Lutford were not yet down, but Sir Charles was there, talking with great animation to a short, stout man with keen eyes in a harsh-featured face. Rachel gasped and would have withdrawn, but at that moment Miss Lutford entered behind her.

"Miss Lutford, Miss Ross," said Sir Charles urbanely. "Allow me to make you known to Mr. Roth." Lady Barrett hastened in, apologizing for her tardiness, and was presented. Rachel pulled herself together and was introduced to her uncle.

"Miss Ross and I have met, at her father's house in London," he said with a twinkle in his eye.

Rachel thought bitterly, He is just as good at this as James and my father. I am sure Miss Lutford can see that I am utterly confounded, and how will I explain it to her? She managed some polite reply and took refuge over by the fireplace. This proved to be an error, as her uncle was able to join her, out of earshot of the others, and ask her quietly if she had any news of her brother. She shook her head.

"We will speak after dinner," he said. She wondered how he would contrive to draw her apart in a manner which did not arouse suspicion, but he resorted in fact to the simplest solution: the truth. When the gentlemen joined the ladies after a hasty interlude with their port, he announced that he had some news of her family for Miss Ross, and requested permission to enjoy a cigar on the terrace in her company. Even Miss Lutford could not see anything odd about this, and Rachel dutifully followed her uncle out through the French doors. He wandered over to the balustrade and pulled on his cigar with obvious relish.

"So, you have not seen James?" he asked.

"No, only Silvio," she said. There was no point concealing anything from him at this point. "I think James must be making more unauthorized runs to the French coast; I have had to give him French money, and when he is traveling on legitimate army business they arrange for the funding themselves."

"I would not be surprised," he said, blowing out a curl of smoke. It drifted off into the garden.

"Uncle . . . you must think me a complete fool."

"Not at all, my dear," he said gently. "Merely a very devoted sister and daughter."

"I suppose that all this time, I had only to ask, and you would have postponed Anthony's visit? I could have stayed in London and tried to keep James out of trouble, and advanced him funds?" Rachel had control of her own inheritance from her mother, but her brother's portion was still in a trust.

He nodded. "James has moved back into his old rooms in our house, in fact—at least when he is in town. But this is not a bad scheme of yours. It would be very dangerous for James to be coming into London all the time; it is much easier for him to be followed in the city, which is swarming with Bonaparte's agents. And he does not see things my way at all. I am a planner, and he is a doer. He thinks I move far too slowly, and I find him somewhat rash. You could not have found a better situation; I trust Sir Charles completely. I would advise you to consult him should you find yourself in any difficulty at all. Even one involving James or your father."

"Have you—have you any news of him? Of my father?" said Rachel, hoping against hope.

"No," said Roth heavily. He put his arm around

her—he had to reach up slightly to do so—and said in a warm voice which Rachel had seldom heard from him, "My little Rachel, you must be brave. It is harder to be a planner than to be a doer, but even harder to be the one who waits. Try to be patient."

"How nice to see you again, Captain," said Minton, ushering him into the hall. "Lady Barrett is at Chanterfield for the morning, and Sir Charles has ridden over to take luncheon with her and Mrs. Southey. Would you like me to announce you to Miss Lutford? I believe she is in the stillroom."

"That's quite all right," said Drayton hastily. "I think I shall seek out my wards." A squeal of excitement could be heard at that moment from the side of the house. "William?" he asked Minton. The butler nodded. "I apprehend, sir, that he is having his first riding lesson." Drayton was not surprised. His sister believed that children should learn to ride as soon as they could talk. He left his hat and coat with Minton and strode around the front of the house towards the stables.

An odd procession met his eyes as he rounded the corner and came up to the yard. In front was Samuels, leading an ancient pony towards the drive. Next to the pony was Jem, holding a very small boy in the saddle. Behind the pony were Amy and Mrs. Mott, wringing their hands in alarm and uttering small cries of concern and caution. William was bouncing with all his might up and down on the saddle, disappointed at the slow pace set by Samuels. Having endured untold horrors at the hands of Masters Ned and Jamie Barrett, the pony did not find this odd, but the two women were imploring Jem to hold Master William more snugly, and wasn't this long enough for the first ride?

"Unca! Unca!" screamed William as he caught sight of Drayton. "I ride!"

"So you do," said Drayton, coming over and scooping his nephew out of the saddle for a hug. At this, however, there was a wail of protest, and Drayton restored William with a laughing apology. "Should have known any child of Harry's would prefer a horse to an uncle," he said ruefully to Mrs. Mott. "Is Caroline about?"

Mrs. Mott sniffed. Caroline and Miss Ross, she allowed, were at their French lesson upstairs. "French," muttered Drayton. "How appropriate." He lingered for a few minutes watching William bump back and forth between the yard and the drive, attended by his acolytes. Finally, with a heavy heart, he went into the house. No use putting it off, he told himself sternly. You will have to see her sooner or later. He climbed slowly up the narrow back stair and paused in front of the nursery door.

It was open this time, and he could see Caroline inside, pirouetting in an ancient ballgown. She caught sight of him halfway through a revolution and stopped, causing her skirts to fly round to one side and tangle her as she ran towards him.

"Uncle Richard! You're back! Look, Maria fixed the dress so that it isn't too long! I almost fit in it! And Miss Ross made me a crown! I'm going to be a princess today!"

"What's French for princess?" he said, smiling and catching her arms to twirl her around.

"That's easy! *Princesse!*"

"Where is Miss Ross?" he asked casually.

"She's changing into her dress. We found one

that wasn't too small, or only a little bit, and Maria fixed it, just like she did mine. She's going to be my *dame d'honneur.*"

"Your lady-in-waiting? May I be something as well?"

"You can be my knight, but first you must pay a forfeit." Caroline had remembered that she had a bone to pick with her uncle. "You left without saying good-bye, or where you were going, or anything," she said accusingly.

"You're right," he said, wondering if anyone else had been offended by his abrupt departure. "I apologize. What is my forfeit?"

"Mmmmmmm." Caroline was thinking hard. "Fight a duel?"

"Perhaps not at the moment, sweet. I was wounded, remember? And who would be my opponent?" Caroline sighed. Twice, when she was very young, she had been allowed to watch her uncle practice fencing with his friend Mr. Southey, and she had thought it the most beautiful thing she had ever seen.

"Could you write a poem, then? That's what the knight does in my book, when he loses the favor of his lady."

"A poem it shall be," said Drayton, smiling. He went into the small, inner room that served as the schoolroom and rummaged around for foolscap and ink. "Caroline Drayton!" he called out from behind the door. "Don't you ever sharpen your pens? Never mind, that will be part of my forfeit." He was sitting on the edge of the scarred wooden lesson table and trimming the pen with his pocketknife when he saw Rachel, halfway into the nursery, framed in the schoolroom door.

He had meant to be very cool and firm, to tell her that he must speak with her privately at her earliest convenience. Instead he found that he could not speak at all, that he had risen and was staring at her like someone who sees a ghost. She might almost have been a ghost, he thought, the ghost of some great Jacobean lady, in the blue satin gown with its lace-edged sleeves, her hair tied up on top of her head, her feet glittering in silver-heeled pumps. She too had stopped dead as soon as she had seen him, and a flush rose slowly up her neck.

"Good afternoon, Captain Drayton," she said.

"Mademoiselle Ross," he said slowly. It seemed appropriate to bow, so he did. "Please excuse me, I am writing a poem for Caroline."

"It's his forfeit, because he left without saying good-bye, and he can't fight duels," Caroline explained to Rachel. The explanation left something to be desired, but Rachel accepted it without comment. She retreated to the far corner of the nursery, opened the hamper, doing her best to keep her eyes lowered, and began to get out the other things they would use for the lesson—the brittle old fans, the broken parasol, the pasteboard crown. Drayton emerged from the schoolroom.

"*Vôtre poème, princesse,*" he said, bowing to Caroline and presenting her with the sheet of foolscap. Caroline accepted it gravely and read through it, her lips moving slowly, then handed it to Rachel.

"Can you help me read it, Miss Ross? I mean, Mademoiselle Ross? Some of the words are too hard for me."

"*Certainement,*" said Rachel, though her voice trembled slightly.

> *" 'Beauté dont la douceur pourrait vaincre les rois,*
> *Renvoyez-moi mon coeur qui languit en servage,*
> *Ou, si le mien vous plaît, baillez le vôtre en gage:*
> *Sans le vôtre ou le mien, vivre je ne pourrois.' "*

Her accent was flawless. The light from the window behind her framed the edges of her gown with a blue glow.

> *" 'Beauty, whose grace might vanquish royalty,*
> *send back my heart which lies enslaved to thee,*
> *or, if my heart doth please, thine own do give:*
> *without thine or my own, I may not live,' "*

quoted Drayton softly, translating from memory. "There is more, but that is all I could remember. It may not be a proper forfeit, Princess, since I did not write it. It was written by a French poet named Ronsard."

Caroline was puzzling through the lines, sounding out the words. "It's very nice," she said graciously. *"Très gentil, mon . . .* What is the word for 'knight'?" she appealed to Rachel.

"Chevalier," said Rachel absently. "Caroline, why do you not mark the words you do not understand, and then you and I can read it again together. It is a lovely poem."

Drayton was moving towards the door.

"Aren't you going to stay?" demanded Caroline, disappointed.

"No, *ma chérie,"* he said, managing somehow to produce a smile. "I have to go check on Sleet, and see where they have put Robson, and find some friends who are staying in Charing." Some friends of Miss Ross, he thought wearily.

He made it through the door, shut it behind him, and then slumped against the wall at the head of the stairs. He felt faint, and his heart was pounding against his ribs. Behind his closed eyes, he could still see Rachel's face, her dark lashes sweeping her cheeks as she had looked down at the poem, in the blue light of her dress. Damn it, he thought. I'm falling in love with her.

Chapter Twelve

As Sir Charles sipped perfunctorily at his port and prepared to rise to join the ladies after dinner that night, Drayton pulled over his chair and laid a hand on his arm. His brother-in-law looked up, surprised. Drayton was not normally one to linger in the dining room at Leigh End; he was far too fond of his sister.

"Something amiss, Richard?" he said, scrutinizing Drayton's face.

"I might well ask you the same," said Drayton. "What do you know about Miss Ross—or Miss Meyer, as she is more properly known?"

Sir Charles looked relieved. "You don't mind, do you, Richard? I am delighted that she has seen fit to tell you. I felt deuced awkward concealing it from you, but I thought myself bound by Sara's word."

"I have been seconded to Colonel White and asked to remain here as though still on medical leave," said Drayton abruptly. Sir Charles said nothing. He did not think this was a change of subject. "Evidently our courier service is having a problem with—shall we call them infiltrators? or unauthorized exporters? And the interference seems to be centered on the Maidstone-Dover route."

Sir Charles raised one eyebrow, his eyes fixed on Drayton. "You are looking into the situation?" he said. "And have become concerned about Miss Ross's presence here?"

"I think it could be very ugly indeed," said Drayton curtly.

"You know that her uncle was here last week? While you were in town?"

"No, I did not know that," said Drayton, leaning forward, astonished. "Had he known she was here?"

"Yes, although Miss Ross was not aware until he came to dine that he had discovered her scheme. But he felt that indeed she was best here, rather than in London."

"Where we can keep an eye on her, and strangers are easily spotted," suggested Drayton, thinking God! What a cold fish Roth must be!

"Exactly," said Sir Charles. "I must confess I am very glad to hear that you will be looking after things, Richard," he added. "In spite of your numerous attempts to convince all of us, especially your father, that you have no sense whatsoever, I have great confidence in your abilities." With which oblique compliment he pushed back his chair and headed for the company of his wife, a commodity he was finding in very short supply at the moment.

Drayton sat for a moment longer, a bit stunned by his brother-in-law's reaction. Then he shrugged.

If Barrett felt that the situation was of such importance that personal embarrassment must take second place to tactical advantage, so be it. Miss Meyer was none of theirs, and presumably he and Sara could claim to have been deceived by her false identity as Miss Ross. It was more of a surprise that the uncle was not making an attempt to protect his family name—and the person of his niece. Evidently his commitment to Wellington overrode family feeling. Drayton could not but respect him for it, while wondering if he would have the strength of character to make the same choice. He was to discover the answer to that question all too soon.

The next afternoon, Drayton took the chaise and drove to Charing. He refused Hickman's offer to send Jem, telling the groom that he was well enough now to be trusted to drive on his own for brief excursions. A suggestive wink at the end of this reply led Hickman's thoughts in the direction Drayton hoped; he snickered and wished the captain a lovely drive. Sometimes, thought Drayton, it was useful to have a reputation as a ladies' man. In reality, he wanted to be sure that no one would report on his itinerary to Samuels or Rachel. It would be hard to explain why he was going to visit every posting house in Charing.

At the first inn, the largest, he discovered that the ostlers worked in shifts, and the night ostlers had not yet arrived. The place was so large and bustling that he doubted whether any of the servants would notice if Napoleon himself walked in, so that it was probably no great loss that he had missed interrogating the evening staff. He moved on to the second inn, the Abbot's Key, an ancient establishment in the heart of town. It had a number of dim, tiny rooms and seemed a likely meeting place for persons not wishing their business to be overheard. But when he asked, in various roundabout ways, whether a fashionable young man was wont to stop in late at night every ten days or so to meet with some foreign man or men, he drew a blank. The innkeeper told him bluntly that he had not seen anyone from out of town—man or maid, foreign or English—in weeks. " 'Tis mostly local folk here, sir," he said earnestly. "Seeing as we be down the alley by the church, not easy to see from the high road."

He thought at first that he had found something at the third inn, which lay at the southern edge of town. Here the ostler immediately nodded when Drayton put his query, and asked if he meant the young gentleman who came midnights on Tuesdays. This sounded very promising, although Drayton did not think it had been a Tuesday when he had caught Rachel on Sleet. It turned out, however, that the object of the young gentleman's visits was a barmaid, and the midnight visitor had a Scots accent. Drayton gave him a few coins and thanked him, feeling almost relieved that it had been a false lead.

It was growing late, and Drayton turned the chaise for home, a bit tired from the strain of driving, to which he was unaccustomed now, and fuddled from the pints he had purchased in each of the three hostelries. Perhaps it was weariness which made him decide to stop again at the first house, the Golden Pheasant, and to his surprise the ostler who had assisted him on his first stop came running out to the chaise, calling to him that the head ostler had arrived early to take his supper with his aunt, the cook, and was he still wishful to speak with him?

Tom, the cook's nephew, came out a few moments later and stood shyly by the chaise. "I heard you was asking after the young gennulman as comes in the middle of the night sometimes," he said, blushing with the effort of speaking. "A slim chap, with a great hat what he hides his face under? And goes off in the corner of the yard with some odd men what don't speak to anyone else?" Then he recollected his duty to protect the patrons of the house, and said with some dignity, "What would you be wanting with him, sir, if you don't mind my asking? He's a nice polite gent, and we want no trouble here."

Drayton had anticipated this, and was ready with a story about a wager and unexpected winnings which the young man needed to go claim in London. "Would you have any idea when he might come next?" he asked. "I am staying nearby, as it happens, and could ride over and give him the letter he needs. I would prefer not to leave it for him, as it is quite confidential."

"Monday, sir; if he comes, 'tis always Monday. Not every week, mind, but he was not here this past Monday, and has not missed two in a row for these three months now. I'll wager you can find him here in three days' time, nigh on one in the morning." Drayton gave him a substantial tip and submitted to some questions about Barrett's horses, a beautiful pair of bays. He was bitterly regretting this final stop. It was increasingly clear to him that he was not a good intelligence officer; he had been hoping against hope that he would turn up nothing and could report back to White that the treasonable activity must be located further down towards the coast.

The three days until Monday he spent in a dull, feverish haze, wandering about the grounds, skipping meals, avoiding everyone in the house. Even in his miserable fog he could tell that Caroline was hurt by his neglect, but he could not think of a way to see her without risking an encounter with Rachel. The hours went by, too quickly, too slowly, and it was Monday night. Shortly after eleven, he excused himself from a conversation with Sir Charles and went to his room. There, after sending Robson off on a trumped-up errand, he changed into pantaloons and a dark jacket, and slipped out to the stable.

He had thought long and hard about the best way to go about it. Riding out to the inn in advance he rejected at once. If he left early to be in place before she arrived, Rachel would notice that a horse was gone when she came to take her own mount. He could wait again in the stable but would then have no evidence of what she had done in Charing. Pursuing her on his own horse after she left seemed best, although very risky. He decided to hide up in the hayloft, so that he could see what she put in her saddlebags when she left, and then follow. He would not need to ride close behind her, where there was a chance she might hear him, because he knew where he was going.

The hay was stale and dank after a whole winter up in the leaky loft. It prickled even through his jacket, and he heard the skitter of mice under the clumps as he moved them to make a more comfortable backrest. Hours passed; he grew impatient, and then drowsy, but forced himself over and over back to wakefulness. He had convinced himself that his sense of time was distorted when he noticed that the light was changing. Stiffly he staggered to the loft window. It was dawn. She had not ridden out.

What could this mean? he thought, as he slowly walked back to his room. Could she have been aware that he was ready to pursue her? It was true that he was not good at concealing what he felt; if Caroline had noticed his odd behavior, then obviously she must have, as well. Yet how would she know to connect his avoidance of her with danger to her insidious mission? They had certainly quarreled enough since he had arrived to provide ample excuse for his ill humor. White had told him that no one except Southey would know of his assignment; surely her source in Whitehall could not have warned her? He did not know if he could stand another week at Leigh End, waiting for the next Monday night.

Exhausted and longing for his bed, he turned the handle of the door to his room and went in. Sitting by the bed, on a trunk, was Robson, with a ferocious scowl on his face. Drayton suddenly realized what he must look like, haggard from lack of sleep, with bits of hay all over his clothing and hair.

"Might I ask where you been and gone?" said Robson in an icy voice. "Not that it needs much guessing, as I look at you. Hickman told me you was gone to Charing the other day, but your lady friends used to be a touch more class than this one."

"Stow it," said Drayton wearily. "Help me out

of this jacket. My arm's gone numb. I'm going to bed."

It was only by chance that he saw Rachel slip out of the house that night. He had slept so late after his ordeal in the loft that he was still very wakeful when he retired from the library at midnight. Not expecting to hear or see anything, he at first ignored the brief flash of light outside his window. When it was repeated, however, he sprang out of bed and threw open the casement. Leaning out, he could just see a figure carrying a lantern, headed for the far end of the terrace.

Now what? he thought. If it was not Monday, the meeting place might well be different. He was not dressed; by the time he could follow she might have met her accomplices and departed. The thought of riding out to Charing and storming into an empty inn was not attractive. And he was tired, and still feeling the effects of his night-long watch in the barn. Comfort was worth something, he decided.

Rachel dragged herself up the stairs and bit her lip to keep herself from weeping. James had been there tonight, instead of Silvio, and they had had a terrible quarrel. She had accused him of taking unauthorized trips to France, and he had not only admitted it but had let slip that he was planning to go inland this time, all the way to Lille.

"But there is a huge garrison there!" she had protested. "With a counterespionage office! That is Arnaut's headquarters!"

"That is why I need to go there," James had said stubbornly. "I have a reliable guide waiting for me at our rendezvous point on the coast. There is no more danger at Lille than on the beach. They are both enemy territory."

She had called him an idiot, an arrogant fool, a disobedient officer, and even an unfeeling brother who did not care if his sister was left a lonely orphan.

"What do you mean, orphan?" he had blazed at her. "Papa is not dead!"

"How do you know?" she countered. "I have heard rumors that he is. Have you had word of him? Silvio says you have not. And our uncle has heard nothing either."

"He is not dead!" he repeated, so fiercely that he frightened her. But he would not tell her more, nor give up his plan. When she threatened to withhold the money she had brought he sneered at her and told her he would take it by force if necessary. That was when she had flung it at him and left the back porch of the inn in tears.

"Thank God Samuels will be well enough to ride soon," he had hissed after her, "and I may be spared these female melodramas." The phrase echoed through her head all the way back to Leigh End.

Returning at last, at around half-past two, to her room, she noticed with surprise that it was dark; she had left a candle burning, a stout new one. Candles could go out, though, she supposed. She groped to the hearth and reached for the tinderbox. Feeling her way to the side of the bed, she found the candle and struck a light. At that moment she felt a hand clamp down over her mouth and sensed a pistol in her back. A familiar voice spoke quietly in her ear.

"Do I have your word you will not scream?"

She nodded, but as soon as his hand was removed, she turned to face Drayton, her eyes flashing. "You would not dare to fire that thing in here!" And then, as her situation came home to her, she added angrily, "What are you doing in my bedchamber?"

"I grew tired of the stable," said Drayton coolly. "Your room seemed a more civilized place to wait."

"You must leave at once!" stormed Rachel. "This is outrageous!"

"Is it?" Drayton said sternly. "Charing again, I take it? The Golden Pheasant? Your 'brother'?" This last was said with heavy sarcasm.

"Yes," said Rachel, tears filling her eyes as she remembered James's harsh words. Then, rallying, "Did you suppose, sir, that I went out to meet a lover?"

For some reason this had not occurred to Drayton as a possibility. He paled. It was by far the most plausible—and least serious—explanation, but illogically he found that the thought of Rachel meeting some man at an inn in Charing was so dreadful that he preferred to find her a spy. "Is that it, then?" he asked, swallowing. "You came to my sister's house to be near some . . . man?"

"What do you think?" snapped Rachel. "It would not surprise you, would it? Given my well-known tendency to behave improperly?"

Drayton stared at her for a moment, stupefied, and then said grimly, "Let's see, shall we?" Without warning, seizing her arms in an implacable grip, he dragged her closer and kissed her. It was a fierce, angry kiss, at least at first, as though he were hunting for traces of the imagined lover on her mouth. But he could not help recalling that other kiss, and the tiny drop of blood. Slowly, imperceptibly, he softened the embrace until he held her quite gently. He drew back; she was looking up at him with the strangest expression. My God, what must she think of him? A wave of self-loathing so violent that it made him physically ill washed over him; his arms dropped to his sides and he turned his face away.

"You do not bring out the best in me, Miss Meyer," he managed to say. There was a lump in his throat; he could barely breathe. "I apologize; that was unforgivable. We will take it that you were not involved in a romantic tryst. Shall we move on to other explanations?"

"Apparently you believe that you are entitled to more than explanations," she said, her voice shaking. "Must I be assaulted by you every time I leave my room at night? Am I a prisoner? By what authority do you interrogate me? What business is it of yours?"

"What business is it of mine? If a guest in my sister's house disgraces herself, betrays my brother-in-law, deceives her own uncle? The governess of my ward?"

Rachel lifted her chin. The candlelight glittered on her skin, on the tears in her eyes, on the proud set of her mouth. "I have done nothing shameful, Captain Drayton. And I am no longer deceiving any of the people you mention, save Caroline. It is true that even I, so sadly lacking in knowledge of deportment"—Drayton flinched at her savage tone—"even *I* realize that these expeditions are not appropriate for a young woman, but it is an emergency. As soon as Samuels can ride again I will be glad to give up my midnight rides. Nevertheless I do not see what right you have to interfere with my meetings with my brother, unconventional and clandestine though they may be."

Because I am an officer of the king, Drayton wanted to say. Because I arrest you in his name for espionage in the service of the enemies of England. But that was not what he actually said. Instead, to his astonishment, he heard himself say in a strange voice which seemed to come from some other person, "Miss Ross—Miss Meyer—Rachel—is it possible that you would give me that right? That you would allow me to protect you, with my name? I am an English officer; were you to marry me, and become an English citizen, and forswear your French allegiance, I think—I hope—I could shield you from arrest and imprisonment."

Rachel stood as though turned to stone. "You think I am working for the French?" she whispered at last. "You think I am working for the French, and you ask me to *marry you?* To protect myself?" She stood aghast, her eyes wide, so horrified that she could barely breathe. "What kind of Englishman are you?"

"A very poor one, I think," said Drayton. His eyes were clouded. "You must despise me, in a way. At least your loyalties are whole."

"May I ask, Captain Drayton, what nationality you suppose me to be? Or do you think Jews have no country?"

Drayton was bewildered. "I don't know," he stammered. "I suppose I had thought you German, like your uncle. Or possibly French."

"Captain Drayton," said Rachel coldly, "my uncle is an English citizen. He and my father were naturalized many years ago. My uncle's children are English citizens. My headstrong, idiot, pepperpot brother is an English citizen. I am an English citizen. When you offer to protect me from the consequences of my alleged dealings with the French, you are shielding a traitor. I ought to arrest *you*. Now please leave my room. At once. Or I will scream, in spite of having given you my word. I thought I was speaking to an officer and a gentleman at the time I pledged myself."

"It appears you were wrong," said Drayton bitterly. He moved to the door, still facing her, and said in an odd, neutral voice, "I take it you reject my offer."

Rachel nodded; she could not speak. Dazed, she put one finger to her lips and traced them. They were still burning, and her shoulders were throbbing where Drayton had clutched her. I must leave, she thought, Caroline will never understand, she will be so unhappy, but I must leave. Today. She looked up and saw Drayton standing there, the fine features drawn, the dark eyes wistful. Then he turned and left, and she sank onto the bed, fully dressed, crawled under the coverlet, and lay shivering in the candlelight. She did not even remove her boots.

It was past noon when Drayton finally came downstairs. He had sat at his writing table with an empty sheet in front of him while he heard the bustle up and down the hall, and the thump as trunks were brought down from the attic, and Caroline's voice wailing, and the wheels of the carriage rolling on the gravel. He waited for another hour before he descended. But Sara was waiting for him at the foot of the stairs. She had been listening from the library and sprang up as soon as the first tread creaked at the landing.

"What have you done?" she said hotly. "Why has Miss Ross left?"

"Do you mean Miss Meyer?" he said, his face bleak. "It's for the best, Sara, believe me."

"Richard," she said, pleading, "please tell me what is going on. I have defended you—how many times!—to our father, to Aunt Estelle, to those horrid dames in London. I know you are not really a rake, but I am not blind, either. I have seen the way you have been behaving around Miss Ross. You are in love with her, are you not?"

"Yes," he said heavily after a moment.

"Richard, please, please tell me that you did not—that you did not insult a guest in my house?"

Drayton lost his temper. He forgot that he had, in fact, kissed Rachel, had gagged her and held her at gunpoint in her bedroom, had grabbed her in the stable, had mocked her for wearing boy's clothing. First Rachel had accused him of condoning treason, and now his sister, the one person he thought completely loyal, was accusing him of assaulting a woman who might or might not be considered gently bred, but who was certainly a guest, and his ward's friend and companion.

"Insult her, hell!" he shouted. "I asked her to marry me!"

"What?" said Sara faintly.

"Don't worry," said Drayton with an odd grimace. "She refused. Please excuse me, Sara. I need to go to Charing." And he strode off towards the kitchen without looking back, leaving Sara standing openmouthed at the foot of the stairs.

He rode to Charing with the firm resolve to clear things up for once and for all. Rachel's vehement denials had shaken him, he was obliged to confess. Yet he found her protests a relief, in a way: If he did find evidence that she had been meeting anyone suspicious at the inn, he would feel no compunction about exposing such a brazen liar to the authorities. Only when he reined in at the Golden Pheasant did he remember that Tom would not be there yet. The same pleasant youth who had helped him previously brightened when he saw him (perhaps remembering the coins he had received) and said eagerly, "Oh, sir, Tom did be telling me that if you came by I was to direct you to his mother's place. He has word of that young man you was asking after. Tom'll still be there; it's straight down the second lane up the road, all the way to the end."

Drayton pressed another coin into his hand and rode off swiftly, not staying to hear the thanks or further directions. The house was easy to find, because Tom was out in front, smoking a pipe and chatting with an elderly man who was sitting on the stoop. He looked up as Drayton approached and then came to the gate and touched his cap. As he saw Sleet, his eyes widened.

"Has you already found him, then, sir?"

"No," said Drayton, puzzled. "I thought you had word of him for me."

"Beg pardon, sir, but I thought you must have seen him—that being his horse you have under you."

Drayton swore under his breath. "Was he here recently, then?"

"Yes, sir, and meeting with his friends, like I said."

"Perhaps I know them," said Drayton. "Ross—the young man I seek—Ross and I have many mutual acquaintances. Are they local gentry?"

"Oh, no, sir. Furriners, I am sure. Italians, I think

they said. Very close-mouthed lot. And not gentry, either. Even furriners can be gentry, I suppose, sir, but this lot are very plain folk. Quietlike, rough and homely types. Sailors or such, I shouldn't wonder."

Drayton remembered to thank him, and gave him a few crowns, but he rode away in the middle of a query about how to find him, should the young Ross come again next week. His thoughts were black. "No brother of yours, Rachel Roth Meyer," he said between his teeth. "You lied to me, damn you." He would leave for London at once.

Chapter Thirteen

The young lieutenant was apologetic. "Colonel White is expected back momentarily, Captain Drayton. Is it urgent?" Drayton nodded. The lieutenant looked at his haggard face and took pity on him. "He'll likely go directly to Captain Southey's office when he returns; he and the captain are meeting one of the couriers there. Would you like to go down the hall and see if you can intercept him? It's the fourth door down on the right. Knock loudly; there's a small antechamber behind the outer door and sometimes it's difficult to hear from inside."

Mechanically, Drayton thanked him and went back out into the twisted hallway. He had forgotten Southey might be here, and the agonizing ache in his stomach eased slightly. He would explain the whole situation to South and ask his advice. Perhaps things were not as bleak as they appeared to be. But then common sense reasserted itself. He knew perfectly well what Southey would say: female or not, friend of the family or not, a spy was a spy. His mind slid hastily away from the word *traitor.* He realized that he was standing in front of the fourth door, and he collected himself and knocked firmly. There was no reply. He tried again, a rattling fusillade. Nothing. He grasped the handle; it turned, and after a moment he went in. There was a small dark hall, and then an inner door, slightly ajar, with light behind it. He pushed it open, knocking softly at the same time.

It was understandable that White would want to meet in here, thought Drayton. The office was impeccably neat and organized; although smaller than White's it appeared bigger, without the litter of papers everywhere. Southey's desk was empty, but there was another person in the room, seated at a small side table, looking intently at some documents. A slender figure, in the uniform of a lieutenant of rifles, with dark waving hair and a familiar profile. A very familiar profile. Drayton's heart seemed to stop beating. How could she be so reckless? To come here, in such a disguise, in broad daylight! He could never save her now; putting on an enemy uniform was a hanging matter. Did she think Southey would not recognize her, after spending days in her company? Or had she hoped to slip in and out of the office unobserved while Southey was away on some errand? Enraged, he strode over to the table and seized her by the shoulder.

"Rachel!" he started to say, "This is the outside of enough! Have you . . ." Then his voice died in his throat. The shoulder under his hand was packed with muscle. The face that turned to stare into his had recently known a razor. An extremely handsome young man was looking at him in astonishment, then in angry comprehension. The stranger rose; he was considerably taller than Rachel. Dark eyes blazed.

"You make very free with my sister's name and person, Captain Drayton," said the young officer, his temper flaring. Even in his stupefied trance, Drayton recognized the clipped accent and the keen eyes, narrowed now in fury. A miraculous light broke through the confusion and suspicion which had oppressed him for weeks. It was the stranger from the cave, the one who had helped Rodrigo get him back through the French lines. How could he not have realized that Rachel looked like the man in the cave? The eyes were nearly identical. And how could he have failed to connect her fear of dogs, her scar, with Rodrigo's story of Rover's children? The brother must be Little Rover. So far from being a Bonapartist agent, she was assisting her brother on his trips to France.

Overwhelmed by relief, he sagged against the table momentarily. Then he groaned inwardly as he recollected the accusations he had made two nights ago. He was an idiot. He had jumped to conclusions and acted rashly, as usual. Would she ever forgive him?

"By God, Drayton," said the lieutenant, enraged, "when I heard my sister was at your brother-in-law's house I had some qualms, but White assured me he was the soul of discretion. He even spoke up for you, said your reputation for philandering was vastly overblown. And I, fool that I was, believed him. If you've insulted her, abused her situation—"

Drayton looked at that fierce face and came back to the present. "Have I compromised her, do you mean?" he said slowly. "You give your sister too

Take A Trip Into A Timeless World of Passion and Adventure with Kensington Choice Historical Romances!

—Absolutely FREE!

little credit, I think, if you suppose that any actions of mine could tarnish her."

"I must ask you to be more explicit, sir. To which *actions* do you refer?"

"Let me see," said Drayton, who was suddenly seeing the humorous side of this bizarre conversation. "I have spent the night with her, alone, in a hut in the woods. We had to take some of our clothing off, we were soaked. Then, while she was nursing me after my surgery, she fainted in my bedroom and I tore off part of her dress trying to revive her. I waylaid her in her bedchamber night before last after she went to meet you. It was you, was it not? And I have kissed her. Twice. Without her consent, I should add. Is that what you wanted to know?"

There was a stinging crack across Drayton's cheek; the blow was so sudden and so forceful that he staggered. "You unprincipled scoundrel!" stormed the younger man. "Did you think her so unprotected? I will call in the account with interest, I promise you." A shocked cry came from the doorway; Southey stood staring in dismay at the two of them.

"Can't you ever control your temper, Nathanson?" he said fiercely. Striding over and standing between them, he caught Drayton's arm. "Drayton, listen to me," he said urgently, "you can't meet him! Nathanson is Little Rover! White and Tredwell will take us apart limb from limb if anything happens to him." Southey turned back to Nathanson. "I thought you promised to stop brawling with everyone who insulted you," he snapped.

"He didn't insult me; he insulted my sister," said Nathanson, rigid with fury.

"If you knew Drayton better, you wouldn't take anything he says seriously," said Southey calmly. "He outranks you, in any case. You could lose your commission if you force a quarrel on him." Then he recalled something. "What happened to your promotion, then? Were you demoted for fighting? White told me they had offered you a vacant captaincy."

"They did," said Nathanson. "Twice. I wasn't demoted; I simply refused both promotions."

"Well, you don't need the six shillings a day," commented Southey; then, seeing the junior officer bridle, "Take a damper, Nathanson! I'm not making gibes about your family fortune, just wondering why you refused. Surely the rank itself has some value for you?"

"At the moment, it does not," said Nathanson. "Couriers are rarely in uniform, and I work mostly with Rodrigo. I suppose that if I were in the field with a regiment I would take my proper rank."

"Why is he calling you Nathanson?" interjected Drayton, puzzled. "Isn't your name Meyer?"

"My *nom de guerre,*" said that gentleman curtly. "Roth and Meyer are a bit conspicuous."

"Does anyone in your family ever use their real name?" said Drayton, exasperated. Then he turned to Southey. "I have no intention of calling him out, have no fear. If he insists I will delope, and he can shoot me or not, as he pleases. I can hardly kill the man I hope to make my brother."

Nathanson turned white. "You will not marry my sister!" he said furiously.

"Well, God's Blood, man, be consistent!" retorted Drayton. "If you think I've insulted her, why will you not permit me to prove that my intentions are honorable by offering for her hand?"

Southey stared at Nathanson and then at his friend, puzzled. "Drayton, what are you talking about? How could you have met Nathanson's sister, or any of his family? They are Hebrew; they live in a very quiet way. Don't go into society at all."

"I would hardly call Miss Meyer's recent activities quiet," observed Drayton sardonically. "Are you blind, South? Nathanson's sister is Miss Ross. You spent a good part of last month with her at Leigh End." Southey's mouth opened and closed; he looked for a moment like a fish gasping for air. Then he sat down weakly in the chair Nathanson had vacated and tugged at his shirt collar.

"You don't have to marry her, you know," he said to Drayton, looking uncomfortable. " I'm the only one who knows you were not unconscious in that hut after you were kidnapped, and I gave you my word." Nathanson was frowning in bewilderment, but his expression was still hostile.

"I don't think you quite understand," said Drayton, looking at both men. "It has nothing to do with that ridiculous abduction. I love her. I want to marry her. I've asked her three times."

"It is impossible," said Nathanson flatly. "Completely impossible."

"Your sister said the same thing," observed Drayton. "Perhaps you can give me some reason why."

Nathanson looked at him, the anger fading gradually from his face. "I wouldn't mind some explanations myself," he said after a moment. "For example, about that hut. Let me just file my report with the colonel."

Drayton picked up his hat, which had been knocked out of his hand by the force of Nathanson's blow, and moved towards the door.

"I'll wait for you outside," he said to Nathanson, who nodded.

"But Richard," said Southey, "didn't you come here to meet Colonel White? Have you found anything? I know I was supposed to come down to Kent and brief you, but I couldn't get away."

"I thought I had some information, yes," said Drayton. "But I realize now that I was misled. I shall have to go back to Charing and make further inquiries." I should contact the man who sold Sleet to Harry, he realized. Someone else has a horse with markings like mine and Southey's. Chances are it's another foal from his mare.

Nathanson took him back across the river to Jasper and Sons, a coffeehouse near Whitehall popular with the younger officers. It was crowded, and Drayton without thinking went over to a table with space at one end, nodded to the occupants, and took a seat. Smiling grimly, Nathanson followed him. At once the three men who had been seated there rose and left. A murmur arose and rolled across the room from table to table, then an ugly silence fell. Some officers at adjacent tables edged their chairs away. Conversation resumed, but there was a tense feeling in the air. Drayton realized that several acquaintances of his in the room were pointedly looking the other way.

Nathanson looked at him impassively.

"Is it as bad as that?" said Drayton, slowly understanding what was happening.

"Do you see why you cannot marry my sister?" said Nathanson softly. "I will set aside her part of the story—that she would be completely abandoned by many in our family, possibly including my aunt and uncle, who are like parents to her, that she would never be received in polite society, would be despised by your servants, snubbed even by the local tradesmen. And I will assume that you are prepared to be ostracized yourself, although I think you do not really understand what that means. Suppose you love each other. Suppose it is worth it, to you, to pay that price. Is it fair, though, to ask your children to pay it?"

He gestured around at the uncomfortable crowd, sipping their coffee and pretending Nathanson and Drayton were not there. "Do you want them to face this every time they go into a public place? Do you want them to be bullied at school—if any school will even admit them? To be insulted constantly, to realize that when they, in their turn, fall in love and wish to marry they are likely to be refused?" He added, after a moment, "Do you know what I find to be one of the most difficult aspects of my work? I spend days, weeks sometimes, pretending to be Christian—usually Catholic, of course, when I am in Spain. But even so I get a glimpse, a tantalizing glimpse, of what it would be like to actually belong to the world for which I am in every other way fitted, by wealth and education and inclination. Can you understand now why all the Roths and Meyers marry their cousins? Because there is no one else we can marry. We are like some exotic animals which can only find mates within their own dwindling numbers."

"Is it not changing, though?" said Drayton, fighting against the black picture Nathanson presented. "I had heard talk of making your uncle a peer."

"That is true," said Nathanson. "And my uncle Leon, in Austria, is a baron. The patent covers all the Roths; technically my uncle Eli is already ennobled, at least on the continent. But an English peerage would be meaningless, in a certain sense. My uncle has not sought it."

"Why?" asked Drayton. "Surely that would be a signal to the aristocracy that your family's worth counted more than its religion."

"My uncle would not be able to take his seat in the House of Lords," said Nathanson. "He cannot take the oath. That is why I refused my promotion, also. Officers are required to affirm that they are loyal sons of the Church of England, and my perjury is tolerated only up to the rank of major. It seemed pointless to accept a captaincy under those circumstances." He added bitterly, "Even as couriers we are not respectable. My father agreed with Tredwell that we would use code names, so that our reports would be accepted more readily by the regimental commanders."

"Nathanson!" called a friendly voice from the door. Evrett had come in, and limped gracefully over to their table. "And Drayton," added Evrett, smiling. He pulled up a chair, apparently unaware of the glares and whispers at adjoining tables. "May I join you?" He looked more closely at Drayton, and saw the mark of Nathanson's palm still visible on his cheek. "I beg your pardon," he said, "perhaps I interrupt some personal business?" He rose again. "Feel free to call on me, should you need a second," he said to Nathanson.

"Sit down, Evrett," said Drayton. "He won't need any seconds. I told him I would not fight him."

Evrett folded back into his chair and looked at both men quizzically. "You, Drayton? Refuse a duel? What next? Will the sky fall in?" Then his face darkened. "If you have refused him because you do not consider him a proper opponent you will have to fight me in his place, you know. We served in Portugal together."

"My thanks, Evrett," said Nathanson stiffly. "But Captain Drayton and I were the victims of a misunderstanding. We do not plan to meet—at least not at the moment," he added, with a meaningful look at Drayton.

Evrett grinned. "You and Drayton are a well-matched pair," he commented. "Between the two of you a surgeon could build an entire practice."

"My dueling days are over, I think," said Drayton with a smile. "I'm planning on getting married."

"Congratulations, my dear fellow!" said Evrett warmly. "Who is the young lady? Not Miss Waite, I know, since I saw the announcement of her engagement to Courthope. This must have happened quite recently."

"Yes, just this past month," said Drayton, watching Nathanson. "It is Nathanson's sister. She has been staying at Leigh End, and we became acquainted there."

Evrett looked a bit stunned. "Is this true?" he said, turning to Nathanson.

"No!" said Nathanson.

"Yes," said Drayton, at the same moment.

"You see?" said Nathanson to Drayton, ignoring Evrett. "Did you see his face? He was shocked. It is unthinkable."

"What I saw," said Drayton between his teeth, "is that the best man in this room came straight over to this table the minute he entered. And greeted you, not me. So don't try to fob me off with horror stories of my children's dreadful fate."

A wry smile appeared on Evrett's face. "Is your

sister anything like you?" he said to Nathanson. "I wish I could be there."

"Be where?" said Nathanson, puzzled.

"In the room. With Drayton and your sister. When they have their first fight."

"Our first!" said Drayton bitterly. "We've had nothing but."

"Somehow I am not surprised," said Evrett, a twinkle in his eye.

It was impossible, of course, to have any sort of confidential conversation at Jasper's, as Nathanson had known very well when he selected it. "You wanted to put on a little demonstration, did you not?" asked Drayton. They had walked down along the Strand towards London Bridge, and Drayton had filled Nathanson in on Rachel's visit to the Barretts', the kidnapping, and his involvement in investigating the courier route. Now they had reverted to Drayton's courtship of Rachel.

"As you saw," said Nathanson shortly. "Perhaps we should try White's, where they will refuse me entrance. Jasper's doesn't seem to have done the trick."

"You could fill an amphitheater with good men who have been blackballed from White's by some country squire whose grandfather got him in before he was breeched," said Drayton impatiently.

Nathanson sighed. In spite of himself he was warming to Drayton. The description of the battle with Rachel at the dinner table had made him laugh so hard that he had been forced to grab the wall in front of Somerset House. "I shouldn't tell you this," he said, "but it is not completely out of the question. If it were, I would not be taking the time to persuade you what a dreadful mess it would be. One of my French cousins married a Christian. My uncle Jacob is much more liberal than my father and my uncle Eli. And Paris is a more open society than London. It has still been very, very difficult. My grandmother will not even hear her name spoken."

"Do I—might I have your permission to try, at least, then?" said Drayton, stopping in his tracks. "It's not much of a risk," he added after a moment. "She has refused me with more vehemence each time."

"I have no authority to give you that permission," said Nathanson.

Drayton was disconcerted. "But your father is dead, is he not? Or is your uncle the head of the family?"

"My father is not dead," said Nathanson after a long pause. "And if you disclose that information to anyone else, including my sister, many lives are at risk. I must ask you to swear on your word of honor that you will not reveal it, under any circumstances. And please do not ask me how I know, or where he is."

"Very well," said Drayton. "You know your sister took the report of his death very hard," he added, subdued. "I let it slip inadvertently while she was nursing me. That was when she fainted. I did not understand that at the time, of course."

Nathanson looked troubled but said only, "It was concealed at first even from senior officers like Colonel White, and I am probably wrong to tell you. But we cannot let Rachel know; her distress is an important confirmation of the news. I almost gave the game away myself when we quarreled the other night; I had forgotten that she must not be told. Luckily I am a pugnacious fellow, and I trust she will ascribe my remark to my well-known habit of contradicting her." He looked around; they had turned away from the river and were walking up towards the Bank of England. "Where are you headed?" he asked in surprise. "I had thought your family's home was in Berkeley Square."

"I am not staying there," said Drayton. "But in any case, I am not returning to my lodgings just yet. I must apologize to your sister. The last time I saw her I accused her of being a French spy."

Nathanson raised his eyebrows. "Before or after you proposed?" he asked caustically.

Drayton sighed. "During, actually. I offered to protect her from the consequences of her activities by marrying her."

"My God!" said Nathanson faintly. "I had thought you to be a man of address, Drayton. How on earth did you get such a reputation for success with the fair sex if you proceed in such a bone-headed fashion when you propose?"

"I don't seem to have any address at all when I deal with your sister," said Drayton ruefully. "First woman I ever wanted to marry, and I provoke a quarrel every time I speak to her."

They had reached the narrow lane behind London Bridge where Eli Roth had his house, which was attached to his bank. Drayton squared his shoulders and marched up to the door of the residence. Nathanson stayed in the street. "Are you not coming in with me?" said Drayton, turning around in surprise. "You may play chaperone if you wish. Although I swear I will be a model suitor."

Nathanson snorted. "If you think I want to be in the same room with you when my sister tells you what she thinks of your conclusion that she was spying for Napoleon, you are even more of a fool than I had thought. She won't need a chaperone. I had best get back to Greenwich. Southey and I are setting up new schedules for the couriers, to try to avoid the problems on the Dover road. My next run to France will require me to travel fairly far inland, and I need to make sure that my arrival is not broadcast to Arnaut and his thugs."

Her father's study had always been her favorite room in the house in London, and although it was off-limits while he was in residence, Rachel had his permission to use it whenever he was out of town. Everything about it was soothing and familiar: the distorted view of the courtyard through the ancient glass in the windows, the dark wooden bookcases, the battered old desk, the painting of her mother on the wall above the tiny fireplace. She had taken refuge there now, and was frowning at an enormous pile of letters when there was a knock at the door.

"Come in!" she called, thinking that it was her aunt. But Sweelinck, the Roth's Dutch butler, was accustomed to young men in uniform arriving at all hours requesting speech with either Master James or Miss Rachel. It had not occurred to him to ask the captain to wait while he went to ask Rachel if she would be at home to the visitor. She was utterly unprepared, therefore, for Sweelinck's announcement that a Captain Drayton was here to see her, and even more unprepared for the sight of Drayton. Her firm resolve never to speak with him again crumbled in an instant. She had never seen him in uniform, and he seemed to glitter everywhere: the polished blue cloth, the white lace, the buttons, the dark, straight hair, the fine eyes.

"Miss Meyer," he started to say, and then cleared his throat. He looked at the floor and said helplessly, "Please forgive me. I do not know what to say. There is no excuse for the dreadful way I have harassed you and misjudged you. I really have no hope that you will ever want to see me again, but I wished to assure you that in my deepest heart I do not think I ever truly believed you to be a French agent; I could not feel about you as I do if I had been completely convinced you were working for the enemy and deceiving my sister." He paused and then continued, with some difficulty, "I also wish you to understand that my offer of marriage was sincere, if poorly phrased. I admire you more than I can possibly say. Your brother and I met this afternoon, and I asked him for permission to pay my addresses."

"What—what did he say?" faltered Rachel, her gaze fixed on the anguished face above her.

"He disapproves, but he did not forbid me to see you," said Drayton truthfully, if a bit ambiguously.

Rachel had recollected her original resolution. "Captain Drayton, must you offer me marriage every time we are alone together?" she said severely. "My brother cannot disapprove of the notion more than I do myself. How could we possibly be married? English law would not even recognize such a marriage. Or did you assume that I would convert to your faith?"

Drayton had indeed assumed exactly that, and his face told her as much.

"*You* convert, then!" she flared at him. "And at that time I will consider your offer!"

There was an appalled silence. At length Drayton's face relaxed again. "You have made your point," he said quietly. "I had not thought you especially pious, but I suppose you must feel the same loyalty to your faith that anyone would, even if you are not as observant as some others in your family."

Rachel sighed. "I think that with my father's constant masquerades I have been in church more often than in synagogue, it is true," she said. "But it is as you say; it would be a betrayal. I do not think I could do it."

"We could be married abroad," argued Drayton.

"Do you never give up?" said Rachel, beginning to smile. She was still marveling that Drayton had not stormed out when she had made that angry comment about conversion.

"I am noted for my stubbornness," said Drayton with an answering smile. Then, growing serious again, "Miss Meyer, of all things it would be most distasteful to me to annoy you with my attentions if they are unwelcome. I have told you how I feel about you, in part by way of apology for my boorish behavior and in part because I could not help myself, but I am not certain that you have any real liking for me, and that is a matter of much more moment than whether we can be married by an Anglican parson. If you can assure me that you do not return my regard, even my stubborn nature will know how to yield."

Tell him, Rachel said to herself sternly. It is by far the easiest way. Tell him that you do not care for him. You coward, speak! It will only be painful for a moment. It is better for both of you. But she could not do it. Drayton saw her shake her head numbly. He could not tell what that meant but assumed the worst. Rachel saw his face flicker for a moment in pain, and then his jaw tightened. Involuntarily, she gave a small cry.

"I am sorry," she said, very white. This preamble confirmed his misinterpretation, and he bowed and turned to leave. "Captain Drayton—stop. This will be very difficult for both of us, but you have been honest with me. I cannot tell you in good conscience that I have no regard for you. On the contrary. And I find your suspicions of my activities at Leigh End entirely understandable, and would have acted just as you did." She saw a light come into his eyes that was so disquieting she looked away. "Please do not misunderstand me. I cannot marry you. It will not do. But I want you to know that in spite of all that has happened between us, I have come to esteem you very highly." She looked up at him again, and added in a low voice, "I have never met anyone like you. But I must ask you not to repeat your offer of marriage, ever again. I cannot accept."

Drayton stood for a moment considering her, and then said very gently, "You have my word, Miss Meyer, that I will not propose to you again without your permission." He bowed again, and left quietly. It took Rachel a minute to realize that what he had promised did not precisely correspond to what she had requested of him.

When he arrived back at his lodgings with Fielding in Mount Street, Drayton was whistling cheerfully. He took the stairs two at a time up to the third floor hall, and went straight to the cupboard to drag out his valise. Perhaps he could make it back down to Kent this evening. Should he go straight on into Charing? No, for then he would arrive very late at Leigh End, which would be most disconcerting to the tidily organized world of Mrs. Tibbet. In fact, best to go down tomorrow morning, after all. He kicked the valise back into the cupboard. Only then did he notice the envelope on the tray by the door of his room. His heart sank. The writing was well known to him.

"Hell and damnation," he muttered, ripping it open and tearing off one corner of the enclosed sheet in the process. It was a note from his father, requesting that Drayton call in Berkeley Square at his earliest convenience. In a panic, Drayton wondered how long the note had been lying there. Had his sister already told their father about his offer to Rachel? He was forced to acknowledge that if she had taken him seriously she might have done exactly that. Well, best to get it over with, he thought. If he went at once, he might find his father at home, before his normal round of evening engagements.

Alcroft was, in fact, tying his neckcloth when Drayton was shown into his dressing room. Splendid in knee breeches and starched linen, he surveyed his son with a sigh. There was dust on one side of Drayton's coat, where he had brushed against the inside of the luggage cupboard. His hair looked as though he had been dragging his hands through it, which he had, and his boots were scuffed.

Well aware of his parent's scrutiny, Drayton flushed. "I beg your pardon, sir, for calling on you in this rig, but I feared to miss you if I delayed long enough to change. I only received your note twenty minutes ago; I have been down in Kent and then went straight in to report to Whitehall this morning."

"No matter, no matter," said Alcroft, waving his hand in dismissal. "I did not ask you to come and see me in order to discuss your sartorial failings." He paused. Drayton, who had rarely seen his father at a loss for words, waited apprehensively. "The truth is," Alcroft went on stiffly, "I owe you an apology. Colonel White stopped by the other day. Evidently I have, as is my wont, underestimated you. He could not tell me the details, but he said enough to make me realize that I ought to be rather proud of you. And instead I came down and all but disinherited you while you were so ill you could barely lift your head, let alone defend yourself. I hope that you will forgive me." He was studying the Indian carpet in front of the dresser as he spoke.

For a moment, Drayton was tempted to shake his father's hand and leave, which was clearly what was expected. He could let Alcroft discover his plans for a scandalous mésalliance at some later date. But for some reason the thought of someone else telling his father about Rachel distressed him. "I take it that Sara has not told you about my marriage plans, sir," he therefore said, knowing that the word *marriage* would instantly command his sire's full attention.

Alcroft looked up in astonishment. "No, she has not. I am delighted to hear that you are finally thinking of settling down," he said with something approaching warmth. "There had been some talk of Miss Waite, had there not? When I saw that she was promised elsewhere I assumed that you were not yet ready to give up your—shall we call them youthful pursuits? This is very welcome news."

"Don't kill the fatted calf too quickly," said Drayton with a rueful grimace. "You have not heard the name of my prospective bride." He felt a pang of guilt for the grief his announcement would cause, and understood suddenly what Nathanson had been trying to tell him earlier that afternoon. "I have asked Miss Meyer, the niece of Eli Roth, for her hand," he said, looking squarely at his father. "I met her at Leigh End; she has been staying with Sara and Barrett."

There was a stunned silence, and then his father's brows snapped together. "This is a jest, surely? Such a marriage is impossible!"

Drayton sighed. "I suspect you are right. You are the third person to tell me that today, and the other two are even more closely involved in my hopes than you are. But I did not want to deceive you, sir. If she consents, and her family will allow the match, I mean to have her."

"I do not believe I could recognize such a marriage," said Alcroft slowly. "It is only fair to warn you. I am sure you suspected as much." Drayton nodded. "I appreciate your willingness to confide in me, however," his father went on awkwardly. "Perhaps, at least for the moment, we might try to remain on better terms than our misunderstandings have permitted in the past?"

"It is my fault that we quarrel so often," said Drayton, feeling wretched. "I will try to curb my temper, sir."

A rare smile lit his father's face. "I can hardly reproach you for your temper," he said, clasping Drayton's hand. "I need only look in the mirror to find its source."

Chapter Fourteen

Originally Drayton had planned to take the post-chaise into Charing and go immediately to the Golden Pheasant to try to get back on the track of the French agent. It had become clear to him, recalling his conversation with the ostler, that the gentleman he was after had probably come on Monday, as usual. Drayton had assumed that Rachel's expedition the following night was the one described by Tom, but that was obviously wrong. Nathanson had told him about their meeting, and it did not match Tom's description in the least. Before he had reached the turnoff for Leigh End, however, he recalled that his man would not yet be at the inn. In addition, he thought it might be useful to have Sleet with him; perhaps other servants at the inn would recognize what they thought to be their patron's horse and have further information. Accordingly, he had the driver take him straight to Leigh End.

As he pulled up in the drive he was astonished to see two coaches standing before the front door, being loaded with parcels and luggage. The front door was wide open, and servants were running back and forth in the hall, apparently in the grip of some mass frenzy. He had just paid the post charges when Sara emerged from the house, carrying a basket whose cloth cover rippled as Drayton watched it. "Richard!" she said, relieved. "I did so hope you would come back down before we left. I had no idea what to do with Sleet, or whether I ought to send Robson up to London or not."

"But where are you going?" asked Drayton, mystified. "Had you told me you were leaving? I have been a bit distracted of late; I beg your pardon if my absence has delayed your departure."

At that moment, the basket in Sara's hand erupted, and a gray kitten vaulted neatly over the side and disappeared into the shrubs beside the drive. "Drat!" said Sara, irritated. "That is the third time! I scolded Caroline twice for letting her escape and have just done the same thing myself!" She sighed. "Never mind. I think I will wait until everyone is in the carriage and then have Jem lure her out at the last minute. I should never have agreed to take her, but Caroline was so torn between the puppies and Miss Ross, I thought a bribe was in order."

"Miss Ross? Miss Meyer, rather?"

Sara glanced around instinctively to look for Barrett's aunt. "We are still using her other name, Richard, if you please. It is too difficult to explain to everyone at the moment. Caroline was very distressed at her departure, and Charles is forever going to London, so that when Miss Ross wrote to Caroline and expressed the hope that she might see her if we came to town, I decided to go up at once." She smiled at him. "Which means that you may now stay with us in Harland Place, if you choose, instead of in that rickety set of rooms Fielding has taken in Mount Street."

"I will probably be staying at Berkeley Square when I return," he said lightly.

Her face lit up. "Oh, Richard! You have seen him and are reconciled again. How wonderful!" On impulse, she stood on tiptoe and kissed his cheek. "When are you returning to town, then? We are not closing Leigh End; you may stay here as long as you need to. Charles says you have some business down this way."

"Yes, I do," he said, frowning. "I should go and find Robson. Will you mind if I do not stand on the front steps and bid all of you adieu? I got off on the wrong tack in this work I am doing and need to set about repairing my error as soon as may be."

"I saw Robson going over to the stable a few minutes ago," said Sara. "You may omit the fond farewells if you promise to come see us as soon as you are back in London. But pray do not leave your valise here on the steps; it will likely be loaded into one of the coaches if you do."

"Then I would be forced to visit you in London, would I not? To reclaim my shirts," said Drayton, laughing. He picked up the case and turned to walk around the side of the house, but Sara laid her hand on his arm and stopped him.

"Richard," she said, biting her lip, "you do not have to tell me anything if you do not wish to, but were you serious when you said you had offered for Miss—Ross?"

He set the bag down and looked at her gravely.

"Will you refuse to receive us if I do marry her, Sara? I have asked her brother for permission to court her, and have so informed our father. Thus far I have no great hopes of success, but I am prepared to be patient." Patience was not normally one of Drayton's virtues, as Sara knew, but there was a look on his face she had never seen before.

"Oh, this is all my fault!" she said, agitated. "I should never have proposed my silly scheme about the Shropshire Rosses to her! You would not have even considered marrying her had you known her real name when you first met her."

"You are probably right," said Drayton. "But fortunately, I did not. You did not answer my question, though."

"Of course I will still receive you," said Sara, horrified. "How can you even ask?" And she hurried back inside the house before he could see that she had tears in her eyes.

Robson was in Sleet's stall looking at one of her hooves when Drayton came in. "This shoe will be off before the day is out, Master Richard," he said. "Shall I take her over to the smithy?"

"I'll take her," said Drayton absently. "Been cooped up in that chaise all morning. And Davies always likes to hear war stories while he shoes the horses. Has she been out yet today?"

"No, nor yesterday afternoon, either. I was just about to give her some exercise, when I saw that there shoe was loose," said Robson. "She's a bit fresh, if I may say so, and won't take kindly to being walked. Even by you."

"She doesn't take kindly to anything when she's been in her stall that long," said Drayton dryly.

"Come to think of it, after sitting in that chaise for hours, I sympathize with her." He patted her softly while Robson saddled her, and rode off cheerfully toward the smithy, holding Sleet to a trot.

Davies, an enormous man with bristling white hair, was wrestling with a broken roasting spit when Drayton came up, and he abandoned it with a wide grin. "Captain Drayton, good day, sir! I'll wager your mare needs a shoe. Have a seat, sir, have a seat!" He dusted off an old crate with a polishing cloth which left black smears on its surface and rolled over to examine Sleet's hoof. "Aye, you would not get far on this, sir. Just a few minutes and she'll be fit for a gallop. Sit you down, then, this other can wait." And forgetting that he had already done so, he smeared yet more polish on the crate.

Hiding a grin, Drayton politely refused the proffered seat and obliged the old smith with news of the war while he heated the iron. Wellington was Davies's hero, and every traveler was interrogated mercilessly for the duration of a shoeing job until Davies was satisfied that they had nothing new to tell about the campaign. Sleet was shortly fitted with her new shoe, and Drayton had overpaid the smith, as always ("to drink Lord Wellington's health"), when the old man recollected something.

"Might you be stopping by Chanterfield, Captain?" he asked. "The Southey's wagon is here and all repaired, but my 'prentice, young Malton, warn't here yesterday and like as not I'll not see him today; his grandma tells me he is feverish. I was wishful to send him with a message; 'tis weeks now the wagon has been ready, and Captain

Southey may have forgot 'tis here." He waved his hand towards the small yard in back of the forge, where Drayton saw a battered wagon sitting with blocks under the wheels. One of the wheels had a brand-new rim.

"Certainly," said Drayton, thinking that he had not seen Mrs. Southey at all since he had returned from Spain. "It will be no trouble to call on my way home." He glanced idly at the wagon and froze. There was an iron bar above the backboard. Very few wagons had such a bar. He walked warily over to the back and looked in. There, on the left side, towards the front, was a large dark stain. He knew what it was. It was his blood.

Even then the truth did not really occur to him; he turned to the smith and said intensely, "Are you sure that Southey brought this in, Davies? Or if he did, did he say how the wheel rim was broken? Had someone borrowed the wagon, stolen it perhaps, and then abandoned it?"

Puzzled, the smith looked at the wagon and then back at Drayton. "He brought it in himself, sir. With his Spanish man, who let on as how he had taken it into the woods and gone off the track."

"What Spanish man?" asked Drayton, dreading the answer. "The Southeys have no foreign servants, or did not when I last called."

"He's Cap'n Southey's new groom and batman, or so they say. Not like any groom I ever saw! That fellow is dreadful hard on Captain Southey's animals, sir. Time and time again I've been shoeing the horses and seen their poor hooves nigh shredded. I suppose"—with a condescension very common in rural England—"that being a Spanish chap he don't know when the shoe is coming loose until it goes and falls right off. As for being his batman!

He calls the captain 'commander,' as if he was in the navy!'' And Davies shook his head and pursed his lips.

Drayton stood stock-still as the smith spoke, hardly able to assimilate what he was hearing. Fragments of memory assailed him: Southey, white with horror, rushing into his room as he lay recovering from the kidnapping. The rivalry for Miranda. His friend's uneasy reaction to the revelation of Rachel's true identity. Then shock and disbelief were succeeded by blinding rage. Without a word to the smith, he seized the mare's bridle and leaped into the saddle. Sleet seldom felt his spurs, but she felt them now. He galloped her down the lane, across two fields, up the drive and into the yard at Leigh End, slid off her back, and roared for Robson. He wanted Barrett's curricle, and the bays, and he wanted them now. They were going back to London. It was urgent.

He drove like a madman through Maidstone, over the heath, and across the southern edge of London. It had started to rain and his shoulder was aching, but he could think of nothing but finding Southey. As they neared the city he had a moment of panic; he had been to Southey's new lodgings recently but could not recollect where they were. He turned to Robson, who was grimly clinging to the side of the curricle. He had stuffed his hat under the seat, to prevent it blowing off, and his bald head glistened in the rain dripping from the alders lining the streets of Deptford. ''Robson,'' he yelled over the noise of the wheels and the wind, ''where is Southey staying now?''

These were the first words he had uttered since they had left Leigh End.

His batman looked at him in astonishment. "Master Richard, never tell me we've been risking our necks for some engagement with Mr. Southey you had forgot?" Drayton gave him such a ferocious look that he quailed.

"Devil take you, do you know his direction or not?" Robson told him. They tore through Southwark and nearly ran down a pedestrian on the bridge; recalled to some sense of his responsibilities, Drayton slowed in the heavier traffic closer to Charing Cross and held the horses in until they reached Westminster. The sight of Whitehall looming over him reminded him with renewed force of his misery, and he groaned aloud; then he had turned up towards St. James and slowed the horses. He pulled up at the address on Clifford Street, jumped down without even handing the reins to Robson, and pounded on the door.

Sievert, Southey's valet, came down the stairs in haste when he heard Drayton shouting at the servant who had admitted him. Drayton whirled on him. "Where is he, damn it? Don't tell me he's out of town! I just saw him in Greenwich yesterday!"

Sievert shrank back, terrified. "Is it very important, sir?" he said, hesitating. Southey had given him strict instructions to tell no one where he had gone, but Captain Drayton was his oldest friend, and working now for Colonel White.

"Very," said Drayton, his face gaunt.

"You've missed him, sir," said Sievert. "He's gone to Dover, in a tearing hurry, some two hours since."

Drayton swore softly. He had very likely driven

right by his target without even noticing. "Where does he stop in Dover?" he asked curtly.

"I don't know, sir," said Sievert helplessly. "I wish I did. He never takes any of us when he goes down to the coast on army business."

Suddenly Drayton realized that he himself had the information he needed. Southey had given him the names of the two inns in Dover used by the couriers, along with a list of boatmen, to use in his investigation. It was back in his rooms on Mount Street. He ran out the door and leaped back into the curricle. Robson, who had been walking the horses, barely had time to scramble back in before Drayton jerked the horses around and headed off. "Master Richard!" gasped Robson. "These animals are exhausted! You'll cripple them an you drive them more today."

"We're only going to my lodgings," said Drayton, not looking round. He pulled up in Mount Street a few minutes later. "I'll need a fresh pair. Get them harnessed while I run up and get a few things from my room." For the second time in twenty-four hours, he took the stairs two at a time, but he was not whistling now. A frantic search of his chamber turned up the list, which he stuffed into his coat pocket. Then he tore back down the stairs. Robson had not yet returned from the livery stable with the new team. He went back into the town house. "Fielding won't mind," he muttered. "In fact, he would give me his blessing." Opening the door to the ground-floor parlor with a jerk, he crossed the room in two strides. Above the fireplace, elegantly crossed, was a pair of rapiers. Drayton ripped them down, wrapped them in a throw rug, and headed out. Robson was just pulling up with fresh horses.

Drayton looked at him, soaking wet and shivering, and said with belated remorse, "Robson, you're done up! Get out at once! I can handle a curricle on my own; take yourself inside, man! You look dreadful."

"As if you looked any better," muttered Robson. But he dropped thankfully down onto the street as Drayton sprang back into the vehicle. A minute later he was driving away, with the rapiers lying at his feet.

The Roth house, too, had seen an urgent inquiry for one of its residents. Sweelinck had come to the parlor, where Rachel was helping her aunt make up a guest list for a luncheon, to advise her that an Ensign Lawrence was asking for Master James, and was most distressed to find him away. Did she know where the ensign might find him?

"I will come down," said Rachel. "Where is he, Sweelinck? In the bookroom?" She set aside the portable desk she had been writing on and excused herself to her aunt. There was a brief delay while her aunt settled one or two matters pertaining to the menu, and then she hurried downstairs behind the portly butler.

Ensign Lawrence's round face was unusually serious. "Miss Meyer?" he said. "My apologies for disturbing you, but it is vital that we find your brother at once. Have you any idea where he might be?"

Rachel shook her head. She turned to Sweelinck. "Sweelinck, can you find out if anyone has seen him leave, or if Silvio is in the house?" The butler went off and returned a few minutes later to report that Silvio had just gone out on an errand, but that one of the footmen had seen her brother, dressed for travel, leaving the house over an hour ago.

Lawrence turned pale.

"Oh, what is it?" cried Rachel. "He has gone down to the coast, is that it? And there is something wrong?" She saw that Lawrence was holding an envelope addressed to Captain Nathanson, and she stretched out her hand. "Can you let me see the note?" she pleaded. He shook his head. Rachel wrung her hands. "Do you know what is amiss?"

"Only that Captain Southey sent me here with the most pressing command to find Captain Nathanson as soon as possible, no matter how great the expense or trouble."

Rachel made up her mind. "Ensign Lawrence, I must see that note. I understand that it would be most improper for you to give it to me. I will therefore ask you merely not to stop me if I take it." He nodded, hypnotized by her fierce stare. She tugged it out of his hand and opened it. Numbly she read it, and reread it. It was from Southey, advising Nathanson that the time and place of the rendezvous had been discovered by the French. They would almost certainly be waiting for him when he reached the house north of Sangatte. If he received this message, he was to come down to the coast with all speed and try to find Southey, who had gone on to Dover with the hope of intercepting him there.

Paradoxically, the discovery that one of her worst nightmares was well on its way to being realized had a calming effect. She looked up from the note. "Sweelinck," she called. The butler reappeared instantly; Rachel suspected he had been listening outside the door. "Sweelinck, please find Samuels and ask him to have the carriage brought round at once. And tell Maria to pack me a change of clothing." She turned to Lawrence. "Ensign Lawrence, are you authorized to go as far as Dover in order to deliver your message?"

He considered this for a moment. "I believe so," he said.

"It will be fastest and most efficient, then, if we travel together as far as Canterbury," she said. "I should explain that my uncle's bank has long had its own system of couriers to send information to London from the continent quickly and reliably. My brother is accustomed to using that system to arrange speedy passage to and from France on small boats, and there are two agents he may have visited. One is in Dover and the other in Ramsgate. If we part company in Canterbury and go on separately to the two ports, one of us may be able to find him before he sets sail. I can assure you that my uncle's carriage receives very good service at the posting houses; we will make excellent time to the coast." She refused to think about what she would do if she arrived and found he had already set sail for France.

Jeremy Applethwaite sat on his bench in the corner of the Blue Boar's taproom and pulled on his pipe. It was a fine, misty May night, a likely night for sailors with shy passengers and illicit cargoes, and he anticipated good business. The war had brought hardship and distress to many along the coast, but not to Jeremy Applethwaite. Now that regular shipping did not go to France, folk who wanted to reach that country were compelled to seek the assistance of men such as himself, men who could call on "fishing boats" which had not sold a catch in months. Not a catch of fish, at any rate. Already one of the bank's messengers had come through, paying handsomely for a boat to take him over to the French coast. He was in such haste that he had refused to stay at the inn, but had gone down to the beach to wait there while the boat was rigged. Just now a young redheaded fellow had arranged for a similar trip, and was waiting upstairs for the boatman. And here was another prospect, unless he was much mistaken. An older man, a bit grizzled, looking about uncertainly and finally approaching a barmaid for assistance. Sure enough, here he came, pushing his way through the tables to Applethwaite's corner.

"Be you by chance Master Applethwaite?" said the new arrival. Applethwaite acknowledged as how he might be so, indeed. "My mistress would take it very kindly, then, if you would step outside, so as she could have a word with you. Her carriage is right by the door."

Applethwaite raised his eyebrows. Females, now that was unusual in his line of work. It was drizzling outside, but he did not demur at the prospect of standing in the rain to speak with this mysterious lady. Any woman who wanted to hire his services was likely to be willing to pay very well indeed. Clamping his pipe between his teeth, he rose heavily to his feet and made his way slowly to the door. Under the lamps he could see a coach and four and a female figure, veiled, looking anxiously out the window. He approached and touched his cap.

"Jeremy Applethwaite, ma'am. You was wishful to speak with me?"

The figure opened the door to the carriage and leaned out. "Is there a private parlor in the inn where we might discuss some business, Mr. Applethwaite?"

The Blue Boar did not cater to gentry; there was only one private parlor (a room which might more charitably have been called an attic, although it did have a fireplace). Applethwaite informed her with some regret that the private parlor was already bespoke.

"Then please step inside the carriage for a moment, sir. It is far too wet for you to remain out there while we talk, and I would prefer in any case to be private."

Applethwaite heaved himself into the carriage, which rocked alarmingly at his weight. The older man who had summoned him from the inn sniffed in disapproval and immediately took up a watchful position by the carriage window. Meanwhile the woman had extracted a stiff folded paper from her reticule. It was covered with seals. Applethwaite did not read well, but he knew those seals.

"By any chance," said the lady, "has a messenger from my—from this bank come through already this evening and booked passage to France?"

Applethwaite's instinct was to deny that he had any part in such havey-cavey business as arranging illegal trips to France. This usually produced a hefty coin, which he took as a prelude to his eventual fee, only reluctantly admitting that perhaps he knew a fisherman or two who could sail across, for a price. As to revealing anything about another customer—never. The sight of the bank's authorization letter, however, reminded him that he earned a comfortable retainer arranging passage for their messengers, on top of the normal fees. Surely his usual rule of never answering questions about his clients would not apply here; the woman was clearly connected with the bank herself. Probably a mistress of one of the owners, he thought, assessing her figure and expensive pelisse.

"A young, dark-haired chap?" he said.

The woman threw back her veil. Applethwaite gasped. Even in the dim light inside the carriage he could see the resemblance.

"Cor! Is he your brother, then, ma'am?"

"Yes," she said, "and I must reach him as soon as possible. It is vital that I find him before he lands, or immediately afterwards. Do you know where the boat is to take him? And when they left?"

"One minute, ma'am, and I will see if I can find out." He put his head out the carriage window, startling the guardian standing there, and bawled, "Pete! Pete, I say!" A boy of about eight darted out of the inn and ran up to the carriage. At the sight of Applethwaite inside this luxurious vehicle he gawked, which produced a cuff on the ear. "Mind your manners, Pete. This lady needs to know sommat about that young man as sailed with Robey and his son just now. Did you hear where they was going to set him down?"

"Just above Sangatte," replied the boy promptly.

"And did you see them set off?"

"Yes, sir, but half an hour past."

"Is there any chance I could catch them?" said the woman, clenching her hands together. "I will pay double if we can come within sight of them before they land."

Applethwaite thought a moment. "I would have to send Pete, here, down to Noakes's place, and then he must fit up his boat—chancy, ma'am, very chancy. The Robeys' craft is fast, the gentleman asked for them by name." Then he snapped his fingers. "Wait!" He turned to the boy. "Pete, is

Mowatt ready to take the gentleman upstairs yet? Has he come back up from the beach?"

"No, sir, but he should be here any minute, I reckon."

A lady in distress, connected to the bank that provided so much of his custom, and—most importantly—willing to pay double fees was in Applethwaite's view entitled to some special consideration.

"When Mowatt comes up, have him take this lady. And then run straightway down to Noakes. He can take that other gentleman, 'twill be only a slight delay."

Very satisfied with his evening so far, Applethwaite retreated to his bench in the corner. The barmaid brought him another pint, and he relit his pipe. He heard the carriage moving off, and Pete dashed in, caught his eye and nodded, and then dashed out again. Applethwaite applied himself to his pint and considered this flurry of business. Odd to have two men in one evening book passage to Sangatte. The area above Calais was a more normal destination. A second pint appeared and was duly consumed. He was thinking that he might not have any more clients that night when there was a commotion at the door. A tall, dark-haired young man had burst into the room and stood staring around like an eagle surveying its eyrie. He was soaked to the skin and quite handsome, but so fierce-looking that the barmaid shrank back instead of hurrying over to help him. The new arrival strode over to the tap.

"Have you seen a young gentleman with red hair? Perhaps asking for a Mr. Applethwaite?"

"He's upstairs, sir," said the innkeeper timidly. "Is he expecting you?"

"No," said the stranger grimly. He turned on his heel, went out the door, and reentered a moment later carrying a large cloth bundle. His teeth clenched, he started up the stairs. Then he paused, came back down, and went over to the tap again. "Could I ask you to see that we are not disturbed?" he said pleasantly to the innkeeper, handing him a coin of a color not frequently seen in the Blue Boar. Then he went back up the stairs.

Southey was sitting at a table, sealing up a large packet of papers, when Drayton came in and softly closed the door behind him. "Richard! What are you doing here?" he said, bewildered. "How did you find me?" Drayton did not answer; instead he dropped the peculiar bundle he had been carrying onto the floor and unwrapped it by the simple expedient of tugging violently upward on one end of the rug. The dueling swords fell onto the floor with a ringing crash. Drayton picked them up and tossed one to Southey, who caught it instinctively.

The long, wretched trip had muted Drayton's consciousness of the reason for his pursuit of Southey, but as he looked at the familiar hazel eyes, the boyish features, the freckles standing out against a sudden pallor, a cold fury welled up again. "Stand up, you sneaking bastard!" he said, spitting out the words. "Stand up and fight, you meddling matchmaker, you cowardly kidnapper! I had not realized that your friendship extended to choosing my brides for me. I am honored. It must have been a dreadful blow when you heard I had been unconscious in that hut. How poignant, too, that you eventually learned the truth, but only after being sworn to secrecy. And then—the ultimate irony! I am so very obliging as to offer for my designated bride after all, your path is clear to the dazzling Miranda, but no! She accepts the lowly Courthope. And now you have lost your bride, and your friend both. Get up, I say. The god of love may have had his revenge already, but I am waiting for mine."

"Richard—" said Southey, in a pleading tone.

"I am not interested in your excuses," Drayton interrupted savagely. "Please observe my consideration in bringing my own swords, by the way. And in choosing rapiers instead of pistols. So noisy, pistols, do you not agree? So inconvenient for private quarrels. They attract so much attention. While here we may be quite cozy with our swords."

"Richard," said Southey quietly, not rising, "I cannot fight you."

"Then I'll kill you where you sit," said Drayton fiercely.

"I cannot let you do that either," said Southey, looking haggard. "After I catch up with Nathanson you can do whatever you like with me, but I have to reach him. If you force me to defend myself, I will, and in a small space like this I will have a great advantage over you."

Drayton looked around. The room was barely ten paces long, and the ceiling sloped on one side. But he believed that for once Southey would not be the superior fencer. "Advantage be damned!" he said, raising the point of his sword and leveling it at Southey's chest. "Defend yourself, then, or I'll ruin your shirt."

Southey shook his head and did not move. "Don't soil your blade, Richard," he said bitterly. "The kidnapping is nothing."

"Nothing?" snarled Drayton. "You abuse me,

Barrett, Miss Meyer, Miss Waite and Courthope, and call it nothing?'' But then the self-hatred in Southey's words forced itself into his consciousness; he lowered his weapon and stared in horror at his friend. ''What do you mean?'' he whispered. He already knew. It was so obvious, when he remembered the Spanish ''kidnappers,'' and the ostler's remark about his horse.

Southey's eyes were remote. ''I mean what you think I do. I have been selling information to the French. I thought I could outwit them, but Arnaut has caught me out. They're waiting for Nathanson at a boathouse near Sangatte. I'm going to try to find him before he reaches the rendezvous, and I pray to God I can do it. The man who is sailing me across should be here any minute.''

''It was you,'' said Drayton numbly. ''It was you all along. You were the traitor.''

Southey nodded.

''My God!'' said Drayton, leaning back against the door in anguish. ''South, how could you?'' His voice broke. ''You're the only person besides Harry I ever completely trusted, did you know that? When I saw you in that hospital, after I'd been wounded, it was like—it was as though I were a ship, reaching harbor. If someone had accused you of this, I would have defended you to my last breath, against every man in the king's uniform.''

''I know,'' said Southey faintly.

''But why, for the love of God? Why?''

Southey looked down at his hands and smoothed the hilt of the rapier. ''I was a fool. A desperate fool. My family was facing complete and utter ruin, Richard. That is no excuse for what I have done, but I thought—well, never mind.'' He pressed his fingers to his eyes briefly. ''When my father died, there were a lot of legal problems with the estate. For a few months I believed it could all be straightened out. But about eight months ago I discovered that it was even worse than it had first appeared."

He got up and began pacing back and forth next to the table. "I don't know how I could have failed to see it—the horses, the gambling, the women—those things all cost money. And yet there always seemed to be more for him to spend. The estate was prosperous, but not that prosperous. I finally learned the truth: He had hired some attorneys from Salisbury, some crooked swindlers who make their living giving people like my father what they want. And they managed to break the entail."

"What?" said Drayton, shocked.

"By the time he died, everything was mortgaged except the manor itself and the dower house. Everything. Not just my mother's and sister's holdings, which were not entailed, but my lands, as well. And the mortgages were due and overdue. The sale of both houses might have partially satisfied the creditors, but my mother and sister would have been left completely penniless at best and more probably we would all have been in Newgate. I went to the man who held most of the notes and begged for some time to arrange something for them. I didn't care for myself—I've never fancied the life of a country gentleman—but I could not bear the thought of Alice and my mother cast out of their home, in debtor's prison. For God's sake, Richard, Alice is still a schoolgirl!"

He paused. "I thought first of marrying an heiress. I began to court Miss Waite. She had always been friendly to me, and I thought, correctly, that my courtship would hold off the other creditors. Then an émigré approached me, very discreetly, to enquire if I might be willing to pass certain items on to the French, for a fee. It seemed like the answer to a prayer. I had always done well in school, you know that—examinations, lessons, everything came easily to me. I thought I could forge a few letters, give them the names of some of their own double agents. No one would be harmed, no one would be the wiser. And they pay well. Very, very well, Richard. I was earning more in a week than I would see in two years as an officer.

"Everything went smoothly at first, and I realized that if I could ever extricate myself I had a gold mine of information for White." He gestured to the sealed packet on the table. "I did get quite a bit, but I am not sure it is reliable, now. Arnaut took over at Lille, and Meillet replaced Jarron as my contact. He drew me on, asked me for names and documents which were harder and harder to falsify. At first I had convinced myself that I was actually acting in Whitehall's best interests—a private double agent, as it were. But once they got involved, it all changed. They seemed to know everything before I did it; they were always one step ahead. Meillet demanded that I give them information about Little Rover's movements in France. So I sent them a copy of a real letter, establishing a meeting, and then I changed the time of the meeting at the last minute. The French arrived and could see evidence that we had been there, but Nathanson and the French informant got away. Then he demanded that I try again.

"That was when I arranged the kidnapping. I was frantic to get out from under their thumb. I convinced myself that I was not really harming anyone—that you were, whether you recognized it yet or not, attracted to Miss Ross, as I then thought her. And everything went wrong—the French couriers were bunglers; they hurt you, they let Miss Meyer hear the plans; Miss Waite accepted Courthope; Meillet pressed me again for one more attempt to catch Nathanson."

"So now you tried the same scheme of switching the meetings, and this time it did not work," said Drayton harshly. His original expression of bewildered horror was giving way to one of disgust.

Southey began to laugh, a mirthless laugh which turned into a kind of gasping shudder. "You talked just now of irony. Would you like to know what went wrong? Nathanson and I set up the schedule. We sent off the carrier pigeons, and I told Arnaut's people where to 'find' one of them. At the last possible minute—as I thought—I changed the meeting place. And then *Nathanson changed it back.* He had become suspicious of me, with good reason, and the cursed fool changed it back. And now unless I can come up with him before he gets to that boathouse, I will have his life on my conscience along with everything else."

There was a knock at the door, and a boy's voice, calling that Mr. Noakes was waiting for the gentleman downstairs. Southey picked up the packet and his satchel and moved towards the door. Drayton stepped back and blocked his way, his sword raised.

"I can't let you go," he said coldly. "You're a confessed traitor. You must be mad to think I'll stand by and watch you board a boat for France."

"And Nathanson?" said Southey, his eyes flashing. "Your prospective brother, whose challenge you refused so courteously the other day? You won't fight him like a gentleman, but you'll let the French take him and execute him?"

Drayton bit his lip. "Give me your word"—he

looked rather contemptuous at this phrase—"such as it is, that you will remain here, and I will sail in your place," he said.

"And then what?" said Southey. "You have no idea where to go when you land—and they may put me ashore in one of several places, depending on weather, patrols, and tide. What is more, should you fail to come up with him, and find him already in French hands when you arrive, you can do nothing for him. I have met some of Arnaut's men; I know the passwords; they believe I am one of them. I may well be able to contrive something."

Drayton acknowledged the force of these arguments. "Very well," he said curtly, lowering his weapon. "But I am going with you. Not," he added, with a curl of his lip, "that I would seek your company if I had any choice in the matter. I have a pistol in my belt, by the way, in case you are thinking to sell me to the French as well. I would not bring in nearly as much as Nathanson, but money is money."

Southey flinched, his face white. Without answering, he opened the door. Drayton waved him through courteously. "Traitors first," he said.

Chapter Fifteen

Rachel paused at the top of the cliff and peered uncertainly down into the dark hollow below her. There was no moon, and it was very black. It had been a difficult climb up from the cove where she had landed, even in her boy's clothing; several times she had regretted ordering Samuels to stay behind. But he had suffered one of his dizzy spells on the boat and could barely walk; and she had been afraid he would collapse in some dangerous spot on the steep path. She had not been here for many years; her original confidence that she could find her way was deserting her. Patiently, she tried to let her eyes adjust, to distinguish the smoother darkness of the water from the jumbled shoreline, and find the square intrusion into the smoothness which represented the boathouse.

Perhaps she had made the wrong decision, coming up the cliff. The path along the beach, from the north, was easier, although she would have had to walk all the way around behind the headland to reach it. And it would have taken her much closer to the boathouse. But she had thought time was more important than safety, and now she was facing a dilemma. The path down the cliff was too difficult for her to attempt in the dark; unlike her father and brother, she did not see well at night. But she knew that at any moment James might be approaching from the other side of the cove, walking towards the boathouse in complete ignorance that the French lay concealed inside. She could shout, and draw out the men who were presumably waiting for her brother. Or she could play a more cautious game, and hope to hear or see something in time to warn James.

In the end, she elected to wait, at least for a bit. The climb had taken nearly two hours because she had had to feel her way by hand in many spots; at this time of year it should begin to grow light soon. At least, she thought, as she settled herself on her stomach looking down over the edge, it was so uncomfortable that she was unlikely to doze off. There was a faint gray cast to the sky when she saw something at last, a dim movement along the shore which resolved itself into an agile figure picking his way over the rocks. At first she thought it could not be James because the shape was wrong. Then she realized that he was probably carrying a rucksack. She pulled her whistle out from under her shirt. She would need to get this right: over the sound of the water, the whistle would be hard to hear until he was fairly close. But the shed—and the men inside—were closer still. She did not want to alert them unless James could hear the signal also.

The figure had slowed down perceptibly. She

was sure now that it was James, even though it was barely visible. He never approached a meeting place quickly; he was always prepared for trouble. This was the time, when his senses would be strained for any sign of something wrong, before he came past the outcropping onto the part of the beach visible from the boathouse. She put the whistle in her mouth and blew two notes, twice, as hard as she could. At once, she saw the figure stiffen and lift his head. An answering whistle came faintly up from the beach; he was loping carefully into the protection of the rocks. A moment later he had vanished, and Rachel was sobbing with relief.

Lanterns flared inside the boathouse, and three figures came running out. Behind her she heard a smothered exclamation. She twisted her head. A dimly seen form rose from a crouch and ran swiftly over the rise. The French guide, thought Rachel, glad he had not been trapped in the boat shed. She had been concentrating so hard on protecting James that she had forgotten that she too needed to retreat. Hastily she pushed herself up on her elbows and started to get up and move away from the edge. But she had been lying in one position too long; her right leg had gone to sleep. She slipped to her knees with a soft cry, and her foot dislodged a small stone. Aghast, she watched it bounce down the face of the cliff and land directly in front of the tallest figure. A shout, an oath in French, and he was pointing up the cliff; all three men were running, their lanterns bobbing up and down. It was growing lighter by the minute; a fourth man emerged from the boathouse and bent down over a dark shape. She heard a bark. He must have been slipping off the muzzle. They had a dog.

Why had she not thought they might have a dog?

she thought in despair as she hobbled back towards the path down the ridge. The French agents had had a dog last time she was here. Her leg was still not working, and she had lost track of which direction to go in order to find the top of the path. She could hear the men scrambling up the cliff and, far closer, the barking of the hound. There were no trees, only scrub and rock. Frantically, she slid down into a narrow gully and crept along, hoping that it would bring her down towards the path. There was a bark at the top of the gully, and she caught her first glimpse of her pursuer. It was not light enough to see color properly, but she thought it was a tan mastiff. It was running swiftly now along the edge of the gully. Now it was above her, barking ferociously and then growling. The gully had petered out; she had no place to go. She pressed herself against the rocks and watched as the dog leaped in slow motion and landed four feet away. Its hackles rising, it crouched, ready to spring.

I'm not afraid of dogs, Rachel said to herself. This is an animal just like Belinda and Bertha. I am in charge, dogs are friendly to humans. She put out her hand; the dog growled again and snapped. "Down, sir," she commanded sternly. Then her common sense reasserted itself. This was not Belinda or Bertha. There was nothing wrong with being afraid of it. This was an attack dog, and it was about to pin her down and rip open her flesh. She pulled out her pistol and fired just as the dog leaped for her arm.

"Good shot, Nathanson," said a voice from the top of the gully in French. "What a pity that you have only the one pistol. Or am I mistaken? No, I see that I am correct. Please do not bother to reload. I'm afraid that I have two." Rachel saw them gleaming against the brightening sky as she looked up. Slowly she lowered her weapon and spread out her hands in a gesture of surrender. He stood back, the pistols still trained on her, as she climbed back up to where he stood, immaculate in lace and fine woolens, his blond hair neatly tied back. Cold gray eyes looked into hers. Another man came running up and, at a nod from the first man, ran his hands along her coat looking for more weapons as she held her arms out from her sides. Then he gasped in shock and tore off her cap. Her hair was bound neatly on top of her head.

"*Nom de dieu,* Meillet," said the second man breathlessly. "It's a woman!"

"So I see," said the man with the pistols. He looked at her thoughtfully, and Rachel felt a chill run through her. "This becomes very interesting, does it not?" He placed the muzzle of one gun against her chest. "Where is Nathanson?" he demanded. "What was that whistle?"

"I warned him off," said Rachel wearily.

"How very romantic," said Meillet with a sneer. "Let us see if he will be equally romantic and come back to rescue you. Tie her hands," he ordered the other man. "Take her down to the boathouse. I hope she enjoys it as much as I did these past two hours. Lock her in, and keep a good watch for anyone approaching. I don't like this; it smells like one of Arnaut's tricks. I'm going down to the other hut to see if anyone is on duty there. I'll be back shortly." He started down towards the back side of the hill, and then turned. "Jarron, don't touch her. And don't let those other two even near the shed; they're animals. I suspect that she is very valuable, and I don't want her harmed. Yet."

* * *

Desperate to reach the cove quickly, Southey and Drayton took the risk of a lantern. They had come in at an inlet two miles north of the boathouse, and Southey, who had only been there twice before, knew that they could more than double their speed if he had some light. His main concern was to recognize the rock formation that guarded the cove, so that they could extinguish the lantern before it was seen. He was therefore slightly ahead of Drayton, peering up at the outline of the cliffs against the charcoal sky, when he heard the faint echo of a gunshot. A startled cry escaped him; the next moment he was suddenly seized from behind; a knee went into his back, and he found himself on the ground with a dagger at his throat. "Tell your friend back there to raise his hands and approach us slowly or you are a dead man," hissed his assailant in French.

"Drayton!" called Southey, forgetting momentarily that he was himself a French agent, "I'm taken, run for it!"

There was a disgusted exclamation from his captor. "For God's sake, Southey," said a well-known voice in English. "What is Drayton doing here? What was that shot? And how did you get down from that cliff so quickly after you whistled me off? I thought just now that you were a French agent, coming up to intercept me." Approaching at a run, Drayton held up the lantern and saw Nathanson sitting on top of Southey's shoulders, sheathing his dagger.

"An interesting surmise," Drayton drawled, overhearing the last phrase. "And not far from the truth. Don't let him up, Nathanson. Now that we know you're safe, he's under arrest. He's been selling information to the French. Mostly false, but the money was real enough. You almost walked into a trap just now. He was juggling too many balls and let one slip."

Nathanson shot a glance at Southey. "So I was right," he said slowly. "You could have come to me, you know. At the very least you might have realized that rumors of financial difficulties would reach me fairly quickly through my uncle."

Southey had rolled over onto his back and was staring up at the cliffs. Straight up from the beach they rose, gray and rugged, notched with scars from the unending attack of the water. His face was bleak. Then he sat up suddenly. "What whistle?" he said. "Drayton and I just arrived. Did you actually go to the boathouse?"

Nathanson frowned. "Yes, I was nearly there when someone signaled with our whistle code and warned me off. I was on my way back and heard you blundering up the shore like a quarry gang." Southey flushed. This was a sore point; he had always suspected that he had been given the liaison job in London because he did not have the same tracking skills as some of the more experienced couriers.

"We did not signal," he said. "It must have been Silvio."

"Silvio stayed in London," said Nathanson, looking worried. "I asked him to check on something I heard about a Spanish delegation to the Regent. Who else knew that I had changed the rendezvous?"

"Lawrence," said Southey absently. "I sent him to your house, to try to stop you before you left this afternoon."

"Lawrence does not know the whistle code," said Nathanson impatiently.

"Rachel," whispered Drayton. "Rachel. She found out from Lawrence, I'll wager. God in heaven, it's her." He started to run down the path. Dawn was breaking; silver streaks were visible in the east behind the massive towers of dark rock. As he came around the last outcropping, the top of the bluff above the boathouse was clearly visible. A slender figure was starting down the face of the cliff, hands behind its back. A second figure was walking warily in the rear, with what looked like a gun. Without thinking, Drayton rushed forward, only to be jerked to his knees. Nathanson had his hand over his mouth, and Southey had pinned his arms from behind. They looked at him grimly, and he lowered his head, contrite. Cautiously, the three retreated behind the rock tower once more.

"I'm sorry," said Drayton, dragging his hand over his eyes. "It was her, though, was it not?" Nathanson nodded. "Well, there are three of us—two at least," he amended harshly, looking at Southey. "How many men do you think the French have here, Nathanson?"

"Four or five," said Nathanson. "And they often have dogs; I thought I heard one a few minutes ago, in fact. But sound carries oddly around here. It will not be easy, now that it is getting light," he went on with a worried frown. "We picked this spot for a reason, you know. Anyone coming down the cliff is completely exposed and helpless while they are on the steep part of the path. And when you come around the corner here, into the cove, you are directly in the line of sight from the boathouse window. One man with a rifle could pick us off easily. You are lucky, Drayton, that we stopped you before you had completely emerged on the other side of the rock. We may have to wait until dark to go in after her."

"And leave her in their hands for fifteen hours?" snapped Drayton. "I think not."

"There is no need to use force to get her out," said Southey. "You are forgetting something. There are advantages to being a double agent, you know. I can walk right up to them, and they will shake my hand and offer me snuff."

"And how does that help us?" said Drayton contemptuously. "Do you think us so gullible that we will let you join your friends, and increase the odds against us?"

"Drayton, stop playing the fool," said Nathanson sternly. "This is no time for personal rancor. Southey is right, he can walk into the boathouse, and that is of enormous value to us in our situation. He has shown no signs of any desire to betray us; he could have been safe in London right now if he had not tried to rescue me from the consequences of his error. And when I surprised him back there on the path, and he thought me a French sentry, his first thought was to save you. If he has a scheme to get my sister out of that boathouse without risking all our lives, including hers, let us hear it."

"I don't know if it would work," said Southey. "But it seems fairly obvious. I go in, I find some excuse to send any other guards out, and then I come out. Only it is Rachel, not me, who comes out. She is tall for a girl. And I am no great height."

"You are jesting, surely," said Drayton. "They would spot her in a moment."

"Not necessarily," said Nathanson thoughtfully. "People see what they expect to see."

"And their expectations will convert dark hair to red?" said Drayton in a cutting tone.

Southey smiled, the first smile Drayton had seen on his face since they had left. He reached into his jacket and pulled out an odd, bristling lump. "I found my auburn locks a bit conspicuous when I visited the continent," he said dryly. "My colleagues here believe me to have brown hair." And he held up a neatly folded wig.

In the end, it was Nathanson who delayed and argued. Drayton had capitulated at once; the thought of Rachel in that boathouse was suffocating him. But, he was to learn, Nathanson in the field was a very different article from the impetuous young man he had seen in London. Calmly, he made Southey answer questions about every possible contingency. They discussed Rachel's exit route, signals to summon the two who would remain hidden, even which articles of Southey's clothing Rachel did and did not need to wear.

"Who is likely to be here?" said Nathanson. "Meillet and his crew?"

Southey nodded. "This is their area," he said. "When I sent the message with the false information—well, I suppose it was not false this time," he corrected—"when I sent that message, I sent it to a man who normally reports directly to Meillet."

"He's an ugly customer," said Nathanson. "I think before you make your appearance I had best look around a bit." To Drayton's astonishment, Southey nodded, and Nathanson rose from his seat on a lichen-covered rock, took off his jacket, and pulled on a gray smock which he had taken out of his rucksack. In another minute he had sprinted over to the base of the rock tower and was climbing lightly up the side. Then he vanished. Bewildered, Drayton scanned the landscape of boulders and gravel. He could not see Nathanson anywhere.

"Incredible, isn't he?" said Southey. Drayton did not reply, and Southey turned his face away and did not speak again. Twenty minutes later, Nathanson materialized.

"There appear to be three of them outside, as near as I can tell," he said. "Two rather loutish types, very heavy, young, and one older fellow with a gray mustache. The older man is watching the cliff face; the younger ones are lounging by the wall of the boathouse. They are probably supposed to be guarding this path, though. I didn't see anyone else, but someone might be inside with my sister. I had to stay rather far away, of course, so I cannot be sure of anything."

"The one with the mustache is Jarron," said Southey. "The other two are likely a pair of brothers, real filth, whom Meillet uses for rough work. If they are outside that is good news for Miss Meyer. Jarron is not a bad sort, but Meillet dominates him completely. Meillet may have gone off somewhere; he has a lookout site he supervises a few miles away on top of the cliffs. I would be very surprised if he were in the boathouse; it is foul in there and he is extremely fastidious."

Nathanson nodded. "I think your prospects are quite good," he said.

"Well, then," said Southey, standing up and adjusting a slouch hat over his wig, "I'm off. Keep an ear out for my signal in case there is trouble."

Drayton suddenly realized that in all the detailed planning one topic had never been mentioned. "South," he said suddenly, inadvertently using the old nickname, "how are you going to get back out?" The other two looked at him in silent pity, as grownups regard a child who has been trying unsuccessfully to follow a difficult conversation.

"Why would I want to, Richard?" said Southey gently. "I did think, for a while, that the proper course would be to turn myself in. I wrote down everything I could remember in that packet I sent off to White from Dover, but there might be things that I omitted that our investigators could, shall we say, persuade me to recall. I suppose I am a coward, really. I couldn't face it, and most especially I couldn't face seeing White once he knew what I had done. The man has been like a father to me, you can't know—" Tears were burning the back of his eyes. Then he mastered himself. "My job is to make them think Miss Meyer is still in there, for as long as possible, so that you are not pursued once she leaves. And when I am discovered, I will be much happier with my gun than I would be with a hangman's noose in England." He turned to Nathanson. "My apologies, Nathanson," he said. "You deserved a better colleague."

Awkwardly, Nathanson put out his hand, and Southey clasped it gratefully. He looked at Drayton. "Richard," he said in a low voice, "I hope you will be able to forgive me someday. I shall never forgive myself, you can be sure of that. I ask you for nothing on my own account, but for the sake of our old friendship, I beg you to make sure that my mother and sister do not suffer for what I have done any more than is unavoidable. I know that legally they are not entitled to the monies I was paid by the French, and I have written as much to White, but I am almost certain that he will not take any action against them. If I am wrong, though—"

"I will look out for them, you have my word on it," said Drayton stiffly. He did not move towards Southey, or extend his hand.

Southey looked at him for a long moment, then turned and walked away towards the cove. Drayton sank down onto his rocky seat and put his head in his hands.

"You are too hard on him," said Nathanson fiercely. "I have only known him for a year, and you have known him for more than ten times that long, but he is a good man. He deceived us all, it is true, but he was never a real traitor. He was simply trying to protect his family. And he has not hesitated for an instant to do his best to set things right, at a price few men would be willing to pay. What more can he do? Are you made of such fine stuff that your friends must be faultless?"

"You are right," said Drayton. He felt himself trembling. "You are right, but it is too late now."

Originally, the boathouse had been a single long shed: a wooden-floored entry from the shore side, leading to a sloping stone ramp enclosed on both sides by stone walls, with double doors opening out onto the water's edge, the whole roofed over with a wooden frame. At some point an interior partition had been constructed between the entryway and the stone boat ramp, with a low door allowing passage in between. That door was now nailed shut. Rachel sat on a crude bench in the small wooden-floored room, her hands still tied behind her, and tried to hold her breath against the odor of rotting fish, rotting wood, rancid oil, and rodent droppings. There was a window, facing north, but it was shut. Except for the bench she sat on, and a few splintered boxes, there was nothing else in the room.

It was very quiet; she was exhausted and terrified. She leaned back against the plank wall and closed her eyes. It had not occurred to her that in a state of such anxiety she would actually be able to fall asleep, but she must have done so, because she was startled awake by the sound of the door opening. Light washed across the threshold; it was full day now. Two men entered—the mustached Frenchman who had taken her down the cliff and a second man. Rachel blinked, and looked again. It was Michael Southey, she was sure of it, although something looked odd about him.

"Here she is, Captain Southey," said Jarron in French. He pronounced the name *Sow-tay*. "Do you recognize her?"

Any chance Southey might have had to pretend that he did not was ruined at once by Rachel's reaction to this question. She dragged herself to her feet, struggling to keep her balance as she rose with her hands behind her and looked straight at Southey.

"You filthy traitor!" she said with contempt. "Thank God Miranda Waite would have none of you."

The recipient of these remarks looked astonished; then he removed his hat and bowed politely. Now Rachel could see what was wrong: he must have dyed his hair. It was brown.

"Your servant, Miss Ross," he said in English. He turned to Jarron. "I do indeed recognize her, but I confess I am mystified as to why she is here. She is a Mademoiselle Ross, the governess at an estate which borders my lands in Kent. I presume that was a cover for her real activities, but I have met her several times and had no suspicion she was other than what she seemed. Where did you find her? What happened to Nathanson?"

"As I told you, monsieur, she whistled some signal; we heard an answer but could not find anyone else. Presumably she warned Nathanson away. Meillet caught her up at the top of the cliff path."

"Where is he, then?" said Southey casually. "I had thought he would be in here guarding Mademoiselle Ross."

Jarron spat. "Meillet? He would not stay longer than two minutes inside here, now that the trap is sprung, monsieur. When we were waiting for Nathanson he had his kerchief to his face the entire time. Pah! This is no work for the queasy, I think, but Arnaut is still using him. Perhaps not for long; I have heard rumors that Arnaut is not pleased with some recent events." Jarron meant the earlier incident, when the raiding party had arrived too late to intercept Nathanson. "He has gone over to the lookout, to see if he can bring more men back here. I fancy he means to take the mademoiselle to Lille and wishes to leave a guard here, to intercept any rescue attempts."

"Have you searched her?" asked Southey.

"She had a pistol, which is no longer loaded, and a dagger." Jarron held up the latter, which he had jammed into his belt.

"Papers?"

Jarron was silent and fidgeted uncomfortably. "Meillet did not want her disturbed, at present."

"Did not want her disturbed? What on earth do you mean?"

"He said that—he ordered us not to touch her."

"For the love of God, Jarron, she could be carrying all manner of documents which might require urgent action! Are you a total imbecile? What he meant, I am certain, is that you should keep Jean-Luc and his pig of a brother away from her. But if you are afraid of Meillet, I'll take the consequences. Go out and find Jean-Luc, in case I discover anything. I'll search her myself." Rachel went white and shrank back against the wall.

Anxious, Jarron nodded and went out, closing the door. Rachel could hear him walk around the side of the building; Southey came over and pulled open the shutters. "We'll need some light," he said brusquely. Now she could see the Frenchman heading down towards the northern edge of the beach. The fresh air tasted wonderful; she stood for a minute simply breathing. Then she turned to Southey, her eyes flashing. To her surprise he pulled out a knife, whirled her around, and sawed neatly through the thongs that bound her hands. Then he sat down on the bench and was tugging at his boots.

"Miss Meyer," he said, "you must put on my clothing, or at least the hat, jacket, and boots, and you must make haste. Jarron might come back in, or Meillet could return at any moment. Take off your jacket and boots. I know my boots will be too big for you," he continued as he pulled them off, "but the difference is too noticeable, you will have to manage." Southey's boots were glossy black Hessians, taller and far darker in color than Rachel's, which were an old pair of James's riding boots from his schoolboy days. Southey was taking off his stockings now, and stuffing them into the toes of the boots. "Do you by any chance have something written on you? A note, a letter of credit, anything? I might be able to use it as a pretext to get rid of one of the guards."

"I don't understand," said Rachel, bewildered. "When you came in with Jarron I thought—"

"So does he," said Southey dryly. "I would prefer that he not discover that I am here to rescue you until you are actually rescued, so I shall ask you to set modesty aside and put my things on as quickly as you can." Obediently, Rachel took off her jacket and boots. She inserted her feet into Southey's boots; they were still too large, but not obviously so.

"Oh!" she said, remembering. "I do have a piece of paper with something written on it." She reached down inside her shirt and extracted a much-creased scrap. Southey took it and scanned it. It was four lines of verse, in French, with six apparently random words shakily underlined in ink.

"What is it?" he said, baffled.

Rachel blushed. "It's a poem—part of a poem. Captain Drayton wrote it out for Caroline, in our French lesson, and she underlined the words she did not know."

Southey looked at her thoughtfully. Then his mind returned to their dilemma. "This may do very well," he said. He had started to shrug out of his jacket, but now he put it back on, and leaned out the window.

"Jarron! Hi, Jarron!" he called. The older man came hurrying up from the beach. "Here," Southey said, handing him the paper. "Can you make anything of this? It's some kind of code, clearly." Jarron took it and looked at it for a minute, then shook his head. "Someone should take it in to Lille, to Arnaut, right away," said Southey crisply. "Did you get Jean-Luc?" Jarron gestured farther down the beach, where a stout young man was puffing up the path over the rocks. "Send him off with this, then—wait, perhaps he should go up the cliff, so that he can catch Meillet as he returns. I'm going back up towards Calais, so you can stand guard here and put Martin at the foot of the cliff. If I see anything on the beach path, I'll double back here." Jarron nodded, took the paper, and trotted off towards Jean-Luc, waving it.

"That man will do anything anyone tells him," Southey muttered, stripping off his jacket again. "Such folk are dangerous." He took a critical look at Rachel after she had donned the jacket. "Here, try the hat." He shook his head. "Your hair is too dark; you'll have to have my wig. I'm delighted to make you a present of it; it's hot and scratchy." He adjusted the wig quickly and put the hat back on her head, then nodded to himself and pushed the shutters closed.

"Go now, quickly, but do not look as though you are hurrying," he said. "Take the path you just saw Jean-Luc—that gross young man—leave. About five hundred yards down the path, the cliff has a triangular fissure running up it from below. Drayton and your brother are waiting there for you." She started, he saw, at the sound of Drayton's name. Slipping over to the door, he eased it open a crack. "Wait until I tell you to go and then leave." His eyes on Jarron and Jean-Luc, he said without turning around, "Does Drayton know you kept that poem?"

"No," said Rachel softly.

Southey turned and studied her face. "I had thought this romance a bit more one-sided than it now appears to be," he said carefully. "I suppose I am hardly in a position to give advice on matters of the heart, but I should tell you that if your reluctance to marry Captain Drayton derives from a fear that he will be cut off by his family, your scruples are groundless. Drayton and his father are long estranged, his older brother died in Spain, and I am quite sure that the Barretts would eventually be reconciled to the match. As for Caroline and William, they would be overjoyed." He did not wait for her reply, but turned back to his vigil. A few seconds later, he beckoned urgently.

"Wait!" said Rachel. "How are you going to leave, with no boots? And what will happen when they see I am gone?"

"Oh, Meillet and I have an arrangement," Southey said easily. "He owes me a debt, and I intend to collect. Go on then, while Jarron is still up at the base of the cliff with Jean-Luc and his brother."

Rachel moved to the door, peered around, and straightened up. Then she turned suddenly and pressed Southey's hand. "Thank you," she whispered. "Thank you for the advice, and the rescue, both." The next moment she was gone, and Southey could not resist opening the shutters just a crack to watch her stride away. She remembered to walk like a boy, he thought, impressed. Two minutes later, she had rounded the corner and was out of sight behind the great pier of rock which rose from the northern edge of the beach. Southey sank down onto the bench with a sigh of relief. Only then did he realize that he had forgotten to take his pistol and knife out of the pocket of his jacket. Desperately, he picked up Rachel's coat and pawed through it. A brief flare of hope as he discovered her weapon was dashed immediately: as Jarron had said, it was no longer loaded. With a sigh, he folded the jacket into a rough pillow.

"Time for a change of plans, Michael, old boy," he muttered. He stretched out on the floor, tucked the folded jacket under his head, and waited for Meillet to return.

Chapter Sixteen

It was bitterly cold in the shade of the damp rocks, although out on the water the sunshine was beginning to glitter on the whitecaps. Drayton hunched inside his coat and nibbled absentmindedly on a piece of dry bread. Nathanson had insisted that he eat something, pointing out, quite reasonably, that they might have to move fairly quickly once Rachel emerged. His eyes went constantly to the farthest edge of the rock face, where the path from the boathouse emerged. Nothing was stirring.

Nathanson was sorting out the various items in his rucksack and repacking them. He avoided looking at the path, Drayton noticed, but his face was taut, and there was a mechanical quality to the repacking. "It's too soon," Nathanson said, not looking up. "He has to talk his way in to see her, and change clothes, and then she must wait for a good moment to leave."

"I can't stand this," said Drayton weakly. "I've been in combat for almost a year now, and this is more terrible than anything—well, almost anything," he corrected, remembering the dreadful sight of Harry's cavalry troop being hacked down by the French infantry.

"Rachel is not good at waiting, either," commented Nathanson, packing some ammunition and powder back into an oilcloth bag. He deposited the bag very carefully in a side pocket of the rucksack and laced it up. "But, in fact, waiting is what couriers do best. At least good ones. It is certainly what we do most often. My father taught himself to fall asleep and wake again in fifteen minutes so as to make good use of all the hours he spends lying hidden."

Birds were wheeling overhead; the water danced and rippled. Illogically, Drayton resented the beauty of the scene. It was a distraction, and although part of him longed to have something else to engage his attention, part of him seemed to believe that if his concentration strayed at all, some kind of lifeline linking Rachel to safety would snap. A movement at the far edge of the path caught his eye. Straining, he tried to focus better. It was nothing; his eyes were playing tricks on him. He gave up and closed them. The metal rings on the rucksack were making little clanking noises as Nathanson shoved his spare clothing back inside it.

"Someone's coming," said Nathanson calmly.

Drayton's eyes flew open. A figure had come around the point of rock and was walking slowly down the path towards their hiding place. Squinting, he tried to see better. It was becoming difficult to look out of the shadows under the cliff into the brighter light of the morning. The figure was limping slightly. It grew closer; he could see more clearly. With a groan, he said, "It's Southey. He must not have been able to get inside the boathouse. Or they have already taken her away."

Nathanson had abandoned his pretense of calm patience and was staring intently down the path. Then a broad smile spread over his face. "Look again," he said. "Look again, enamored one. A fine lover, who cannot recognize his own maid! What will you give me not to tell her you thought she was Southey?"

"You can tell her anything you like," said Drayton, a wild joy flooding him. His face was burning. "You can tell her I thought she was Napoleon and almost shot her." He stood up. "You can tell her that if she ever does anything like this again, I *will* shoot her. You can tell her that she is now hopelessly compromised, and if she doesn't marry me she will have to marry Meillet."

"Tell her yourself," said Nathanson. "I may withdraw my approval for your courtship if you do not show more enterprise, sir suitor. Rescued from dire peril, your damsel approaches, and you stand there gawking."

Drayton swung around and looked at Nathanson. "Have you changed your mind, then?" he asked, astonished.

"I suppose so, for what it is worth," said Nathanson. "Which is not much, since my uncle and my father are unlikely to agree."

"It is worth a great deal to me, whether she ends by accepting me or not," said Drayton gravely. Then he grinned. "I have given her my word that I will not propose to her again without her permission," he said, his tone casual.

"Go ask her permission," said Nathanson. "This might be a propitious moment. I fancy that she will find you rather a refreshing sight after Meillet."

But, in fact, Drayton said nothing, only moved out into the path and stood in silence as Rachel walked up in a state of exhausted happiness and relief. He was watching her face closely, shadowed though it was under the stained hat, and he saw the quiet brightness spread over her features as she saw him waiting for her.

Rachel felt her fatigue drop away at the sight of that familiar tall figure. She abandoned decorum and prudence; she was running, so eager to reach him that she kept tripping over the toes of Southey's boots, and he was catching her, and embracing her so ardently that she gasped for breath. Tearing off the hat and wig, he kissed her hair and ran his fingers through it. Then he cupped her face, but drew back, his hands on her shoulders, and looked at her with a question in his eyes. The chivalrous fool, she thought helplessly. He remembered to ask me, this time, and I should say no. It was beyond her to meet this particular obligation, she decided.

"Just this once," she said desperately. "I cannot marry you, but just this once."

He gave an odd little smile, pulled her closer, and set out to make the best of his one chance. For a moment time stood still: she could hear the noise of the water on the rocks and see brightness behind her closed eyes, and somehow those sensations became entangled with the others, so that she felt as though she were swimming in a sunbeam. Then cold air washed over her face and she opened her eyes. He had suddenly drawn away, looking rather startled.

"You kissed me," he said sheepishly. "I wasn't expecting . . ." His voice died away.

"It is customary," she said tartly, "for young ladies who have agreed to be kissed to participate. Or are you quite out of the habit of obtaining consent first?"

"Does that count as my once?" he asked humbly, ignoring her question.

"No," she whispered. "No, I think not."

"And precisely what does she imagine she is going to do if she does not marry him, after that?" muttered Nathanson as he turned politely away to avoid seeing any more; one glimpse of that kiss had more than convinced him that Rachel's heart was irreparably given. "A fine pickle she is in now, my wise, cautious sister."

French patrols might be anywhere, Nathanson warned, and they moved very cautiously as they worked their way back to the hollow where Rachel had left Samuels. There was no reason to hurry, after all; the boat could not come in to pick them up before darkness fell. Until Southey's ruse was discovered no one from Meillet's group would be searching for them, but anyone moving about near the coast was liable to be stopped and questioned by troopers, whether there had been an alarm raised or not. Best was not to be seen at all, by anyone. Drayton knew Nathanson could have moved more quickly and more safely without him; he seemed always to be accidentally straying out into the light, or stepping on twigs which cracked so loudly that he flinched.

The morning was half gone when they found Samuels, watching anxiously from a makeshift couch under a gorse bush. He stood eagerly, if a bit shakily, as they approached. "Miss Rachel!" he said, beaming. "And Master James, safe and sound. Lord be praised! Captain Drayton, if you had aught to do with this, I would be honored to shake your hand, sir." And he pumped it energetically.

"Are you recovered, Samuels?" asked Nathanson. "I gather you were ill on the boat. We must get on down the coast; my man is coming in tonight about ten miles south of where he landed me this morning. This neighborhood will shortly become rather unhealthy for anyone wearing Captain Southey's clothing."

Samuels was bewildered. "Captain Southey? Is he here then, as well, Master James?"

"He took Miss Meyer's place in a shed where the French were holding her," said Drayton tersely, "and they exchanged clothing. Once they find him there, they will undoubtedly circulate a description of what he was wearing when he arrived."

It was Rachel's turn to be bewildered. "But he is leaving also, is he not? He told me he had an arrangement with Meillet. How will he find us, if we move too far down the coast?"

"He is dead by now, almost certainly, Rachel," said her brother gently. "He has been selling false information to the French without approval from Whitehall; a scaffold awaits him on both sides of the Channel. It was his idea to go and exchange identities with you, not ours," he added defensively as incredulous horror dawned in her eyes. "He told us he thought his pistol far preferable to a noose."

Wordlessly, Rachel reached into the pocket of

Southey's jacket and pulled out a pistol and a small knife. She held them out so that they could see them clearly, her hands shaking. "He has my gun," she said faintly. "It's still in my coat pocket. But I fired it. It's unloaded. That is why they didn't take it away."

"God, no," whispered Drayton. "Please, no. Are you certain, Rachel? He didn't have a second pistol?" She shook her head. He had known the answer already; Southey hated guns. It was surprising he had even had the one.

"We were in our shirts and breeches," she said. "He had nothing when I left. Not even shoes. Mine did not fit him. He was barefoot." She was crying.

"I'm going back," said Drayton with sudden decision. "There must be something I can do. They won't be expecting anyone to return, now. I can't leave him there for the French to interrogate; he knows too much. You go on without me, and if I can I will meet you tonight. Where will the boat come in?"

"You still haven't gotten over being deceived by him, have you, Drayton?" said Nathanson coldly. "What are you afraid of, that he'll send them after you? That he'll talk?"

"No," said Drayton, his jaw set. "That he won't. Were he a less valuable prisoner, they might be willing to put him to the question for a few hours and then kill him. But South is too important; he's White's right-hand man. They'll keep at it until he cracks, and I know him. It will take days." He swallowed and said in a low voice, "He's had some practice. His father used to beat him for over an hour, sometimes." He gave Rachel a pleading look. "I'm sorry," he said, "but you understand, don't you? I have to go back. I can't bear it, I couldn't live with myself if I didn't." Slowly, she nodded.

"Very well," said Nathanson, after a pause. "I will go with you."

"Then I am coming also," said Rachel, lifting her chin.

Drayton and Nathanson spoke simultaneously: "No."

Nathanson raised one eyebrow and looked at Drayton. "I find you more acceptable as a brother-in-law every minute," he observed. "Samuels, take my sister to the caves above the old pier north of Gris-Nez. Do you have food and water?" The groom nodded. "We will meet you there at sundown. Stay completely hidden, and if we are not back by sundown, watch for Master Robey. His boat will come partway in, light a lantern, and then row back out. Flash your own lantern four times, and he will come in for you."

"May I ask what right you have to dismiss me so?" said Rachel, incensed. She was looking at her brother, but it was Drayton who answered.

"I am a captain, Rachel," he said, "and your brother only a lieutenant, but I am putting myself under his orders. He is the expert here; we are a danger to him, all three of us. You are ill-shod and exhausted; Samuels may collapse again. It is lunacy for either one of you to go back up to the top of that cliff. Moreover, it will take you longer to reach the caves than it will take us. You might seriously delay us if you do not start out now." Rachel lowered her head; her anger was giving way to a dull ache of grief. He was right, and she knew it. "You have done more than your share already, after all," said Drayton with a smile. "Your brother might well be dead now had you not signaled him in time."

"I will hold you to that, you know, Drayton," said Nathanson, looking at him intently. "You will obey my orders? Without question? And not interfere with me?"

"I swear it," said Drayton. "Unless you order me to walk silently through the brush. I cannot promise something I am incapable of performing."

"Oh, I don't know," said Nathanson, to Drayton's surprise. "You are really not so bad, for an amateur."

They reached the top of the bluff above the boathouse without much difficulty, and Nathanson dropped onto the ground and wormed his way cautiously to the edge. After a moment, he beckoned to Drayton, who imitated his example. The boathouse sat in crooked splendor at the edge of the cove, with its elegant frame of rocks at either end. In front of the door to the boathouse, he could see three figures: two standing, one on the ground. Three more men, in uniform, were visible in a rough perimeter around the boathouse; sentries, presumably. One was standing almost directly beneath them. Nathanson took out a pair of field glasses and scanned the scene below intently. Then he pushed himself quietly backward until it was safe to rise to his knees and withdrew to a small outcropping. Drayton followed.

"Southey is on the ground by the door of the shed," said Nathanson very quietly. "Meillet is with Southey, along with the man called Jarron; others might be on the side of the boathouse we cannot see from here. For example, I do not see the two brothers who were here this morning. Meillet has brought some soldiers back with him, obviously. If we are lucky, there are no more than those now visible, plus perhaps the brothers."

"Could you see anything of his injuries? Is he badly hurt?" asked Drayton, dreading the answer.

"I could not see much, no," said Nathanson curtly. "There was some blood on his face, and quite a bit on his shirt. They are probably planning to take him to Lille, you know; this is just an hors d'oeuvre. We are lucky he is still here; I thought they might move him immediately."

"Was he—" Drayton started to say, but Nathanson made an imperative gesture. Holding very still, Drayton heard footsteps coming over the top of the hill behind them. Barely moving his head, Nathanson indicated that they should slide back into the shadow of a boulder. A moment later, a very stout young man came trudging down the path, sweating profusely and muttering to himself. Without making a sound, Nathanson had slid around behind him, and just as he reached the boulder, Drayton stood and stepped out in front of him. He opened his mouth to cry out, but it was too late. Nathanson's arm was around his neck, and Drayton's dagger in his stomach.

"Good," said Nathanson to Drayton, as though he were teaching a boxing lesson. "Never use pistols when you may not be able to fire them without endangering your purpose. There is a ridiculous fondness for firearms these days, but what good would it do to threaten this oaf with a pistol when he might be shrewd enough to realize that we could not use it? Then again," he said, considering the terrified young face of the Frenchman, "he might not be that shrewd. I think this is one of the brothers who was guarding the shed earlier this morning.

"Talk, *canaille*," he said in French, applying more pressure to the back of the man's neck. "Where were you? Who is down at the beach? What does Meillet want with our friend?" There was an incoherent babble in response. "Try again," said Nathanson grimly. "We will take it one question at a time. Where were you?"

"Calais," stammered the youth.

"Why?"

"To take a message from Monsieur Meillet, monsieur, to his cousin, who commands a troop there."

"Do you know what the message said?"

"No, monsieur."

"If I were Meillet, I would not tell you either," commented Nathanson. "How many men are down at the beach now?"

"Six, monsieur. Messieurs Meillet and Jarron, three troopers, and Monsieur Southey."

"Where is your brother, then? He is your brother, the other young man?"

"Yes, monsieur. Monsieur Southey sent him with a message to Lille. That was before we knew that he was a traitor." He spat with disgust after this last word, and Drayton pushed the knife slightly further into the paunch under the smock.

"Mind your manners, filth," he said sternly. "What will happen to our friend now?"

"Meillet waits for me to return, messieurs," gulped the Frenchman. "Then he will take the prisoner to Lille."

"What shall we do with him?" said Nathanson to Drayton in English. If he advised Nathanson to kill him, Drayton realized, he would do so. It was probably the right thing to do.

"Knock him out and tie him up somewhere out of the way," said Drayton, hating himself for his own squeamishness. This was war just as much as a cavalry charge, but somehow he could not bring himself to kill an unarmed boy, no matter how foul he might be. Nathanson nodded; then his elbow tightened slowly and the face above it turned blue. With a small belch, the youth collapsed.

"I hope I brought enough rope," muttered Nathanson, fishing down into the bottom of his knapsack. "Have you anything to use as a gag?" Drayton tore off his neckcloth, which at one point had been white but was now a soggy gray lump. "I should have made him walk over into the rocks before I knocked him out; he must weigh twenty stone," he added ruefully. "We'll have to drag him."

Once the Frenchman was safely bestowed, Nathanson and Drayton returned to the problem at hand. "Meillet will not wait much longer," said Nathanson. "Let me take a look and see what is happening down there." He returned a minute later, puzzled. "Southey is on his feet; something very odd is going on. If we cut down to the northernmost edge of the bluff we will be lower; I think we should risk it. It will be more difficult to get away if we are seen, and we will no longer be able to watch this path, but we may be able to hear something."

Five minutes later, they had crawled on their stomachs to another point on the edge of the bluff. Here the drop to the cove was only forty or fifty feet, and they had a better view of the front of the shed. Four people were there now: Southey, leaning against the wall; Meillet, Jarron, and a trooper. The trooper and Meillet were arguing; Drayton could not quite hear what they were saying. Jarron joined in. Meillet was getting angry, that much was clear. Then he said, loudly enough to be audible to the hidden listeners, "Enough! I am in charge here, for the moment. I will not damage him seriously, I promise you. He is said to be quite good; it will pass the time until Martin returns." Then Drayton understood what the argument had been about. Reluctantly, the soldier drew his sword and handed it to Meillet. The latter passed the weapon on to Jarron. Then he took off his jacket and drew his own sword. Southey had moved away from the wall and was talking urgently to Jarron, who nodded. Nathanson had the glass out and was studying the scene intently.

"Jarron is taking off his belt," he reported. "He's strapping Southey's arm to his side—my God, it's broken, and his hand as well, it's all black and swollen. What is Meillet about?"

"I surmise that he fancies himself as a swordsman," said Drayton. He spoke very quietly, as did Nathanson; they were much closer to the Frenchmen now. "He means to make Southey fight him. South is an extremely fine fencer, you know."

"With his right arm broken and bound to his side?" said Nathanson scornfully.

"Meillet has made a slight miscalculation," said Drayton thoughtfully. "That is, if he told his thugs specifically to go after South's right arm. He is left-handed."

Nathanson stared. "He is? But I have seen him write, and eat. He uses his right hand, does he not?"

"Yes," said Drayton. "He was forced to do so, at school. His handwriting is atrocious as a result. But he fences left-handed. It gives him an enormous advantage. Meillet is in for a surprise."

"Not much of one," said Nathanson. "I am not sure Southey can stay on his feet very long. But this gives us an opportunity, and perhaps we should take it."

"What do you mean?" said Drayton.

"Look," said Nathanson, gesturing. All three troopers, as well as Jarron, had gathered over towards the northern side of the small flat space on that side of the boathouse where Meillet and Southey now stood opposite each other. The soldiers were almost directly underneath the two Englishmen, and were watching the duelists with great interest. "I was not sure what we would be able to do once we arrived here. To be honest, I suspected we would have to shoot him ourselves, and I will still do it rather than let him be taken to Lille. But now I think we may be able to get him clean away. What we need is a diversion."

He wriggled his way back a few feet from the edge and reached for his rucksack, which he had leaned up against a rock. Then he took out a small pistol from his pocket, emptied the bullet out of the barrel, and began to pack it with powder from the oilskin bag.

"What are you doing?" asked Drayton, mystified. Nathanson gestured for silence. Drayton turned his attention back to the duel; the two men were circling each other now. Southey was stumbling on the gravel in his bare feet, but he was managing to keep Meillet facing towards the glitter of the water.

"Tell me when Southey begins to fail," said Nathanson as he wrestled with the gun. "This may not work, but if it does, I want to time it right. I can only afford to sacrifice one pistol."

"He is doing well," reported Drayton. "It is difficult for him to move properly, though; the stones are probably hurting his feet." Raising the glass, he saw traces of red on Southey's left heel, and bit his lip. It was a rather unconventional duel. Southey could not use his right hand to balance and was struggling against pain and exhaustion. He was fighting a purely defensive battle. Meillet was handicapped by his lack of experience with left-handed opponents, and by the necessity to avoid hurting Southey seriously. Drayton watched an endless series of thrusts and parries, trying to discern what Meillet had in mind. Then Meillet broke through Southey's guard briefly, and Drayton understood. He swore under his breath.

"What is it?" said Nathanson, binding something around the bottom of the gun. He reached into the rucksack again and took out two coils of rope. He secured them around the boulder behind him and began to tie knots at intervals in one of them.

"He's trying to cut him on the face. He wants to scar him. It's a very clever ploy, in a way. It forces South to defend high, which is not normal in a duel, and makes it more difficult to balance. And it will humiliate him terribly if Meillet succeeds. Nor does Meillet risk a fatal accident, with his blade that high. Lower, South might well run himself onto the sword deliberately, even if Meillet had not intended to kill him."

Nathanson crawled back over next to Drayton. "It's incredible that he's still moving, let alone defending that well," he whispered. "Look at his arm." Drayton picked up the glass and took one look, then shuddered and put it down. In the brief glimpse he had taken he had seen a huge purple lump protruding from Southey's arm just above Jarron's belt. Southey was concentrating grimly on keeping Meillet's blade away from his face. He did not riposte at all, except when it was necessary to complete the movement of a defensive parry. Meillet took advantage of this to land a sudden blow on the thigh; Southey ignored him and kept his blade high. He had begun to sway slightly.

"He can't last much longer," whispered Drayton, his throat tight. As he spoke, Southey sank to his knees and then collapsed completely, blood trickling down his leg.

"I'm ready, then," Nathanson whispered back. "Let us pray that this works, and that the soldiers forget that they were originally on guard in different spots. Once one of them runs off, I am hoping the others will follow automatically." He backed away from the edge again, and moved silently down to the lowest point on the bluff, where he was concealed by some shrubs. Then he stood up and, arcing his arm, threw the oddly wrapped pistol as hard as he could towards the rock chimney which guarded the entrance to the path up the beach. It sailed through the air and then hit the rock. They heard nothing.

"Peste!" swore Nathanson soundlessly. Then suddenly there were two explosions, one right after the other, from behind the stone spire. Instinctively, the three soldiers ran toward the water's edge, drawing their weapons as they went, and turned down the path, followed by Meillet. Only Jarron remained behind, bending over Southey. Nathanson had paid out his rope and was down the cliff in four seconds; he clubbed Jarron viciously on the back of the neck and looped the rope through the belt around Southey's arm. Then he waved imperiously to Drayton, who threw down the second rope, the one with the knots. Nathanson

started to climb, but shook his head and dropped once more to the ground. He raced over to the water and threw something white into it. Then he raced back and came up the knotted rope so fast that Drayton's jaw dropped. As he reached the top, he yanked it quickly up behind him.

"Hurry," gasped Nathanson. He was hauling on the other rope; Drayton ran to help him. "Thank heaven for that belt of Jarron's; it gave us an extra ten seconds. He's not that heavy with both of us lifting, but we must get him up before any of them come back around the corner."

They barely made it; they had just tumbled Southey's unconscious form over the edge when Meillet strode back up from the side of the shed and spotted Jarron lying on the ground. An urgent shout brought two of the soldiers racing around the corner. They began to search feverishly, and one of them spotted the white object floating in the water.

"What is it?" whispered Drayton, barely moving his lips, although he knew they were not easily audible from below.

"One of my shirts," whispered Nathanson in reply. "I thought they might be less inclined to deduce that we used a rope if we gave them something else to think about."

There was a faint groan, and Drayton whirled, placing his hand gently over Southey's mouth. Hazel eyes blinked open and looked at him in utter confusion, then closed again.

"Get him on his feet," said Nathanson, pulling a flask of brandy out of the rucksack and thrusting it at Drayton. He was stuffing the rope back into the top of the bag. "If we can just get him over to the back of the bluff, there are some woods on the other side. Now I wish Rachel were here. We're going to have to splint his arm, and I don't know how."

"Nathanson, how is he going to walk?" hissed Drayton, pointing to the soles of Southey's feet. They were a mass of bloody welts. "And he still has no shoes." Cursing, Nathanson dove back into the rucksack and thrust a wad of cloth at Drayton.

"Start bandaging," he grunted. "Let us hope our fat friend is still there up the hill. I'm sure he would be delighted to lend us his boots if I ask in just the right way."

Somehow they got Southey over the crest of the hill and took refuge in the scrubby wood on the east side. Drayton looked down at him with concern as he tightened a makeshift splint around the upper part of his arm. They had given up on his broken fingers, but between the two of them they had managed to partially straighten out the pieces of the large fracture above his elbow. The cut on his thigh, luckily, was only a graze.

"Now what?" whispered Southey, opening his eyes. His skin was tinged with gray, and sweat was trickling down his temples.

"Good question," said Drayton, realizing with sick horror that he might well find himself executing his friend after sparing Meillet's bully boy earlier.

"If I were a horse, you would shoot me," said Southey in a slightly stronger voice, producing a faint grin.

"What do you want us to do?" said Nathanson. He was sitting off to one side, looking at Drayton.

"Give me a pistol, first of all," said Southey, his

eyes closed again. Drayton went white, then pulled the pistol out of his belt and set it in Southey's left hand. "My thanks," said Southey weakly. "I'm not planning on using it immediately, but I had an opportunity in the shed to reconsider my dislike of firearms." He looked up at Drayton. "I didn't tell them anything, Richard," he said. "I only talk for money, you know."

"Don't say things like that," said Drayton, his eyes full of pain.

"I had a lot of time to think about what I wanted, when I realized I didn't have my knife or my pistol," Southey went on. "Once they put me in a proper cell, in Lille, I knew I would never be able to hold out. It wasn't so hard out there, with the ocean and the rocks to look at. Meillet should have worked on me inside the shed, but he hates the smell." He sat up a bit. "Give me some more of that brandy, would you?"

"Just a sip," warned Nathanson, passing the flask over to Drayton.

"I'm all right," said Southey, taking a pull. He was starting to regain his color. "Except for the arm and hand, they didn't hurt me too much. Meillet told the other fellow to be careful; I had to make it on my own two feet out to the road behind the hill so they could cart me off to Lille for the real thing. Where was I? Oh, yes. At any rate, it doesn't matter what I thought I wanted then; I didn't expect to have any choices at all any more. But of course, Meillet didn't expect me to live either, and he told me a great many things that he should not have, especially considering there was a trooper there with us." He took another small sip of brandy. "The man is the veriest fop; he kept adjusting his neckcloth while he was hitting me. It is all of a piece, I suppose, because the reason he was so indiscreet is that he could not resist boasting to me. At any rate, I am fairly certain that I ought to go back to England and turn myself in. White will want to talk with me personally about what Meillet said."

"What did he tell you?" asked Nathanson, suddenly very alert.

"Quite a bit," responded Southey. "For example, did you know that your father may be alive, Nathanson?"

"Yes. Not may be, is."

"Meillet was asking me about Miss Meyer, whom he called Miss Ross, and he suddenly started raving when he realized that some man in Lille he suspects of being a double agent resembles your sister. He sent off Martin to Calais to have his cousin bring a whole troop up and meet us on the road to Lille."

"We met Martin, on his way back," said Nathanson. "He is resting right now, just off the path up there."

"I see," said Southey. "Do you think this man is your father?"

"I am almost certain of it," said Nathanson. "Only four or five people know this, but he was not killed in Spain, although it was intended that everyone, even our people, should believe him to be dead. He went over to France and has been in Lille for some time. What I do not understand is why Meillet should take a troop from Calais when he has a whole garrison already in Lille. How difficult can it be to arrest one clerk?"

"That is something else I discovered," said Southey. "Jarron told me. Meillet and Arnaut hate each other. The old chief of intelligence in Lille was very lax, and Meillet was really in charge. Then

Arnaut arrived and cleaned house. Also, Meillet has a passionate loathing for deformity or disease of any kind, and Arnaut evidently has a twisted leg, or some such thing. I'll warrant Meillet wants a troop personally loyal to him, lest Arnaut somehow turns the situation to his advantage."

"I may have to go to Lille," muttered Nathanson.

"Are you mad?" demanded Drayton. "If Meillet noticed the resemblance between your sister and your father, what do you suppose will happen when he sees you?"

"We have some time," said Nathanson, ignoring him. "They will be wondering where Martin is, and searching for you," he said, looking at Southey. "Do you think you can walk eight miles?"

"Haul me up and we'll see," was the response. Southey took a few cautious steps and winced. "Lucky these boots are so big; my feet are swollen to twice their normal size, I think. I'll do for the moment. We will have to go slowly."

Drayton snorted. "You may rest easy. When Nathanson here is leading the way in enemy territory, *slow* is the watchword. They should call him Little Tortoise."

Chapter Seventeen

Nathanson was slightly in front, feeling out the easiest path for Southey, when he saw the footprints in the sand below them. "What on earth?" he muttered. "Wait here," he said to Drayton, who was holding up Southey with one hand and leaning on a rock with the other. Both men sank gratefully down, heedless of the sharp stones beneath them, the minute Nathanson had moved away.

"I didn't realize it was possible to move so slowly and expend so much effort simultaneously until I fell in with your couriers, South," said Drayton, exhausted. He pulled out a canteen and started to offer it to Southey, but observed just in time that the auburn head was nodding. It looked like an attractive option. He decided reluctantly that one of them had best stay awake. Already they had taken two detours to avoid other parties—one definitely a French troop, the other apparently fishermen. No point in taking chances.

He stared absently at the drawn face of his friend. The light eyelashes lay unmoving on the freckled cheeks; Southey looked very young and frail. He had not uttered a word of complaint since they had left the wood, although he had nearly passed out once. They must be close to the caves, Drayton thought, but this fact brought him no comfort. After the caves came the boat, and after the boat came England, and Southey would be arrested. He remembered, with a peculiar sense of recalling someone else's actions, that less than twenty-four hours earlier he had tried to kill the man who lay dozing beside him. Rachel's words came back to him, the despairing phrase she had uttered after his father had left the sickroom: "I don't know what to believe anymore. Everything is a muddle." He sipped the water slowly and waited.

Half an hour later, scanning the landscape around them mechanically, he sensed a movement next to him and saw that Southey was awake. Silently he passed him the water and watched the other man drink. "We're nearly there, I think," he said. "Not that I have a great fondness for caves, after my Spanish adventures."

"You won't care for these, I assure you," said Southey. "I've already had the pleasure once. They are very wet, and full of seaweed. The good news is that they are too wet for the smugglers, so we will probably have them to ourselves." He handed the water back to Drayton. "Why did you come back for me, Richard?" he asked abruptly. "Nathanson told me it was your idea." The hazel eyes looked at him steadily. A bruise was darkening beneath the skin on one cheek.

"I was afraid you would decide to play at being

a hero," said Drayton. "Most unsuitable, with those freckles and the red hair."

"Auburn," said Southey with dignity.

"Besides," said Drayton in a low voice, "I didn't say good-bye properly when you left before."

A shadow flickered across his shoulder, and Nathanson reappeared, scowling.

"What is it?" demanded Drayton, suddenly dreading that something had happened to Rachel. "Did you reach the cave? Have you seen them anywhere?"

"They are already there," said Nathanson, fuming. "But Samuels left footprints in the sand in at least half a dozen places, and Rachel never noticed. I tried to cover them, but damp sand holds prints very well, and the tide will not come back in for hours. Anyone with a trained eye will not be fooled for an instant."

"Then we should get there as quickly as possible," said Drayton, rising stiffly to his feet. "In case the artwork in the sand attracts visitors." Southey pushed up with his good arm, and Drayton bent down to give him a hand. He heard Nathanson draw in his breath and then felt a firm pressure on his shoulder, preventing him from straightening up.

"Soldiers," said Nathanson in a barely audible whisper. "Behind us. About half a mile away. At least ten of them."

"Hell and damnation," muttered Drayton. His eyes met Nathanson's. Both knew that Southey could not move quickly or unobtrusively at this point. "Can we remain here until dark?"

"No," said Nathanson. "They will spot you easily once they come across the inlet." He jerked his head towards the northeast, where a shallow creek ran out into the Channel around a sandbar. On this side of the sandbar was a slight rise, and Drayton realized that even from his crouch the top of the rise was clearly visible. "This is most inopportune," grumbled Nathanson. "I should be heading back to Lille. But first I will see you safely disposed."

"Another diversion?" said Drayton.

Nathanson nodded. "I'll draw them off," he said. "Can you and Southey reach the cave? Southey knows where it is, if he can stay awake."

"I'm awake," said Southey with a grimace. "The word *soldiers* had a most wondrous rousing effect." But Nathanson was already gone, and after a minute Drayton heard a shout and a distant gunshot.

"Don't worry about Nathanson," said Southey, gasping slightly as he put his weight back on his feet. "He'll lead them a merry dance." Then he dropped suddenly back down beside Drayton and said in a completely different tone of voice, "Did he leave the field glass?" He was opening the rucksack and fumbling around with his left hand inside it as he spoke. With a grunt he pulled out the instrument and cautiously rose to his knees, squinting off towards the rise. "I spoke too soon," he said, handing the glass to Drayton. "What do you see?"

Raising the lens to his eyes, Drayton scanned the rise. Four figures appeared in blurred outline; they appeared to be three troopers and a tall man with a cane. As he watched, the tall man gestured with his cane, and then limped rapidly towards the east. Swinging the glass over, Drayton could see eight troopers strung out in pursuit of something—Nathanson, presumably.

"Eleven soldiers; three on the rise and eight chasing our decoy; one tall man with a cane."

"It is the latter who commands my interest,"

said Southey, reaching for the glass and packing it awkwardly away. "I have never seen him, but I have very little doubt of his identity. It is Arnaut. The one man on this coast who is up to any trick Nathanson can devise. We had best be on our way. It would be a pity to waste our lovely decoy."

By going on their knees most of the way, they reached the approach to the cave without being spotted. Southey was drenched with sweat; he had been crawling one-handed, and Drayton had not always been able to help him. Drayton gave a sigh of relief as he saw the entrance; no sign of soldiers, no evidence of a struggle. He had started to gather himself for a dash to the mouth—the approach was a small, open stretch of beach—when he felt an iron hand reach out and pull him back with a jerk.

"You fool!" whispered Southey. "Do you want to get killed? They are likely on guard in there, and nervous as cats!" Drayton remembered then the whistle code Rodrigo had used in Spain. His blood ran cold at the thought of what might have happened had Southey not stopped him.

"Confound it," he said, shaken, "I'm just an ignorant cavalry captain. This courier business is for subtler heads than mine. You had best go first." Southey glanced around quickly, gave a low, two-note whistle, and hobbled with surprising rapidity to the dark hole in the rock. Drayton saw a small spray of water come up as he took the last few steps.

"Very wet indeed, it appears," he muttered. Then a cautious arm beckoned, and he sprinted across the strand with the rucksack and tumbled into the hillside. He landed on his side in a mass of gravel and seaweed, cursing as water soaked instantly into his breeches. The rucksack was rescued from a similar fate by an unseen hand at the last minute.

"I believe I will demand an apology for the remark about tortoises you made earlier, Drayton," drawled a haughty voice in the darkness. The effect was slightly spoiled by the panting breaths which the speaker could not quite suppress.

"Nathanson!" gasped Drayton. "We thought you miles away."

"As did the French," said Nathanson coolly. "Come farther in; we cannot have a light this close to the entrance." Farther back, Drayton could see a faint glow, and a wavering shadow as someone—Southey, presumably—preceded them toward the source of the light.

"Did South tell you that he believes the man commanding the soldiers to be Arnaut?"

"He did. I suspect he is correct. There is at least one commissioned officer among those troops, and I do not know any other civilian who would outrank a captain in this sector. I did not get a good look at him, however. He had a stick, but it might have been a walking stick rather than a cane."

Drayton shook his head and then realized that Nathanson could not see the movement. "No," he replied. "I got a good look with the glass. It is a cane, and he limps. A tall, gray-haired man."

"That is Arnaut," said Nathanson heavily. "I am sure of it. And he will see those footprints. One of us must keep watch here at the entrance." Drayton saw a brief gleam and realized that Nathanson had unsheathed his dagger.

"No gunshots?" guessed Drayton.

"If it is possible to avoid them," said Nathanson, moving back towards the opening. "It may not be." A soft footfall sounded from the back of the cave, and Drayton saw a dim but beloved form approaching them.

"Richard!" she called softly, and then corrected herself. "Captain Drayton, I mean. Are you unhurt?"

"My knees are bruised from crawling," he said ruefully. "But I think Southey requires more immediate attention than your brother or myself."

She had moved up beside him and, unthinking, he slipped his arm around her. For a moment she dropped her head onto his shoulder, and then she straightened and said in a calm tone, "Yes, Samuels is taking off the old splint now, and soaking it to soften it a bit. At least we have plenty of water, even if it is not drinkable. I must go back and try to redo that arm, and then if there is time I will see what I can do for his fingers. I came to see if you had James's rucksack; it has more bandages in it." Then she noticed the dagger, and her brother's tense stance.

"What is it?" she said. "James, I thought you told me you had lost your pursuers."

"I did," was the reply. "Unfortunately, Arnaut is commanding them, and I do not think him a man to take lightly. I would prefer to be ready for company, even if no guests arrive. It is many hours until full dark; in some ways we are lucky that they spotted us this early. My hope is that they will give up and move on before the boat comes in. Smugglers do not use this cave; the locals are unlikely to have pointed it out to Arnaut as a possible hideout, and it is very difficult to see it until one is directly opposite the mouth." He was trying to reassure her, Drayton realized. It apparently worked; she picked up the rucksack and moved off again towards the back of the cave.

Drayton and Nathanson took it in turns to watch the shore in front of the opening. It was cold, wet work; the sentry had to stand in several inches of water in order to get a reasonable view. Drayton's teeth began to chatter after only a few minutes. Even when Nathanson relieved him and he was able to dry off he shivered convulsively for several more minutes. On his third watch, as the sun was moving towards the western portion of the sky, Drayton saw with a sinking heart a tiny figure with a cane making his way slowly up the beach from the north, followed by six troopers. An urgent gesture brought Nathanson to his side.

"He's stopped," reported Drayton.

"So I see," said Nathanson. "I believe he is looking at a print of Samuels's right boot at this moment."

Drayton swore softly. Then he frowned, puzzled. "What the devil?" Arnaut had sent four of the troopers back in the direction from which they had come. Taking a slight risk, Drayton pushed his head a bit farther out and saw the four waving to five more, and gesturing that they should turn around. Arnaut and the two remaining troopers waited for a few minutes until they had moved off; Arnaut appeared to be pounding the sand with his cane. Then the three moved slowly but inexorably towards the stretch of beach which concealed the cave.

"Can you throw a knife?" asked Nathanson softly.

"No," said Drayton, his heart thudding in his chest. "Dare we shoot?"

"I think not," said Nathanson. "We will have to let them get very close. If it looks hopeless, we must run out and hope that they believe we are the only ones here. And—" He broke off. Arnaut had halted at the edge of the water, about fifty yards away. He was looking directly at the cave. Now he raised something to his eye, and the two men shrank back instinctively, although they knew the darkness protected them.

"He's seen it," said Drayton, a cold ache rising in his chest. More gestures with the cane, and then, to their surprise, the two soldiers unslung their rifles and stood at ease down by the water. Arnaut continued speaking and then turned and strode, alone, towards the mouth of the cave. When he reached the line of rocks where Drayton and Southey had lain concealed, he gave a short two-note whistle, and then proceeded onward.

"The arrogant swine!" whispered Nathanson. "Does he think us such fools? Meillet has given him the code after hearing Rachel this morning, that is obvious." He hefted the knife in his hand. Drayton watched the Frenchman limping onward, twenty yards away, now ten, apparently unconcerned. He had not drawn his pistol, nor his sword. This was sickening, Drayton thought. He was the enemy, yes, but he was walking on so confidently, with no weapon at hand. Think of Rachel, he told himself. Think of Southey, of what this man would be doing to him now in Lille. It was no use. He could see the features now, the gray hair, an arrogant face, eyebrows raised in curiosity as he neared the entrance, keen dark eyes, a clean-shaven chin. It was an intelligent face, an interesting face. He hardened his heart and turned away as Nathanson poised his arm and aimed.

Suddenly a dreadful recognition forced itself upon him, and with a shout he flung himself in front of Nathanson. It was too late; Nathanson could not stop the motion of his wrist. The dagger tore into Drayton's right hand and sliced open his palm; he sank into the salt puddle with a cry of pain. Arnaut already had his pistol drawn, the trigger cocked.

"You meddling idiot!" hissed Nathanson in savage despair. "I should have known better than to trust your promise to obey me! You have betrayed us all with your childish scruples!" Stumbling footsteps were running towards them; Rachel threw herself down next to Drayton, gasping in terror and trying to pry his fingers away from the blood welling up inside his other hand. Then she looked up at Arnaut. He stood calmly surveying them, framed in the late afternoon sun. He had lowered his pistol. Drayton felt her stiffen. She gasped out one word, so faint that he could not hear, and then she staggered to her feet and ran out of the cave, flinging herself at the Frenchman.

"Papa! Papa!" she sobbed, flying across the sand, throwing her arms around him, kissing his cheek over and over again. "They told me you were dead, I thought you were dead!" The man called Arnaut embraced her, smiling and soothing her in some language Drayton did not know. Then he looked over at Nathanson.

"I suppose I should be flattered that my disguise fooled even you," he said dryly. "Or were you concentrating so hard on your aim that you neglected to look at my face?" Then, seeing Nathanson's pallor and his trembling shoulders, he added gently, "I would have shot it out of your hand had this gentleman not anticipated me."

Southey spoke from behind them. "Mr. Meyer, may I present Captain Drayton? Drayton, Mr. Meyer is known to you by reputation at least. He is Rover."

Meyer bowed, as though introductions to gentlemen who knelt bleeding in tidepools were an everyday occurrence. "It is a great pleasure, Captain Drayton," he said formally. "I have heard something of you from Rodrigo. My apologies for leaving that survey unfinished; when the real Arnaut fell into our hands and proved to resemble me, it was too good an opportunity to let slip." He added, glancing sardonically at Nathanson, "You must tell me how it is that you recognized me more easily than my son, without ever having met me."

Drayton tried to rise but realized that he might not succeed. He compromised by dragging himself to the side of the puddle and leaning back against the side of the cave mouth. He looked up at Meyer and said with a rueful grin, "I am afraid, sir, that I have recently had the family features impressed upon me most forcefully. I mistook your son for Miss Meyer and so addressed him."

"Indeed?" said Meyer, glancing at Nathanson. "Since I doubt that my son has been wearing gowns lately, I take it that my daughter has not abandoned her youthful custom of wearing James's castoffs?"

"Papa, it was only once or twice," said Rachel in a pleading tone. "Samuels could not ride, and I had to deliver a message."

"If your brother would confine himself to his officially assigned duties instead of trying to win the war single-handed, you would not need to deliver such messages," commented Meyer. But he was smiling.

"Sir!" stammered Nathanson, suddenly remembering. "Meillet has summoned a troop from Lille! He is on his way to arrest you; belike he is there already. Robey is coming for us in a few hours; he will have room for you as well." He shot a glance to the two troopers down by the water; they were looking at the group in front of the cave with some curiosity.

Meyer followed his gaze and waved his hand lightly. "Those are my men; do not concern yourself with them. And Meillet can hardly arrest me; he is under arrest himself. I have had my eye on him for some time. He has been accepting bribes from his cousin to concoct incidents along the coast; the cousin fears that his troop will be ordered into combat in Spain if he does not show himself busy in the service of the emperor. But the evidence against Meillet was dubious, and such affairs are not seriously regarded here.

"Now, however, he is utterly in my power. First, he failed to have a prisoner properly searched and thus missed an important document." He bowed to Southey and Rachel. "I am sure I can concoct some sort of coded meaning for it, eventually," he added. "Then, he allowed that prisoner to escape. His new prisoner"—here he did not bow, but looked at Southey with such feeling that the latter turned away—"his new prisoner, I say, was improperly interrogated and subjected to a grotesque abuse of authority which risked both Meillet's life and that of the prisoner. Subsequently this prisoner was also allowed to escape. I take it you roped him up the cliff? Monsieur Meillet will be well occupied in explaining himself for quite a while."

"But in that case," said Nathanson in a respectful tone Drayton had never heard from him, "why are you here? Surely the risk you take in meeting us is not worth the pleasure of seeing Rachel so briefly."

"I did not come to see Rachel," said Meyer evenly. He smiled at her. "Although I am happy to have that opportunity, as well. I came to see Captain Southey. I gather from one of the troopers that Meillet was extremely indiscreet this morning. Unfortunately this particular soldier has a rather poor memory. His main expertise appears to be in wrestling." Meyer glanced pointedly at Southey's arm.

"Indiscreet is hardly a sufficient term to describe Monsieur Meillet's revelations," said Southey with a grim smile. "Would you care to come inside, sir? It is drier in the upper part of the cave, and we have a lantern. I would prefer not to be seen by any more French troops today, even those under your command."

Meyer stepped down onto the floor of the cave, somehow managing to avoid the pool of water. He looked over towards the edge of the entrance, where Rachel was now pressing a pad of cloth over Drayton's palm. Drayton returned his gaze, and then glanced down at his nurse.

"Miss Meyer," he scolded, "you should be splinting Southey's fingers. This can wait." Then he turned back to Meyer. "If it would not be too much trouble, sir, I will beg the favor of a private word with you before you leave." Meyer considered him thoughtfully; his gaze swung to Rachel and then back to Drayton. "I would be delighted," he said.

The conversation between Southey and Meyer went on past sundown. Drayton began to fear that Robey would put in with his boat before he had managed to speak with Meyer. But at last Meyer emerged from the back of the cave. Rachel escorted him to the entrance and then embraced him once more. "Take care, Papa," was all she said. He bent down and kissed her, and murmured something Drayton could not hear. Whatever it was, her face brightened, and she turned lightly and went back to Samuels and Southey.

Meyer turned to Nathanson. "That was quite a performance, your alluring escape in front of the sandbar," he said, laughing. "It almost makes up for your attempt on my life. I haven't seen those bloated soldiers run so fast in weeks. Let me have a word with Captain Drayton, and then we can walk down to the water together, and I will introduce you to my two guards. It might be useful for you to know them by sight." His son nodded and discreetly withdrew back into the cave.

The cane was propped up against the wall of the cave by the entrance; Meyer picked it up and stepped out, resuming his limp. Drayton swung out beside him and they stood for a moment, watching the clouds roll across the sky as darkness spread out towards the west. "There is something you wish to discuss with me?" Meyer said, keeping his eyes on Drayton's face. He had seen the glances that had passed between his daughter and the young officer earlier, but something was wrong, that was clear. Drayton did not have the look of a man who was about to discuss marriage, even a difficult and unlikely union such as this one.

"May I ask you to treat what we say as completely confidential?" said Drayton abruptly. "It involves very grave matters; please do not agree lightly."

"Very well," said Meyer, after a pause.

"I would like your approval to commit an act of treason," said Drayton. His face was expressionless, but he knew that his voice was strained. To his surprise, Meyer received this request calmly. He looked at Drayton for a long time, and then looked at the ground and poked his cane into the rocks, frowning. Drayton started to speak again, but Meyer held up his hand and stopped him.

"I will not ask for explanations," he said. "To do so would compromise both of us irretrievably. I will merely say that were I in your place, I would likely consider the action I believe you are contemplating. I would consider it very seriously, although the risks are enormous."

"Do you understand why I felt I must ask you?" said Drayton. "I apologize for burdening you, but I cannot think clearly anymore. It seemed to me that if anyone had the right to say yea or nay, it should be you."

"Legally, of course, neither of us has any rights in this matter whatsoever," commented Meyer. "But for what it is worth, I will at least abstain on the question you bring to me. Will that do?" He saw a look of relief on the other's face.

"That will do, yes. I am very grateful, sir. I have placed you in an impossible position."

"Impossible positions are my specialty," said Meyer with a dry smile. "By the way," he added, "should there by chance be other matters requiring my approval, you may consult my son in my absence."

"I think it unlikely, now, that I will need to approach you or Nathanson further," said Drayton. "It is probably for the best." He looked at Meyer with regret, but with resolution.

"That would have been my own opinion, before today," said Meyer. "Now I too find that I cannot think clearly anymore." He clasped Drayton's uninjured hand briefly, and then limped off towards his two sentries. Nathanson caught him at the water's edge, and Drayton's last view of the famous courier Rover was of him leaning on his son's shoulder and stabbing his cane energetically into the air as they walked up the beach.

Chapter Eighteen

Robey's boat was old and smelled of fish. There was a tiny hold—suspiciously tiny, for the boat was not that small. Drayton guessed that there was a second, concealed space for illegal cargo. At least the false hold had a makeshift berth, allotted at once to Southey. His protests were only token; he was on the verge of collapse from nothing more than the effort of wading out from shore. Nathanson and Samuels, who had clearly made such trips before, were busy at first helping Robey and his son get the boat back underway. Then the four of them fell into an argument of some sort; Drayton could hear various references to tides and sandbars. After a few minutes he smelled tobacco and heard the argument settle into a well-worn groove. He sensed Rachel moving to his side. In silent agreement they clambered forward and sat down together on the deck with their backs against the gunwale.

All his life he would remember that trip across the Channel. It was a warm night for mid-May, with very little wind, and what there was came fitfully blowing straight out from Dover. The boat was forced to tack again and again, sometimes hardly making any way at all; at other times a sudden breeze would lift them and they would scud along gaily for half a mile before slowing again to something like a controlled drift. This would be a long voyage, compared to their outward trip. Drayton knew it, and yet he was neither impatient to reach shore nor anxious about what would happen once they arrived. He felt very peaceful.

Rachel sat beside him, her head tilted back, looking at the sky. She was relaxed and still, but he knew she was not asleep. Absently he reached out occasionally and touched her arm with his bandaged hand, as though assuring himself that she was still there. Tendrils of cloud floated gently overhead; there was no moon, but stars came and went behind the light mist. This will probably be the last time I will see her, Drayton realized. Even that thought could not spoil his happiness. He felt Rachel sink finally into a doze, and started instinctively to take off his jacket to cover her. Then he remembered that one side was still very wet; he had slipped into the water nearly up to his chest while helping Southey into the boat. He contented himself with drawing her closer in under his arm.

After a very long time, Rachel stirred and sat up. A faint pale streak was growing in the east; it would be dawn soon. "Richard," she said in a drowsy voice.

"I am here, love," he answered, thrilled to hear her say his name. She did not object to his arm, which was still around her, or to the endearment.

"You spoke to my father."

It was a statement, but he knew it was meant as a question. He sighed. All idylls must end, he thought. "I did. I am afraid that the omens for the success of my courtship are not favorable," he said evasively.

He heard her draw in her breath. "I suppose it is for the best," she said, unconsciously echoing his own words to her father.

"Probably so," he agreed. But he had never felt this way about anyone before, and it was still quite dark, and she was there beside him, her shoulder settled beneath the crook of his arm, her head on his chest. So that he could not bring himself, after all, to renounce hope completely, and he asked with some hesitation, "Should circumstances change, is it possible that you would consent to see me again?" She tensed and turned her face away. "I beg you, forget that I spoke," he said, distraught. "I have broken my word; you did not give me permission to broach the subject. Please forgive me; I never know what to say when I am with you."

"Oh, no," she said, agitated. "It is only that it seemed so fortuitous, that Southey should tell me this morning that your sister might not object, and that we should encounter my father—I was not even sure he was still alive, and to see him, and think you might have spoken with him about us—it made it almost appear possible, for a brief while. But I should have known better."

He saw in the growing light a streak of silver on her cheeks.

"What, tears from Miss Ross?" he said lightly. "Surely you must have adventures like this every month. You will go back to your world of masquerades, and I will go back to my horses and my sour-faced sergeant, and you will forget that you ever knew such a clumsy amateur."

At this she shook her head. "I will not forget you," she said fiercely. "If—if circumstances change, I will be happy to receive you. But if not—" She paused.

"If not?" he prompted after a minute.

"In case they do not, I think you should kiss me again now," she said in a rush. "It will be light in a few minutes."

"And you accused me of being a rake!" he said, laughing. But he looked at her for just a moment with such warmth that she had to close her eyes, and the next thing she knew he had taken her in his arms.

"Is it always like that when people kiss each other?" Rachel said in a faint voice a few minutes later.

"No," said Drayton, still a bit dazed. A line of pink shot across the sky, and the outlines of the boat grew markedly more visible around them. Thank God, he thought. A man can only hold to his good resolutions for so long without some external assistance.

It was long past sunrise when they finally docked at a small pier in the lower part of Dover's harbor. Although the port was far quieter than in the days before the embargo, several large merchant ships lay at anchor, and their crews were scurrying about readying them to sail as soon as the wind should come up. The docks and streets were already busy, and faint echoes of shouted orders from the ships mingled with the church bells calling the folk of Dover to Sunday worship. Drayton felt the quiet loveliness of their night-long sail vanish away. With a sigh, he stood up, groaning as his stiff limbs protested. Rachel had fallen asleep again; he left her there, curled up on her cloak, with one last glance. Then he climbed over the bulkhead to the stern and went to seek out Nathanson.

He found him down in the hold, helping Southey shave. The sight of a razor made him put his hand to his own chin, and he winced. "Might I beg the loan of that item?" he said politely. "It hardly behooves the gaoler to be less well groomed than his prisoner." At this reminder of Southey's situation, Nathanson looked up, startled.

"Hey!" cried Southey indignantly. "Watch what you are about, sir barber! You could do me an injury!" A tiny red weal had opened on his chin where Nathanson's hand had slipped. Then the incongruity of such a complaint from a man with three broken bones and a warrant for treason out against him struck him, and he began to laugh.

Drayton laughed, too. "We will be gentle wardens, South." He turned to Nathanson. "I assume that you will want to take your sister up to London? In any case, I outrank you, and he is properly my charge. If he gives me his parole, I see no difficulty in escorting him up to Whitehall on my own." Nathanson considered this and agreed. "I have one stipulation, however," Drayton said to Southey. "I have not had a decent meal in nearly two days. Before I do my duty as your accessory in this patriotic self-immolation, I insist that we go to the best inn in Dover. I want hot food. I want coffee. I want it served to me by someone wearing clean clothing. Preferably a female. And I want to eat it sitting down, on a chair. With cutlery. Not sitting on a rock, and not with my fingers."

It might not have been the best house in Dover,

but it was a far cry from the Blue Boar, thought Drayton. They were seated in a cheerful coffee room, with chintz curtains drawn back to let in the morning sun. The innkeeper's wife, a pleasant woman with apple-red cheeks, had taken them up to a chamber and brought them hot water and towels, exclaiming in concern at the sight of the bandages and splints on Southey's arm. She had wanted to send for a doctor, but Drayton had glibly assured her that they were going up to London to consult a specialist. Now she fluttered over them, plying them with biscuits and ham and sausages and tubs of jam and butter. The round wooden table was already loaded with food. Drayton called her back as she bustled off towards another table.

"Is there a likely lad about, mistress, who could take a message for me to the docks? And to the posthouse? We will be needing to hire a chaise, and to make some arrangements for friends who have just landed here."

"There's Dan'l, sir, my grandson. Only nine, but a sharp one, he is. Shall I send him in? He'll be just across the yard, I reckon; 'twould only take a minute."

"I'll go out," said Drayton lightly. "Daniel, did you say?" And he pushed back his chair. He had no trouble finding the boy, or making his requirements understood. He went back in and had a second round of food. Southey had not eaten much, which was understandable, but he sat sipping coffee and looking around hungrily at the cheerful ordinariness of the room. Poor devil, thought Drayton. I'll warrant this all looks very good to him just now. The boy reappeared at the door leading out to the taproom, and Drayton got up again.

"Where is that coffee?" he said, frowning. "Ah, there is the young imp I sent to the stables. Excuse me for a moment, will you?" He reappeared two minutes later, carrying a small coffeepot. "Our chaise will be here shortly," he said. "And I stole the coffeepot. No sign of our hostess anywhere." He poured Southey another cup and topped up his own. Then he turned his attention back to the biscuits, chatting between mouthfuls about safe topics such as the weather and Sleet. But he must have betrayed himself somehow, because in the middle of a rambling story about a snowstorm down in Sussex, Southey interrupted him. His speech was slurred, and he was swaying.

"Richard," he said, with an effort, trying to stand up. "What did you put in my coffee?"

Drayton thought about feigning ignorance and decided against it.

"Laudanum," he said curtly. "It won't kill you."

"But why?" whispered Southey. He was leaning on the table.

"I owe you a kidnapping," said Drayton. Southey attempted a puzzled frown, and then slumped quietly down to the floor. The hostess, who had just come back in, shrieked in horror.

"Pay him no mind, ma'am," said Drayton. "He has these turns, sometimes. I've sent for a sedan chair to take us to the posting house."

Daniel had told him that there were four ships sailing that morning for "furrin parts." One was bound for Genoa; Drayton rejected that as too distant. In any case, although the Italian officials were rumored to be very lax, Genoa was officially in French hands. Two were headed for the Channel

Islands and then Lisbon. One was destined for Stockholm. Eventually, Drayton had chosen this last boat, the *Maid of Eastbourne.* He would have preferred a boat without an English captain, but only the ship sailing to Genoa met that criterion.

Certainly spending a few days with Nathanson had improved his acting ability, Drayton decided. He had no difficulty whatsoever convincing the captain of the *Maid of Eastbourne* that Southey was his younger brother, wounded in a duel which had proved fatal to his opponent. Now he was forced to flee the country and, as an extra flourish, Drayton added the detail that remorse had so overwhelmed his rash sibling that he had consumed an entire bottle of brandy late the previous night. Looking at the bandages and at Southey's torpor, the captain clucked in sympathy.

"Dreadful things, these duels," he said earnestly. "Should be outlawed."

Drayton reminded him tactfully that they were, indeed, illegal, and hence the need for his brother to leave the country. A large purse was handed over, "on behalf of my brother, for his passage, and to assist him in finding lodgings in Stockholm." The purse contained nearly every penny Drayton had; he had barely left himself enough to get up to London on the stage. He wished momentarily that he had thought to ask Nathanson for some funds, but then recollected that he did not want to involve him in this—especially when his sister held such a dim view of shielding traitors.

A crewman helped Drayton carry Southey down to a tiny cabin, which had not originally been mentioned by the captain, but had apparently become available when he saw the fat purse designated for "passage." Banging his head twice on the low door,

Drayton managed to get Southey laid out on the bunk in a way which did not threaten to do too much damage to his arm. Then he took out a folded sheet of paper and tucked it into his friend's shirt. Southey was snoring slightly. "How very mundane," muttered Drayton. "You're spoiling my heroic parting scene, you dolt."

He backed out of the cabin with a last glance at Southey's sleeping face and paused, remembering a July day fifteen years earlier. It was the summer after his first year at Winchester. Sara had just been married, and he was visiting her at Leigh End and had ridden over to call on his new school friend—the first time he had been allowed to ride out without a groom. He had dismounted, proud of himself for needing no assistance, and led his horse into the stables, nodding shyly to Southey's father, who was striding off, riding crop in hand. And inside he had found Southey, huddled in a corner, beaten so badly that he could not stand and clenching his teeth to keep from moaning. In an agony of schoolboy embarrassment Drayton had fled, and neither of them had ever mentioned it since. Now, as he walked back up on deck and climbed down into the longboat, Drayton found that for the first time he was able to remember that day without hating himself.

Springing up onto the dock, his thoughts were busy. He must go book a seat on the stage; once he arrived in London he would need to go to Mount Street in order to change clothing and get hold of some funds. Tomorrow he would call on his solicitor. Perhaps he should send a note to White immediately, informing him of what he had done, and of his intention to present himself at Whitehall. A dark-haired man loomed up in front of him; he brushed by without looking at him. The man stepped directly into his path.

It was Nathanson. "May I ask what your business was with the captain of that merchantman?" he said in a dangerous tone.

"You may not," said Drayton wearily. Why had he not thought to make sure that Rachel and her brother were gone before he took Southey out to the ship? A sedan chair disgorging an unconscious man into a longboat could hardly have been an inconspicuous sight.

"In that case," said Nathanson, "I will have to go ask the captain myself." And he raised his hand to signal a dinghy hovering next to the pier.

"Lieutenant Nathanson," said Drayton formally, "I order you to leave this dock immediately."

"It won't do," said the other, his eyes cold. "A serving officer is not required to obey orders which he knows to be unlawful or treasonable."

"I rather suspected you would say something of the sort," said Drayton with resignation. His fist shot out and caught Nathanson on the side of the jaw. The younger man collapsed onto the pier and lay stunned for more than a minute. Drayton stood unmoving and waited. At last his victim pulled himself up on one elbow and caressed his jaw carefully. Drayton's glance had moved out to the harbor, and Nathanson turned to follow it. The *Maid of Eastbourne* was pulling up her anchor; as they watched, two sails unfurled on her mainmast.

"What did you do? Knock him out with that right?" asked Nathanson.

Drayton shook his head. "Laudanum." He reached down and helped Nathanson to his feet. The other man was looking at him with curiosity.

"I left him a note, and nearly all the money I had on me," said Drayton.

"What are you going to tell White?"

Drayton looked at Nathanson in astonishment. He had assumed, once Nathanson had seen him, that he would report him immediately.

"The truth," he said. "I intended to all along, even had you not discovered me."

"You'll be ruined," said Nathanson. "If not gaoled or executed."

"I know," said Drayton.

"When did you change your mind?"

Drayton thought for a minute. "I'm not sure. When I caught up with him, at the inn here, I was so angry that I wanted to kill him. But when it came to it, as soon as I thought about what the French would do to him—well, you know about that. And after we hauled him up the cliff, when he told me he wanted to come back and turn himself in to White—I respected that at first. Clearly Meillet had let some rather valuable items slip out while he was watching his henchman break South's arm. But once your father had a chance to speak with him, it seemed to me that it was no longer so imperative that he talk to White. Surely passing the information on to your father would serve as well, if not better. And that was when I realized that I could not do it. I could not march him into the Horse Guards and watch them strip him and take his sword, and shut him up somewhere with people who work for our side but are likely just as brutal as Meillet. And I could not tell his mother, who has been almost a mother to me as well, that I gave them her son to hang, or put in prison."

They were walking side by side up the pier and onto the quay.

"Where are you headed now?" asked Nathanson.

"Up the hill, to book a seat on the stage."

"You may as well share my post-chaise," commented Nathanson. "It holds two. If you insist, you can pay half the charges when we reach your lodgings in London."

It suddenly occurred to Drayton to wonder why Nathanson was still in Dover.

"Where are Samuels and your sister?" he asked. "Did you not return with them? Samuels said the carriage was here."

"I sent them on without me," said Nathanson. "I thought your notion of a hearty breakfast an excellent development. It gave me time to make some arrangements of my own. You gave me quite a turn, you know. I had someone on guard at the posting house, so I should have known you had not left for London, but when I found you gone from that coffee room I thought you had given me the slip. I'll confess I did not think of the laudanum. I was planning to resort to cruder methods."

"As one who has experienced those methods," said Drayton, fingering the bone beneath his ear reminiscently, "let me recommend the virtues of laudanum."

"Ah, I had forgotten that Rachel had showed you that trick." Nathanson smiled. Then he grew serious again.

"Did you ask my father for permission to court her?"

"I did not," said Drayton. "I am, at least at the moment, a man without a future. And your sister made it very clear, during one of my more disastrous attempts to propose marriage, that she takes a dim view of those who aid traitors."

Nathanson stopped, astounded. "What did you ask him, then? I had assumed, when you requested a private word—"

"He assumed the same thing, I think," said Drayton slowly. "I am sure he would have preferred that topic. I asked him for his permission to do what I have just done. Not directly, of course. It was all most hypothetical and elliptical. Your father grasped what I was after immediately."

"You *what?*" gasped Nathanson. He looked at Drayton with respect. Then, against his better judgment, he gave in to his curiosity. "What did he say?"

"I cannot answer that question," said Drayton, "Or you might have to report him to Colonel White also. If we keep on at this rate we could have the entire courier service under arrest."

Chapter Nineteen

The smell of hot chocolate woke Rachel at last, and she peered up to find Maria, looking very concerned, standing over her with folded arms. A tray sat steaming on the nightstand, the curtains were drawn wide, and the sun was high in the sky.

"Miss Rachel, do you know that your aunt is about to send for a physician? Samuels told her that you slept in the carriage all the way back from Dover, and now you have been in your bed since you arrived yesterday afternoon."

Rachel suppressed a yawn. "What time is it?"

"Past eleven, *señorita.* Your uncle is wishing to speak with you, and Master James has been in twice, and you have had a caller."

Sitting bolt upright, Rachel said, "I have?" Her heart was hammering, although she knew that nothing could possibly have changed in the thirty hours since Drayton's bleak announcement on the boat.

"A Lord Alcroft, *señorita.*"

The name meant nothing to Rachel, and she sighed. But she could not remain disappointed for long. James was safe, and her father was alive, and somehow she and Drayton would find a way to persuade their families to allow them to marry. And best of all, she was in love, and it was a beautiful morning. Her glance fell on the hot chocolate, and she realized that she was ravenously hungry. She bounced out of bed and beamed at Maria.

"I am feeling quite well, Maria. Please let my aunt know that I am up, and tell her that I will go down to my uncle's office as soon as I have eaten something. Do you think Cook would make me an omelet?" She tugged at the bell.

Forty minutes later, bathed and fed and combed, she picked up the skirts of her cream and beige gown and ran lightly down the stairs to the door which connected the house to the bank. Her uncle was just coming down the hall in the opposite direction and looked very relieved to see her up and about.

"Your aunt was worried," he scolded her. "I was coming back to inquire how you did. James tells me that you had a narrow escape over there." He added, with a frown, "You should not have gone, Rachel."

"I hope I shall not have to go again," she said in sober tones. "We were very fortunate to come away safely." Not all of us did, she thought, wondering what was happening to Southey. A brief shiver ran over her.

"Come into my study," said her uncle abruptly. "I would like to be undisturbed for a few minutes." Rachel followed him into the austere little room, sure that he would ask about her father, and trying desperately to remember whether James had said that he was one of those permitted to know. Best to play it safe and deny any knowledge of the truth. To her surprise, however, her uncle's concern was on quite another head.

"James tells me that a nobleman's son, a certain Captain Drayton, has been seeing you very frequently of late," he said, looking very stern. "Is this true?"

"He visited Leigh End, yes, it is his sister's home. And he came across on this last trip to help Captain Southey intercept James." Her uncle waited, saying nothing. Rachel gave in. "He has asked me to marry him, Uncle. I have refused him so far."

"And what should I tell your Cousin Anthony, who will be arriving in London within the fortnight?"

Rachel had forgotten about her cousin's visit, and the long-anticipated betrothal. It seemed like something which had happened in another life. She sank down into a chair and put her head in her hands.

"I cannot marry Anthony, Uncle. It is impossible. Please forgive me."

"What are you saying?" said her uncle, looking horrified.

She realized what he must be thinking and blushed in mortification. "No," she stammered, "it is not—I have done nothing truly improper, Uncle, you must believe me." She remembered the kiss on the boat and hoped that God would permit her a small distortion of the truth. "I wish we were Papists," she said miserably. "I could enter a convent."

Roth knew what this sort of wild declaration meant. His niece fancied herself in love with the fellow. Well, in time, he hoped, she would forget him. But the marriage contract with young Anthony would have to be postponed.

"I will not press you, Rachel," he said gently. "I am not your father, after all, although he had agreed to this match before he went abroad. But you must see that it is most unsuitable for you to make these journeys, at your age, and with your position to think of. It is past time for you to be married, and if you are not careful you will find yourself with such a reputation that none of your cousins will have you."

Sweelinck appeared at the door of the study.

"Sweelinck, I am not at home," said Roth. "Please tell any callers that I will return to the bank at two o'clock."

"Excuse me, sir," said Sweelinck, "but the caller is asking for Miss Meyer. It is a Lord Alcroft, and he insists that it is urgent."

Roth turned to her. "Do you wish to receive him?"

"I do not know the gentleman," said Rachel, bewildered. She remembered that Maria had told her that this person had called earlier.

"He is a very influential man," said her uncle. "The family name is Drayton. I assume he is your captain's father." It must be more serious than he had thought, he realized, if the father was here. Presumably he had come to try to persuade his niece to renounce any claim to the boy, and illogically this angered him, although his own aims were identical.

"Show him in," Roth told Sweelinck. "Wait, bring him to the bookroom." He looked around at the tiny study, with its antique desk piled with ministry papers. Best to fight this sort of battle in the elegantly furnished front rooms of the house, without reminders of his work for the government staring Alcroft in the face.

Was it only three days ago, thought Rachel, as she opened the door of the bookroom, that she had come down to find Ensign Lawrence here? A trim gentleman, unmistakably related to Drayton, turned as she entered. He was not as tall as his son, and the features were more delicate, but he had the same clear eyes, the same slightly square face. He bowed, and nodded briefly to Roth, who had followed Rachel into the room.

"I am Miss Meyer, Lord Alcroft," she said. "I believe you wished to see me? May I present my uncle, Mr. Roth?"

"Your uncle and I are acquainted, Miss Meyer," said Alcroft. "And I beg your pardon for disturbing you like this, but I hoped to speak with you alone, if your uncle will permit it."

"I would prefer to remain," said Roth shortly.

Alcroft inclined his head. He was considering Rachel, who was not at all what he had expected. He knew Roth, and respected him for his ability and intelligence, but he was in fact if not in law a foreigner—a dumpy little German, as one of the newspapers had called him. This girl was most decidedly not dumpy, and her voice was that of a well-educated Englishwoman. Her wide dark eyes were fixed on him; he began to feel uncomfortable and glared at Roth.

"Miss Meyer," he began, and stopped. This was not going to be easy. "Miss Meyer, I have received, early this morning, a rather disquieting letter from my son advising me that he wishes to meet with me"—he glanced at his watch—"in less than an hour to deliver some legal papers which will require my signature. Have you any idea what these documents might be?"

She was astonished, he could see, and her surprise was clearly genuine. The uncle was frowning; he was surprised as well, and angry.

"I do not, my lord," she said. "I infer, since you approach me for an explanation, that you must be aware that your son has mentioned marriage to me. But that is as far as it has gone, I assure you. We are both well aware that there are many obstacles to such a match."

Alcroft was taken aback. He plunged on, nevertheless. "Can you perhaps tell me where he has been for the past two days? His sister has been trying to find him, and came to me. I could discover nothing of his whereabouts, and my resources are not paltry. I could ascertain only that he had been both at Leigh End and here in London on Friday, and left Mount Street in the early afternoon."

"He has been in France, my lord." Alcroft drew in his breath sharply. "One of Wellington's couriers was betrayed, and your son went, together with another gentleman, to warn him." She anticipated his question. "I know this because I also was there, on the same errand. He has returned safely; I last saw him in Dover, preparing to escort a prisoner up to Whitehall." She saw that he was shocked and bewildered, and she sat down on a brocade sofa. "Please be seated, my lord. My uncle was also upset to find that I had traveled to France without a proper escort, but I assure you that my groom Samuels is a faithful guardian, and that there is no question of requiring Captain Drayton to marry me. It was a matter of life or death, or I would not have gone."

Shaken, Alcroft moved to a chair, but he remained standing. "But then, what can it be?" he said, talking more to himself than to Rachel. "His letter was most odd. It seemed as though he was saying farewell—forgive my candor, Miss Meyer, but I had told him that I could not recognize a marriage with you, and I assumed when I received this note—"

"I understand, Lord Alcroft," said Rachel. "But I am afraid that I cannot help you." She was frantically trying to recall everything Drayton had said yesterday; Alcroft's anxiety was contagious. But nothing came to her.

"Beg pardon, sir," said Sweelinck, opening the door of the bookroom. Roth looked up in annoyance; he had asked not to be disturbed. "A note has just come for Miss Meyer, by special messenger, sir. From Whitehall."

"Excuse me, please," said Rachel, and she went out into the hall with Sweelinck. She returned a minute later, white-faced. "It's James," she said. "Uncle, it is from James. He is under arrest."

Alcroft moved towards the door. "I will take my leave," he said. "Please forgive me for troubling you. I am very sorry to have intruded at such a time."

"Wait," said Rachel, trembling. "Please wait one moment, my lord. I do not know why my brother is under arrest. But Captain Drayton has been in his company for the last thirty-six hours. It is very possible that he has been arrested, also."

"Dueling?" said Alcroft, curling his lip.

Rachel shook her head. She was beginning to be very worried. Something was horribly wrong. "He would never fight my brother; indeed, he took a blow from him and still refused to call him out."

She turned to her uncle. Roth was not a volatile man, but even he was concerned.

"Alcroft," he said, "it may be our turn to beg a favor from you. If you return home, and your son is waiting, would it be too much to ask that you send us a message with any information he might be able to give you about my nephew?"

"No trouble at all," said Alcroft. "I am sure it is nothing serious; belike they have been in a brawl. My son has a hasty temper."

"As does my nephew," said Roth, his anxiety easing slightly. It was probably a fistfight; they had been unlucky and run afoul of the watch, that was all.

Drayton was standing by the fireplace in the parlor when his father came in and paused in the doorway, astounded. His son was not known for being well groomed, but at the moment he could have had his portrait taken for a painting entitled "Officer in Dress Uniform." Every button glistened. The boots were a black mirror. Epaulettes lay in perfect symmetry across his shoulders. The sword hilt gleamed; there was not a crease in the jacket. The dark hair was perfectly combed, and even as he watched, Alcroft saw Drayton start to reach up to run his hands through it and then restrain himself. Only the face was wrong; it was very pale, and the lips were pressed together.

"Richard, what is all this drama of notes, and documents for signature?" demanded Alcroft testily. "Do you know that I have made a fool of myself going over to Roth's house to see if you and his niece had decided to get married?"

"Did you see her, then?" said Drayton.

"I did," said his father. Drayton waited. "Very well," spluttered Alcroft. "I admit it, she is not at all as I had pictured her. But that is nothing to the purpose. It is not the girl herself I object to, it is her faith. Is that why you wished to see me?"

"No, sir," said Drayton, recalling his mission. He gestured to a pile of papers on the table. "I have been to my solicitor and have had him draw up certain documents which will require your signature, as they involve my guardianship of William and Caroline, and you are a trustee of Harry's estate."

"I am afraid that I do not understand," said Alcroft.

"You had best sit down," advised Drayton. "If you do indeed wish to understand, it will be a long story. Do you remember my friend Michael Southey?"

"Of course I do," snapped Alcroft. "He is a captain in the army, is he not? One of White's men?"

"He has been selling information to the French," said Drayton. "False information. But he had no authorization to do so; he needed money badly, and he thought he could hoodwink Napoleon's intelligence service."

"Good God," said Alcroft, stunned. As advised, he sat down in a side chair and looked at his son.

"White knew there was some kind of leak," said Drayton grimly, "and he asked me to look into it. With the result that I initially suspected Miss Meyer, behaved most shamefully towards her, and in the end was forced to arrest my closest friend for treason and espionage."

"I cannot believe it," said Alcroft, his voice shaking. He got up and went to the sideboard; there was a decanter of brandy there, and he poured himself a glass, lifting his brow at Drayton. His son shook his head.

"It gets worse," said Drayton. He told Alcroft as much as he could, omitting the kidnapping, which he judged to be a personal matter between himself and Southey. Alcroft listened in growing dismay, interrupting only to exclaim, appalled, when Drayton described the travesty of a duel.

"So now he means to turn himself in," said Alcroft, shaking his head. "It will kill his mother, Richard. How could such an intelligent boy do something so idiotic?"

"I am glad you agree with me, sir."

"About what?" said Alcroft, puzzled.

"That what he did was idiotic, but not truly treasonable."

"What of it? Whitehall will not see it that way, of course."

"I did not think they would," said Drayton. "That is why I drugged him and put him on a ship for Stockholm instead of escorting him to the Horse Guards. I am on my way to report myself to Colonel White, but I stopped here to resign the guardianship of Caroline and William. I have transferred authority to Barrett, but the transfer requires your signature."

Alcroft turned red and slammed the glass down on the sideboard. "Are you demented?" he roared. "Will you never be done courting disgrace? You send the real malefactor off to Sweden and march in to surrender your sword? Have you no respect for our name, for me, for your brother-in-law? Why must you drag yourself through the mud, for no good reason? How can you begin to imagine that what you did is treason? What does it matter, now, where the fool boy is, or who put him on that ship?''

But as he saw Drayton standing there, remote and unyielding, he fell silent.

''You mean to do it, then,'' he said, his voice so low as to be nearly inaudible.

Drayton nodded. His father looked away.

''Sir, please try to understand,'' Drayton said in an anguished voice. ''Let me try, for once in my life, to do something right.'' He strode up and down in front of the mantel, clenching his fists. ''I never completed my training at the academy—no''—as his father stretched out a hand to object—''I did well enough at my studies, but my after-hours behavior did not endear me to the masters. I would have been asked to leave, even had you not decided that Harry and I were to have no part of His Majesty's forces. I wasted three years in London drinking and fighting, and gave at least two honorable young men wounds they will live with for the rest of their lives. Thank God I did not kill anyone, but apart from that negative accomplishment I cannot say that I have one single thing to boast of from that period of my life.

''Then I defy your orders and join the dragoons—principally to be with Harry. A fine job I did there,'' he said bitterly. ''The only time he truly needed my aid, I did not manage to reach him until it was too late. Not my fault, you will say: very well, let us suppose that I was adequate as a cavalry officer. But as soon as I was sent on an important mission which required a bit of caution and self-control, I nearly got myself and my guide killed, and risked two weeks' worth of painfully collected information because a thirsty Frenchman made a crude remark. Now I am asked to investigate some problems with our French couriers, and while my oldest friend is sending off false information to the enemy, I, completely duped, have been terrorizing the woman I hope to marry."

He stopped and looked straight at his father. "It is not up to me to decide whether I have committed treason. It is for Colonel White to decide whether to indict me, and for a tribunal to decide whether I am guilty. I myself see no ambiguity at all: I helped a man whom I knew to have sold information to the French to escape the country."

Alcroft said nothing. After a moment, Drayton continued, with some difficulty. "I think I must take my leave of you, sir. If your optimistic view is correct, and I am not guilty of treason, I plan to marry Miss Meyer. I understand that you will not wish to acknowledge me once the marriage has taken place."

"She told me she had not accepted you," said his father numbly.

"Not yet," said Drayton. "That is the next thing I plan to get right. If there is a next thing." Before Alcroft could move, he had inclined his head respectfully and left the room.

Alcroft stood gazing after his son as the tall figure disappeared. Then he sighed and crossed the hall into his study. A savage tug on the bell rope brought a footman.

"My lord?"

Alcroft was seated at his writing table, scrawling something on a small sheet of paper; he raised his hand to indicate that the footman should wait. He folded the sheet and sealed it.

"Have this conveyed immediately to Mr. Roth, at his banking house," he said. "There is no need to wait for a reply."

Chapter Twenty

Two sentries stood outside the door of what had been Southey's office as a tight-lipped lieutenant boxed and corded the papers from his desk and cabinets. Two more sentries were on guard outside a room farther down the hall, where White sat, his face devoid of expression, behind a surprisingly clean desk. The piles of papers were gone from the floor and chairs, and the door to the inner office was closed. Southey, in his shirtsleeves, was sitting in a wooden chair facing the colonel. He wondered bitterly if the sudden neatness in White's office was to guard against his inadvertently catching a glimpse of something important. His arm throbbed, his fingers were so swollen that the skin felt tight, and his feet were covered with blisters. At least they had found him a pair of boots that fit, he thought.

"Is that all you have to say?" said White.

"It is."

"You expect me to believe that you bribed a stranger to convey you on board that ship while you pretended to be unconscious? And that you later changed your mind and arranged to return here?"

"Yes."

White controlled his temper with difficulty. No point telling Southey that he had a letter from Drayton advising him of his role in the affair, and a page of depositions from the harbormaster at Dover and the captain of the *Maid of Eastbourne,* furnished by the constable who had escorted Southey up to London after he had compelled the ship to turn back.

"If I thought that the information you have just given me from Meillet was as suspect as that ridiculous tale of the stranger, I would be forced to conclude that I had wasted the last two hours," snapped White.

Exhausted, Southey closed his eyes briefly. "Everything I passed along is exactly as Meillet told it me," he said. "Please believe me, sir. It is the only reason I came back." White would probably have him interrogated, he realized. It was only reasonable, under the circumstances.

There was a knock at the door, and Ensign Lawrence came in. He studiously avoided looking at Southey and handed some papers to White. The door closed behind him. White grunted and got to his feet.

"I believe we are done here, then," he said, to Southey's surprise. "You understand that for public consumption you will have been killed in action." Southey nodded. "It has been difficult to arrange on short notice, but we have retroactively purchased a commission as a major in your name, to increase the pension your mother will receive, and there will be bonuses for the trips to Spain, as well."

It was more than he had dared to hope for. No public trial, and some chance for his mother and sister to keep the house at Chanterfield; the income would be sufficient to pay the interest on the mortgages. He felt tears of gratitude blurring his vision and turned away hastily. Probably they would not hang him, then. If he were to be killed in action, they would need to shoot him. He leaned back in his chair with a sigh of relief. Then White's next words sank in.

"Excuse me, sir?" he stammered.

White repeated himself patiently. "Should you wish to send additional moneys to your family, you may do so through my office. They will be paid out as part of the pension."

For a moment, Southey could not make sense of this. "You mean—I will not be executed?" he said, incredulous.

With great difficulty White maintained his air of cold restraint. "You have forty-eight hours to leave the country," he said. "Obviously, you should not expect to be able to return." He passed Southey a set of papers. "We have provided you with identification papers under a different name. You will be well advised to alter your appearance, as well, since Rover, in his capacity as Arnaut, has published a substantial reward for your death or capture, and there are French agents in every capital in Europe. It is up to you where you go, once you leave the country, of course. But if you believe that we can trust you for some small services, we might have some use for you in Vienna."

Totally overcome, Southey put his head down

on the desk in front of him. Then he raised his eyes, and White looked quickly away. Dammit, the boy looked ready to lay down his life for him then and there! And he still had Nathanson and Drayton to deal with. He cursed Tredwell and the foreign office under his breath in two different languages. Southey was getting shakily to his feet; White summoned the sentries hastily. He was afraid the young man might say something which would cause him to step out of his part.

The minute Southey was out of the room, White strode over to the inner door and pulled it open. Tredwell was sitting behind it, looking thoughtful.

"I hope you enjoyed yourself," White said, his voice cutting. "The French merely broke some bones. This filthy little scheme has destroyed him."

"Don't be so theatrical, White," said Tredwell. "If he were indeed a broken man he would have put a bullet through his head already. Instead he came back here and gave you information on the French coastal patrols that even Rover did not know." He held up a sheaf of rumpled papers. "This report he sent you from Dover is remarkable, as well. You've done a very fine job with him."

"I've done a very fine job, have I?" shouted White, the repressed emotions of the past hour boiling over. "What has the ministry done? They took my best aide, exploited a family tragedy to press him into what he thinks is treason, and put a price on his head in France only rivaled by the reward for Rover and his son, simply in order to provide Rover with credible information in Lille and then send that boy on to the Austrians carefully 'discredited.' He sat here in front of me, so ashamed of himself that he could not look me in the face, refusing to tell me why he sold information to the French, refusing to admit that it was all fabricated, refusing to implicate Drayton in the attempt to get him away from Dover, and all you can say is that I have done a fine job?" And he glared at Tredwell.

Tredwell glared back. "Very few men have Rover's skills. If he does not believe, truly believe, that he is disgraced and exiled, he will never fool the Austrians."

"Does Rover know about this?" asked White abruptly.

"No," said Tredwell. "He would not approve."

"How fastidious of him," said White acidly.

Another knock at the door, and the harassed lieutenant who had been down in Southey's office appeared. "Lieutenant Nathanson to see you, sir."

"Have him wait for a moment down in Southey's office," Tredwell said. The lieutenant saluted and withdrew.

"Well, sir," said White in icy tones to Tredwell. "You allowed the foreign office to play puppeteer. You perhaps forgot that there were other characters in the drama. Just what do you propose to do with messieurs Nathanson and Drayton?"

"I will admit that I did not think Nathanson would become involved, if you will admit that you underestimated Drayton," said Tredwell, frowning. "I need to go back over to the Horse Guards. Have Nathanson wait here, and Drayton too, when he comes. It will not hurt those hotheads to cool their heels for a few hours and reflect on their sins."

If, in a blaze of dutiful self-sacrifice, a young man comes to his commanding officer intending to denounce himself as an accomplice to treason, it is a bit of an anticlimax to find that the commanding officer is at a meeting and will not return for an hour or more.

"Would you care to wait, Captain Drayton?" said the young lieutenant politely. "We are allowed to use the college's refectory; you could go down and get yourself a cup of tea."

And so, incongruously, Drayton found himself sitting by a window sipping tea and watching ensigns scurry about carrying logbooks while he waited to be arrested. He could just glimpse the stone steps leading down to the river from where he sat, and the twinkle of the water was reflected in the play of light on the balustrades. Gulls wheeled overhead, and a ship—only its sails visible—was struggling to tack in the light breeze. He wondered idly what happened when an officer was arrested for treason. Did they rip off his epaulettes then and there? Confiscate his shako and jacket? Would he still be addressed as "captain?"

He was on his second cup of tea when the lieutenant appeared at his table. "The colonel has returned, sir," he announced. "You may see him now."

For the third time in two weeks Drayton walked into the oddly shaped office. White was sitting impassively behind his desk, which now was completely clear of papers. Drayton said nothing, but unbuckled his sword belt and dropped it, sword and all, onto the bare desk.

The colonel looked at him with no change of expression whatsoever. "How very unoriginal," he said coldly. "You may wait in there"—nodding his head toward the small back office, whose door was now closed. "Tredwell is in town; when he returns from Whitehall we will hear your report."

The lieutenant, with an odd glance at Drayton, opened the connecting door. Seated in one of the two chairs in the tiny room was Nathanson, his jaw somewhat swollen. His sword belt was gone. Nathanson's eyebrows rose.

"I have you by three hours, Drayton," he said. "Been here since half-past one."

"Two hours," said Drayton. "I had a cup of tea over at the naval academy while I waited for the colonel."

It was nearly six before Tredwell returned and summoned Drayton out of the back room. Nathanson had been escorted off somewhere shortly after Drayton's arrival. Drayton longed for his company, silent and arrogant though he might be. He grew hungry, and ever more anxious. Once he was allowed out to use the privy and was shocked to notice that he was escorted there and back by one of the sentries posted outside White's door. That small detail brought home to him with a vengeance the grim realities of his situation.

Now, as he emerged into the larger office, Drayton saw that Lawrence and the sentries were waiting by the door. White was conferring with the lieutenant over by the desk; a messenger came in, picked up a dispatch bag, and raced off. An air of urgency and disquiet hung over the room.

"Drayton," said White, looking up, "I am afraid we will have to detain you overnight. Wellington has arrived unexpectedly and Colonel Tredwell and I must leave immediately for Westminster; evidently he has pushed up the date of his advance towards Madrid and is here to confer with the Secretary. Lawrence here will take you over to a room in the college and provide you with some spare gear. May I have your parole to remain at his orders until we have time to see you tomorrow morning? I would prefer to dispense with the sentries; in the college they will be quite conspicuous." Without waiting for an answer, he turned to the ensign. "Get him some food," he ordered. "And bring him over to Whitehall in the morning. Around ten. If our meetings continue into the morrow, I will send word to you here."

Mechanically, Drayton followed Lawrence back through the twisting halls. He felt naked in his uniform without his sword, and imagined that every eye—fortunately, there were very few—was drawn straight to the empty space at his hip. Lawrence glanced at him with something like sympathy. "Would you like to borrow a sword?" he asked. Tight-lipped, Drayton shook his head.

"In that case," said Lawrence, "I will have one of the porters go out to the Pipe and Anchor and bring food back to your chamber. We will be too noticeable if you go out in public like that, and the colonel is anxious to avoid attention. I could lend you a shirt, but my breeches will never fit you." He looked ruefully at Drayton's long legs.

The chubby ensign duly conveyed Drayton over to Whitehall the following morning. Drayton had surprised himself by sleeping quite well; Lawrence had been impressed to find him rather difficult to awaken when he came with clean linens and shaving gear just before seven. But then, Drayton reflected grimly, he had had precious little sleep for the three prior nights. Even a condemned man cannot stay awake forever.

He was shown to a small, elegantly furnished sitting room on the first floor of the Horse Guards, evidently part of some senior officer's quarters, since a connecting door opposite the entrance offered a glimpse of a large and rather untidy bedchamber. White was sipping tea at a mahogany escritoire, and sealing up some papers. One of the ubiquitous messengers stood impatiently next to him. Tredwell was in an armchair by the window. The messenger accepted his packet and left; White turned his chair to face Drayton and looked at Tredwell. Not having been given permission to sit, Drayton perforce remained standing.

"Captain Drayton, would you care to explain why you have turned in your sword to Colonel White?" said Tredwell in a mild voice.

His carefully rehearsed speech flew out of his head. After a minute, he managed to say, "I believe that I have failed in my duty as an officer of the king, sir."

"In what way, Captain?"

Drayton swallowed. At times during the previous night he had convinced himself that what he had done was not, in truth, treason, but that conviction had never been very secure, and now it evaporated completely.

"I helped a suspected traitor leave the country, sir. No, a known traitor; he had admitted it to my face."

"Do you refer to Southey?" interjected White, leaning forward in his chair.

Drayton heard the omission of the word *Captain* and felt a chill spreading through his ribs.

"I do," he said faintly.

"Perhaps it would interest you to know that Mr.

Southey surrendered himself to me yesterday,'' said White, looking intently at Drayton.

Drayton was stunned. "He came here? But how?"

"He came to in the cabin of the *Maid of Eastbourne* about one hour out of Dover,'' said Tredwell. "You did him no favors, Drayton. Had it never occurred to you that it takes a great deal more money to persuade a captain to turn back once under sail than to buy passage? Southey was forced to tell the captain that he was wanted for treason, with the result that he was turned over to the harbormaster in Dover and escorted up here, in chains, by a constable.''

"No,'' gasped Drayton, horrified.

"What made you think he would stay on that boat, once he awoke?''

"I left him a note,'' said Drayton slowly, pushing his hair back from his forehead. "I told him that I thought he had done enough. He had already told Rover everything Meillet had said, you know. And I thought he would be far out to sea before he came to; he must not have had enough of the coffee. I should have known he would simply turn around and come back.''

"Ah, you drugged him,'' said Tredwell, nodding to himself. "I thought as much."

"He did not tell you?'' said Drayton, more and more bewildered.

"He claims,'' said White, with a smoldering glance at Tredwell, "that he bribed a stranger to take him on board the ship while he pretended to be unconscious. Later, he says, he changed his mind.''

"That is ridiculous!'' exclaimed Drayton. "No one could believe that!''

"Nevertheless,'' said White, with a sour smile,

'it might be rather difficult to convince a tribunal hat you are guilty of abetting the escape of a traitor vhen the traitor himself has voluntarily surrend-ered and denies your involvement."

"He is only trying to protect me," said Drayton iercely, forgetting that he was arguing in favor of iis own condemnation.

"Then you are quits," said Tredwell. "Because ou were trying to protect him, were you not?"

"I have so admitted, sir," said Drayton, looking iaggard. "I couldn't bring him back here, after vhat he had already undergone at Meillet's hands. did arrest him, you know, in France, once we ound Nathanson unharmed, but I couldn't go hrough with it. And I cannot pretend now, simply ecause he overturned what I did, that it never iappened."

"You would be surprised at how much pre-ending goes on in this branch of the service," ommented White under his breath.

"Might we give him a chair?" said Tredwell per-emptorily to White. "My neck is getting stiff, and ve have a great deal to discuss." At White's nod, Drayton perched gingerly on the edge of a settle. 'We would like an account of everything you did from the time you left Barrett's house on Friday until you came into White's office yesterday. If it will ease your mind, we have already spoken to Nathanson and have pledged to keep Miss Meyer's part in these events completely confidential."

The narrative took quite some time, because White and Tredwell kept interrupting with ques-tions. When Drayton had finished, White drummed his fingers on the desk. "His account agrees almost exactly with that of Nathanson. Only the descrip-tion of the events in the harbor at Dover diverges."

"I take it Nathanson claims that he did not see me returning from the *Maid of Eastbourne,*" said Drayton acerbically. "If I am going to nerve myself to help a friend escape the king's justice, I would at least like to get the credit for it."

"Would you prefer the credit to the fact?" asked White, watching him to gauge his reaction.

"What do you mean, sir?" said Drayton after a moment.

"I mean that your friend is at this moment on his way to Vienna. In a way, I must disagree with Colonel Tredwell. Perhaps your high-handed actions in attempting to rescue him against his will worked to his advantage, in the long run. Any doubts we might have had about his motives and his underlying loyalty were certainly dispelled by the difficulties he had to overcome in order to get off that boat. And since he is now one of only eleven people who know that Rover is Arnaut, it is as well for his sake that we are convinced that he is trustworthy."

Drayton slumped back onto the settle, fighting to make sense of what he was hearing. Relief began to bubble up inside him, but he refused to trust it yet.

"Are you saying," he asked cautiously, "that you do not believe him to have been guilty of treason?"

"Legally speaking," said Tredwell, "I believe that he is guilty of embezzlement—because the French payments should properly have gone to the treasury—and of unauthorized contact with foreign agents. But no, not treason. Not in the strictest sense."

White put his fingertips together and scrutinized Drayton closely. "The situation is a delicate one, and we must rely on you and Nathanson to conceal

is whereabouts at all costs. To be frank"—he
lanced at Tredwell—"there was some debate as
o whether to inform you of the real facts. But
n view of your persistence in tracking down Miss
Meyer and then Southey in Charing, it seemed
afest to tell you the whole. Southey has been
eported killed in action. I am afraid that you may
ot reveal the truth of the matter to anyone, regard-
ess of the provocation. And the provocation will
e extreme, because we would like you to convey
is effects down to his mother at Chanterfield
omorrow or the next day. Nathanson has gone
ver to his lodgings to recover his uniform; he will
end it over to you later today."

"God in heaven, no!" groaned Drayton, before
e could stop himself, picturing Southey's mother
nd sister as they received the news. He flushed
nd amended, "I beg your pardon, sir, but I have
ever been good at playacting."

"I assure you that you will have no difficulty in
ppearing distressed and uneasy, which will be all
hat will be required," said Tredwell. He went over
o the door and spoke a few words to someone
who was evidently waiting outside.

"The sergeant has gone to fetch your sword,
Drayton," he announced as he returned.

Drayton stood, frowning.

"What is it, Drayton?" said White testily. "Are
ou thinking of resigning? I would have thought
ou would be delighted to be walking out of here
with your freedom, let alone your rank."

"That's just it, sir," said Drayton stubbornly.
"Southey may not have been guilty of treason, but
I thought him a traitor at the time, and in that
belief put him on the ship. Am I not, in that case,

still guilty of shielding a traitor, in both intent and action?"

"Devil take you, Drayton," roared White. "What did you do at Woolwich, engineering or philosophy? Take yourself off and take your blasted sword with you! Before your father and Roth come and pester the Secretary about you yet again!"

And as Drayton, abashed, saluted and withdrew he muttered, "Waste of good brains to send that boy back to Bridgwater and his equestrian idiocies. Perhaps I should ask Wellington again about the situation in Gibraltar."

Fielding came clattering down the stairs just as Drayton came into the front hall of the house on Mount Street. "Drayton!" he said in obvious relief, his eye taking in the complete uniform. "Thank goodness. The wildest rumors have been circulating, and Robson has been hovering about and driving me distracted. Do you know they were saying at the club that you had been arrested for treason? Your father has been here, and Sir Charles, and a caller is waiting for you in the upstairs parlor. Hayes told him you were not expected, but he claimed to know that you would be back shortly, and said he would wait." Hayes was Fielding's butler and general factotum and, in spite of his former career as an artillery gunner, was not entirely satisfactory as a butler, due to his inability to prevent unwelcome callers from intimidating him.

"Who is it?" said Drayton, frowning. He wanted a bath, and a shave with a decent razor, and a pair of boots that had not been polished until they were stiff as boards.

"Hayes did not say. A foreign gentleman, I believe."

Uneasy, Drayton decided reluctantly to meet the visitor first and postpone his ablutions. A rotund little man with a beak of a face rose to greet him as he came into the parlor. Drayton recognized him at once; the caricatures in the newspaper were unflattering, but the likeness was unmistakable.

"Captain Drayton?" said the visitor, with a heavy Germanic accent. "I am Eli Roth. I believe my family owes you a considerable debt."

"On the contrary, Mr. Roth," said Drayton, shaking hands. "The debt is mine; I understand that you have been attempting to assist me over at Whitehall. And I wish I could agree with your assessment, but I fear that I have been more of a nuisance than a help, particularly in the case of your niece."

"It is about my niece that I am here," said Roth.

"I rather suspected as much, sir," said Drayton calmly. "Please be seated. Would you care for a glass of something?" He went over to the hall and, to Roth's amusement, rapped on the wall—the bell ropes were all broken at Fielding's. Hayes appeared, looking rather uncomfortable. "Hayes, some refreshments for myself and Mr. Roth, if you please," said Drayton. When Hayes returned shortly with a decanter and two glasses, Drayton took one with a sigh of gratitude and sank into a wing chair across from Roth.

"Allow me to be frank with you," said Roth, refusing the glass Drayton silently offered. "My niece has made it quite clear that her affections are engaged. And my nephew tells me that you seek her hand; I will not accuse you of trifling with her. But I must ask you, for her sake, not to press her in this matter as of yet. It is unfair, and unrealistic perhaps, to expect you to give her up completely. All I am asking is that you allow her some time to reflect."

He leaned forward, and Drayton understood why this man was Wellington's friend. A persuasive intelligence shone out of the hawklike face. "Please consider, Captain Drayton, what my niece's life has been, up to this point. She has led, in alternation, an existence of seclusion and propriety, while residing with me, and an existence of disguise, danger, and recklessness with her brother and father. In my home, she has met very few young men, other than some half-dozen co-religionists. These are the sons of eminent scholars in the synagogue. They are, for the most part, shy and bookish, with no address at all, and very different from her father and brother. Now circumstances have brought her into contact with you, in a sudden and most intimate manner, and you are"—he looked objectively at the clear-eyed face and the tall, athletic figure—"you are everything the sister of James Meyer and the daughter of Nathan Meyer might imagine in her husband. But you are not of her world, nor is she of yours.

"I cannot prevent the marriage, if you are both set on it, and neither can your father, although he has reservations similar to my own. Would you think it unreasonable, however, if I asked you to refrain from seeing my niece for a space of time—say, two months or so—so that you may both be sure that you will face the difficulties attendant on such a marriage secure in your affection for each other?"

It was a clever proposal, Drayton thought bitterly. It was so moderate that any man with even a shred of honor would feel bound not only to acquiesce, but to consider withdrawing his suit entirely. A night in the naval college under arrest had left him feeling somewhat selfish, however, and he said only, "Such a separation seems only prudent. I have no desire to compel my bride to lose the world for love, although I mean to have her at the end of your two months, if she does not object, whether our families give us their blessing or no." His eyes flashed a veiled challenge. "We are both of age, Mr. Roth, and I have sufficient income from my mother to support a wife in comfort without a dowry from her family or any further inheritance from mine."

This was not news to Roth; indeed, at this point he probably understood the state of Drayton's finances better than their owner. He rose. "As from now?" he said, staring at Drayton with a measuring look.

"As from now," agreed Drayton, sighing. It would not be any easier if he saw her again; in fact, it might make it harder. "I suppose it would not be sporting to inform her of the agreement; she might take that as an implicit promise from you that once the time is up she may wed me without opposition."

In spite of himself Roth smiled. No wonder James liked the fellow. "You are very astute, Captain Drayton," he said dryly. "I begin to understand why White and Tredwell think you have the makings of a courier." With which astonishing remark, he politely rose and took his leave.

Chapter Twenty-one

Miranda and Sara had their heads together over a pattern for a bride dress when Rachel was announced. The small drawing room in Harland Place was dark, even in the early afternoon light, for it faced north. As a result, Miranda and Sara had spread out the pattern on the window seat and were indecorously kneeling on the floor with their backs to Rachel when she came in.

"Miss Ross!" said Miranda, jumping up with a mixture of embarrassment and pleasure. "How lovely to see you again!"

"It is Meyer, actually," said Rachel with a slight hesitation. "I—I had had a quarrel with someone in my family this winter and did not use my own name for some months. You did tell Caroline, did you not?" she asked, turning to Sara.

"Yes, since you so requested," said Sara. Then, with a frown, "Where do you suppose she might be? She has been up since before seven, talking of nothing but your visit and the expedition to the waxworks, and now she has vanished."

This exchange had given Miranda time to recover from her astonishment at hearing the name Meyer, and she was able to come forward with some semblance of composure to greet Rachel. There was an uncertainty in her manner, but Rachel was so preoccupied at the moment that she did not notice.

"Lady Barrett," she said, in a worried tone, "I must ask you, before Caroline joins us, have you any news of your brother? Mine was released yesterday evening, but he told me that Captain Drayton had been detained overnight."

"It is true, then?" said Miranda, aghast. "I heard the rumor that two officers had been arrested for treason but could not credit it. And several people told me that Captain Drayton was one of them. I do not remember the name of the other officer."

"It is a dreadful misunderstanding," said Sara, fuming. "Richard evidently reported himself to his colonel for some imagined piece of misconduct. Or so my father says." She turned to Rachel. "No, we have heard nothing, but Sir Charles tells me that Wellington has arrived unexpectedly, and I imagine that Whitehall has come to a standstill while he consults with the War Office."

"Yes, Lord Wellington was at my uncle's house last night, briefly," said Rachel, biting her lip. She had not been as concerned as her brother about the likelihood that Drayton's conduct would be viewed seriously, until she heard that he had not been released along with Nathanson. Even more worrisome, Lord Alcroft had called early this morning and had gone off with her uncle on what she was fairly certain was an expedition to the Horse

Guards—their second, since both had gone the previous afternoon as well.

The sound of voices in the hall caught Sara's ear. It was unforgivably rude, but . . . "Pray excuse me for a moment," she said to Miranda and Rachel. "I believe I hear my husband. Perhaps he may have some news for us." At that moment, however, the door opened and Sir Charles appeared. He was smiling.

"Richard has been released," he said to Sara. "Apparently they simply wanted to hear his report about an incident in France."

"Thank goodness!" she gasped, realizing that she had been holding her breath. Glancing at Rachel, she saw a mirror of her own relieved face, and then something more, an unguarded moment of . . . what? Anticipation? Happiness?

"And I found someone in the front hall," said Sir Charles with a twinkle in his eye. He stepped aside and ushered a small form into the room.

"Caroline!" shrieked Sara. "Whatever have you done to yourself?"

The bizarre little figure burst into tears. Her hair had been pulled up on top of her head, although it was beginning to escape from the clumsily inserted hairpins. Her frock was decorated with an ancient shawl, and she was wearing an old pair of Sara's half-boots, which were sliding off the side of one foot. But it was her face which riveted every eye in the room. It was covered with layers of wax, thickest over the cheeks and nose, but forming at least a thin mask over her forehead and chin as well. Streaks of wax extended up into her hairline, and there were drops spattered across the shoulders of her shawl. Cracks in the layers gave evidence that she had been wrinkling her forehead since applying that portion.

"I wanted to be a waxwork," wailed Caroline. "Miss Meyer told me that they were of real people, and I wanted to be one, too. And I took the wax from the tapers in the drawing room and dripped it to make puddles and put it on my face, but now I can't get it off, and it *hurts.* It is pulling my hair, and my eyebrows won't go down!"

Only Sir Charles maintained his dignity. The women, weakened perhaps by the earlier tension, burst into peals of laughter. Caroline threw her shawl over her head in mortification and sank down to the ground, sobbing.

"Caroline, I beg your pardon, it is very discourteous of us to laugh at you," said Rachel, breathless. She moved over to the lump under the shawl and picked up a corner very tentatively. "I do know how to get it off, you know," she said, peeping in underneath the covering. "And so do you, if you will but think for a moment."

"I do?" said Caroline doubtfully, forgetting her humiliation and letting the shawl slide down to the floor.

Rachel had to dig her nails into her hands to keep from laughing again, but she mastered herself.

"How did you get the wax on?" she asked gently.

"I melted it from the candle into a puddle and . . . Oh! I must melt it!" Caroline looked horrified. "Will I have to put a flame on my face? Oh, I could not, Miss Meyer, truly, I could never do it!"

"Well," said Rachel, "I am glad to hear that you realize that a flame is not the best solution. What else is hot, and useful for cleaning your face?"

"Hot *water!*" said Caroline triumphantly.

Rachel held out her hand. "Let us find Mrs. Mott and give your face a bath. And then we can go see the waxworks. Caroline, when I said they were real people I meant that they were like portraits—not that the museum was full of real people with wax over them!"

"Well, you were not very clear," said Caroline with dignity. But a moment later she was happily pulling Rachel out of the room, chattering away about her kitten.

"I must take my leave," said Miranda, gathering up the patterns into a large portfolio. "Dare I hope that you are going to the Morgan affair on Thursday?" Mrs. Morgan was a wealthy widow, a great friend of the Waites', known for her interminable "evenings" and her fondness for bullying young brides-to-be like Miranda with lectures on Marriage.

"Yes," laughed Sara, "Barrett has agreed to take me. We will engage to rescue you from the hostess if necessary."

"I believe—I am sure," said Miranda, blushing, "that I could obtain an invitation for Miss Meyer, if she would care to come."

"That is most kind, and I will be sure to ask her," said Sara, resolving to do nothing of the sort. She could well picture the dreadful evening a guest named Meyer would have at the hands of the starched-up Mrs. Morgan. And taking her leave of Miranda, pondering, she went slowly up the stairs towards the suite of rooms which had been converted into a nursery when she married Sir Charles. Had Miranda also too noticed the expression on Rachel's face when Sir Charles had made his announcement about Drayton's release? Was that why she had made that unexpected overture?

A splashing sound and a few faint shrieks from Caroline's bedchamber gave evidence that the wax removal was underway. Rachel was on an old divan, playing catch with William, while his nurse attempted to clean up the aftereffects of his luncheon. He ran to Sara immediately, abandoning his game, and she scooped him up with a mock groan and plumped down next to Rachel.

"How is Caroline getting on?" asked Rachel, smiling at the sight of William trying to climb up his aunt's neck.

"Quite well," replied Sara absently. "The new governess is very shy, and I would not have thought they would hit it off, but Caroline has adopted her. When she heard that Miss Montague could barely sit a horse, she was in alt. I suppose after her success with you and the dogs, she believes that her mission in life is to educate benighted females who do not know how to behave around animals."

The nurse scurried off with William's luncheon tray at this point, and Sara seized her opportunity. "Miss Meyer," she said, "please forgive me if I intrude—but may I know how things stand between you and my brother? He himself told me that he had made you an offer," she added hastily, lest Rachel think she was not in Drayton's confidence.

Rachel twisted her hands together and looked down at her lap. "I hoped that you did not know," she said in a low voice. "I suppose that is a coward's wish, for you must feel that I have repaid you very ill for your kindness in inviting me to stay with you at Leigh End. When I realized that your younger brother would be in residence for an extended visit, I should have left at once." She looked at Sara. "I have refused him, of course. But he is very stubborn."

"Indeed, he is," said Sara with feeling.

"I am certain," continued Rachel, "that such a marriage would be very distasteful to his family. And to mine."

Sara could not contradict her, so she remained silent. But glancing over across William's head she surprised an expression of such longing on Rachel's face that her own eyes filled with tears.

"I am afraid that he has been more effective as a besieger than I have been as a defender," said Rachel, lowering her revealing eyes hastily. "When we last spoke, he said that he was not hopeful but asked whether, if circumstances changed, I would allow him to address me again. And I was weak enough to say yes. I thought he was referring to the opposition of my family, but now I believe that he was speaking of the possibility that he would be charged with treason. I think it quite likely, therefore, that he will ask me again sometime quite soon for my answer."

"And you will say yes, this time," said Sara.

Rachel nodded. "Will you mislike it very much?" she asked miserably.

"No," said Sara after a long pause. "It will not be easy, but we will all manage somehow." There was a triumphant shout from the bedchamber; the last of the wax had been removed. "After all, there will be advantages," added Sara with a wicked smile. "I will no longer be responsible for Caroline's education."

"Blast!" said Drayton under his breath as Hayes appeared to announce another caller. He had just gotten rid of his father. During this last visit he had managed to persuade his father to take some refreshment (and therefore had had some himself), but he had still not managed a bath or change of clothing. Nathanson appeared at the foot of the stairs, deposited a parcel on the hall table, and peered up uncertainly.

"Well, if I have come at an inconvenient time—" he said, raising one eyebrow. But then he laughed. "Do the two of us have any convenient times these days?"

"Come up," said Drayton warmly. "As long as you promise not to lecture me. I've had enough of that from your uncle and my father."

"Oh, was my uncle here?" said Nathanson as he came up the stairs.

"Yes," said Drayton, leading Nathanson into his bedchamber and sitting down on the edge of a chest at the foot of the bed. "Robson!" he shouted. "Sorry," he said to Nathanson, "but if I don't get these boots off I can't answer for the consequences to my temper." Robson materialized briefly, grumbled at the gouges on the black boots, and whisked them away.

"Your uncle," resumed Drayton, pulling on an old pair of slippers, "gave me a disquisition on the sheltered life your sister has led and requested that I eschew her company for two months so that she can learn that I am not the only fish in the sea."

"And?" said Nathanson. The eyebrow was up again. He had taken a seat on the edge of the unmade bed.

"I agreed. It seemed a reasonable request, from his point of view. It would be foolish to give up any chance of reconciling your uncle to the match."

"It occurs to me," said Nathanson thoughtfully, "that my sister may not appreciate this scheme.

When she discovers it, woe betide any conspirators nearby. Fortunately, I am on my way out of town."

"Back to France?" Drayton said, concerned. Then he realized that Nathanson was in uniform. A captain's uniform.

"Spain," said the other. "Wellington is about to make his move."

"So you took your promotion," said Drayton slowly. "Are you going back to your regiment, then?"

Nathanson shook his head. He gave Drayton a mocking smile. "Shall we say I discovered the dangers of remaining a lieutenant? Even as a courier, rank has its privileges."

"Where will you be based?" said Drayton. "I suppose I will be back with my unit in a week or so. Shall I see you at all, or will you be behind the French lines?"

"I fancy we might see each other, yes," said Nathanson evasively. He rose to go. "I stopped by to bring you some of Southey's things: his uniform and sword. I got them from Sievert. Someone is bringing a few more bits over from the Horse Guards later today. I don't envy you the job of telling his mother the false news of her son's death."

"At least it is close to Leigh End," said Drayton. "The minute I escape from Chanterfield, I plan to abuse my brother-in-law's hospitality by retreating at once to his cellars and getting damnably drunk."

Bathed, freshly shaven, and in clean clothing at last, Drayton was finishing off an excellent supper and feeling nearly restored to himself when Hayes appeared.

"A gentleman is here from Whitehall, Captain," he said. "Although not in uniform."

It must be the messenger with the rest of Southey's effects, he thought.

"He has a parcel for me, Hayes," said Drayton impatiently. "Tell him to leave it in the hall. I don't need to speak with him."

"The gentleman insists on seeing you, sir," said Hayes, avoiding Drayton's eye.

"Oh, very well," said Drayton, exasperated.

A light step and Courthope appeared in the doorway of the dining room. "I beg your pardon," he said formally, "Hayes did not tell me you were still at table. I shall wait across the hall until you have finished your meal."

"Don't be ridiculous," said Drayton, smiling and getting up to greet him. "Hayes can bring you a glass . . ." He trailed off. "What is wrong, Corey?" Courthope's face wore a strange, cold expression.

Courthope tossed a small bundle onto the end of the table. Drayton saw a book, a watch, and some papers—probably Southey's identification papers. "I went in to Whitehall this afternoon," said Courthope in an odd, tight voice. "I am selling out, as you know, and I needed to sign the new man's contract. And the quartermaster was just sending off a messenger with this lot"—he gestured at the bundle—"to you. So I said I would be happy to take it, since you were an old school friend. I was planning to see you anyway, some arrangements about the wedding." He paused. "Is it true that you were arrested yesterday on suspicion of treason?"

"Yes," said Drayton, "but they released me, of course."

"Of course," said Courthope savagely. "Your father and various other influential men were pulling the place apart on your behalf, I gather." He continued in a stern voice, "Will you swear to me, on your word of honor, that you were not in fact guilty of betraying your country?"

Drayton was silent. Finally, he said, "Whitehall did not so regard it, but in the last analysis, I cannot swear that oath."

"To think," said Courthope almost to himself, "that I was originally calling with the intention of asking you to stand up with me at my wedding!"

"But, Corey—" Drayton began, bewildered.

Courthope cut him off. "Is it true that Southey was intercepted on a mission to France and shot?"

"Yes," said Drayton, swallowing as he told the lie and picturing himself at Chanterfield on the morrow.

"Then you have as good as murdered him," said Courthope, his face implacable.

"Corey, are you mad?" gasped Drayton.

"Don't bother to deny it," said the younger man coldly. "I found the letter. It was folded in with his identification papers, and I thought they had given me two sets by mistake. So I glanced at it"—his voice shook—"I glanced at it, and discovered that one of my *old school friends* had arranged to have the other kidnapped. Admittedly that was a rather nasty prank, and I would not have thought it of Southey, but I would not have repaid him by betraying him to the French, either. I am afraid that in my view that was beyond the pale, even for an *old school friend.*"

Sinking back into a chair, Drayton regarded Courthope with horror. "You cannot really believe this?" he whispered.

"Do you deny that you wrote this letter?" retorted Courthope. He slid it across the table to Drayton. He recognized it immediately. It was the note he had slipped into Southey's shirt in the cabin of the *Maid of Eastbourne.* He could not even remember precisely what he had written. Numbly he unfolded it. It read:

If my plan succeeds, it will be too late for you to return to England by the time you read this. You have done enough, and more than enough. I cannot let you go further. Naturally, I now consider the debt owed me for the kidnapping at Leigh End fully discharged. Do not think me a complete villain; I will do my best to secure such benefices as I may for your mother and sister. I regret most deeply the necessity for such a deception, but as you can well understand, on certain occasions treason appears the only option.

"It's not what you think," said Drayton, ashen-faced, trying to find a way to explain the situation without revealing that Southey was in fact alive. No solution presented itself, and he stared at Courthope helplessly.

"I think," said Courthope, pronouncing every word distinctly, "that you are a traitor and an assassin. And I will so name you publicly. I am asking Chapman and Waite to act for me. Please arrange for your friends to call upon them at their earliest convenience."

Those words, as Drayton knew, made any further explanations impossible. "You will want pistols, I take it," he said, his eyes bleak.

Courthope nodded. "I know that it is by rights your choice, but I am a poor hand at fencing."

After Courthope had left, Drayton sat staring at the tiny remnant of wine in his glass for a long time. He swirled it under the candles and watched the reflection glitter on the surface. It looked like blood. If only Nathanson were still in town, he would know what to do. Or at least would second him. Supposing others, not just Courthope, believed this story? Would he even be able to find two friends willing to stand up for him? What an irony that Corey, of all people, should force him out. He shook himself. He had best get started. It might take quite a while to round up a pair of seconds.

Fielding had arrived home shortly after Courthope's departure and consented at once to help, but Drayton could sense his unease, and his suspicion that rumor had been at work was confirmed when two friends were "not at home" when he called, although it was nearly eleven at night now and in one case he could clearly hear merry voices at the top of the stairs. I'll try Evrett, he thought, and then—then what? He would have to go to the club, and the thought of running the gauntlet of sneering eyes there made him quail.

The upper floors at Evrett's were dark, and this time Drayton believed the manservant who told him his master was from home. Recognizing Drayton, he added that he believed his lordship was at White's. Very well, Drayton told himself grimly, and headed over towards St. James's. To his unutterable relief, however, he had not reached the end of Evrett's street when he saw a link boy approaching, closely followed by a familiar figure.

"Evrett," he said wearily as the other limped towards him. "Are you still speaking to me?"

"Odd you should ask that," said Evrett. "A number of gentlemen at White's had the same question. Am I?"

"I hope so," said Drayton. "I need a second. Courthope has called me out."

"You had best come in," said Evrett, leading the way back to his house. He started to dismiss the servant who had lit the lamps in his study but thought better of it. "Do you need a drink?" he asked. Drayton nodded. "Brandy, then," he told the man. He said nothing more until Drayton had taken a few sips and set down his glass.

"There are some pretty ugly rumors going around," he said bluntly. "And it does not help that you have been seen with Nathanson; he is disliked by many. Roth's movements are very public, and it is known that he has been at Whitehall. He is said to have interceded for you, on the strength of your friendship for his nephew."

"But you do not believe the rumors?" said Drayton.

"No," said Evrett. "But it would help if I had something to put in their place. What did happen?"

"I cannot tell you," said Drayton, gripping his glass tightly. "I will swear to you, however, that I had nothing to do with Southey's death."

"Good God, is that what Courthope accused you of?" said Evrett, horrified. "I had heard nothing more than some nebulous charges of treasonable doings, covered up at the behest of Roth and your father. Where was Southey when he died?"

"On assignment behind enemy lines," said Drayton, thinking that he had best come up with one story and stick to it but keeping his tale as vague as possible for the moment.

"I should have known it would be something dreadful, to provoke Courthope to a challenge," muttered Evrett.

"His charge that I betrayed South is not true, but I admit the coincidence of my arrest and his death is very suspicious," said Drayton, pushing his hair back, as he always did when anxious. "And I wrote a note to Southey just before he died that is tailor-made to support Corey's interpretation of the facts. You can see it, if you like."

Evrett shook his head. "That will not be necessary," he said. "Who is your other man? Fielding?"

"Yes," said Drayton. "Would have been a bit awkward if my own host had refused. But he's been a brick. Even offered to go find another second for me. Chapman and Waite are acting for Courthope."

"Did you agree to pistols?" asked Evrett. "Courthope is not much of a swordsman; it would be bad *ton* to insist on rapiers."

"I ceded him the choice of weapons, yes. Bring a good surgeon. Although one consolation is that if Corey is not shooting to kill, he will not give me a fatal wound accidentally, as has been known to happen with poorer marksmen. Try for Green Park; if we meet early it will be quiet enough, and it is close to both our houses."

He slept in the next morning, and found a note from Fielding awaiting him when he finally rose at noon. The meeting was to be at dawn the following day. Chapman had agreed to Green Park; Fielding and Evrett had agreed to allow Courthope to supply the pistols. On Courthope's behalf, Chapman had reserved his principal's right to set the distance until he could judge the conditions at the site when they arrived.

Slowly, he got dressed. Robson looked at him suspiciously when he spotted the note from Fielding but said nothing. Drayton wondered what he should do with himself. It was out of the question to go down to Chanterfield with the issue of his guilt in Southey's death unresolved. Either he would go himself tomorrow after the duel, or . . . he realized that he had arrangements to make. It was fortunate that he had not had time to formally resume his guardianship of Caroline and William. He sat down at the writing table in his bedchamber and began to write letters. One to his father. One to Sara. One to Fielding, whom he charged with the grim errand to Chanterfield.

Should he write to Rachel? Or call on her? Surely, a voice whispered, your agreement is not binding under these circumstances? Surely you have the right to speak with the woman you love before you engage in such a doubtful affair? A longing to see her swept over him, so powerful that he felt physically ill with the force of it.

Luckily, Fielding returned at that moment. He glanced at the pile of letters and nodded. "Good," he said briskly. "If you are done with your business here, Haverford is selling his black gelding. I'd appreciate it if you'd have a look at him; he's too expensive for me to consider without someone to restrain my tendency to fall in love with anything that can carry me." And he surveyed his bulky frame with good humor.

Drayton grinned. "If it can carry you, it's not a horse, it's an elephant," he commented. "By all means, take me to Haverford, or anywhere else you like; this is the third time in four days I've been contemplating my own demise. It grows wearisome. Never written so many letters in my life."

"Horses first, then," said Fielding. "We'll have to take a little ride to try his paces, of course. And then Evrett has asked us to dinner."

Robson came back in with a handful of clean neckcloths and scowled when he saw the telltale pile of correspondence. "Another duel, I see," he said grimly. "I thought you was done with that nonsense, Master Richard. 'Twould serve you right if I went to your father and had it stopped." It was an empty threat and Drayton knew it.

"I may not be back until late, Robson," was all he said. "Don't wait up. Wake me tomorrow an hour before dawn."

Green Park lay under a light mist; it had been chilly during the night and the dew was heavy. Arriving on foot, Drayton and Fielding found two vehicles already drawn up at the edge of the grass. Evrett was hobbling about with Chapman, looking over the ground. The surgeon, Leacock, arrived next. Evrett must be well-connected, thought Drayton. Leacock did not normally attend duels now that he was established, although he had built his reputation repairing the damage caused by the London aristocracy's obsession with putting holes in their friends.

Evrett came over to Drayton. "It's slippery," he said tersely. "Take care when you turn for your shot." Another chaise pulled up, and Courthope and Waite jumped out. Fielding went over to inspect the pistols. As expected, they were faultless. Drayton buttoned up his coat, although he had always thought it a useless affectation. Courthope, he noted, respected his aim enough to do the same. The seconds took their places, and he and Courthope walked out to the middle of the green. The mist had lifted slightly in the twenty minutes he had been there, but it was still quite foggy.

"Twelve paces?" said Courthope.

"Agreed," said Drayton. He wondered where he should try to put his shot. He could not delope; that would be to acknowledge the justice of the accusation against him. But he did not trust his aim; he needed to select a target which did not offer much risk of a fatal miss. He decided to try for the right arm. If he missed inside, he would not be near the heart.

He felt a lean, muscled back against his own. Then there was space in between; he was walking, counting automatically. Ten, eleven, twelve. He turned, aimed, and fired. Dimly he saw Courthope jerk oddly, but at the same moment he felt an impact push him backwards with tremendous force. I am hit, he thought, unsurprised. Where? He looked down. There was a hole in his jacket, a neat hole, right over the center of his chest. He still felt no pain, but now he was on the ground, and Evrett was tearing open his clothing. Red was flowering out beneath his breastbone. He shot to kill, thought Drayton, noting the fact in an oddly detached fashion. Fielding was cursing frantically, the surgeon was hastening over, pushing him aside. "Corey?" gasped Drayton to Evrett. It was suddenly very painful to breathe.

"Grazed," said Evrett, striving to remain calm. "You get first crack at the surgeon." Leacock had started to cut away the shirt. Waite hurried up next to the surgeon. It was his first duel; he was barely eighteen months from his degree and was an amiable, timid young man. But now his face was harsh. Courthope was just behind him; Drayton saw that he was holding a handkerchief around his wrist.

"Courthope," said Waite through his teeth, "if he dies, I shall have you charged with murder. You said no word to me of this being a killing matter."

"My God, Waite!" exclaimed Fielding, shocked. "You can't have your own principal arrested!"

"Can I not?" Waite fired back. "I would never have acted for him had I known he meant this. Devil take it, Harry Drayton put me on my first horse! I have been in and out of Alcroft Hall since I could walk!"

A last layer of cloth was cut away, and the wound was exposed, an ugly, pulsing pool. The surgeon was trying to staunch the flow. Raising his eyes to meet the surgeon's, Evrett asked a silent question; in reply the surgeon gave a quick, bleak shake of the head. Courthope had seen the exchange; he turned pale.

From his makeshift couch on the turf, Drayton was looking up at Courthope, trying to say something. He tasted blood in his mouth, and his tongue did not seem to work. Courthope dropped down beside him, hypnotized by the ominous seepage under the surgeon's pressing hand. Wrenching his gaze away from the bandages, he looked in anguish at his victim. Somehow Drayton managed to choke out in a faint voice, "I didn't kill him, Corey."

"I believe you," said Courthope hoarsely. "Richard, I believe you. The minute I fired I knew it was all wrong." But Drayton did not hear him. The grass was climbing over him; it was wet and soft, and dark. He sank down inside it.

Chapter Twenty-two

"Why did he not come to me?" demanded Barrett in despair. He was standing by the bottom of the stairs, observing the terrified faces of the servants as they ran up and down at the command of the occupants of the sickroom. Evrett, Waite, and Fielding had taken Drayton to his father's house in Berkeley Square. It was only two streets from the park, but even so, when they had arrived they had not been certain whether they carried in a man or a corpse.

"I could ask the same question," said Alcroft. His face was drawn with pain. "Does the stubborn fool think he must take the entire world on his shoulders?" The confused accounts of Evrett and Waite had sent Barrett off in grim haste to Whitehall, where a horrified Colonel White had clarified matters after extracting a promise of secrecy. "If he did not care on his own account, could he not think of Courthope? The boy is ready to shoot himself, now."

Sara appeared on the landing and came clumsily down to where they were standing. Her father's hand on the banister was trembling, she saw. "Leacock has the bullet out," she informed them. "He cannot tell if it has pierced the lung." She knew they wanted a fuller account, but what should she tell them? That she had seen a hole in Richard that she could put two fingers into? That the surgeon had only just now been able to stop the bleeding? That he did not think his patient would live out the week? "I have sent for Dr. Barnes," was all she said. "Even if the lung is not damaged, the surgeon believes he will develop a fever in the chest."

"Is he conscious?" asked Alcroft in a halting voice.

She shook her head. "Right now it is for the best, though. Leacock warned me that laudanum could be fatal if his lung was hit, so that we could do nothing for the pain were he awake."

Alcroft had not moved from his post when Barnes arrived twenty minutes later. This was the Draytons' family physician, and Alcroft was somewhat cheered by the sight of the familiar face, with its pince-nez and receding hairline. Sara's message must have conveyed the gravity of the situation; he did not stop to greet Alcroft and nearly sprinted up the stairs. Alcroft continued his vigil. After a time, he heard voices from the top of the stairwell, and Leacock descended. He paused when he saw the anxious face waiting for him and then continued down and stopped in front of Alcroft.

"Mr. Leacock, is it not?" said Alcroft. "Has he a chance, do you think?"

The surgeon tried to be objective. Privately, he thought the young man unlikely to survive. But the question had been phrased in such a way that he could answer honestly without terrifying the father.

"I believe the lung is not much damaged, my lord," he said slowly. "And the bleeding is stopped, for the moment. Barnes is an excellent man. He has a chance, yes." A servant brought Leacock his hat and coat, and then unobtrusively fetched a chair from the drawing room and stationed it next to Alcroft at the bottom of the staircase. Eventually, without noticing that he did so, Alcroft sat down.

Sara appeared again, and he sprang up to meet her. He could hear Barrett talking to someone in the upper hall; Barnes, presumably.

"Who is with him?" he said in agitation.

"Mrs. Mott and Robson, for the moment," said Sara. "Barrett is speaking with Dr. Barnes about hiring nurses. I will go back up myself as soon as I have made sure I understand what he advises us to do."

Alcroft looked dreadful, thought Barnes as he joined them. And no wonder, losing first his heir and now his younger son, in the space of a year. Barrett ran lightly down and stood by Sara, his hand on her shoulder as she looked anxiously at her father. He stood very still, hardly daring to breathe.

"I have told Barrett, my lord, and will repeat it to you: This is a very serious wound," said Barnes. "The damage to the lung, if any, is slight, but this sort of injury invariably produces lung fever. I will return in six hours or so and look in on him again. In the meantime, he will need two nurses in the room at all times. He must be kept as still as possible or the bleeding may resume. If he wakes and can

eep anything down, tea or water only. No lauda-
um or strong spirits; he is having difficulty enough
reathing."

"Papa," faltered Sara, "ought we to send for
Miss Meyer?"

"Absolutely not!" snapped Alcroft, coming to
ife.

Sara stood her ground. "She is a superb nurse,
Papa. Harvey had her change the dressings after
he surgery last month and said he himself could
ot have done better."

"I said no," growled her father. "I believe I am
ble to afford the hire of nurses. We need not rely
n the charity of acquaintances."

What are you afraid of, Papa? thought Sara to
erself as she climbed back up the staircase. That
he is not merely an acquaintance? Or that sum-
noning her would be an acknowledgment that he
s dying? Or both?

All day Wednesday, Rachel stayed home, hoping
hat Drayton might call. Her uncle was down in
Bristol at a shipyard, which meant there were many
ewer visitors than there were on a normal day.
This was perhaps fortunate, since at each peal of
he bell, she would start up from wherever she had
perched and wait anxiously for Sweelinck. By early
evening, she had accepted that he would not come
hat day, and she was able to keep her aunt company after dinner without betraying herself. The
following day, however, she had an engagement
to go to a luncheon and would have to leave the
house. Maria was putting up her hair when she
reached a decision.

"Maria," she said, "please tell my Aunt Louisa

that I cannot go with her to the luncheon." Sh
thought of claiming to be indisposed but realize
in time that the servants would then deny her t
visitors. "I am expecting an urgent message con
cerning James."

Maria stared in amazement at her mistress. Th
Roth household was very informal; Rachel ha
never in the nine years she had been her mai
asked her to deliver such a message. "Your aun
will be very surprised to hear such a word fror
me, *señorita,*" she said bluntly. "She will ask m
if you are unwell, that you did not come to he
yourself."

Attempting to imitate her brother's haught
manner, Rachel simply looked at Maria with a col
frown. Hastily, the maid left. But her intuition wa
correct. Not five minutes after Maria had left o
her errand, there was a knock on Rachel's door
and her aunt came in.

She found Rachel engaged unconvincingly i
sorting some jewelry from her trinket box. Louis
Roth had very sharp eyes. She saw that Rachel wa
beautifully dressed, in an elegant silk frock mos
unlike the round gowns she wore when she wa
not planning to go out. Her hands were agitated
she was flushed, and she could not meet her aunt'
gaze. She is expecting this young son of the lord
thought her aunt. She does not know that he ha
agreed not to see her for two months. And althoug
she had concurred with her husband's decision
when he had told her of his interview with Drayton
her heart went out to Rachel as she sat by her
dressing table, her face averted. It would be bes
for her to go out, she realized, rather than sit and
wait alone for a visitor who would not come.

"We are only going over to Richmond, little

Rachel," she said gently in her odd dialect of Ger-
nan, using the childhood nickname. "I will leave
he address with Sweelinck and instruct him that
any callers for you are to be directed there."

If Roth had been in town, news of the duel would
have reached Rachel within hours. But as it was,
she heard nothing, and passed the day in ignorance
of the events at Green Park. By Friday lunchtime,
she had begun to doubt the interpretation she had
given Sara of the "circumstances" mentioned by
Drayton. Perhaps the charge of treason was not
he obstacle after all. Perhaps he had simply
decided that he could not marry her, that the differences were insurmountable. She did not trouble,
any longer, to conceal her agitation from her aunt,
who was growing more and more concerned. Lou-
sa Roth had never seen her calm, self-possessed
niece in this state.

Late in the afternoon, Rachel heard the bell, but
t was long past the hour for social calls, and she
had given up expecting anyone to come. Most likely
t was a family friend who had been invited for the
Sabbath dinner and had come early to visit with her
aunt. When Sweelinck appeared, she was startled.

"Miss Rachel," he began, "you have a caller—"

Rachel rose, hardly daring to hope now, and
hen saw Barrett standing behind the butler. His
face was gaunt.

"Miss Meyer," he said quietly, "Lady Barrett has
ent me to ask for your help. Her brother has been
wounded in a duel and has developed a high fever.
We hoped that you would again be willing to help
with the task of nursing." She was staring at him
n shock. Although she did not ask, he told her
anyway. "He is not really awake, but he has been

talking in his sleep, calling your name," said Bar
rett. "He needs you. Please come."

In spite of Barrett's warnings, Rachel was still no
prepared for what she saw when she entered th
majestic bedroom. Sun was pouring in two of th
west-facing windows, which looked out toward
the square. On the window closest to the grea
four-poster bed, the drapes had been closed, bu
there was enough light for Rachel to see at onc
that Drayton was a shell of himself. His face wa
flushed; his lips were cracked, and there were yel
low hollows under his eyes. His breathing was a
agonized rasping. Robson and a stout young nurs
were attempting to restrain him as he tossed fre
fully on the bed. Sara was rinsing cloths in a basi
and dropped them with a cry of relief as she sa
Rachel and her husband. As Drayton had grow
worse, she had argued with her father more an
more fiercely, until finally she had dared to tel
him that his son was lost to him, and it was hi
choice whether the loss was to death or to an unac
ceptable marriage.

Now she flew to Rachel and the two clung t
each other, weeping openly for a moment befor
Rachel went over to the bed. She felt Drayton'
forehead, although she knew what she would find
He was blazing with fever. "Prop him up higher,"
she told Robson. "It will help him to breathe. Brin
more cold water. We will change the cloths ever
two minutes. Can he sip water at all?" she aske
the nurse.

"Not to speak of, miss," said the nurse, brigh
ening at the presence of someone more know
edgeable than herself. "He can't swallow well, an

earlier today the other nurse told me that he drank some tea but spit it straight back up."

"We will have to give him water from a spoon, then," said Rachel decisively. "Every time we change the cloths, a spoonful. If he can tolerate that, then two spoonfuls."

At first it seemed that Rachel's arrival had marked a turning point. The fever did not abate, but it did not increase, and gradually the three women were able to force some water down him, a little bit at a time. He did not open his eyes, but he seemed a bit more aware of his surroundings. Only gradually did Rachel realize, to her horror, that he seemed to flinch whenever he heard her voice. She drew Sara over to the window and told her what she had observed. Sara looked at her in amazement.

"He has been saying your name, often," she said. "And speaking in Spanish. He was talking about Chanterfield as well, but Barrett talked to Fielding and deduced that he was concerned about an errand to the Southeys. Fielding came in and talked to him very carefully, explaining that he would go down there himself tomorrow, and Richard has not mentioned it since."

Hoping that she was imagining things, Rachel returned to the bedside. She left only to swallow a few mouthfuls of food and was sitting next to the bed with Mrs. Mott, taking turns to change the cloths, when she heard Drayton muttering her name. "I am here, Richard," she said, leaning over and taking his hand. There was an unintelligible protest, and he began to toss wildly. Frantically, Rachel ran to fetch Sara, who had gone to take a brief rest, and she was able to soothe him.

"I will leave," said Rachel to Sara, completely

undone. She could feel the tears pouring dow
her face. "I am doing more harm than good."

"He is delirious," said Sara desperately, "it is al
a jumble in his head, I am sure. Please do no
leave, he is so much better since you came. He ca
breathe now, and he does not shiver so. I thin
you are our only hope." Rachel returned, heavy
hearted, to her tasks, but she now spoke as littl
as possible, and attempted to move away from th
bed when she did so.

Shortly before ten, Barnes came in. He examine
Drayton perfunctorily; he knew what he would find
"I can do nothing for him," he told Sara bluntly
"If you can keep the fever from going any highe
and above all keep him still, he may pull throug
it. But it is out of my hands."

Alcroft had come to the door of the room an
was listening. Rachel turned to him.

"My lord," she said, haggard, "if I might mak
a suggestion, I think we should send for my aunt."

"Who might your aunt be?" demanded Barne
Social niceties had vanished, and he had not bee
introduced to Rachel.

"Louisa Roth," answered Rachel. "She is Benja
min Gideon's sister. They were both trained b
their father." Anselm Gideon had been a note
physician, and his son was now attending the ailin
king. Gideon's methods were often unorthodo
Barnes knew, but he had saved many patient
whose own physicians had despaired of them. H
turned to Alcroft.

"I think it an excellent suggestion, my lord."

"Is it not your Sabbath?" said Sara to Rache
remembering that the Roths were said to be ver
devout.

"Yes, but that makes no difference, of cours

n a case like this," said Rachel absently. "It is a ortunate chance, in fact. We may be sure my aunt s at home."

Within two hours, Louisa Roth had turned the ickroom upside down. Sips of water were replaced y tea brewed with meadowsweet, cooled until it vas lukewarm. She ordered two maids to sit in the all and tear bedsheets into thick strips. Great tubs f cold water were lugged up from the kitchen, nd the strips were immersed in the water. Then)rayton was wrapped, swaddled from head to foot, n the wet cloths. There were three wrappers, and hey worked from toe to head, leaving only his nose nd mouth exposed. After ten minutes, they began gain, unwinding and rewinding with freshly oaked strips. The wrappings immobilized Drayton, vhich gradually distressed him, so that he began o struggle and call out in Spanish.

"What is he saying?" asked Sara. "He was speak-ng in Spanish before, and we heard some of the ame words—the name Rodrigo, for example."

"He is apologizing," said Rachel, her hands shak-ng. "He is apologizing to Rodrigo for some mis-ake he made. He thinks he is in Spain."

At the sound of her voice, Drayton turned blindly nd then began muttering even more frantically.

"I am sorry," Rachel whispered to Sara. "I forgot or a moment that I should not speak aloud where e can hear."

"What is this about not speaking?" said Louisa o her niece in German. She had excellent hearing, nd although her spoken English was not fluent, er comprehension was. Rachel moved across to he windows and explained. "What does he say,

then, when he hears that you are there?" aske
her aunt with a dreadful premonition.

"Something about my uncle, and taking m
away," said Rachel, her voice quivering. "I wante
to leave, but Lady Barrett convinced me that
should stay, and I have been trying to remembe
not to speak when I am by the bed."

"This has gone far enough," said her aun
reaching a decision. "I must send for your uncle.

"But he is in Bristol," said Rachel, bewildered
"And what would he do here?"

"I will let him explain," said Louisa Roth, wh
was normally a very gentle woman. Rachel looke
at her face and drew back. "Let him take the cons
quences of his scheming for once. Fortunately, h
is no longer in Bristol. He returned shortly afte
you left this afternoon."

At one o'clock in the morning, therefore, E
Roth stood in the front bedchamber of the hous
on Berkeley Square. He saw Rachel, bewildered
staring at him; his wife, unwontedly stern; Alcro
and the Barretts, puzzled but hopeful. They ha
taken off the wrappings above the waist, and th
patient's flushed face turned weakly on the pile o
wet cloths. He was still very restless. "If he wer
not delirious," Roth muttered to himself, "sure
he would know that such blind adherence is ridicu
lous. Still, there are worse things to cling to in
high fever than the memory of one's given word

"Captain Drayton," he said slowly, "can you hea
me? It is Roth. I release you from your promise
You are free to see my niece."

Rachel stood for a moment, thunderstruck, an
then comprehension rushed in, followed by sea
ing anger. She looked at her uncle with such
bitter expression that he shrank back. "It was onl

to be for two months, Rachel," he pleaded. Alcroft was looking on uncomfortably, remembering his own speculation about extracting a similar promise from his son's bride-to-be.

Only Sara and the nurse were looking at the bed. Drayton was lying still, for once. He appeared to be trying to say something. Roth turned back to him and repeated what he had said, word for word. There was no apparent reaction at first; then the face relaxed a trifle. After a few minutes, it was apparent that Drayton had fallen into a light doze. Roth took his leave, and the wrappers returned to their sodden work. About an hour later, Drayton was perceptibly cooler, and they began to hope that the fever was breaking. Suddenly he woke, or appeared to wake.

"Rachel," he croaked. She went over and took his left hand, which was the only piece of him save his face not covered by the wet cloths.

"What is it?" she whispered, still afraid to speak out loud.

"Get me out of this horrible wagon," he said in Spanish.

Chapter Twenty-three

It was a long and checkered convalescence
There was the day, for example, when Drayton
began to cough and could not stop, his chest con-
vulsing in spasms which caused his wound to star
bleeding again. At last Barnes gave him some syrup
of poppy and mercifully, when he awoke, th
coughing did not resume. After that, there was th
episode of the pork pie, smuggled in with the bes
of intentions by the remorseful and too-persuad
able Courthope, which provoked a night that Dray
ton fervently prayed would never be repeated. Hi
insistence on being moved up to his own boyhoo
room on the third floor caused yet another setback
A fortnight after the duel, he was sitting up i
bed, despite the efforts of Robson to make him li
back down, when Fielding came in, out of breat
from hauling his huge bulk up to the top of th
house. He collapsed heavily onto a chaise that ha
been moved into Drayton's room for the use o

he nurses, who had been sleeping in the room ıntil quite recently.

"Tell me again why you wanted to be moved up o this poky room in the attic," panted Fielding. 'I take it that since your lungs are a bit damaged ou choose to put your visitors in the same condiion?" Drayton was looking much better, he noted vith relief. Someone had cut his hair and shaved ıim; he was in a proper shirt, and his eyes were lear. But his face was thin, and there were giant ıollows above his cheeks.

"There is nothing wrong with my lungs," said)rayton peevishly. "The problem is my nurses. Apparently they have decided to fleece my father y insisting that I need their care for months to ome. Do you realize that I have spent five of the ast twelve weeks confined to my bed?"

"True enough," said Fielding, struck by this tatement. "I would lay a wager that no one in our regiment, perhaps no one in the dragoons ven, has ever been on medical leave for such a ime, with three different injuries, and none of hem taken in combat."

"A glorious distinction," snapped Drayton. 'Pray enter the bet for me at White's when next ou stop in."

"You will not have many visitors, sir, an you eceive them in such a fashion," said a voice from he hall, and Rachel ducked through the low doorvay and came in with a smile which took the sting ut of her words. She had finally returned to her ıncle's house but still came every day to help care or the increasingly uncooperative patient.

Refusing to be mollified, Drayton glared at her, nd then at Robson, who was standing in a pose f long-suffering patience on the other side of the

bed. "Give me one good reason why I cannot ge
up," he said to Rachel with a pugnacious thrus
of his jaw.

Rachel eyed him speculatively. For the last few
days he had reminded her increasingly of Caroline
Perhaps a change of tactics was in order. "Go
ahead," she said calmly. A protesting gesture from
Robson was suppressed as he saw the quick shake
of her head.

Nonplussed, Drayton hesitated. "I may get ou
of bed?" She nodded. He looked at Robson, who
stood back to allow Drayton to swing his legs ove
the side. "B-but I'm not wearing any breeches!'
he stammered. Rachel refrained from pointing ou
that she had bathed and bandaged him for eigh
days while he was wearing far less than he wa
wearing now.

"I will go out into the hall," she said. An instinc
tive movement by Robson to assist his maste
received a warning frown as she withdrew and
closed the door. She leaned back against it and
listened. First there was a shuffling sound, then a
stifled groan, then a creak as his weight left the
bed. A minute later there was a reverberating thud
and a faint volley of curses, cut short by a hacking
cough. Repentant, she flew into the room as Rob
son and Fielding were helping Drayton back into
bed.

"You perfidious woman," he gasped, with feel
ing. He collapsed onto the bolster and got his
breath back gradually. Then he started to laugh
weakly. "I'll pay you out for that, Madam Nurse
see if I do not."

Rachel promptly forgot this threat, which was a
mistake. She sent Robson off to eat his dinner and
settled herself in a chair in the corner, content to

vatch Drayton and Fielding talk. Eventually she
ıoticed that Fielding was doing most of the talking,
ınd dismissed him with a reprimand for tiring her
ɔatient.

"It is quite gratifying to have so many visitors," he
aid humbly, after Fielding, abashed, had clumped
lown the stairs. "It was only to be expected at first,
ɔut it has been weeks now, and they are still toiling
ıp here."

"Had you fewer visitors and more sleep, you
night be well enough to leave your bed sometime
his month," said Rachel sternly. Drayton did not
ınswer; his eyes were closing. They heard a heavy
read on the stairs.

"Is that Hatchet?" he asked drowsily. The nurse's
ıame was in fact Hitchett, but Drayton's nickname
vas unfortunately very apt, and had been adopted
ɔy both Sara and Rachel, who now lived in dread
hat they would accidentally slip in front of the
ɔrim older woman.

"Yes," said Rachel, straightening the bedclothes.
'She is bringing up your soup. Shall I send her
ıway? Would you like to sleep?"

"No," said Drayton faintly. "Soup sounds good."
This should have made Rachel suspicious; he had
ɔeen complaining for nearly a week about the
estrictions on his food. "Rachel," he said in a
oice so weak she could hardly hear him. Then he
loubled over in agony and clutched at his chest.
She scrambled up to the head of the bed, terrified,
nd pulled his hand away.

"What is it?" she gasped. "What is wrong?" Sud-
lenly his arm grabbed hers and tightened, pulling
ıer down to him. She was being embraced, passion-
tely and dramatically, being kissed with theatrical
rdor; without thinking she returned the embrace,

and felt his hand start to caress her neck and move down, tracing her scar.

Drayton had timed it perfectly. With a shriek of outraged propriety, Hitchett slammed down the bowl of soup and retreated in dismay back down the narrow staircase. A very audible "Well, I never!" floated up behind her.

"I thought you said you were not good at play acting," scolded Rachel, trying vainly to look stern.

"Now," said Drayton, breathing hard and clutching his bandages, but smiling maliciously, "now, Madam Nurse, you absolutely, utterly, and completely must marry me. Southey's kidnapping was the right way to go about it all along. There is no escape. The Hatchet is not susceptible to bribery. I already attempted it, when she brought me yet another bowl of that foul soup yesterday."

"Do you mean it?" whispered Rachel. The subject had been carefully avoided by both up until now. Suddenly serious, he nodded and looked at her doubtfully.

"Please say yes, for once," he begged. The tired eyes were anxious. "I don't think I can bear it if you say no again."

"I don't think I can, either," she said, attempting a smile. "But would you mind making me a proper offer, if I am going to give you permission to ask?"

"If you will excuse me for reclining in the presence of a lady," he said gravely. "Miss Ross, or Meyer, or—for good measure—Nathanson, I cannot live without you. Would you do me the honor of accepting my hand in marriage?"

"Yes," she said, her voice trembling slightly. "Yes, I will." She looked down at her hands, clenched and unclenched them. "If you wish it—if it is needful, I will be baptized, Richard. It is less of a lie than saying that I do not wish to marry you.''

''I would not ask that of you,'' he said in a low voice.

''When I marry you, I will be dead to my grandmother whether I am baptized or not.'' He was still holding one shoulder, and he felt her shiver slightly as she pronounced the stark words.

''Let us go slowly, even so,'' he said gently. ''Marrying me is quite enough for the moment. I am trying to learn to be more patient, remember?''

''I am delighted to hear it,'' she said with forced lightness, pulling away and picking up the tray. ''I take it that means you will eat this soup?''

''Yes, dear,'' he said meekly, but unable to keep the possessive joy out of his eyes as they followed her across the room.

''Now you sound like a husband,'' she said approvingly. She stirred the soup. ''It's gotten cold. Would you like me to take it down and have it reheated?''

''No,'' he said, eyeing her bodice with interest. Her gown was still partly off one shoulder as a result of his assault. ''I would like you to feed it to me, though. Suddenly I am feeling rather faint.''

Another week saw him venturing downstairs, dressed for the first time since that fateful Thursday. Sara and her father had cannibalized a good-sized study which had been fitted up for Alcroft's secretary. Since that gentleman had lasted approximately three weeks and had never been replaced, the room was not in use at the moment. The chaise was dragged back down three flights of stairs, some side chairs and an armchair introduced, and a small table brought in, which could be pulled up for meals. Sara stood surveying her handiwork with satisfaction as Robson helped Drayton down the last few steps and into what Caroline now called the "getting-better room."

"Excellent," she said approvingly as Drayton sank down onto the chaise and permitted Robson to tuck a quilt over his legs. "You are just in time. You have a caller. I had hoped the first one to visit you in here would be Fielding, since he has complained so vociferously about the stairs up to your bedchamber, but never mind."

Catching sight of the visitor looming up behind his sister, Drayton choked in surprise and kicked off the quilt, but not before Nathanson had seen it.

"Oh, put the silly thing back on," said Nathanson. "To hear my sister tell it, you can barely sit up, so don't try to feign health for my sake."

"I thought you were in Spain," said Drayton, and, looking at his uniform, "and I thought you were a captain. Of Rifles. Did you decide to take another promotion and switch regiments to boot?"

Nathanson sat down in the armchair and crossed his long legs gracefully. "I am going to Vienna, as it happens," he said. "The promotion is temporary, as are my identification papers." His eyes met Drayton's with a significant look. "I may see some acquaintances there; I will have to be careful." Sara had gone, and now Robson took a hint from Nathanson's tone and withdrew quietly.

"Give him my regards," said Drayton. "Tell him your sister and I are to be married."

"So I heard, and high time," said Nathanson. "Perhaps your engagement could have been arranged without resorting to that bullet-ridden pre-

ude, but it was certainly effective. My aunt no
onger opposes the match."

"Are you suggesting I nearly got myself killed so
hat your sister would be permitted to marry me
out of pity?" demanded Drayton, incensed. "I
assure you that if I could have thought of a way to
avoid that duel, I would have. And don't tell me I
could have gone to White. He has already told me
so himself, and it is arrant nonsense. A fine thing
f junior officers are to run to their colonels every
ime they are challenged."

"Speaking of Colonel White . . ." said Nathanson, eyeing the invalid.

Drayton frowned. He considered Nathanson
houghtfully. "I take it," he said slowly, "that your
visit just at this moment is not a coincidence. White
was here yesterday, you know." Nathanson inclined
his head. "And he made me a proposal, and told
me to take a day to think it over. You have not, by
any chance, been sent to assist me in my cogita-
ions?"

"A crude description," commented Nathanson.
'But, yes. White seemed to feel you might need
persuading."

"Why on earth," said Drayton fiercely, "would
you encourage the man who is about to marry your
sister to accept White's offer?"

"Are you going to sell out, then? Like Cour-
hope?" said Nathanson, without answering the
question. "Many do, when they marry." He left
unspoken the other half of the sentence: many did
not. Nearly two-thirds of the officers in Drayton's
regiment were married.

"No," muttered Drayton, "not while that pint-
sized emperor is running loose. But it's not the
same."

"Your post at Gibraltar would be safer by fa
than the Fourteenth," observed Nathanson. "It i
not as though White wants you to go behind enem
lines. We simply need someone there in the for
to act as a clearinghouse for information from th
south of Spain. Wellington has held open the posi
tion as second-in-command of the garrison forc
purposefully, hoping to find a suitable man."

"I am not suitable!" said Drayton desperately
"Surely there must be someone else more experi
enced, more—oh, I don't know!" He gave a savag
kick at the quilt.

"That is what is really troubling you, I think,'
said Nathanson quietly. "It is not the thought o
Rachel, although it cannot be easy to leave a wif
behind in times like these. Indeed, she could g
with you to Gibraltar, should you wish it. But i
anyone will understand, she will. She has lived wit
it her entire life. No, you have decided that yo
cannot do the job, haven't you?"

"Yes," said Drayton curtly. "And with good evi
dence. I have bungled more times than I can count
on only two missions. I lost my temper in Spain,
followed a false trail down in Kent, I nearly ruine
our chance of rescuing your sister from that boat
shed, I failed to use the signals, and I made enoug
noise in the woods to attract forty Frenchmen."

"Perhaps you have forgotten," Nathanso
replied in dry tones, "that you are speaking to
man who shot his sister in the shoulder and nearl
knifed his own father. A rather unfilial error whic
was prevented only by your discernment." H
leaned forward, and his face was suddenly ver
serious.

"Everyone makes mistakes," he said passion-
tely. "No one can become a good intelligence
fficer overnight, any more than children can learn
ɔ ride well overnight. It takes experience, and
eflection. If White and Tredwell never asked any-
ne to serve in our branch save those who had that
xperience, that knowledge, there would be no
ntelligence service. And Wellington would be los-
ng this war. White is not asking you to take a post
which will require you to exercise skills you do not
ave. For this position, there is no masquerading,
o tracking through the hills. There is simply judg-
nent, and discretion, and integrity."

Shaken, Drayton stared at his interlocutor.
Nathanson's intent gaze did not waver. Suddenly
Drayton felt very tired. "Why," he demanded indig-
antly, "do I sometimes feel when I am with you
s though you are the one who is six years older?"

Nathanson glanced at him with a wry smile. He
ould afford to smile; he knew he had won. "Imag-
ne how I felt, growing up with my father," was all
e said.

On a sultry June day that promised an evening
torm, they were married very quietly at Leigh End.
The groom was still a bit shaky on his feet, but
when Rachel had discovered that Nathanson was
assing through on his way back to Spain, she had
egged Sara to move the date up so that at least
ne member of her family could attend. To her
urprise, her aunt came down from London, as
well, announcing that although she did not feel
hat it was proper for her to attend the wedding

itself she hoped to be invited to luncheon afte wards.

The vicar in Haythorn had refused to officiate the ceremony. With Rachel's assistance, howeve Barrett had located the clergyman who had helpe Nathanson in the sham conversion required fo his commission. Whether it was the opposition c the vicar which swayed her, or the informatio she had somehow unearthed that the Roths wer distantly connected to the Spanish royal family, wa not clear, but Barrett's Aunt Lutford pronounce with a magisterial air that she thought the Barre name would carry them through even this affai and said little more on the subject.

Caroline was to be allowed to attend. She ha harbored visions of a splendid ball, after hearin Sara's description of the elaborate London wed ding of Miranda and Courthope, but Rachel tol her gently that this would not be that kind of wed ding.

"This is not even the real wedding, for me," sh confided, sitting on Caroline's bed in the nurse the evening before the event. "This is only to mak sure that the government of England thinks we ar legally married."

"Where is the real wedding, then?" said Car line.

"In Gibraltar," said Rachel. "We will have drumhead wedding, like the other officers wh have married while serving abroad. Your uncl thinks it is silly to be married twice, but he was ve nice about it."

"Can I come to the wedding in Gibraltar, then? asked Caroline eagerly.

"No, sweet, because you are not coming t

ibraltar to live with us until October. You are to
pend the summer here."

"Why?" asked Caroline, yawning.

Rachel recognized the first of a chain of "why's"
hat would extend far into the night if firm mea-
ures were not taken immediately.

"Because that is what your aunt and uncle
ecided," she said crisply. "Now go to sleep or you
night not be allowed to come to the first wedding
omorrow."

Caroline persisted. "When are you going on the
oat? Right after tomorrow?"

Rachel shook her head. "First we are going on
wedding trip, and then we will come back and
ay good-bye and pack our trunks, and then we are
oing to Gibraltar. Go to sleep, Caroline."

"Where are you going on your trip?" demanded
he irrepressible questioner.

"I don't know," confessed Rachel. "Your uncle
ould not tell me. Not France, I am sure of that."

The ceremony itself was a ten-minute blur. After-
ards, Rachel remembered only a vague impres-
on of Drayton in his uniform, looking impossibly
istant at the other end of the drawing room as her
rother escorted her in the door. The luncheon of
old meats, poached turbot, jellied asparagus, and
niniature tarts, which had cost Mrs. Tibbet and the
ook many apprehensive moments, was unnoticed
nd virtually untasted by either the bride or the
room. A last, sticky embrace from Caroline, who
ad been given a sample of the fruit tarts by Betsy;
handclasp for Drayton from his brother-in-law,
nd the exhausted newlyweds found themselves
uddenly alone in the Barretts' carriage, heading

down the drive under an increasingly threatenin sky.

"Well, that was not as bad as I expected," sai Drayton, closing his eyes and slumping back again the cushions. Then, as he realized how Rach might take his remark, he sat up remorsefull "Dear heart, I only meant that I had never hope to have both your brother and your aunt ther Nor to escape a vicious scolding by Barrett's aunt.

"Your father did not come, though," sai Rachel, and instantly regretted it as she saw Drayto stiffen.

"How stupid of me!" he said, reaching into h pocket. "I meant to give you this right after th ceremony." He handed her a small box wrapped i cream-colored paper. There was no subscriptio "My father sent this down, with no note. He do not like to admit he has changed his mind. It ma be some time before he addresses you as Mrs. Dra ton, but that did belong to my mother."

Rachel had pulled off the paper and opene the small case. Inside was a stunning seventeent century brooch consisting of a circlet of pearls s in a garland of gold leaves. "It is beautiful," sh said sincerely, feeling as though a small cloud ov the day had just blown away. She was fishing in h reticule. "I may as well give you this now, in th case," she said, still fumbling. "I was going to wa until after the proper wedding, but my father co siders the Anglican service binding." She held u a small chamois bag and untangled a hairpin fro the tiny drawstring.

"I'll have you know," said Drayton with a gli in his eye, "that I have the greatest respect for th opinions of your father, and must warn you th I, too, consider us married as of this moment.

There was a pause as he wrestled vainly with the tangled drawstring. "What is in this infernal bag?" he grumbled.

"It was sent from Lille; I believe it is a wedding present of sorts," said Rachel, looking smug.

He could feel some sort of hard, cylindrical object inside the bag. Not a ring, then, or a stickpin. Finally he ripped the knot open and tipped the contents of the little bag into his hand. It was a small silver whistle, with two notes.

"Does he think that like you I cannot whistle properly on my own?" he said in mock outrage.

"I think it is more of a reminder," said Rachel primly.

"You'll pay for that insult, my girl, when we arrive," said Drayton, attempting to produce what he thought was a menacing frown.

"Arrive where? Where are we going, Richard?" asked Rachel. "May I know, now?"

"Bettham's Keep," he replied, looking at her from under his lashes. "I was a trifle indisposed when we were last there, as you remember, and unable to take up the suggestion that we have our honeymoon at that point. So I thought we could return there now."

"You cannot be serious!" said Rachel, appalled, and then saw the twinkle in his eye. "You are still indisposed, in any case," she said, fuming.

"And likely to be more so, if I do not cease making sport of my bride?" Drayton laughed. A distant rumble of thunder echoed his laugh, and it began to rain lightly.

"Richard," demanded Rachel, "would you please tell me where we are going?"

"My house," he said simply. "I have a small estate in Sussex, you know. Nothing like Leigh End," he added hastily. "And there are tenants there, of course; I rented the place out as soon as I bought my colors. But my father's agent, who manages the land for me, told me that the tenants were up in Scotland at the moment, and I could not resist taking you there, just for a few days. The tenants were most accommodating when I wrote to them. You do not mind, do you? Once the war is over, I promise we can go to Venice, or Paris, or anywhere you like." He was watching her face anxiously, but as she gazed back at him, lips parted, the anxiety slowly dissolved, replaced by something else. Something dangerous, and compelling.

"No," whispered Rachel, mesmerized by the look in his eyes. "No, I do not mind."

Drayton swung across the carriage and sat down next to her in one sinuous movement. "Do you realize," he said casually, "that for the first time since we met, we are alone together and neither one of us is behaving improperly? That will never do."

"I suppose not," said Rachel.

The rain was coming down harder, and flickers of lightning were visible over the tops of the hedgerows when Robson pulled up at an inn just outside Tunbridge Wells. With his coat held over his head, he jumped down and ran to the carriage window.

"Master Richard," he shouted, "I think we should stop here a bit until this blows by us. Would you and the mistress be wishing to come inside and wait in a private parlor?" There was no answer, and he recollected suddenly that Drayton was still far from well, and had looked a bit haggard when they had set out from Leigh End. Worried, he ugged open the carriage door. Then he hastily losed it again.

"I'll take that as a 'no,' " he muttered, and went nto the inn to order himself a pint of ale.

Historical Note

The Roth-Meyer family is fictitious, but there i
some basis in fact for my portrait. Converts such a
the Schombergs, for example, boasted numerou
senior naval officers during this period. Professin
Jews might still be active in the war effort by partici
pating in home militias or, in the famous case o
Nathan Rothschild, by providing Wellington's cam
paign with both money and information. On th
domestic front, however, unconverted Jews—eve
wealthy ones like the Goldsmids and Rothschilds—
lived in a sort of social limbo. Men who had busi
ness dealings with them would visit them at thei
homes, but their wives and daughters were rarel
welcome in the homes of the British aristocracy
The complaints made by Rachel's brother abou
the restrictions on his military career—and hi
uncle's political career—are true. Jews and Catho
lics were barred from commissioned ranks in th
services, and not until 1858 was a Jew allowed t

ake a seat in Parliament. On the continent, espe-
ially in cities like Berlin, there was far more social
ntercourse, and larger scope for political advance-
nent. Patents of nobility were also granted to Jews
ar earlier in Germany and Austria than peerages
n England.

Intermarriage in elite circles was uncommon,
ut not unknown. In the mid-eighteen century,
Elizabeth Gideon married a viscount; however, her
nother was Christian and she herself had already
een baptized. One of Nathan Rothschild's daugh-
ers converted and married the son of a British
eer in St. George's, Hanover Square, some years
fter Napoleon's defeat. The Rothschilds were bit-
erly opposed to the match.

Characters in this story refer to Jews in terms
which are now sometimes considered offensive: *Jew-
ss* for a female Jew, *Hebrew* as a synonym for Jewish.
This is a reflection of actual practice; the characters
nay not intend any insult, but the terms themselves
o convey something of the "foreign" qualities
ttributed to Jews in a country which expelled them
n the Middle Ages and did not readmit them until
he seventeenth century.

Finally, a note on terminology. There was no
eparate intelligence service in Wellington's army.
ntelligence work was supervised by Adjutant-
General or Quartermaster-General, or, in a few
ases, by Wellington personally. The status of the
agents" varied wildly. Some were commissioned
fficers scouting behind enemy lines in uniform;
ome were soldiers or officers who took the enor-
nous risk of operating undercover; some, like the
rivate couriers used by the Rothschilds, had no
fficial connection to the army at all. No consistent

term is used to refer to the men who performe these tasks. I have therefore adopted the word *cou rier* to serve this purpose; it is not entirely accurat but the courier services and information-gatherin services were closely connected.